Marion Lennox has written over one hundred romance novels and is published in over one hundred countries and thirty languages. Her international awards include the prestigious RITA® award (twice!) and the *RT Book Reviews* Career Achievement Award for 'a body of work which makes us laugh and teaches us about love'. Marion adores her family, her kayak, her dog, and lying on the beach with a book someone else has written. Heaven!

Annie O'Neil spent most of her childhood with her leg draped over the family rocking chair and a book in her hand. Novels, baking, and writing too much teenage angst poetry ate up most of her youth. Now Annie splits her time between corralling her husband into helping her with their cows, baking, reading, barrel racing (not really!) and spending some very happy hours at her computer, writing.

Also by Marion Lennox

Mistletoe Kiss with the Heart Doctor
Falling for His Island Nurse
Healing Her Brooding Island Hero
A Rescue Dog to Heal Them

Also by Annie O'Neil

A Family Made in Rome
The Princess and the Paediatrician
Hawaiian Medic to Rescue His Heart
New Year Kiss with His Cinderella

A FAMILY TO SAVE THE DOCTOR'S HEART

MARION LENNOX

IN BALI WITH THE SINGLE DAD

ANNIE O'NEIL

MILLS & BOON

First Published in Great Britain 2022
by Mills & Boon, an imprint of HarperCollins*Publishers* Ltd,
1 London Bridge Street, London, SE1 9GF

www.harpercollins.co.uk

HarperCollins*Publishers*
1st Floor, Watermarque Building,
Ringsend Road, Dublin 4, Ireland

ISBN: 978-0-263-30125-0

05/22

MIX
Paper from
responsible sources
FSC® C007454

This book is produced from independently certified FSC™ paper to ensure responsible forest management.
For more information visit www.harpercollins.co.uk/green.

Printed and Bound in Spain using 100% Renewable Electricity at CPI Black Print, Barcelona

A FAMILY TO SAVE THE DOCTOR'S HEART

MARION LENNOX

MILLS & BOON

For Helen.

With love and gratitude for so many years
of friendship, encouragement and support.

You are my hero.

Marion

CHAPTER ONE

'MUM ALWAYS MAKES stew when we find fresh bull kelp. This'll make heaps.'

Jenny stared at the heap of sodden seaweed the kids had hauled up from Kelpcutter's Bay. It was oozing seawater onto the kitchen floor, and already starting to smell. They thought she should cook it? Really?

'We'll never get it fresher,' Ruby yelled excitedly. 'And there's piles down there for the racks. Soon as the storm stops, we need to get the tractor out.'

And they were gone again, Sam, Ruby and Tom, twelve, eight and six years old respectively. Followed by Nipper and Pepper, their two kelpie-type mutts.

She should stop them. For two days now the weather had been wild. Who knew what sort of junk had been washed up? A good parent would have her children inside, home schooling, sharing educational children's programmes, keeping them clean and dry.

Staying safe.

But safety was not on these kids' agenda, and she wasn't their parent. For these kids, safety seemed almost a dirty word.

When she'd watched them build a campfire in the backyard so they could bury potatoes to cook, she'd bitten back warnings, though she had insisted they light it further from the house. But when six-year-old Tom had spooned out the innards of his first spud, she'd lost it. 'Be careful, you'll burn yourself.'

The kids had looked at her incredulously and then ignored her. Tom had thus scalded his tongue when he'd bitten into the too hot potato. He'd cried, but he'd folded into himself, not wanting her comfort.

'Dad says we gotta learn ourselves,' twelve-year-old Sam had said briefly, and Jenny's grief at the death of her brother and his wife had verged on anger.

There was no doubt that Chris and Harriet had loved their kids, but safety hadn't seemed to be in their vocabulary. Self-sufficiency seemed to have been their mantra, but sometimes she wondered if it had verged on neglect.

That lack of concern had seen the family hiking to the far reaches of the island on one of the last hot days of autumn—*'Because the waterfall at the head of the river is the coolest place to be in the heat,'* Sam had told her. Then they'd pitched tents under one of the vast eucalypts that even Jenny knew were nicknamed by the locals as 'widowmakers'. The massive branches were known to drop without warning, and Chris and Harriet were never to realise the appalling consequences of their actions.

They'd died instantly, leaving three bereft children. Sam, aged twelve, was still suffering the effects from a major infection—the boy had hiked five kilometres in bare feet to get help. 'My shoes were in Mum and Dad's tent.' His voice had been a bare sob when rescuers had found him. 'I couldn't reach anything. I couldn't reach Mum and Dad.'

And that was why Jenny Martin, twenty-nine years old, emergency doctor at Sydney Central, happily single, happily a city girl, was staring at a pile of fresh bull kelp, thinking with searing longing of the menus pinned to her fridge back in Sydney. Thinking of a takeaway Thai feast. Even a pizza would be great, she decided, and sighed, and then picked up the bull kelp and carted it outside, across the wind-blasted yard to hang on one of the long lines of drying racks.

No, she wouldn't eat it—her sister-in-law had left the freezer loaded with cooked kelp and she wasn't going there either—but it might as well make them some cash. Bull kelp had many commercial uses— pharmaceuticals, toothpaste, shampoo, dairy products… The kelp dried on these racks, and every few months a boat would arrive and cart the dried product away.

It was a living—just—but it wasn't a living Jenny would ever have chosen for herself. She used the winch to heave the kelp over the racks, and then stood back and stared at it in dislike. Jenny Martin, highly qualified doctor, carting seaweed to make ends meet.

She couldn't go on like this.

What choice did she have?

'Jenny!'

And that brought her out of her reverie. Eight-year-old Ruby was screaming her name as she raced up the path from the beach, and she sounded terrified.

These kids pretty much lived their own lives. Jenny had come when Chris and Harriet had died, expecting to comfort, expecting…well, she wasn't sure what. What she'd found were deeply traumatised kids, but kids who'd been raised to be fiercely independent. They didn't want comfort, at least not from her. Sam had had to spend two weeks in hospital on Gannet Island because of the infection that had taken hold of his foot, but once he was home they'd gathered together into a self-reliant group.

Jenny was the outsider. An aunt they barely knew. An aunt whose role, they'd decided without discussion, was to be their adult base so their lives could stay exactly as they'd always been.

They couldn't. She knew that, and she suspected the kids knew that too, but months later she was still trying to figure whether transplanting them to Sydney would break them. And break their future?

'Jenny!'

She abandoned the kelp and ran. Ruby's cry had almost been lost in the wild wind, but she'd definitely heard fear.

These kids didn't call for her. When they cried into the night, they called for each other.

But now she saw Ruby, her tangle of red curls flying, her feet—in sandals now; there'd been some things Jenny had insisted on—barely touching the ground.

Jenny reached her, caught her shoulders, squatted and steadied her.

'What is it? Ruby, it's okay, I'm here. Tell me what's wrong.'

For a moment Ruby couldn't answer. She stared wildly at Jenny, and Jenny had visions of some new horror, some new tragedy. Why hadn't she insisted on going with them?

But these kids knew Kelpcutter's Bay far better than she did. It was their backyard, their playground. They all swam like fish. Chris had knocked basic water safety into their heads early and let them be, and they regarded their aunt's qualms with bewilderment bordering on distress.

Marc, the physician on Gannet who'd cared for Sam, had taken her aside after he'd dropped in for a 'home visit' when Sam had come home from hospital. 'Jenny, as far as possible you need to let 'em be.' These kids have been raised like wild creatures. You'll need to tame them, but if you move too fast you'll cause more problems.'

All very well for Marc to say, she thought bitterly, but now…

'Ruby, what's happened?'

'We've found…' Ruby could scarcely get her words out. 'Jenny, there's a boat. It's smashing into the rocks. And Jenny, we've found a man.'

CHAPTER TWO

CALIFORNIAN PAEDIATRICIAN SILAS BRADEN had made a mistake, and mistakes weren't what Silas Braden was known for. He'd never been a man to squander opportunity by lack of planning.

As the only child of almost obscenely wealthy parents, Silas's astonishing good looks, his athletic body and his quick brain had meant the world had been his oyster from the start. He'd been to the best schools, the best colleges, and he'd risen quickly to a prestigious position as a paediatrician in one of Los Angeles' best hospitals.

He owned glorious cars. He'd dated beautiful women and he'd eventually married one. The perfect one. He and Charlotte had had one perfect little girl—on the surface they'd been the perfect family.

And then, for all his planning, life had thrown in a grenade and perfect was nowhere.

The last couple of years had seen him doing just what was expected of him. One step after another. Pretending life was normal. He'd gone back to planning, obsessively determined never to leave himself exposed again.

And then this opportunity had presented itself and planning—his way of avoiding that untouchable section of his heart—was called to the fore.

His parents were both doctors, or they had been. Four

years ago his father had had a stroke. He'd recovered well, but his career in orthopaedic surgery was over—his hands had lost the finesse such a career demanded.

But they'd always owned yachts, classic ketches they spent a fortune on. After the stroke, they'd retired from medicine, hired the very best of skippers and sailed their way leisurely around the world.

But then had come the death of their daughter-in-law and seven-year-old granddaughter. They'd been in Sydney when they'd heard, and had abandoned the boat and taken the first available flight home. The pandemic, with its myriad consequences, had struck soon after.

Two years later, *Sea Raven* was still stuck in Sydney, and Charlotte and Harper's deaths were still a shadow over them all.

'Your father's deeply depressed,' Silas's mother, sitting in their magnificent beachfront mansion, had confided to her son on his last visit home. 'You know he feels for...what happened to you. I can't distract him. If he had his boat he could play with it, take our friends out, potter, but no one's doing international boat transfers any more.'

'So let's buy him another,' Silas had suggested, thinking a cool new yacht would make a great gift for his father's seventieth birthday. He was already starting to plan in his head. Planning was his place of peace, the only way he could get away from the grief that still overwhelmed him.

But, unexpectedly, his mother had hesitated. 'Silas, your father...that yacht...he does love it.'

Really? *Sea Raven* was a vintage beauty, but his father had always had yachts. The notion that he couldn't just buy another felt weird.

But his mother had been firm. 'Silas, he dreamed of

this yacht for years. He researched and researched, looking for just the right one—you know how many he bought and sold, looking for perfection. And now he's lost her. He's been so bleak since his stroke. Harper's death has made everything worse, and for some reason he can't stop thinking about the fact that his boat's stuck in Sydney. But, even though the pandemic's easing, we still can't find anyone to sail it home. The red tape to find an international crew...you wouldn't believe it.'

He did believe it. The pandemic had left international travel in limbo.

But then he thought... He knew sailing like the back of his hand—much of his childhood had been spent on his father's succession of boats. He sailed his own boat now, and he was, if he did so say himself, a damned good sailor.

Sea Raven was magnificently equipped, with easy reefing and state of the art assistive equipment. It'd be easy enough to rig her for solo sailing before he left Sydney. Sailing alone, he could travel light. He wouldn't need to step ashore in different places. He had enough funds to organise harbour stops, even for supplies to be air-dropped if needed.

What was more, he needed a challenge. He'd worked harder than he'd thought possible during the pandemic, but now the situation had eased he could leave without guilt. His father was depressed and his own grey cloud wasn't lifting. Two months at sea...

And in an instant he'd thrown caution to the wind and he'd made his mother a promise. 'I'll bring her back.'

She hadn't exactly fallen on his chest in gratitude. She'd looked at him as if he had two heads. 'Dear, you can't. Not by yourself. We always hire a skipper.'

'You're saying I'm not as good as a hired skipper?'

'Of course not, but she's a big boat. Think of the dangers.'

'There won't be dangers,' he promised. 'It's mid-season in both hemispheres—the safest time to sail. Weather forecasting's great now, and *Sea Raven*'s engines hold enough power to get me out of trouble if I need to outrun a storm. You know me, Mum, I don't take risks. I'll plan it to a T. It'll be a challenge, to get her home for Dad's birthday.'

Which was looking a lot less likely now, he thought faintly, as *Sea Raven* lurched and wallowed towards the small cove marked on his incredibly detailed map. He was heading for Kelpcutter's Bay, Albatross Island, part of the Birding Isles group.

The Birding Isles were three days' sail east of Sydney. He hadn't planned to go anywhere near them, but then the weather had exploded. A cyclone, far earlier than could possibly have been expected, had formed north-east of Queensland and, instead of staying out to sea or veering inland to the tropical north as any tropical cyclone should, it'd decided its path lay south.

Sea Raven should have been able to ride out a storm at sea but, with an abundance of caution, Silas had decided to head to the nearest safe harbour. Albatross Island was the most remote of the Birding Isles and the smallest. Its main harbour was on the east side—a bit too exposed, he thought, not sure whether the facilities would be enough to protect his father's precious baby. But the map showed an inlet to the west—Kelpcutter's Cove. Whoever had drawn the map had indicated depth and added a note: *Jetty, suitable for overnight mooring, but no facilities.*

He didn't want facilities. He only wanted to anchor for a couple of nights and be gone again.

And then the storm had veered, and as he'd neared the island he'd found himself fighting for his life. Facing mountainous seas. Realising that staying out in the storm risked breaking the boat. Then trying to get a gracious old lady of a boat into a narrow neck of a harbour, where the lee of the island offered only minimal protection.

And he'd almost made it. He'd come round and round again, trying to find the perfect time to head through the narrow neck of the harbour—which seemed to be a natural rock formation rather than man made. Waiting and waiting. Then gunning for it.

Thinking he'd made it.

And then one random wave had slashed backwards from the rock wall. Another had hit from behind at the same time. *Sea Raven* had skewed at the top of the wave, lurched wildly and then pounded sideways into the rocks.

The smash was immediate, bone-jarring, hurling him to the end of his safety line. He was being thrown against the boat railings again and again.

He felt a searing pain as his leg buckled under him. The pounding was relentless.

His lifeline, this boat, were useless to him. They were, in fact, killing him. Somehow he managed to unclip his safety harness and haul himself to the upper side of the boat. To the rail.

Another almighty crash.

Now or never. He seized the railings and hauled himself over.

And slipped into the heaving wash of the waves.

There was indeed a man. And a boat, wallowing in the waters of Kelpcutter's Bay.

The boat looked gorgeous, a wooden beauty, forty feet or so of classic loveliness. Somehow she'd made it

But there was little to retch. Maybe he'd been sick before, she thought, and looked back at the drag marks up the beach. He'd been conscious enough to haul himself clear of the water.

And, as if on cue, his eyes opened and he groaned.

The groan was deep, guttural…frightened?

Well, I'd be frightened too if I'd just been smashed against the rocks and tossed into the maelstrom of breaking waves, she decided.

'Hey, you're safe,' she told him, assuming her best doctor-in-charge voice. It was the voice she used for trauma patients in the city hospital where she worked. She hadn't used it for months, but she dredged it up now and hoped it was appropriate. 'There's nothing to worry about. We have you.'

And it did seem to get through. She was cupping his face and his eyes widened, his gaze caught hers.

She saw striking blue eyes, set in a strongly boned face. Dark brown hair plastered to his head. A gash ran across his forehead, not deep but sluggishly bleeding.

In his mid-thirties? she thought. He looked fit, weathered, someone well able to take care of himself.

Except he obviously wasn't.

'Don't move,' she said urgently, thinking of neck injuries, spinal injuries. And then she thought of those drag marks up the beach and the fear subsided just a little. Someone with a major spinal injury would never have made it this far.

Though there could be a fracture, about to shift?

Her training as an emergency doctor at Sydney Central was front and foremost. She thought of the paramedics, bringing patients in by ambulance. Every possible spinal injury was stabilised with state-of-the-art equipment before they arrived.

'He's not going to die, is he?' Sam said in a shaky voice and, amazingly, it was the guy himself who answered. She saw him take a deep breath and then another, and then he twisted his head slightly to look up.

'I think…broken leg. Won't die,' he muttered but that seemed all he was capable of.

'Of course you won't,' Jenny said, but her words didn't seem to register. The guy's eyes closed again.

She bent her head so her face was right against his. An urgent question had to be asked.

'Was there anyone else on the boat?'

'N…no.'

'No crew? No passengers?'

'No.'

Well, thank God for that, but what to do now?

Twenty-three years ago Jenny's mother had left Albatross Island and taken her six-year-old daughter back to what she termed civilisation. She'd also abandoned her kelp-cutter husband and her twelve-year-old son.

It had been a decision Jenny had never been able to fathom. For her parents to irrevocably split the children… for her mother to walk away from her son, for her father to say goodbye to his daughter and never try to make contact… Six-year-old Jenny had been shattered, and the pain she'd felt then had stayed with her for ever.

She'd made contact as soon as she was old enough—of course she had—and she'd returned to visit her childhood home. Brother and sister had rekindled their relationship, but Jenny's few visits as an adult had left her understanding exactly why her lovely, flighty mother had left.

Albatross Island was a tiny speck of an island, the most remote of the Birding Isles. There was a small settlement on the other side of the island, but little industry. It was mostly inhabited by people who wanted to retire from the world. Artists, writers, a couple of ancient boat-builders who spent their lives restoring boats no one else wanted—and then there were recluses who simply wanted to be alone in this admittedly gorgeous landscape. There had not been a medic on the island—except of course now there was Jenny.

Only Jenny.

A daily ferry connected them to the much bigger Gannet Island, and immediate help could also come via helicopter from the same place. Gannet Island had an excellent medical centre, but in this storm the ferry wouldn't be running and a helicopter would be useless. She was alone.

What to do now?

Her hands were running over the man's body as she thought through options. There seemed no major bleeding. The guy's breathing seemed secure. He'd dragged himself up the beach.

His leg… Yeah, there was a problem. His trousers were torn mid-calf, and she could see a massive lacerated bruise, oozing blood. He'd said the leg was broken and in her experience patients often knew. He'd have felt it break. The leg didn't seem out of alignment, thank heaven—a compound fracture was something they could both do without.

There was more to worry about, though—like how long had he been unconscious? That laceration on his head… She could already see the signs that there'd been a vicious blow. And water in his lungs?

She wanted the magnificently equipped emergency department of Sydney Central, and she wanted it now.

She had nothing.

So get on with it, she told herself, fighting back panic and trying to put herself back into doctor mode.

First things first. She needed to get him off the beach. The tide was on its way in. In an hour the beach would be under water, and the rain, mercifully holding off right now, could start again at any minute.

She looked again at the guy's face. It had changed subtly, and she had the impression he was simply regrouping. Holding his eyes closed while he did an internal check?

'Hey,' she said. She was kneeling and now she stooped further so her face was level with his. 'I'm Dr Jenny Martin. The kids who found you are Sam and Ruby and Tom. You've been battered, but you're now in safe hands.'

And his eyes flew open again.

Whew.

He looked sick, ashen-faced. There was a couple of days' stubble on his chin.

He looked up at her and she thought… Paul Newman? There was a weird thought. How long was it since she'd seen an old Paul Newman film?

The Sting? Butch Cassidy and the Sundance Kid? As a teenager she'd binge-watched every one of his movies, and when other teenagers were sticking pictures of hip hop stars on their bedroom walls she'd put up a poster of Newman grinning wickedly, standing incongruously by a horse on a fairground carousel.

And, even more weirdly, here she was, twenty-nine years old, mature, sensible, a doctor coping with an emergency—yet still feeling the lurch she'd felt as a teenager, pleading with her mother to buy that poster.

Oh, for heaven's sake...

'You're a doctor?' the guy whispered and, despite the hoarseness, he sounded incredulous. But at least that brought her back to earth.

He might well be incredulous, she thought. She was crouched on a windswept beach in the middle of nowhere, wearing her brother's ancient oilskins. Her team consisted of three scared kids plus two dogs who'd edged close enough to see what was happening on their deserted beach.

Still, this was what she had, and she needed to make the most of it. One of the priorities drilled in during medical training—secondary only to the ones about danger and airways—was to imbue the patient with confidence that they were in good hands.

She could do this.

'I am a doctor,' she confirmed, managing to sound a lot more confident than she felt. She badly wanted her medical kit. She had one up in the house but by the look of the storm clouds sweeping across the sky in their direction she didn't have time for anything but the barest of essentials. 'When you breathe does it hurt?' He was wearing a sodden shirt under his lifejacket. A polo with the emblem of one of the world's most expensive fashion icons.

'I'll live,' he muttered.

'Yeah, I know you'll live,' she said dryly. 'Tell me what hurts.'

'My leg.'

'It looks broken.' She might as well say it like it was. This guy needed to have confidence in her, and honesty was the way to go. 'You've hit your head. You seemed unconscious when we found you. Do you think you could have been unconscious in the water?' She needed to know that. She needed to figure if he had lungs full of water.

And maybe he got it. She saw him take the time to think it through, form an answer and then summon the strength to speak. His voice was weak but he got the words out.

'I cut my lifeline when the boat smashed. I felt my leg

go. The waves pushed me in, and I let them. I hit my head on a rock, but it was only as I made it to the shallows… I tried to stand and felt…'

Yeah, she knew what he'd have felt. To try and stand on that leg… She might have passed out as well.

That was okay though—even reassuring. Passing out because of pain—she could handle that. Passing out because you were breathing in seawater would have brought complications she had little chance of dealing with.

She'd still like to listen to his chest. She needed her stethoscope.

Priorities? She had to get him off the beach.

How? He was a big man, tall, strongly built. She was five foot three. The kids were tough and wiry, but they were kids. And that leg…if he put any weight on it at all he'd pass out again.

'You have an ambulance on this place?' he asked. 'A hospital?

In your dreams. 'No,' she said bluntly.

'But you're a doctor.' He was starting to sound a bit more confident now, less slurred. She could hear pain but his voice was strengthening. He was thinking for himself. Thinking that he needed a hospital.

'I'm afraid Albatross Island Medical Centre is here at your service, neatly packaged as me,' she said wryly. 'Sorry, mate, I'm all there is. And I need to think for a minute. Shush.'

He blinked and stared up at her. She gave a decisive nod and then sat back on her heels.

He stayed looking at her. They all did. The guy. The kids. Even the dogs.

Jenny to the rescue. Jenny, who only months ago had been carefree as a bird. Jenny who wanted a genie right now, a magic carpet to transport her back to her own life.

There was no genie, and she needed some way of dragging this guy off the beach.

Carpet? There was a rug in the living room.

Too heavy.

A door? She'd seen pictures of disaster scenes where doors could be used as emergency stretchers.

There was no way she and three kids could carry a door.

She turned deliberately away from the many sets of eyes watching her. Thinking… Thinking…

And then she saw palm fronds, torn by the wind, littering the high-water mark.

Palm fronds… The cubby hut the kids had made for themselves behind the house had a roof made of fronds, tied together with twists of bull kelp.

She'd admired their cubby and Sam had explained its construction with a certain amount of incredulity that she didn't know. 'You cut and dry bull kelp strips and cure them, then plait them together. Dad showed me. They make a really strong rope. We used them to tie all the palm fronds together like we were making a raft.'

Palm fronds, already roped together. Like a raft.

'Sam, we need your cubby house roof as a stretcher,' she told him, and Sam looked at her with a gravity far beyond his years—one adult to another? She hated that look, but she had no choice now but to use it.

'I reckon we could put…' She stopped, missing an important piece of information. 'What's your name?' She turned back to her patient.

'Silas Braden.' He was lying still, watching her. They were all watching her.

She was the grown-up. She would have given anything right now to be a kid with someone else to look to.

Deep breath. *You can do this*, she told herself, as she'd

told herself so many times since that dreadful call informing her of her brother's death.

Why didn't she believe it?

She had to. She had no choice.

'We need to cut your cubby roof to make it stretcher size,' she told the kids, trying her hardest to sound confident. Who knew whether it'd hold together, but she had no choice. She could hardly leave the guy… Silas… where he was while the tide came in. 'It's light, and you told me the ropes you made are strong. We could put Mr Braden on it and pull him up to the house.'

'I think… I can walk,' Silas said faintly. 'If you get me a stick…'

He had to be kidding. There was no way he'd be able to stand, much less walk. 'If that leg's broken you'll pass out again and then I'll have a limp body to deal with. Sorry, but you need to let us organise things.'

'If you could find someone else to help…'

'There's no one else,' she said brusquely. She was watching the waves, knowing the wind was rising again, knowing if another squall hit before they got him off the beach they'd be in real trouble. 'Sam, can you and Ruby cut the roof off the cubby? Use the big kitchen knife.' Dear heaven, how she hated saying that, but there was no choice but to once again treat Sam like an adult. 'Chop the roof in half length-wise—we need a long skinny bit, stretcher size. Got it?'

'Yeah.' And she heard the relief in Sam's voice, that he was being told what to do, that he was being given direction. His expression had subtly changed. Turning into a kid again?

'Bring the plastic sheeting from the shed,' she told him. 'We'll use that underneath, to make it easier to slide and to stop the fronds splitting apart. And we'll need ropes. Six ropes.' She was guessing as she went, trying to think things through. 'You'll need to cut them off the cray pots. Drag everything back on the stretcher.'

'Dad's cray ropes?' Sam questioned, uncertainty flooding back. 'Dad will…'

'Your dad won't…wouldn't mind.'

'But…'

'I'm sure,' she said, and she reached out and gave him a hug. 'You're doing great, Sam. We're all doing great. Take the kids with you and hurry.'

And seconds later kids and dogs were flying up the beach on a mission. Even an exciting mission.

Leaving Jenny alone on the beach, feeling not excited at all.

Silas Braden was looking sick, exhausted—and also confused. He was staring at the retreating kids as if he was trying to make things out, and then he tried to twist to look out to sea.

She put her hands on his shoulders and held him still. 'Please… I need you not to move. I don't know what's been damaged and, until I know, you need to stay still.'

'But she's already smashed. The rocks… Her forward hull…'

'I'm not talking about your boat. I'm talking about you.'

'Can you see? If you could get a line to her…'

She glanced out into the bay, at the mass of white water, at the boat foundering towards the shallows. What was he suggesting? That she fight through the waves, swim out, somehow get a line attached to the foundering boat?

'You know, I'm on my own here, and that water's rough,' she said, keeping her voice almost conversational. 'There's me and three kids on this side of the island, and no one else. You want me to swim out and try a bit of marine salvage on my own?'

'She's worth a fortune.'

'More than me?'

There was silence at that. He closed his eyes again and she wondered just how much he was hurting? A lot, she thought.

'Sorry,' he managed. 'My dad'll break his heart. Stupid, stupid, stupid.' His voice was weak, husky, and she thought again about water in his lungs. She should have asked the kids to bring her medical kit.

There wasn't a lot she could do here though, she thought, but the idea pushed her back into medical mode.

She checked his lower leg again, ripping his trousers so she could see the extent of the damage and carefully tugging off his sodden yachting shoes. Expensive, she thought. Nice.

But what was nicer was that his foot had a decent pulse. No circulation blockage, she thought, but she needed it to stay that way.

'I need to find something to splint your leg before we move you,' she told him. 'The kids have gone to fetch your stretcher. Now I'm heading along the beach to find a decent piece of driftwood. Don't move.'

'Do I have a choice?'

'Nope,' she said, trying to sound cheerful. 'Just lie back and admire the scenery while I see what I can scrounge to make shifting you easier.'

CHAPTER THREE

SILAS LAY ON the sand and watched her.

He was soaked. He was chilled to the marrow—or was it shock that was making him shiver uncontrollably? The pain from his leg was unbelievable.

His head hurt.

At some time in his medical training a pain expert had given a lecture, talking about neural pathways. 'The brain seems to be able to focus on only one source of intense pain at a time.' Yeah, right. Pain seemed to be coming from everywhere. He sent a silent message of invective to his long-ago lecturer, and then decided his neural pathways needed something else to distract themselves with.

Watching the woman scour the beach looking for driftwood seemed as good a path as any.

She was worth looking at.

She was slight, he thought, five feet three or four. Neat. Compact. She was wearing wellingtons and a vast oilskin coat. On this beach, in this setting, she was dressed for sense, not for style, but right now sense was what he appreciated.

And more. Her warmth. Her smile. Her reassurance.

When she'd bent over him, her green eyes creased in concern, her auburn curls clinging damply to her forehead... When she'd bent so close he could see a snub nose, freckles, a wide mouth… When he'd seen worry, and that worry was all for him…

Crazy as it seemed, he'd wanted, more than anything in the world, to reach up and hug her close. Even maybe… kiss her?

His guardian angel.

Whoa… Where were his thoughts drifting? He was simply reacting to the events of the last few hours, he decided. To his fear out there in the water that he was probably going to die. And now he wasn't. Some slip of a girl had taken control, had assured him he was safe, was organising him a stretcher, and was now scouring the beach to find a piece of wood to make a splint.

Anybody would have wanted to kiss her.

'Got it.' She'd been raking over piles of seaweed, methodically searching. Now she raised a stick and called. 'Yay, this looks perfect.' She looked like a kid showing off a treasure.

How old was she?

She'd said she was a doctor. That was a bit much to take in. His head was decidedly fuzzy, but if he was to let her anywhere near his leg he should check to see exactly what she meant by 'doctor'. A doctor of…basket-weaving?

Hell, did it matter? She was all he had, and she was a whole lot better than the nothing he'd been facing an hour ago.

She reached him, knelt beside him again and started hauling off her coat.

'No!' He put out a hand and was astonished at how heavy it felt. His whole body felt heavy. 'I don't need your coat.' He managed to put his hand on her arm. She looked down at it for a moment and then lifted it and placed it back on his body. For some reason, the touch of her hand felt amazing.

She was warm, she was real and she was here. His neural pathways were reacting to the situation he'd been in, he told himself, not to the woman herself. But still…

'I'm not offering it,' she told him. 'Your own jacket's cutting the wind, and changing you into dry clothes here isn't an option.' But she wasn't stopping with the undressing. She finished hauling off her coat to reveal an ancient windcheater. That came off fast as well.

There was only a bra underneath, a slip of gorgeous black lace. The contrast was so mindboggling that his dazed mind was struggling to take it in.

'It's okay, I'm not doing a striptease,' she said. She grinned and the way he felt… He must be more battered than he'd thought. This woman had him mesmerised.

But now she was hauling her oilskin back on, and the vision reverted to prosaic. She was holding her windcheater up, examining its threadbare state. 'It's my brother's,' she said. 'Who knew second-hand clothes could be so useful?' And before he could figure what she was about, she grabbed both sides of the front and ripped. Then she took the ribbing at the base and ripped that free. The sleeves seemed a bit harder—she bit into the seam at the shoulders though and they came free as well.

'Hooray for me,' she said as he stared up in dumb confusion. Why wasn't his head letting him think? And then, maybe seeing his look of confusion and deciding to take pity on him, she smiled. It was a kindly smile, doctor to patient.

Maybe she wasn't a basket-weaver then—and her next words confirmed it.

'I now have a splint and strapping,' she told him. 'I'll

be as gentle as I can, but I need to fix your leg so we can get you onto a stretcher without hurting you more than we must. Once we get you to the house we'll get you warm and dry, but I'm afraid the next few minutes will be uncomfortable.'

'You really are a doctor?' Had he already asked that? Everything was still a bit…fuzzy.

'I really am.' She was holding the stick, tearing off a couple of attached twigs, then wrapping the rough part with the back of the windcheater. 'That'll do. Lie still.'

He had no choice. He lay still. He felt her carefully pulling together his ripped trousers. She'd be trying to get as much padding as she could between an open wound and her makeshift splint.

Hell, he wanted to see.

'I'm actually an emergency doctor,' she told him, chatty doctor exchanging niceties with nervous patient. 'My department's full of high-tech equipment for just such an injury as this, but for now we'll have to make do with a ripped windcheater and a stick. Hold still—I'm sliding the wraps under your leg.'

He held still. She was skilled, he thought. She dug sand from under his leg, but just a little at a time so the cloth could be edged inch by inch into place.

He held his breath, but his pain level didn't increase.

'Done,' she said in satisfaction. 'Now for my high-tech stick.'

And once again she burrowed, this time edging the stick under both leg and padding.

He hardly felt it—and what he felt was reassuring rather than excruciating.

She was wrapping now. The front of the windcheater was over his shin, and she was using the ribbing and the sleeves to tie it in place, all the way up past his knee. The length of the stick and the amount of tie meant his leg was now rigid from the thigh down.

'There,' she said in satisfaction and sat back. 'Done.'

'Th...thank you.'

'Think nothing of it. If I have to be marooned in the middle of nowhere, I might as well make myself useful.'

'You're marooned? I thought...isn't it me who's marooned?'

'We're all stuck,' she said, mock-morosely. 'Me, three kids, two dogs and a shed full of kelp. And now a stranded stranger.'

'This island's on the map.' He was struggling to get a grip on things here. His throat felt thick and dry. It hurt to talk but he was trying to understand. 'It said it's inhabited.'

'So it is. Albatross Island's almost the centre of civilisation—if you can call civilisation four hundred permanent residents, a general store, a pub-cum-café, a school, a boat-builder, several artist studios and a bakery. Oh, and a kelp-drying facility, but that's us. But, sadly, everyone but us is on the other side of the island, and if you haven't noticed, we're in the middle of a storm. The track overland will be unusable because of sand blow, and communications seem to be out. There's supposed to be a satellite connection, but my phone's been dead for hours.'

Then she glanced across to where the boat was still wallowing. 'I don't suppose,' she said doubtfully, 'that you've set off one of those emergency beacon thingies they have in boats. Is someone about to launch an air sea rescue mission?'

An emergency beacon thingy... That'd be his EPIRB—an Emergency Position Indicating Radio Beacon. They were used the world over to let emergency services know someone was in trouble, and where.

He hadn't activated it. He'd thought he was running into harbour, that he'd be safe—until he wasn't. *Idiot, idiot, idiot,* he told himself. 'No.'

'It's probably just as well,' she said prosaically. 'An Angels of Mercy rescue mission might lose a few angels if they tried searching for you in this. We're on our own until things die down—but, hooray, here come the kids.'

And here they were again, the kids who'd found him. He'd opened his eyes and they'd been looking down at him, three scared faces. They'd rolled him over, clearing his face of sand. They'd saved him.

He remembered saying, 'Please, fetch your parents.'

The oldest—a boy with burnt red hair; they all had burnt red hair—had said bluntly, 'Mum and Dad are dead. There's only Jenny.'

'Then fetch Jenny…'

So this was Jenny.

'Yay, well done.' She was rising, greeting the kids. 'Sam, that's perfect.'

They were dragging what could vaguely be described as a stretcher-type object behind them. A raft of palm fronds. On top was folded plastic sheeting—bright blue—and a pile of ropes.

Jenny reached out and hugged the oldest boy—Sam—but Sam pulled back. His face wore a look of concern beyond his years.

'We took ages,' he muttered. 'It started to fall apart so we had to find stuff to tie it again. We used more of the ropes from Dad's cray pots. Dad'll be…' He stopped, caught himself, looked about to cry.

'Your dad'd be proud of you,' Jenny said stoutly. 'You've done brilliantly, you all have. But we have more work to do. We have to get Mr Braden to the house.'

'Silas,' he said weakly, trying not to think about what

lay ahead. Jenny's splint was holding his leg rigid—as it must. If he had indeed broken his leg—and it surely felt like it—then movement might allow bones to shift, cutting circulation. And the pain…

He'd never felt so helpless. He'd never been so helpless!

There was a slurp to the side of his face and suddenly he had a face full of dog. A black and white collie, wagging his tail, slurping from chin to eyebrow.

'Nipper,' Jenny said sharply. 'Back.'

The dog looked reproachfully up at her, and she had the temerity to grin. 'Sorry. This isn't exactly hospital hygiene we're practising here, but Nipper likes to know everything about his world. He's a dog who likes control.'

'Me and him both,' Silas muttered. 'I hate this.'

'Yeah, you need pain relief,' Jenny told him. 'I have drugs up at the house, but there's no time to get them on board or give them time to work before we move you. The next front's coming in fast. Let's get you onto this amazing stretcher and get you home.'

What followed was twenty minutes Silas would prefer to forget but would probably stay with him for ever.

Jenny was competent, organised, managing, but this was no normal paramedic's stretcher, and she had no adults to help her.

He could help a bit. His arms seemed undamaged, so she reluctantly agreed to let him hoist himself as she and the kids slid the stretcher under him.

'I didn't hit my back. There's no spine damage, and there's no choice.'

'Yeah, but once you're on the stretcher you're to lie still.'

So he did, and it nearly killed him. Not the pain,

though that was bad enough, but the embarrassment of being helpless. And he had to make it worse.

Jenny had attached the plastic sheeting under the fronds as a base—'It'll make it slide better and it has reinforced corners strong enough to tie ropes to.'

'Tie me up too,' he told her, and she blinked.

'Pardon?'

The last thing he wanted was to increase his sense of helplessness, but he had to make their job as easy as he could.

'If you tie me down there's no risk of me falling off. You can forget about me and just pull.'

'You wouldn't mind being tied?'

'Yes,' he conceded. 'But it makes sense.'

So he was trussed to the palms—and then they pulled. Jenny had one rope, Sam, Ruby and Tom had the other.

This was a massive effort. He was no lightweight, and the ground was rough, but every one of them put their all into tugging.

And then, stunningly, Jenny declared what was needed was a song.

'This is like when sailors had to haul up huge sails in the olden days,' she told them, suddenly sounding cheerful. 'We need a sea shanty. Do you guys know this one?' And she started singing, loud enough to make the dogs lurch away and stare at her in astonishment.

It was an oldie but a goodie. Even he knew it. Her voice was clear above the wind. *'Heave away, you rolling king, heave away, haul away...'*

The kids listened in stunned silence—they all did—and then Ruby giggled and joined in. And then Sam and Tom started as well, tugging and singing together.

Stupidly, he felt like laughing. If his throat didn't feel

so painful he'd sing himself. It was hysteria, he thought. It needed only this.

Finally they were over the dunes and Jenny called for a break. 'We're on the track now,' she told him, bending to check on him. He'd closed his eyes—did she think he'd died? 'We could get the tractor out and put you on it from here, but we're almost home.'

'Tractor…' He was feeling so damned helpless—and also not a little sick. The thought of motorised transport, no matter what it was, was infinitely appealing.

'Bertha. We use her for hauling kelp, but we can't take her over the dunes when the beach is sodden,' she explained. 'We'd lose her, and that's our income gone. You're important, but not that important.'

He wasn't important at all. He was totally, absolutely discombobulated.

'Home soon,' Jenny called. 'Right, kids, ten more verses and I reckon we're there.'

There was nothing he could do but submit.

CHAPTER FOUR

SILAS WOKE AND he was warm. He was dry, he was in a soft bed and the agonising pain of the night before had receded to a dull throb.

The sensation was unbelievable.

He opened one eye very cautiously, thinking the pain might flood back at any minute, but there was nothing but warmth and softness and safety.

Yesterday he'd been almost certain that he was about to die, and such an experience changed a man's perspective. He'd woken to the fact that he was in the middle of nowhere, he'd smashed his father's boat, his leg was almost certainly broken—but now, finally, he opened both eyes and felt nothing but relief.

He was on the floor, on a mattress heaped with pillows and covered with a gorgeous patchwork quilt. Some sort of frame had been fashioned to keep weight off his leg, but the rest of the bedding seemed almost cloudlike.

There were hot-water bottles on both sides of him. The warmth was unbelievable.

He lay still and let his mind drift over the events of the night before, trying to patch together a myriad of impressions he'd gained through a drug-induced haze. Definitely haze, because as soon as they'd reached the house Jenny—Dr Jenny—he knew enough now to accept her credentials—had administered enough morphine to put a horse out of pain.

For which he'd been pathetically grateful.

Then, as soon as the morphine had kicked in, she'd eased the palm frond stretcher out from under him so he was lying on a rug before the kitchen range. Then she'd sent the kids flying to find bedding, to bring warm water and towels and to check and see if the satellite phone was working. Anything to get them out of the way while she'd done a full examination. She'd cut away his soaked clothing, gently washed away salt and sand, cleaned abrasions and reorganised the splint. Then she'd helped the kids lug a mattress into the room. Finally she and Sam had helped him into a pair of men's pyjamas. After they'd chopped off one leg.

'They're Dad's,' Sam had said roughly when he'd protested. 'Dad wouldn't mind. He says we gotta help people in trouble.'

Hooray for Sam's dad, he thought hazily as he tried to remember the events of the night before—and then the door opened and Jenny entered.

Where last night she'd been wearing outdoor gear, now she was wearing a vast woolly dressing gown—faded pink—and a pair of thick sheepskin boots. The Jenny of last night had had her hair caught back. Now her auburn curls were tumbling to her shoulders, tangled, as if she'd just woken from sleep.

'Hey,' she said softly, crossing the room and squatting beside him. 'You're awake. And alive. Two out of two, hooray.'

'And not hurting,' he told her, and discovered his voice was husky and it was harder than he thought to talk. Too much salt water? Too much sand? No matter, he was alive; the fact that his throat was raspy was insignificant. 'So three out of three. Thanks to you.'

'To all of us,' she said. 'We make a great team. My next plan is to train our dogs, though. What we needed yesterday was a sled team, with me behind just offering the odd *mush*!' And she smiled.

He was silent, giving himself a moment to take in the warmth, the gentle crackle of the fire in the range, the sensation of this woman kneeling beside him.

Her smile!

'My ministering angel,' he murmured.

'Yeah, well, no one's ever called me that before,' she said prosaically. 'You want a bottle?'

He opened his eyes again and she was still smiling. Even laughing?

'Do ministering angels dispense bottles?' she asked, and she was teasing.

A bottle. He realised what she was asking and, dammit, he did need it. He had vague memories of last night, of her helping him drink, and now he regretted…

'Yes,' he said helplessly, and her grin widened.

'Coming right up. Pain, one to ten?'

'I… Two?' It was a lie. In reality it was probably somewhere about five, but compared to the night before it was fine.

She gave him a considering look. 'I topped up the morphine at four,' she told him, 'when I refilled your hot-water bottles. 'Let's hang on until we get you some breakfast. We'll top up again in an hour. At eight?'

'You gave me drugs at four?'

'Two-hourly obs,' she said, straightening but still smiling. 'I know, the best hospitals advise hourly, especially as you've obviously been hit on the head, but there are five people who need to survive in this place, Silas

Braden, and one of them's me. I can't cope with no sleep at all, so I took a professional risk. And hey, you still look alive, so that's a win. Now, let's get you sorted before the kids appear. They'd be fascinated by your bottle, but I suspect you'd rather not have your ablutions turn into a spectator sport. Right?'

'Right,' he said helplessly, and she grinned again and headed off to find a bottle.

What was she supposed to do with him?

She'd dressed and headed outside to see the damage. The roof—her main concern—seemed intact. The house was safe. She'd then fought her way down to the bay to see the wreckage of the boat, but one quick foray over the relative shelter of the sandhills had her heading back to the house fast. Now she was stirring pancake batter and worrying about the weather. Without her phone she had no clue as to how long it would be before she could get outside help.

But her main concern was the man dozing on the mattress on the far side of the kitchen. She could see no obvious danger, but he still had that contusion on his forehead, and that leg needed to be X-rayed. She had it splinted as firmly as she dared, but if the bones moved he was in real trouble.

Plus there was the possibility of water on his lungs. She'd listened to his chest, and it had seemed clear, but he'd coughed and his voice was husky. She'd started him on antibiotics—thanking the heavens again for her well-equipped medical kit—but he needed a scan. Pneumonia after such immersion was a real risk.

Bottom line? She needed him to be out of here. Her life was complicated enough already.

But still, as she tried to get the lumps out of her

batter—cooking had never been her skill—she was also aware of a sensation that had nothing to do with the urgency of getting this man off the island. He was an adult, someone to talk to, even if he could hardly answer. For Jenny, the last months had sometimes seemed like solitary confinement and it was driving her crazy. Rotten situation or not, this man's arrival had broken the solitude.

And that brought another thought, a thought she didn't need but it was there regardless. Silas Braden was every inch a man, and an attractive one at that. He was tall and tanned, with dark rumpled hair, a strongly boned face that looked almost sculpted, amazing blue eyes and a smile... Well, she'd only seen a hint of it, but it was enough to make a woman draw breath...

Oh, she missed her life. She missed...

No. She'd made the decision to come here, to give the kids the time they needed to grieve, to come to terms with their parents' death, and also to let her lawyers figure the complexities of wills that seemed just plain crazy.

'You beating that stuff because it deserves it?' The voice behind her made her jump.

She started and then stared down at the bowl. She *was* making the batter in a china bowl and the way she'd been beating she might well be risking sending broken china and batter mixture all over the kitchen.

'Lumps,' she said brusquely and set the bowl aside. 'Breakfast in five minutes. Pancakes.'

'Are you sure you have enough to feed me?'

'We have plenty of provisions,' she told him, and she couldn't get the bleakness out of her voice. She heard it and made an attempt to pull herself together. 'It's normally an hour's drive across the island to the general store, but the road's rough. We knew bad weather was coming—not this bad, but bad enough—so I made a special trip. As long as this storm breaks within a fortnight, we're good.'

'A fortnight!'

She greased her pan then concentrated on spooning batter into perfect circles. It helped to concentrate on small things, she'd found.

'It won't be that long.' *Please...*

'The forecast?'

'Who knows?' She tried to make her voice sound light. 'The satellite connection seems to have been cut, so there's no way I can find out.'

'No internet?' he said cautiously.

'And no phone.'

'And outside...?'

'Raining cats and dogs, and a sixty- to seventy-knot gale. Or higher—who knows? I actually don't understand knots, but we're cut off, Mr Braden. Just don't let that leg shift until we get you out of here.'

He lay in silence while she kept on cooking. Pouring, waiting for bubbles, flipping, ladling cooked pancakes into the oven to keep warm. The little things—they were all she could control.

'It won't be a fortnight,' he said, and for some reason he now sounded as if he was reassuring her. 'I watched the storm cell while I still had connectivity on the boat. Massive, and with what looked like two tails. This must be the second, but it looked relatively fast-moving.'

'Excellent,' she said, trying to sound pleased. 'So maybe another day of filthy weather, then a day for the islanders to get connectivity back up again.'

'You don't have a radio?'

'Nothing so fancy.'

'There's a radio in the boat.' But then he thought of the boat as he'd last seen her, broken and wallowing in the surf. Heaven knew what was left of her. 'Though I can't imagine that'll be useful.'

'It might be.' She frowned and flipped. 'I headed out for a bit when you went back to sleep. Fought my way down to the bay to take a look. She's beached. She has a big hole in her side, but she's now washed up on the sand, stuck fast. I got some decent ropes and attached her to a couple of palms above the high-water mark. The next high tide might shift her around a bit, but she shouldn't go anywhere. If your radio's still working it could be useful when the wind dies. It's not much use calling for help now, though—there's no way a chopper or boat could reach us.'

'Yeah?' Here at least was a little good news. Or…not so bad news.

'My boat…fixable?' he queried.

'I have no idea. I can't see you sailing off into the sunset any time soon, but with your leg you won't be doing that anyway. It's hospital for you, as soon as possible.'

He thought about that. He didn't like it, but she was right. He knew, as he imagined this woman knew, the ramifications of a leg fracture.

'It feels like a stable fracture,' he told her. 'I've felt along it and there's no sign it's compound.'

She frowned. 'You know fractures?'

'You're a doctor. I'm a doctor. Snap.'

'You're kidding.' Her eyes narrowed. 'A people doctor?'

'A paediatrician.'

'You're kidding. American?'

'Californian.'

'So why were you on that boat?'

'It's my dad's. I was sailing it back to the US as a birthday surprise.'

'As you do,' she said wryly. 'So now, instead of a boat, he gets a kid with a broken leg.'

'Not so much of the kid, thanks very much. I'm thirty-five.'

'Really? What you're doing sounds like something straight out of a *Boys' Own* adventure novel. Definitely a kid. Leaving that aside, though… I'll accept you're a doctor but, even though it's *your* leg, you can't be sure the fracture's stable. I just wish I had an X-ray machine tucked into the pantry.' She turned back to her pancakes. 'Sorry, but the pantry's filled with kelp chutney, which isn't much use when you want a bone scan.'

'Kelp chutney,' he said cautiously. He was still filled with painkillers, struggling with the shifts in conversation.

'My sister-in-law was a cook.' She still had her back to him. 'Sort of. If you like kelp. The freezer's still full of kelp casseroles, but since the day I cooked sausages the kids have abandoned their allegiance to their mother's cooking. Hooray, I've made one inroad into these kids' lives.'

There was so much here he didn't understand, and it wasn't just the drugs that made him feel confused. What was a trained doctor doing in the middle of nowhere—a doctor regarding kids eating sausages rather than kelp as a triumph?

'Right.' She flipped the last of her pancakes onto a plate and yelled, 'Breakfast!'

He was, he discovered, ravenous. She helped him prop himself up, and gourmet pancakes had never tasted so good.

While he ate, she sat with the kids. The kids hoovered up their breakfast like there was no tomorrow, but strangely they ate in near silence. Jenny asked a couple of questions and received terse responses. This was no happy family, he thought. There were so many questions.

But then she rose and handed him coffee, and those questions went out of the window. Coffee! Jenny had returned to the table but when he looked up from his mug she was smiling.

'Good?'

'Not just good. Is it just because I haven't had coffee for two days, or is it...?'

'Extraordinary,' she said, and her smile turned smug. 'It absolutely is. I thought of having my gorgeous espresso machine shipped over, but the generator's overloaded as it is. However, my wonderful colleagues gave me a farewell gift—a year's supply of coffee beans, with a coffee pot and grinder included. It'll be cheap instant stuff when I run out, but just this once I'm willing to share.'

Then she went back to eating with the silent kids. The conversation was at an end.

He was aware that he was being watched by the kids. They didn't speak to him though, and his attempts to break the ice were ignored. He tried to thank them for their efforts of the night before, but they simply waited politely until he'd finished speaking and then went back to their pancakes.

'Please can we leave the table?' It was a rote question, asked as the last pancake was demolished.

'Of course,' Jenny said. 'I'll be upstairs to help you with your lessons in a few minutes.'

'We can do them ourselves,' the older boy said flatly, and Jenny nodded.

'I know, but I like to help. See you soon.'

And then they were gone. Jenny looked after them for a moment and then closed her eyes—and then she opened them again and started prosaically clearing the table.

There was so much he didn't understand.

'So where are their parents?' he asked at last. She had her back to him, starting to wash dishes, and he saw her still. Her shoulders slumped a little, and then she braced herself and kept on washing.

Then she told him. He lay back and listened, shocked. Dead parents. Bereft kids. A twelve-year-old boy, wounded and traumatised. A young woman, hauled from her career, stuck on an island…for ever?

'You can't take them back to Sydney?'

'I can't,' she said, her voice bleak. 'Chris and Harriet… I guess they never imagined they'd die, and their will's awful. It was written by Harriet on a form they bought from the general store. They own…they owned almost all this side of the island and there's nickel underneath. Mining companies would pay a fortune for it. It's bequeathed to the kids in equal shares, but on the proviso that they stay here until the youngest turns twenty-one. Otherwise it reverts to a dodgy marine research group Harriet found on the internet.'

He frowned. 'That's crazy. Can't you appeal?'

'I'm trying,' she said tightly. 'But it seems watertight. There's nothing the research group would like better than for us to walk away—if we left they'd sell it in an instant. Meanwhile the kids have been brought up almost wild. Settling them in a cheap suburban house or an apartment in Sydney while I go back to work to support us all… How can I do that? I can't even afford to settle us on the other side of the island.'

'Would you want to?'

'There'd be people there,' she told him, and he heard the desperation in her voice. 'If we move into town—or what Albatross Island has in the way of a town—at least there's a school. It stops after eighth grade, but then the kids could take the ferry across to Gannet. There's a boarding facility on Gannet in case of bad weather, and the kids who go there seem to love it. What's more, with the kids at school I could start a small medical practice. With only four hundred on the island it'd be a meagre living, but it'd stop us relying on kelp curry.'

'You don't really rely on it?'

'Not yet, but the freezer's crammed and ready.' Suddenly her eyes creased again into that smile he was starting to look forward to. 'Come to think of it, it's supposed to be healthy and you're an invalid who needs building up.'

'Um…no, thank you,' he said hastily, and her smile grew.

'Brave, but not that brave?'

'Exactly.' His own smile faded. 'Jenny, I'm so sorry about your circumstances, and here I am, adding to your problems. I can't stay here on your kitchen floor.'

'You have no choice,' she told him. 'There's a spare bedroom but it's upstairs. When this next front passes I'll head back to your boat and see if I can work the radio. The medical service on Gannet'll send a chopper. Looking at this storm, though, I'm afraid that won't be until tomorrow, so for now you need to rest, stay still and don't move that leg. Meanwhile, I need to get these lessons going. These kids will get educated if it kills me.'

CHAPTER FIVE

HIS SITUATION WAS doing his head in. Jenny's drugs, however, were keeping the pain at bay and making him woozy. So he gave in to sleep, and woke a few hours later to a rush of wind blasting in from the back door. Jenny.

The hood of her oilskin was ripped, her curls were riotous and her face looked…sandblasted? She threw off coat and boots and headed for the sink, and he watched as she splashed her face with water. Over and over again.

One of the dogs had slunk in beside her. Once she'd dried her own face, she squatted and washed his face as well. He knew the dogs by now. Pepper was obviously elderly, his coat and muzzle greying with age. He'd obviously decided home duties were sensible, but Nipper must have been out in the storm with her. He watched as Jenny towelled Nipper's face and then did the same for Pepper, who'd nudged her leg as she'd stroked Nipper. If Nipper was being stroked, then Pepper was up for it too.

Finally she straightened, looked down at the dogs and grinned. 'Well, wasn't that worth it?'

The collies almost grinned back, wagging their tails fiercely, and Silas saw… Jenny as she should be? A Jenny who wasn't weighed down with kids and responsibility… and him. For a moment she looked almost happy.

And then she looked across at him and he almost saw the cloak of responsibility slip back on her shoulders.

'Good walk?' he asked, because he couldn't think of anything else to say. He glanced at the window, at the sand blasting against the glass, and winced.

'Bracing,' she said, and tried to resurrect her smile. 'That's how I feel. Braced.'

'Not like you've just spent an hour being sandpapered in a wind tunnel?'

'That too,' she told him. 'But the rain eased for a while, and we walked up the inland track. The wind was at our back for most of the way, but then we had to turn round. You have no idea how tempting it was to keep on going. With this wind at my back, I could have almost flown to Sydney.' She shrugged. 'However, like a good aunt I came home. I need to get lunch on; the kids'll be in soon.'

'They're out in this?'

'Of course,' she said simply. 'We've had almost two hours without rain, so we went looking for your radio. The kids helped me make doubly sure the boat's secure—the sand's driving into her side, but she's not going anywhere. Then Sam figured out the radio.'

'Sam did?'

'Sam's a boat nut,' she told him with a hint of pride. 'Boats seem pretty much the only thing he's interested in. Their schooling's basic, to say the least—my brother and his wife didn't see it as important—but I've bought him books on all things boating and he's been devouring them. One of them was on radios. He gave me a lecture on EPIRBs and why you should have been wearing one. But then he conceded that you might not have had time to activate it.'

'Good of him.' He grimaced. 'I *was* wearing one, attached to my lifejacket.'

'Whoops,' she said. 'I ripped it off when we found you. That'll be something for the kids to hunt for later. Anyway, once we had the boat secure Sam checked your main radio, but he says it's been soaked. It seems useless. But…' and here the note of pride deepened '… Sam said unless you're an idiot you'd also have had a portable radio, so he went hunting. He found it half filled with sand, but the thing still works. He couldn't get a signal though, so that's why we headed inland. Channel sixteen, Sam said, and something knowledgeable about repeater stations being all across the Birding Isles. So once we reached the old mine he tried, and magically a nice man on Gannet Island answered and patched…is that the right word?…us through to the hospital. The bottom line is that as soon as this next front passes they'll send the chopper. Probably not until tomorrow, but that's better than I hoped. So there you are, Dr Braden, rescued by Sam.'

Wow. He lay back feeling winded. They'd fought their way inland in this…

'I can't thank you…' he started.

'You don't need to. Everything's great. There's also a mountain of kelp washed up, so as soon as the storm's passed I have a week's work ahead of me, enough kelp to keep us fed for a month. Hooray.'

'You don't really eat kelp?' She had him fascinated, her ability to bounce with enthusiasm even when surely she must be feeling bleak and trapped.

'No,' she said. 'But it's our income, drying and selling it for commercial use. The kelp forests are dwindling and dumps like this are less and less frequent, but it's still enough.'

'So you'll spend the next week carting kelp.'

'And racking it so it'll dry. Yep.'

'But you're a doctor.'

'I was, but my dad was a kelp farmer. I've just come back to my roots.'

'Oh, Jenny…'

'Cut it out,' she said sharply, her bounce fading. Then she caught herself and smiled again. 'Tell me about you. Mum and dad? Kelp farmers too?'

'Um…no. Dad's a retired orthopaedic surgeon. Mom's a retired paediatric psychologist. They live in California, on the coast near Los Angeles. *Sea Raven*'s normally anchored near their home, but they sailed her to Australia before the pandemic hit. They've been trying to get her home ever since.'

'So you decided to sail her home by yourself?'

'Yeah.'

'Did your parents sail her alone?'

'Um…no,' he admitted. 'They hired a skipper. Plus a couple of deckhands.'

'Sam said that would have been more sensible. He said, "Bloody idiot".' She raised her brows and smiled, taking the edge off her criticism. 'His words, not mine. He mimics his dad.'

'He's right.'

She smiled—doctor comforting dope of a patient? 'Don't fret,' she told him kindly. 'Nothing can be changed by worrying. Meanwhile, the kids'll be here any minute; the sleet will drive them in. Nothing else will, but when they come they'll need lunch. How do sausages sound?'

'Awesome.'

'Excellent because that's our basic menu. Sausages, pasta, soup. Plus pancakes.'

All cheap. He thought of what she was trying to do, raise bereaved kids in such a place.

'Jenny, how can you possibly stay living here?'

'There's no choice. Not a single one that I can find.'

'Can you tell me the background?'

She gave him a considering look and then shrugged, folded her arms and leant back on the kitchen bench.

'Okay. Long story, but here goes. I was born here. My parents split when I was six. Mum took me back to Sydney, but my twelve-year-old brother stayed here with Dad. I went on to become a doctor, Chris stayed here. By the time Dad died, Chris had met Harriet. They had their kids and raised them to think Albatross Island was the centre of their universe. Meanwhile Mum never earned much, and I ran up a huge debt putting myself through med school. Then, after I graduated, I had…fun. Why not? The thought of having to take on the care of three kids was never in my orbit. Thus when Chris and Harriet were killed, I didn't have the money to care for them anywhere but here. So now I'm stuck.'

She dredged up an echo of her lovely smile. 'So that's it,' she said. 'Now it's one step at a time and next step is to make lunch.'

She turned away. He lay back and watched as she cooked, and he thought how she had the weight of the world on her shoulders. And how much he owed her and her blessed kids. If they hadn't found him…he might very well have died, he thought. He'd been injured, shocked, soaked, and the tide had been coming in. He must have been close to having hypothermia, and with his broken leg it would have been impossible for him to find shelter. Okay, he would have died, he conceded. He owed them big time.

The kids returned, rushing in as a pack, sitting at the table, eating as if they needed to make a fast getaway, looking sideways at him—and at Jenny—as if they were aliens in their world.

He tried to think of a way in. What did he know about them?

Sam's a boat nut.

'I need to thank you, Sam,' he said, wishing he could sit at the table with them rather than lie on the floor and look up. Not for the first time he cursed himself for his idiocy.

'Jenny said you understand radios,' he persevered. 'She says she wouldn't have been able to contact the hospital without your knowledge.'

'I read it in a book,' Sam said curtly, without looking up.

'Yeah, Jenny said she'd brought you books on boats.' This woman needed credit and by the look of the closed expressions on the kids' faces she wasn't getting enough. 'Do you know what my boat is?'

Sam stopped eating for a moment and stared down at his plate.

Silas was a paediatrician. He'd dealt with traumatised kids in his career—a lot of traumatised kids. He knew enough not to push. He let the silence hang, not rushing in to tell him.

'It's a yacht.' That was Ruby, glancing at her brother and then stating the obvious, scornful of someone who didn't even know what type of boat he owned.

And finally Sam responded. He put down his fork and sighed, clearly about to enlighten his dumb audience.

'It's a gulet,' he told them. 'She's a classic wooden double-masted schooner. Old, I think, but I reckon she's been restored. She's small for a gulet, they can be up to thirty metres, but I reckon this one's not even twenty. She's got plenty of sail area, and with easy reefing and good assistive equipment she might be okay for one person to handle. In good weather.'

And his tone said exactly what he thought of Silas risking such a beauty by sailing her alone.

But Silas wasn't abashed. He was stunned by the boy's knowledge, and while he had his interest he wasn't about to let it go.

'They're about to take me to hospital,' he said, talking straight to Sam now. 'I gather you and Jenny have her safely beached.'

'I wouldn't say safe,' Sam said dourly. 'She's holed, and at high tide the water's still coming in.'

'So any suggestions?'

That created more silence. Sam ate another sausage, but Silas could practically see the cogs whirring.

He glanced across at Jenny. She'd stopped eating herself. She looked…to be almost holding her breath.

How hard had it been, trying to get through to these wounded kids? How impossible was the future she was facing?

How important was it that somehow, someone could get though the barriers Sam had put up to protect himself from pain?

And finally, blessedly, he cracked.

'Mr Robbins and Mr McArthur would help,' he said, and stabbed another sausage from the plate in the middle. 'You can't contact them till the storm dies, at least I don't think you can. They'll probably have a radio but I don't know their channel.'

'Mr Robbins and Mr McArthur?' he queried, and looked at Jenny.

'Doug and Fred. They have a boatshed on the town side of the island,' she told him. 'They've been here for ever, fixing boats and making new ones. Commission only. They both must be pushing eighty now but they're good.'

'Sam goes there,' Ruby volunteered, while Sam concentrated on his sausage. 'Whenever Mum goes to the store he scarpers and Mum has to drag him out. Mum gets cross 'cos she hates that side of the island. And she says he's a nuisance.'

'They like me,' Sam muttered. 'And they let me do things.'

'Do you think they might help with my boat?'

He considered. 'Maybe. They'd have to get her off the beach, though. Take her overland. They'd probably need a low-loader—Craig Jennings' big truck. You'd have to pay. A lot.'

Silas glanced at Jenny—who was carefully not looking at him. Not looking at anything. This was important, he thought, but suddenly it wasn't all about a damaged boat. Just how dissociated had this boy been?

Okay, he needed to plan. Planning was his forte, his only thing to hold on to. If these guys really were boat-builders he could ask Jenny to contact…

But then he looked again at Jenny. She was staring at her plate, and he could almost read her body language. *Don't ask me, don't ask me, don't ask me.*

And he got it. It wasn't that she didn't want anything more heaped on her; it was just that Sam was actually talking. Actually interested.

Okay, he'd take her cue.

'Do you think,' he asked, speaking directly to Sam and only to Sam, 'that you could contact these men as soon as you can and explain what's happened? Could you tell them that the boat belongs to a crazy American and he's wealthy and he's happy to pay whatever's needed to get her mended? They'll be able to contact me at…' He looked at Jenny.

'Gannet Island Hospital,' she told him, still not looking up.

'Gannet Island Hospital. I'll give them any authorisation they need. But Sam…'

'Mmm?' The kid still sounded suspicious.

'I don't know them. Do you think you could clear out anything you think might be valuable from the boat before they take her away? Could you keep my stuff here? And if they take her to fix her… I'm guessing you all need to cross the island to the store every now and then?'

'Yeah,' he said shortly.

'Could you ask Jenny if she'd mind dropping you off at the boatyard to see how she's going? Just until I can get back. I need someone to keep an eye on things—to tell me what's happening. Do you think Jenny would mind taking you to the boatyard?'

Sam stared at him in astonishment—and then turned to Jenny.

'C…can I?'

'Of course,' she said promptly. 'I know nothing about boats, and someone has to take charge. I usually only go across once a week,' she said. 'But if the boat's there it wouldn't hurt to go every couple of days.'

The look on the kid's face was a gift.

In his work as a paediatrician Silas saw many kids—sick kids, damaged kids. The look on Sam's face now… Well, that was why he was a paediatrician, to search for that look on a child's face. Or on their parents' faces.

And then suddenly Harper was with him again, the memory of his daughter's torn expression as Charlotte propelled her to the car. 'You'll love skiing with me, Harper. Your father will be fine by himself.'

It must be the drugs, Silas thought because, dammit, for some reason he was suddenly close to tears.

He shook away the vision and looked at Jenny, and she wasn't looking at her plate any more. She was looking right at him, and her look…

It was as if he'd given her the world.

Where had this emotion come from? It was such a small thing…

'That'd be great,' he said a trifle unsteadily, because suddenly he was feeling as if he needed to retreat. Back to where that corner of his heart could stay untouched.

Sam was pushing back his plate and standing—a man with a plan? 'It's starting to rain again now, but as soon as it stops then me and Ruby and Tom will head back to the beach,' he decreed. 'We'll watch her for you, Mr Braden.'

'Silas,' he said. 'Please call me Silas.'

'Silas,' Sam said, as if he was sounding out the name to see how it felt. 'Silas,' he repeated and grinned and headed for the stairs.

Then they were gone, and he was left with Jenny.

'Do you have any idea of what you've just achieved?' she asked. 'Silas Braden, I could kiss you.'

'You're very welcome.'

There was a moment's silence while the weight of those words seemed to hang in the air. It had been a light statement, an equally light response. Sexual tension was the last thing intended or desired, and yet… What was it with the way he was starting to feel?

'Um…probably not wise,' she said at last, sounding a bit breathless.

'No,' he agreed.

And then she pulled herself together. They both did.

'Definitely not wise,' Jenny said briskly, moving on. 'Let me give you a bottle instead.'

* * *

They came for him just after dawn the next day—and adding to his sense of pain and helplessness was a strange sense of loss.

The medics from Gannet, arriving via helicopter, were competent, sympathetic, efficient.

Marc, introducing himself as head of the island medical service, seemed almost jovial. 'You never know what the storm'll blow in,' he told them. 'We've had an entire shipping container washed up on the far side of Gannet. The locals got it open and discovered it's chock-full of outdoor furniture. Designer stuff, a bit waterlogged but basically good as new. Chaises longues, cabanas, the works. How do you feel about a trendy outdoor setting for your patio, Jenny?'

'My patio?' Jenny asked, and they all looked out at her sandblasted porch. It was littered with ancient cray pots, plus what looked like years of detritus, most of it half buried in sand. 'I guess it'd give us a touch of class.'

'It would indeed,' Marc said cheerfully. 'And I'll keep you in touch with any other offers. Apparently a few boats lost things overboard. Every local worth his salt is out scouring beaches—it's beachcombers' paradise.'

And then they were loading Silas onto a stretcher and preparing him for the flight. Jenny had topped up his drug dosages. He was feeling hazy, slightly sleepy—but when he looked at Jenny he was aware of a sweeping sense of regret. And…shame? This woman had so much on her plate, but she'd taken him on, cared for him—what could he do for her?

Right now, nothing.

'At least you don't need to worry about your boat,' she told him as they made sure he was secure. 'Sam has it in hand.' And he heard a note of pride—and something else. Hope? He glanced across at the kids, watching from the sidelines as the medics made him secure.

'You all saved my life,' he told them. 'You've been brilliant. You'll talk to the guys about my boat, Sam?'

''Course,' Sam said, and Silas glanced at Jenny and saw a flush of pleasure.

'You've given me this,' she said quietly. 'He woke up this morning and all he could talk about was the boat. But he did talk. We may have pulled you off the beach, Silas Braden, but you've pulled Sam out of a hole where I couldn't reach him. Thank you.'

And then, because they were about to lift him into the chopper and it seemed…well, maybe it seemed like the right thing to do…she stooped and kissed him. The promised kiss from the day before?

No. It was a feather kiss, a kiss of farewell from someone who'd saved his life.

He reached up and took her hand—and he had an almost irresistible urge to tug her down again. To make that kiss deeper.

Which was stupid. It was the drugs, he told himself again. This situation was complicated enough already.

'Stay safe,' he told her stupidly, and she managed a chuckle.

'Look who's talking. You're the one who sails around the world in a bathtub. Me, I get to stay here and eat kelp.'

CHAPTER SIX

THE HOSPITAL ON Gannet Island was surprisingly well equipped. There were competent nursing staff, excellent doctors, state-of-the-art equipment. He was in the best of hands.

His leg was swiftly taken care of. X-rays confirmed a broken tibia, but no displacement meant that once the swelling went down it could be splinted, braced and he could get on with life. Even if his life was now a lot more complicated.

More problematic, though, was the condition of his lungs. 'Messy,' Marc said bluntly when all the tests had been carried out. 'How much sea water did you breathe in? No, don't answer, I expect you didn't measure, but thank God Jenny had the sense to start you on antibiotics. You're already showing signs of bacterial pneumonia. We'll start you on physiotherapy straight away, but if you think you're getting on a plane back to Sydney until it's totally cleared, think again. Aircraft cabins are low pressure, hypoxic environments. Until we get your lungs up to normal performance status, flying's the last thing you need. Meanwhile, unless you go against our advice, you'll stay put.'

So he stayed put. In truth he was even grateful. He needed time to come to terms with what had happened, and also to try to figure what came next. His leg hurt more than he cared to admit, and his chest hurt too. Dammit, just how close to death had he been?

Very close. If it hadn't been for Jenny and her kids…

But they weren't her kids, and as the days wore on he found himself thinking about her situation more and more. Which, in a way, was a relief. Every day since the tragedy that had robbed him of wife and child, he'd woken thinking of them. Well, mostly of Harper. Her bright, sparrow-like face. Her trust in the world.

'Why don't you come with us?' she'd asked that last fateful morning, but Charlotte hadn't suggested that he join them.

He and Charlotte had wed thinking they were the perfect match, but almost from the moment of Harper's birth their marriage had started to fray. Charlotte was a doctor—a good one—but with the arrival of their baby, with Silas's family wealth, her attitude to medicine changed. Apparently she'd achieved her ambitions, and she resented his continued devotion to his career.

Although she still valued her medical identity, it became way down the list of her priorities. They'd hire a nanny and enjoy themselves, she decreed, and there was tension as she was forced to accept how much his medicine meant to him. He loved his family, but his work seemed so important. Surely they could compromise and enjoy both?

But compromise didn't seem to be in her vocabulary, and as time went on, he realised she no longer valued the things he did—or maybe she never had. Maybe, he conceded, he'd never really known her?

Somehow they'd stayed together, but as time went on Charlotte's energy became almost solely directed towards their social life—or *her* social life. When her friends had suggested taking extended leave and heading for the ski slopes, she'd accepted without even talking to Silas.

But she *had* decided to take Harper. She'd loved her daughter—the shared love of their little girl was probably the only thing that held their marriage together. There'd be a ski school and she'd take Harper's nanny, she'd told Silas. Harper could learn to ski.

So Silas had stayed, but as they'd driven away Harper had looked back at him. That look haunted him every waking minute, and it was with him in his dreams. Her loss was so crushing that if he'd died on that beach…

Maybe it would have been welcome, he thought, but somehow now there were chinks of light in the blackness.

He had a challenge—to get his father's precious boat mended and back to the States. That hadn't lifted the blackness, though. What did was the thought of what Jenny was coping with.

He wanted to help. No, he had to help; it was as simple as that.

Money? Well, that'd be simple. Thanks to a great-grandfather and grandfather who'd made a fortune in land speculation, that was one thing Silas's family had never lacked. He could hand her a cheque that should solve all her problems.

Except it wouldn't. Thirty-six hours in that bleak little cottage had made him see exactly what she was facing. He was a paediatrician, and he knew damaged kids when he saw them. He'd watched Jenny's face light up when he'd asked Sam for help, and he knew that she loved those kids. She'd never drag them off the island. Money couldn't solve everything.

But it could solve some things. Lying in his small hospital room, looking out at the truly magnificent vista of ocean and island wilderness—whoever had designed this hospital deserved a medal—he had time to think, and on day three, when the door of his room opened and Jenny popped her head around the door, he almost had a plan.

'Hey!' She'd rung every day since he'd been admitted, checking on progress. The calls had seemed a little stilted but now, as he saw her smile, he was aware of a shaft of delight. And something…more?

Of course it was more. This wasn't a normal visitor. This was the woman who'd saved his life.

This was Jenny, and the way he found himself smiling… People could get extraordinarily fond of their doctors, he thought, fighting to explain his feelings. There were reasons why doctors weren't permitted to date their patients. It could easily end up as something like Stockholm Syndrome, where people grew inappropriately attached to their kidnappers.

Did that explain the way he felt? Surely not.

She looked great. Except she didn't. The women in the circles Silas moved in looked far more beautiful than this. Charlotte had been gorgeous in comparison.

But Jenny looked neat, and that alone was a surprise. She hadn't looked the least bit neat last time he'd seen her. She'd been wind-tossed and sand-blasted on the beach and then, back at the house, she'd been…well, scruffy might be an appropriate descriptor. She'd been cooking, lugging firewood, caring for three kids plus one shipwrecked disaster. She'd worn faded jeans, an ancient windcheater and her hair had been a tousled mass of auburn curls.

Now she was wearing neat white trousers, a pale blue blouse and a cute denim jacket. Her glossy curls were twisted in a knot but cascading a little from their fastening. Yes, she looked bouncy and attractive, but surely not enough to take a man's breath away.

Stockholm Syndrome, he told himself sharply, although this woman had never held him captive. And why the thought…

'Can I come in?' She'd stopped at the door, waiting for permission, and he was aware that he'd waited too long. He'd been staring too long.

'Sorry.' He shoved himself up on his pillows, thinking he'd much prefer not to be sitting in bed wearing strange pyjamas—covered with cartoon-style flamingos floating on inflatable swim tubes. Drinking martinis. These were so not the pyjamas of his choice. 'Please. You're very welcome.'

'Well, I hoped I might be,' she told him. 'I had to bring Sam over for his regular check-up—Marc keeps an eye on his foot. I need to tell you though, Silas, helping with your boat has done miracles. It's fixing more than his foot. We're going across to town every day so he can help Doug and Fred, and he's loving it. He chatted to Marc about the boat while he was checking his foot. Right now Marc's wife, Elsa, has taken them to the baker's for a treat and he's telling Elsa about your boat, too. He's happy and I'm happy—and yay, I have a whole hour free so I thought I'd pop in.'

'You don't have other things to do with a free hour?' He thought briefly of the life she must have been leading back in Sydney—and the life she was leading now. A whole hour without kids…in how long?

'I can do most things with kids,' she told him. 'And they're trustworthy. Elsa's a doctor too. She has two littles of her own and she'll help out when I'm stuck, but Sam's pretty dependable.'

'I can see that.' He frowned. 'And I've met Elsa. She came to visit me yesterday, checking me out, I thought. But she also came to be helpful.' He grinned and motioned to his pyjamas. 'She brought me these, courtesy of the Gannet Island Haberdashery. I gather it was flamingos or nothing.'

'And very attractive they are too,' she said promptly, and grinned. 'I like their inflatable tubes, a reminder to you that life-preservers are important. Though I wouldn't suggest martinis while swimming. I assume you weren't drinking those as your boat went down?'

'As if,' he said, and he smiled back and there it was again, that frisson…

Which had to be ignored. He had a proposition and he needed to clear his head to spell it out. 'To be honest though, Jenny, we talked about you. Hell, Jenny, your life…'

'I'm not here to talk about me,' she said, her smile fading a little. She tugged up a chair and sat. 'I'm in hospital visitor mode. Though, come to think about it, I was the one who called Marc, so I'm your referring physician. Marc tells me your chest is taking time to clear. He's not letting you out?'

'Tomorrow,' he told her. 'But I can't fly home, or even back to Sydney. My lungs need a while longer, and then there's the problem of the boat.'

'She's in great hands. When I put Sam on the line yesterday, I hope he explained. I've left it up to him—he's enjoying the responsibility so much.'

'I guessed that.' He hesitated. 'Jenny, that's pretty much what I wanted to talk to you about. Sam tells me the boat's been carted across the island and it's in the Albatross boatyard.'

'Being lovingly cared for. Doug and Fred have pretty much put everything aside to work on her. I assume they've contacted you already—they told me they would. They seem to think money's no object.'

'It isn't,' he said shortly. 'Jenny, I have an idea that might help both of us.'

She frowned. 'I don't want help.'

'I'm pretty sure you do, and it's not only money I'm talking about.' He'd had a long talk with Elsa, who'd spelled out Jenny's situation, and the more he thought about it the more he hoped he could do something. Elsa had been really helpful. The young mum-cum-doctor had been born here and seemed to know every single thing about the islanders. 'Jenny, I have a plan to help us both.'

'I don't need…'

'You do need.'

But how to put it? This was a lot harder than he'd thought. Part of the problem was that he was sitting in a hospital bed wearing flamingo pyjamas. Charlotte and Harper's death had smashed the illusion that life could be controlled. He should be used to the feeling of exposure by now, but he still felt at sea. As if a lot was hanging on the way Jenny reacted to his proposal.

'Jenny, how do you feel about sharing a house with me for a few weeks?' he asked, talking a bit too fast. 'Maybe until the boat's fixed and I can get the cast from my leg?'

Her brow creased. He liked the way it did that—the pucker between her brows was really cute. He could almost see her brain engage as she thought about what he'd said.

'You want to stay with us? I guess,' she said dubiously. 'We do have a spare room. But it's upstairs, and how would you cope with your leg? Also, we're on the far side of the island and you'd be isolated. I imagine you'd want to spend time at the boatshed. I guess you could borrow my car, but I don't like being stuck…being with the kids without a car…'

'Without an escape,' he agreed. 'I can see that. But my

leg won't be up to driving for a while, so I have a better plan. Elsa's suggested a house. She says it's about a block from the boatshed and a couple of blocks from the shops. It looks over the bay and sounds perfect. It's owned by a lady called Joan Heffernan—do you know her?'

'No, I…'

'Elsa said it's a family house, four bedrooms, all on the one level, so I could cope with my leg—I'll be using crutches for a while. Joan's a widow and her family's in Sydney. When the pandemic hit they panicked and insisted she join them. Elsa says she's loving Sydney, she'll probably stay there, but she's still torn about selling.'

He could understand that. Selling a family home, with too many memories… You had to do it hard and fast, he thought—or not at all.

He thought stupidly of the gorgeous home he'd bought next door to his parents', a rambling bungalow overlooking the sea. Properties in that select beachside location were as rare as hen's teeth, and he'd bought it the moment his parents had found out it was for sale.

It had been a mistake. Charlotte had disliked it from the start, and they'd seldom used it. For some stupid reason, though, he'd refused to sell. Keeping the dream alive? That was a joke. The dream was now well and truly gone.

Don't go there, he told himself. Now wasn't the time.

When was the time?

Jenny's furrow had deepened, and she was looking at him in concern. 'Silas, what's wrong?'

'Nothing,' he said a bit too brusquely, and then he recalibrated. This woman was smart and she'd have seen his expression change. 'Just my leg,' he told her. 'It still hurts.'

'Which is why you're in hospital. You want me to call someone? When did you last take painkillers?'

'It's half an hour till I'm due,' he told her, lying again. In truth he'd been managing without them. 'But, back to this house… Jenny, Elsa's made a call to Joan on our… on my behalf, and Joan thinks rental sounds great. Her house is furnished, so all I have to do is move in. But it comes with a year's lease.'

'A year?' That furrow was starting to seem like a permanent fixture. 'You don't want to stay here for a year!'

'I don't,' he admitted. 'But Joan doesn't want the bother of renting for only a few weeks. She'll need to get her friends to take her personal belongings out, and it's not worth it for six weeks' rent. But Elsa says it's lovely. It sounds ideal for me to limp back and forth to the boatshed—or sit on the veranda and look out to sea, like the invalid I'm forced to be. Jenny, it's the only place available.' That actually wasn't true, but it fitted the narrative he needed. 'And money's not a worry.'

'No?' She sounded bemused.

'My family's wealthy.'

She frowned. 'Your parents would pay?'

He grinned at that, at the idea of him fronting up to his dad and asking for a year's rent. 'Um…no,' he admitted. 'I mean…we're *really* wealthy. My grandfather and great-grandfather speculated in land well before my time and there's family wealth. Dad was an only child and I'm the same. I've had a trust available ever since I turned twenty-one and, believe me, a year's lease won't even dent it.'

'*Really?*'

'Really. So here's the plan. I move into this house, and you and the kids do too.'

'Me,' she said slowly. 'And the kids.'

'Jenny, I owe you,' he said, quietly now, and seriously. He was at a disadvantage, sitting in his dumb pyjamas, and he needed to be taken seriously. 'You saved my life—you know you did—you and your blessed kids. As well as that, somehow you managed to get my father's boat tethered so it wasn't completely destroyed, and you can't begin to know how important that is to Dad. And to me. So this could be a small way of me saying thank you. I'd like to rent Joan's house for a year. I'd like to live in it myself for six weeks, but I'd like you to have the use of it for a year. So…if you think it could work, I'd like you and the kids to move in.'

There was a moment's silence. No, more than a moment. She gazed at him, her eyes not leaving his. Searching, as though she was trying to read him.

'But…why?' she said at last.

'Because it'll cost me little. Because it'll make things simple for me while I recover and the boat's being repaired. But also because I believe—and Elsa believes—that it'll make things a whole lot easier for you.'

'The kids won't leave their home.'

'Really? Not even when Sam has the inducement of being chief supervisor of boat repair? I've talked to Doug and Fred. They know and like Sam, and they say he'd be very welcome to spend any spare time he has in the yard. They'd even enjoy teaching him. But we've discussed it and they agree that if he did that he'd probably need to go to school as well.' He smiled, well satisfied with the result of plotting between himself and the two elderly boat-builders. And Elsa. 'They say there's not much use teaching a kid boat skills if he doesn't get the schooling to get through an apprenticeship, and they'll tell him that.'

She was staring at him, open-mouthed. 'You're kidding.' It was he who had the damaged lungs, he thought, but that was how she sounded. As if she was having trouble breathing.

'Elsa seems to think an inducement like this might be the very thing to persuade him out of his isolation,' he said softly now, watching her face. 'Where Sam leads, Ruby and Tom will follow, and Elsa thinks they'll love making new friends. They've been isolated for too long. Also…' He hesitated, wondering if he'd gone too far but there seemed nothing for it but to forge on. 'Elsa says if you're on the town side of the island and the kids are at school then you might have time to set up a small medical clinic.' He was trying hard to say it in an offhand manner, as if it didn't really matter if she agreed or not. 'In a year…maybe it'd be enough to bring in an income. Enough to set yourself up in your own place? I know it's not nearly as much fun as hauling kelp for a living, and you'd probably miss kelp curries but…'

'Oh, Silas…'

'Think about it,' he said and lay back on his pillows feeling winded. His chest did hurt, but it wasn't that that made him feel winded. It was the way she looked.

As if she'd been given the world?

It was enough to make a man…well, feel winded.

For the last couple of years he'd been moving in some strange, numb other life. He'd worked, he'd socialised with his parents and his friends, he'd done what was expected of him. On the outside he might even have appeared normal but on the inside it was as if he'd been living in fog. There'd seemed no colour, no taste, no fire.

And now, when he'd least expected it, lying in a hospital bed in the middle of nowhere, wearing dumb pyjamas, with a leg that ached and a chest that hurt, it was as if the fog had parted. Just a little, just enough to allow a shaft of light. To watch a woman's face and see hope…

He lay back and held his breath and the world seemed to hang.

She wouldn't have to cart kelp any more.

The kids could go to school.

Sam could love it.

Which was more important?

Sam, she thought, trying desperately to get her thoughts in order in the face of this extraordinary offer. *Think about Sam.*

'You need to give him time,' the island's psychologist had told her. 'He's a kid who's faced the most traumatic thing a child could ever confront. The only security he has is his home, his place. I'm sorry, it's not what you want to hear, but take that away from him now at your peril.'

She couldn't. The thought of living in her brother's ramshackle house, dependent on kelp-gathering for a living, had been doing her head in, yet almost as soon as she'd met them she'd loved these kids. Maybe that had something to do with the shadowy memory of a big brother she'd adored, maybe it was the kids themselves, but, no matter what the reason, she couldn't face the thought of tearing them away from the only life they knew.

But to take them somewhere they could possibly be happy… It might just work, she thought, hope invading her thoughts in a way that was almost breathtaking. She'd watched Sam on the beach with the men who'd retrieved the boat. She'd heard him ask question after question, queries she could only guess were intelligent, but they'd surely sounded so. She'd watched Fred and Doug supervising the whole operation, treating him as if they respected him.

This was the first glimmer of interest he'd shown, the first sign that there was life after horror. And if Sam liked the idea…

'They might agree,' she whispered almost to herself. 'I think they'd enjoy school. Ruby loves gymnastics and I know they run classes. And Tom…he said he wants to be a footy player when he grows up, and they have a tiny team. The teachers are lovely, so enthusiastic. And if I had no rent I could afford to set up a small medical practice, enough to keep us fed.'

'On something other than kelp,' he agreed.

'Oh, Silas…' She gazed at him rather helplessly. 'I shouldn't agree.'

'Why wouldn't you? It would give me a place to recuperate, and I could leave with a clear conscience, my debt to you repaid.'

'There's no debt.'

'There is a debt.' He couldn't help himself; he reached out and took her hands, gripping them hard. 'Jenny, let me do this for you. Please.'

She stared down at his hands. They were warm, strong, sure, and the feel of them was…extraordinary. It was a hold that said she wasn't alone, and for the first time since she'd heard of her brother's death she felt… as if she had foundations again.

This man… No. It wasn't anything to do with Silas, she told herself a trifle desperately. It was all to do with the offer he'd made. If this gesture indeed meant little to him in terms of cost… The difference it'd make to her life…

'I need to talk to the kids,' she said a trifle unsteadily.

'Of course.' His hands still held hers. 'I get it that they need to feel safe, but Marc seems to think this setup would be a huge inducement.'

'You've talked to Marc about it too?'

'I've talked to everyone I can about the best way to help,' he said simply. 'Marc's also talked to the psychologist—Donna, is that her name? Because Marc's Sam's treating doctor, Donna felt she could tell him what she thinks, and she seems to believe it'd work too.'

'You've set up a team,' she managed, and for the life of her she couldn't stop her voice from quavering.

'It takes a village to raise a child,' he said gently. 'Everyone knows you've been doing it alone for too long, but there seemed no way to help. But now…if the kids agree then all you need to do is accept. You don't look a gift horse in the mouth, right?'

'It's you. You're the gift horse.'

'Then look at me all you want,' he said gently. 'But just say yes.' And the pressure on her hands intensified.

She stared down at them. The feel of them… He was holding her as if…as if…

But then there was a knock on the door and Marc appeared—head of Birding Isles Medical Services. 'Can I disturb you for a moment?'

'Of course.' Silas withdrew his hands and Jenny concentrated on her breathing. Somehow she needed to ground herself, to find a rational explanation for the weird sensations she was starting to feel.

It wasn't his offer that was throwing her for six. It was the way he'd held her. The way his grip had tightened—as if he'd needed their link?

There was a rational explanation, she told herself. Silas had been close to death. Whether he admitted it or not, he must have been terrified. Human contact—the touch of a hand—would be doubly, triply, important to him now as he tried to ground himself. Surely that was what the touch was all about.

And her? He'd just offered her the world, or if not the world then a way out of an impossible situation. Of course she'd needed to let her hands lie in his. To do anything else would have been churlish. No matter that it made her feel…

Cut it out, she told herself and took a deep breath and turned to focus on Marc.

'You want to examine your patient?' she asked. 'I'm happy to leave.'

'No, this is a business deal,' Marc said, smiling at them both. And his smile… He'd seen the hand clasp, she thought, and she found herself flushing. *Oh, for heaven's sake.*

'You've told Jenny about the house?' Marc was asking, and Silas nodded.

'Great,' Marc said, beaming. 'All Elsa's idea, Jen. She's organised it so you can see the house on the way home tonight. If you're interested.'

'If the kids…'

'The kids'll jump at it,' Marc said, his beam widening. 'But Silas, mate, it's you I wanted to talk about. You're a paediatrician, right? A good one. I've made enquiries…'

Of course he had, Jenny thought faintly. Marc was responsible for assembling a breathtakingly competent medical team on this group of remote islands, and he'd never let an opportunity to garner another if he had the opportunity.

'I'm not interested in a job,' Silas said uneasily, guessing before Marc opened his mouth, and Marc grinned.

'No, I get that you're only here for six weeks. And you want to be back on Albatross with your boat. But Elsa says Joan's house can't be ready for a couple of days. Jenny will be busy packing and won't want a house guest. So I'm thinking… Mate, we have a problem—a kid with cystic fibrosis. Matthew's nine and he goes to Sydney for a full check-up every three months, but his mum's heavily pregnant and can't take him. Matt's looking okay, but I wondered—a full going-over by a paediatrician would allay her fears. I also have a couple of other kids I'd like checked out—development delays, parents worried. I thought…could you stay on with us until Saturday? That'd give Jenny time to sort the kids out, Joan's friends time to clear her personal things and…'

'And give you a captive paediatrician,' Jenny said and grinned. 'Watch out, Silas.'

'It'd be great,' Marc agreed. 'And maybe over the next few weeks we could call on you a bit? Meanwhile, Jen, if you can set up a clinic on Albatross, you'll need equipment. I can get it to you in a heartbeat. Just say the word and we'll have a team setting you up in style.'

'Marc…' Jenny said weakly, and Silas grinned, and suddenly he was reaching out and taking her hand again.

'Do you get the feeling we're being bulldozed?' he asked. 'Well, so we are, but no one will make you do what you don't want. The choice is yours. But if it's this or kelp casseroles…'

She thought of the freezer back on Albatross, loaded to bursting point with so many varieties of casserole she couldn't count. All made of kelp. She thought of the days she'd spent heaving kelp onto racks. She thought of the unbroken, unending loneliness.

School for the kids. Sam with an interest, a passion. Ruby and Tom making friends. A medical clinic, a job with no kelp in sight.

'Yes,' she said, and she said it too fast so it came out almost as a sob. And as Silas's hand gripped hers more tightly she couldn't help herself, the tears started. 'Y…yes, please.'

CHAPTER SEVEN

THERE WAS NOT a qualm from the kids—not one. She talked to them about it on the return ferry trip, but it seemed Elsa had done her groundwork, outlining the great things about moving to the other side of the island. Ruby and Tom were cautiously excited, and as for Sam, the prospect of spending part of every day working with Doug and Fred had him almost stammering his agreement.

And thus the thing was settled.

Until now Jenny had had no idea how much the islanders as a whole had worried about her and her little family, but now she was shown. Offers of help came from everywhere, and things moved fast. Four days later a convoy of small trucks made the bumpy trip across the island and she and the kids drove behind them. Heading to their new home.

She pulled up, the kids and dogs tumbled out of the car and Silas was standing on the veranda, smiling.

And oh, that smile.

Uh-oh. What was she doing, agreeing to live with this man?

Get a grip. He's only here for six weeks, she told herself. *Then he'll be gone, and we'll have the rest of this fabulous house to ourselves.*

And it was fabulous. Joan's niece had shown her through the evening they'd come home from Gannet, and it had been as much as Jenny could manage not to gasp. The house was big and rambling, a home that had always been loved and cared for. It was oriented to face the ocean and the sun. The rooms were furnished with faded rugs, big squishy sofas and chairs, an enormous scrubbed wooden table, a kitchen to die for. A great open fire in the living room. Central heating. Gardens that meandered to the beach, so the beach was almost an extension of their front yard.

'It's great.' Silas was leaning on crutches, smiling as she headed up the steps to greet him. He must have just seen it for the first time, she thought. That would explain the smile.

Though…how had he described himself? *Really wealthy.* She wasn't sure what that meant, but presumably he wouldn't be as gobsmacked as she was by the sheer comfort of this house.

'I've nabbed the master bedroom at the east end of the house,' he told her. 'Cheeky, but the other bedrooms are close together and…'

'And I'd like to be with the kids.'

Except…part of her wouldn't. She was standing on the veranda with a gorgeous guy—and yeah, this guy was seriously hot—and he was happily saying he'd have the master bedroom at one end of the house and she and her kids—*her kids*—would have the other.

And for some reason it was like a slap. What had happened to the Jenny she knew—to the lifestyle she loved? She was part of a new entity. *Jenny and her kids.* Now and for ever.

But then she looked out at the kids, who, with dogs at

their heels, were already heading for the native willows, figuring out how to climb. They already seemed happy.

That was what she was aiming for, so why should a part of her feel empty? Listening to this gorgeous doctor explaining why he'd sleep at one end of the house and she and her kids would have the other. Thinking of the life she'd left behind.

'What's wrong?' His voice became gentle, and she struggled to pull herself together.

'I…nothing. This is amazing. I…we're so grateful.'

'It'll be a better life for you.'

'It will.'

'But not better than the one you had before your brother died,' he said with sudden shrewdness, and just as suddenly she was close to tears again.

Which was ridiculous. This place was such a gift. This guy was such a gift.

Except he wasn't. He was a gorgeous hunk, a doctor, not so much older than she was, but she couldn't even think of him *that way*. Because for now on she was Jenny with three kids and two dogs and…

Oh, for heaven's sake...

'Sorry.' She closed her eyes for a moment and gave herself a fast internal talking-to. *Get your act together, Jennifer Martin. This guy is offering you the world and here you are whinging about it.* When she opened them again she had herself under control—sort of. She managed a bright smile.

'I'm fine,' she told him. 'Everything's great. I… I need to unpack.'

'You seem to have brought a lot,' Silas said. He was watching her face, though, as if he was reading what she needed to keep hidden. But there were four vehicles parked under the veranda now, all loaded with their gear.

The islanders had been aware of her situation from the time Chris and Harriet had died. There'd been offers of help before, but she hadn't been able to accept. Now, though… Not only was she moving into town, Marc had spread the word that she was setting up a medical clinic. She could have had a dozen trucks if she'd wanted.

As it was, Joan's house was furnished. She would have been happy just picking up the kids' clothes and favourite toys, but they'd been anxious and she'd said they could bring everything they wanted. There were two dog kennels, Ruby's dressing table—pink; it seemed her father had made it for her just before he'd died. Tom's go-cart. And more.

'You brought the freezer?' Silas said faintly. Two men were hauling the huge appliance down from the back of the first truck.

'Months' worth of kelp casseroles,' she said, using the moment to push away her own dreary thoughts. 'We had to turn the power off when we left, and the kids seemed appalled that we'd abandon them. So,' she said and tried a smile, 'maybe we could share a couple tonight?'

'Um…no.'

'What, you'll cook for yourself?'

'If you're eating kelp curry,' he said bluntly, and she couldn't stop a grin.

'It's very healthy. Just the thing for a broken leg.'

'If avoiding it means it takes my leg another month to heal, then I'll consider it time well spent.'

'You haven't even tried it.'

He thought about it for a moment—and then, to her surprise, he nodded. He really did look extraordinary, she thought. He might be balancing on crutches, but everything else spoke of a guy who was in control of his world.

He was long and lean and tanned, and his eyes were

creased, as though he'd spent time in the sun. She and the kids had managed to retrieve most of his belongings from the boat, and Jenny had nobly washed his clothes, taking them over to the hospital for him. That meant she'd noticed the designer brand names. The clothes he was wearing might look casual but they were worth a fortune. They didn't look like a fortune though; they just looked right.

And now he was smiling again, which made them… which made him seem even more right.

'Okay, let's try one,' he conceded. 'These kids need to feel at home, and for the next six weeks we're housemates. We're in this together. Right?'

And what was there in that to make her feel like welling up again? Nothing, she told herself, and she headed down to help with the unloading. Fast. Because for some reason she had to get away from the man on the veranda.

He made her feel… Like she had no business feeling. Like she had no space in her life for feeling.

Like she was a twenty-nine-year-old woman who'd like…

Not! Not, not, not, she told herself, and went to supervise a freezer full of kelp casseroles.

'Kelp Bolognese'. That was what the label on the casserole said. 'Cook with kelp pasta'.

There was a bunch of packets down the bottom of the freezer filled with green and black noodles. Kelp pasta. Of course.

She'd far rather have eggs on toast.

For the last few months—after her first taste test from the freezer—Jenny had been feeding them her own choice of food. She was no cook, and she was broke, but the books said baked beans were healthy. As was pasta with tomato sauce, pancakes, eggs on toast. They'd been her go-to. The kids hadn't seemed to care that she didn't touch the freezer, but when Jenny had suggested they leave it behind Sam had got that blank look on his face. Thus the freezer had come. Now, on this first night away from their home, she was prepared to open the freezer and try again.

'The black's from the bull kelp,' Ruby told them. 'The green's from the sea lettuce.' But she sounded dubious.

'But you like it, right?'

'Yes,' Sam said a trifle belligerently, and Silas nodded. He'd been staring into the freezer with the kids.

'Right,' he said. 'Let's have a go at cooking it then. I'm wobbly on my legs but if you help… You tell me what to do and I'll do it.'

'Jenny cooks.' The look Sam gave her was almost scornful—as if that was all she was good for.

'Well, she can if she wants to,' Silas said mildly. 'But there are five people in this house so that's five people to take turns. Maybe four, because Tom might need a hand.'

'But women do the housework,' Sam said stubbornly, and Silas cast Jenny a questioning look. She winced. These kids had been brought up with values she hadn't been able to budge. Where to start?

But it seemed Silas was starting now. 'Everyone should if they want to eat,' Silas told him. 'Sam, this side of the island is civilisation, and here women have rights. Ruby, do you think it's fair that you and Jenny should do all the housework?'

'No!' said Ruby, much struck.

'So vote,' Silas said. 'Equal rights for everyone. Who votes with me?'

Ruby stuck her hand up. Jenny met Silas's eyes and he was smiling, right at her. She raised her hand and felt…

something inside her melting. Silas put up his hand and then Tom, gamely trying to understand from the sidelines, put his hand up too.

'Right,' Silas said firmly. 'That's the house rule then. Everyone helps. So, Sam, you'll have watched your mum. Show me how to make this kelp spaghetti edible.'

Maybe months of eating her type of food had made them soft. Maybe months in the freezer hadn't helped either, or maybe it was the way Sam and Silas had struggled to cook it, but the kelp spaghetti was...well, pretty much exactly as Jenny remembered from the first time she'd made a tentative foray into the freezer. She got a few mouthfuls down, but she struggled.

Ruby ate a couple of spoonfuls and laid her spoon down. 'I'm not hungry.'

Tom, incurably truthful, had one mouthful and said, 'Yuk!'

Silas, on the other hand, ate as if he enjoyed it. He cleared his plate and then sat back and watched Sam struggle with his. 'I can feel this doing us good,' he told them. He nodded encouragement at Sam. 'We could have this every night.'

'No!' said Ruby, sounding horrified.

'I don't like it,' Tom said flatly.

'But Mum made it,' Sam said and sniffed and gulped. He laid down his fork and stared at his plate. And suddenly a tear trickled down his cheek. Then came another, unchecked, dripping on the spaghetti.

It was the first time Jenny had seen him cry. The temptation was to round the table and gather him into her arms, but she caught Silas's gaze and his look arrested her.

'It's bloody hard, mate,' he said, using the Australian

vernacular, which sounded okay, despite his distinctly US accent. 'You must miss your mum and dad so badly. Sam, I lost my little girl two years ago, and I think of her every day. It's like there's a hole in me where Harper should be. A big one.'

Sam's gaze shot up, shocked enough to stop crying. 'You lost…she died?'

'Same as your mum and dad. An accident. For a while I held on to everything she owned. Harper collected fluffy toys—mostly cats—but then they started to get dusty and old. That made me feel worse. Looking at them every day.'

'Like the freezer,' Sam said, staring at his half-eaten spaghetti.

'I guess. And I didn't know what to do. Because they looked a bit worn, no other kids would want them, and I couldn't bear to throw them away. They were making me feel so sad, but then I had an idea.'

'Yeah?' Sam said cautiously, while Jenny seemed to be struggling to breathe. What a thing to come out of nowhere…

'I remembered how my Harper loved birds,' Silas said, almost conversationally, into the shocked silence. The two younger children seemed stunned as well. Sam's tears must have horrified them. He was their rock. He never cried.

But a twelve-year-old shouldn't be anyone's rock, Jenny thought, and she watched him look at Silas now and found herself hoping… Hoping? For allegiance? For trust? Sam wouldn't—couldn't?—give it to her, but somehow he must if they were to forge a relationship. And Silas was only here for six weeks. Would it do more harm than good for Sam to put trust in this man?

Regardless of right or wrong, she found herself trusting him herself. He was a paediatrician. The first rule of medicine was do no harm, she told herself, and he'd have treated traumatised kids in the past.

But he'd lost a child? She was feeling so many emotions and all she seemed to be able to do was hold her breath.

'If there'd only been one or two stuffed cats I might have kept them,' Silas was saying. 'Like you might have eaten one or two kelp casseroles. But Harper had so many you could hardly see her bed. So I made a plan. There's a place near our home that trains puppies to help kids who need a companion dog, a dog to help them be less lonely. I figured puppies would love playing with stuffed cats, and Harper loved puppies, so I took a basketful to them. The puppies loved them. But I kept all the toys that were made of wool, and I cut them up.'

'You cut them up?' That was an appalled squeak from Ruby.

'Most of them,' Silas said, unperturbed. 'Because of the birds. It was spring, my family has a big garden and we have many, many birds. Harper loved them. So I sat on the back deck where they could see me. I chopped the wool into small bits, I separated threads and I put everything into a basket. Then I hung it in one of our biggest trees. And that spring almost every bird came and decided which colour, which piece was the furriest, which one they liked best, and they lined their nests with them. That year we must have had the happiest birds in America, with the comfiest, snuggliest nests. I think Harper would be really happy too, to think of her toys being used like that. Don't you think?'

'Yeah,' Ruby said, wonderingly. 'Comfy birds.'

'My mum liked birds too,' Sam said slowly. 'And fish. She liked all the things on the beach. But…' He'd got it,

Jenny thought. He'd extrapolated Silas's line of thinking almost instantly. 'Birds can't line their nests with kelp casseroles.'

'They'd be soggy nests,' Silas said, smiling. 'But I bet they'd eat some of them. You know…' He looked at the remains of food on their plates. 'This spaghetti is made with flour as well as seaweed, but Jenny says your mum never used much flour, and the ingredients are mostly little plants and herbs she found growing in the sand dunes. I think birds and fish would probably think all their Christmases had come at once if they had these to eat. If we put them on the beach, we could let the birds eat what they want, and what's left could drift out to sea. I think every fish within miles would come swimming, just as fast as their fins would flipper.'

That produced a giggle from Ruby. 'Fins don't flipper.'

'But they'd like it,' Sam whispered. 'And Mum… Mum would say we weren't wasting it.'

'We get into trouble if we waste stuff,' Ruby informed them.

'I think she'd smile,' Silas said, and looked at Jenny. 'What do you think, Jenny?'

'I think it's a wonderful idea,' Jenny said. She was as close to tears as made no difference. She would not cry. She wouldn't! 'But maybe it's up to Sam, because he's the oldest of you kids. Sam, we'll keep eating these for as long as you like, or we'll do what Silas suggests.'

And suddenly Sam was planning, and the desolate look in his eyes had vanished. 'Maybe could build a bonfire on the beach,' he said. 'Like a ceremony? We could tip them out on the wet sand, so when the tide comes in anything the birds don't eat will be washed out to sea.'

'A bonfire!' Ruby yelled. 'Yay.'

'Mum likes…liked bonfires,' Sam said.

'There you go then,' Silas told him. 'But it's up to you guys. It's not up to Jenny and me—it's your decision. We could have a kelp ceremony for your dad and mum, if you all agree.'

Sam stared down at his half-eaten meal and suddenly he smiled. Oh, the lump in her throat…

She looked up and Silas was watching her, his eyes questioning. And she managed a tiny smile back, just a glimmer, made harder by the fact that her stupid eyes were wet.

'What do you say, guys?' Silas asked gently. 'No pressure though, mate, the freezer can stay full for as long as you want it.'

'Mum'd like it,' Sam said, and suddenly he sounded like a kid again. A twelve-year-old with a bonfire on the beach to look forward to. 'And Jenny says we can talk to her in bed at night and she might even be listening. So tomorrow night we can tell her we've fed every fish near Albatross Island. Cool!'

'So how about we pull a few from the freezer tonight?' Silas asked. 'We can't very well feed 'em frozen stuff. What do you all think? We could defrost a few and see how they go.'

'Yes!' Ruby yelled, and Tom looked confused but excited.

But it was up to Sam—they all knew that. And Sam took a deep breath, looked at his plate, looked up at Silas and came to a decision.

'Let's defrost them all.'

CHAPTER EIGHT

JENNY SPENT MOST of the next day sorting the house, getting things in order, trying to come to terms with the idea that this was where she'd be living for a year. This wasn't Sydney, it wasn't her home, but, oh, it was so much better than the outlook she'd been facing only days before.

Silas had suggested he and Sam went to the boatyard, and Ruby and Tom had demanded to go too. It was only ten minutes' walk, but Silas couldn't walk. Jenny had thus packed them all into the car and dropped them off.

Fred and Doug were already working on *Sea Raven*. They'd greeted Silas and the kids with delight, and Sam and Silas were soon deep in boat talk.

She'd intended to bring Ruby and Tom home with her, but Fred's wife had been there as well. 'Leave 'em,' she'd said. 'There's all sorts of ways the kids and I can have fun. How about I find some wood scraps and we'll see if we can make little boats, launch them off the ramp? I brought sandwiches for lunch, and there's plenty. There's a comfy chair in the lunch room, and cushions Doc Silas can prop his leg up on, but if he needs to rest, either me or one of the boys can run him home. You go home and have some me time.'

Me time… The concept was practically breathtaking. The whole island had been aching to help ever since

Harriet and Chris's death—she knew they had now—but, isolated as they'd been, there'd been little they could do. Now she had a feeling she'd be overwhelmed.

'Doc Marc's been talking to us. We're getting rooms set up for you at the back of the general store,' she was told by Thomas Craig, an elderly fisherman who'd retired here from Gannet Island because he liked peace and quiet. He and his wife had dropped by with cake and excitement at the thought of a doctor on this side of the island. 'It'll be great to have a doc here, lass, so we don't have to push our way through all them people on Gannet.'

She had to grin at the thought of Gannet being a major metropolis, and the grin stayed with her through the day. She could work again! The kids would be in school. There'd be time for Jenny Martin.

Thanks to Silas. Her fairy godfather.

Who'd lost a child.

She hadn't talked to him the night before—he'd gone to bed early and the kids had been present until after he'd disappeared. This morning there'd been no chance.

She'd had him down as someone with more money than sense, yachting across the world as pure daredevilry. Now…things were deeper. Harder. He was starting to seem…

Just a fairy godfather, she told herself firmly, but the thought of him stayed with her as she planned a future that was suddenly full of hope.

Thanks to a man who'd lost a child. Thanks to a man who'd made Sam smile.

Thanks to a man who made her feel…like she had no right to feel, but there was no way she could suppress it.

A bonfire. Tonight. The beach.

Why on earth was her stomach fluttering like she was a girl about to go on her first date?

* * *

The bonfire was magnificent. The recent storms had washed up masses of driftwood, and by mid-afternoon the kids, home from the boatyard, were in full construction mode. This was okay, Jenny thought as she watched from the veranda. They seemed…light. Free? It was the first time she'd ever heard them shouting with laughter. Sam was being bossy, and Ruby and Tom were his loyal slaves, hauling wood that was too big for them, scouring the beach for more. Being kids.

'Happy?' It was a sleepy question from beside her and Jenny started. Back from the boatyard, Silas had gone to sleep on one of Joan's enormous deckchairs. Jenny wasn't sitting beside him—she'd been tempted, but the whole set-up was a bit Ma and Pa Kettle, so she'd kept herself busy and she'd opted to check on the kids by leaning on the veranda rail.

Happy? She glanced down at him and thought…was she?

And there was only one answer. Right here, right now…

'Yes,' she told him and smiled. 'I don't know how to thank you.'

'And I don't know how to thank you. That makes us quits,' he told her and smiled and closed his eyes again. It was not much more than a week since the accident. Trauma and infection would still be taking their toll. He should sleep.

'What time should we light the fire?' he asked sleepily.

'I… Soon, I think.' Dammit, why did she sound so nervous? 'I've wrapped potatoes in foil for us to bury once we have some ashes. I popped into the store on the way home from the boatyard—' did he know what pleasure the ability to do that had given her? '—and bought sour cream and salad and bacon. There's dinner sorted.'

'While we feed kelp to the fishes and the birds. Yay us,' he said, sounding deeply satisfied.

Jenny looked at him for a long moment and then deliberately looked away. The sight of this man was doing something to her insides that she seemed to have no control over.

He was American. He was here for six weeks, she told herself. Whatever was happening inside her had no business happening. She had enough to be excited about without getting excited about…

Stop it! Go and light yourself a bonfire, she told herself crossly. Anything else—everything else!—could stay very much unlit.

He had three kids, two dogs and one worried woman geared up to help him down to the beach.

'You could watch from the veranda,' Jenny had told him. 'We'll bring you up your dinner when it's baked.'

But there was no way he was missing out. He had crutches. He had Sam on one side, Jenny on the other in case he toppled in the soft sand. He was feeling stupidly helpless, but not nearly as helpless as a week ago when he'd been dragged up the beach on palm fronds.

The kids had offered to haul a chair down for him, but he'd scorned that. Jenny had produced a picnic rug, the kids had raced up and down from house to beach bringing cushions, and by the time he was ceremoniously lowered to sit beside the fire—on the rug so sand wouldn't get under his cast—he was feeling like he was having an out of body experience.

'I feel like one of those Roman emperors in my school

history books,' he told Jenny. 'My slaves seem to be anticipating my every need.'

'You ask me to peel grapes, you have another think coming,' she said darkly, and her smile broke out.

She had such a smile. There was a dimple right at the corner of her mouth. He knew her age by now, but tonight she looked much younger. Like a kid herself…

A kid with the weight of the world on her shoulders.

'Our spuds will take an hour or so to cook. Apart from grapes, is there anything else you want, or can we get on with our fish and bird feeding?'

He caught himself. He'd done enough. He didn't need to feel…

'Of course you can,' he said, almost roughly, and she cast him an odd look—and then nodded in a way he was starting to recognise.

'Right,' she said. 'Moving on…'

And she did.

They started a convoy, using a wheelbarrow they'd found under the house. Jenny had turned off the freezer the night before. There were now cartons and cartons of defrosted…mush. Kelp casserole times about a hundred, he thought faintly, as the kids carted them down and then figured what to do with them.

Their first attempt was pretty much a disaster. The beach under Joan's house was wide and long, and it was a birds' paradise. Gulls, sandpipers, plovers, oystercatchers…every wader imaginable seemed to feed on the tiny sand creatures and weeds washed up by the sea.

Kelp casseroles? Not so much. The kids spread a little at the shoreline. The gulls thought the kelp spaghetti was delicious, but the rest of the birdlife checked it out and he could almost read their disdain. *What is this?* In fact, Silas thought, watching, they seemed to react almost as he had.

'I don't blame 'em,' Jenny whispered, sitting beside him while they waited for results. 'Gulls don't seem to have taste buds, but I've always thought sandpipers and plovers to be a superior type of bird. Not to mention oystercatchers. Now if we'd laced this mush with caviar…'

'They would have picked the caviar out and washed the kelp off before they ate it.' He grinned, but the kids were looking downcast.

'Mum wouldn't like this,' Sam said glumly, and Silas's desire to smile faded. Had he persuaded the kid to throw away his mum's food for nothing?

'Okay, next step, the sea,' Jenny said, bouncing to her feet. She grabbed a container from the wheelbarrow and carried it out into the shallows.

She was wearing faded shorts and a skimpy T-shirt. Her hair was loose and free. She stood in the shallows and grinned back at the kids, who were staring dolefully at her from behind the barrow.

'Let's go,' she said and tipped the mushy casserole into the sea.

What followed was a few minutes of stillness while the contents spread around her.

This bay was beautiful, pristine, with golden sand and turquoise shallows. The water Jenny was standing in was up to her knees, gentle waves rippling into shore in the sheltered cove.

It seemed a travesty to tip the food out into such a place. Did he have to add pollution to his list of mistakes? he thought bleakly. He glanced at the kids and saw a picture of combined misery.

And then suddenly…movement. A sweep of silver streaked in from deeper water. A school of tiny fish appeared as a flash, just underneath the surface. What had brought them? Scent? The realisation that their crystal-clear environment suddenly contained something of interest?

Whatever had brought them, it wasn't disgust at someone littering their water. The fish, looking as they came like one large mass, hit the clouded shallows and suddenly—chaos. A feeding frenzy. The arrow of fish abandoned its formation and became every fish for itself. The water around Jenny's legs was alive, splashing, churning, a mass of silver breaking the surface, fish gulping down mouthfuls, diving, grabbing as much as they could.

And here came the bigger fish. The kids were whooping now, big-eyed with excitement, heading out to join Jenny in the water, but Silas called them back with urgency. He'd been sitting on the blanket and there was no way he was missing out on this.

'Sam! Ruby! Help me up!'

And they were good kids. Sam and Ruby grabbed a hand each, helping him haul himself to his feet, making sure he had his crutches. And then they were off, grabbing more of the casserole containers and heading into the shallows to join Jenny.

He couldn't join them—his cast was hardly suitable for paddling and the last thing he needed was to fill it with saltwater and sand—but he didn't need to. It was enough to stand balancing on his crutches to watch.

He'd spent time at sea and knew his fish, so even from here he was guessing what they were. Pilchards? Anchovies? They'd be the small ones. Whiting? They'd be the streaks of silver. Now the bigger ones were arriving, trevally, mullet, yellowtail kingfish, silver drummer… he could see them clearly. In their excitement they were surfacing, diving, surrounding Jenny as if she were the Pied Piper of Albatross.

The kids were in the water now, practically exploding with delight. Sam and Ruby joined Jenny, tipping casseroles in, almost hand feeding. Tom, a bit more nervous around the bigger fish, was closer to shore. The smaller fish had moved back as the bigger fish formed a threat in their feeding frenzy. They were now at the edges of the cloud of scattered casseroles, and Tom plonked his small self down in the shallows and put his hands out, content to let the darts of silver brush his fingers.

The little boy looked awed, happy, but every now and then he glanced back at Silas as if to say, *Is this okay?* And Silas, with his long experience as a paediatrician, with his knowledge of his own daughter, realised with a jolt that Tom was looking to him as his security.

It shouldn't matter. He was transient in this child's life. He was transient in all their lives.

But just for a moment it felt good. It felt like…family?

And with that thought, the longing hit with such a searing pain that he almost lost his balance. This was one of those sickening jolts that had formed a continuous agony in the months after his family's death, and that now recurred often enough to cause his world to stay grey. They'd created the fog of grief and helplessness that had driven him to offer to be sole sailor, to skipper his father's boat from one side of the world to the other, to try and drive away the demons he couldn't get rid of, no matter how he tried. Harper… Charlotte… So many mistakes. So much grief.

And suddenly he was aware that Jenny was looking at him from the water, leaving the kids, wading out of the shallows to join him. 'Silas? What's wrong? Pain? Can I help?'

It needed only this, this woman who'd taken on the world, who'd put her life on hold, offering to help him. Had he shown the spasm of grief so clearly? He needed to pull himself together. What did he have to feel desperate about?

A failed marriage. A lost daughter. A dream of family…

'Hey,' she said softly. 'You're pushing yourself too hard—you must be exhausted. Let us take you back to the house.'

'You'd pull the kids out of the water? To help me?'

'They'd come,' she said, turning and smiling at the kids, still whooping it up in the shallows. 'They're good kids. And tonight… Silas, this is brilliant.'

And, as if on cue, Sam came charging out of the water to collect yet another casserole container. But he skidded to a halt before them as he passed, looking up at them, and his eyes were shining.

'Mum would have loved this,' he said gruffly, and Jenny stooped—not very much because Sam at twelve was a string bean of an adolescent, almost as tall as his aunt—but she stooped enough to hug him.

'Yes, she would,' Jenny told him. 'And so would your dad. Maybe… Sam, maybe tonight is for them.'

Sam stiffened. He didn't hug back—but he didn't pull away.

'We had a funeral for your mum and dad,' Jenny told him, continuing to hug regardless. 'But this is better. This is a real send-off, and if your mum and dad are watching I reckon they'll be smiling and smiling. Using all the stuff your dad collected and your mum cooked, to feed the birds and the fish they loved. When the tide comes in it'll sweep every last bit of casserole out to feed more fish. The traces left on the beach will feed sandworms, crabs, everything that lives in the sand, and that means bigger sandworms and crabs for the birds to find. I think your mum and dad must be so happy now. And they'll be so proud, Sam, of the way you've taken care of the littlies, of the decisions you've made.'

There was a moment's silence—and then one very loud sniff from Sam. Then, as if it was almost hauled from him, the kid raised stiff arms, he put them around his aunt's middle and he hugged her back.

They stood there for a long moment, while Silas said nothing at all. There was nothing to say. Finally Sam pulled back and Jenny let him go in an instant.

'Gotta feed more fish,' Sam said, gulping.

'Of course you do,' Jenny whispered, and the boy was gone.

There was silence as they watched him head back to join Ruby and Tom. The silence stretched on—and then Silas reached into his pocket, snagged his handkerchief and handed it over.

Jenny blew her nose, hard. She gulped a few times, wiped her face and then she collected herself—and stared in astonishment at what she'd just used.

'A handkerchief…'

'And I don't need it back,' he said hastily. 'It's yours.'

'What sort of sailor carries handkerchiefs?' she demanded, stunned. 'It's even ironed. Or it was,' she added, looking ruefully at what she'd just used.

'It was in the one part of my kit that stayed watertight,' he told her. 'My mother sent a care kit with me, insisted I pack it. She has very proper standards, my mother. It's a wonder she didn't pack a dinner suit for those occasions when I felt a little more formal on board. You rescued it still unpacked, still watertight because…well, I hadn't actually had a chance to use it.'

'Your mum loves you.'

'She does.'

'I...well, thank you.' She sniffed again, checked out the handkerchief and carefully tucked it into the pocket of her shorts. 'I'll replace it ironed. You can tell your mum thank you.'

'I'll tell her,' he said and smiled at the thought of telling her just how and when it had been used. His mother would love this story.

His mother would love Jenny, he thought, and that was an unsettling thought.

Why? She was just a friend. Why did that make him feel...?

But Jenny had gone back to watching the children. She was moving on.

'These kids...they've been loved as well,' she said slowly. 'Chris and Harriet were odd parents, but there's never been any doubt that their kids were loved.' Her brow was furrowed, as if she was trying to figure things out. 'Maybe that's why tonight seems such a big deal. With Sam ill, we decided not to put them through the funeral—without Sam it would have just bewildered the littlies—so there's been no real chance for them to say goodbye. I suspect that's what's happening now.'

Jenny was right—something seemed to have been released. The kids seemed not such a defensive pack any more. Tom had grown braver, venturing out to join his siblings. They were playing tag with the fish now, trying to touch the smooth, scaly sides of the bigger ones, watching the water almost boil with fish all around them. The dogs were barking, jumping in the shallows, not sure what they were supposed to be doing with these slippery, silver intruders in their domain.

They were kids and dogs having fun.

Harper would have loved this.

'Silas, what happened to your daughter?' Jenny asked softly, almost as if it was an extension of what they'd been saying.

'I… She was killed. A car accident.'

'I'm so sorry.' She paused. 'How long ago?'

'Two years.' He had to remind himself it was that long, though. It still felt like weeks.

'How…how old was she?'

'Seven.'

'And your wife? Partner?' She was still gentle, ready to step back at any minute.

'Charlotte.' He couldn't keep the flatness from his voice. 'My wife. She died in the accident too.' He felt the customary bleakness hit but he might as well be honest. 'Along with a guy she'd apparently been sleeping with for almost a month before the accident.'

'Oh, Silas.' She winced. 'Oh, no.'

Now was the time for him to shut up, as he usually did when they were discussed. Now was the time to fold into himself. This was two long years ago—surely he should have put the pain behind him. But suddenly it was out there again, front and centre, and speaking about it seemed the only option.

'I was a fool to let her go,' he said savagely now. 'I knew things weren't good between us, but I didn't think they were that bad. But Charlotte was desperate to go for an extended skiing holiday, and there was a ski school on the slopes where kids could combine normal schooling with ski instruction. I couldn't—wouldn't—take months off work, so they went without me. "We'll have fun," Charlotte said. "You can come at weekends, but it'll be a mom and daughter bonding thing. You and Harper spend your lives playing happy families, it's my turn." And it was true. From the time she was tiny Harper tended to cling to me. I was absorbed in my work, but I spent most of my spare time with Harper. We played together, we flew kites, we rode our bikes. Charlotte wasn't interested in…most things we did.'

He closed his eyes for a moment.

'I guess…looking back… I was selfish. I didn't include Charlotte as much as I could—after we were married our interests seemed to diverge—but I loved being with Harper.'

'You're a paediatrician,' she said gently. 'You must love kids.'

'I can't tell you how much I loved Harper,' he told her, and he couldn't help himself. His voice was still savage. 'And I loved… I wanted family. I was an only child, but my parents always made me feel like we were a threesome. Us. Family. And I couldn't manage it for Harper. Or for Charlotte. I didn't try to join them at weekends.' He shook his head. 'I wasn't even surprised when I learned she'd been with someone else.'

'I'm so sorry,' she said again, and she sounded…a bit helpless. Tragedy did that, he thought flatly. He hadn't meant to burden her with his story, but the thing was done now. 'Was that why you decided to skipper a yacht halfway around the world?'

'Maybe it was.' Or definitely it was, he thought. After their death his world had seemed unendingly grey. The idea of getting right away…

'So if you'd drowned yourself in my cove you wouldn't have cared?' She was sounding thoughtful now, discomfort put aside as she gently probed, and he remembered that this woman was a doctor. She was switching into doctor mode, he thought. Asking the hard questions. This was a basic tenet taught at medical schools the world over. Ask the hard questions. *Was suicide an option?*

So say it like it was. 'I never meant to kill myself.'

'No,' she said gently. 'But were you actively trying not to? Lone sailing…'

'I couldn't hurt my parents that much.'

'But what about you?' Her voice was still gentle but she wasn't backing away. 'What do you live for, Silas Braden?'

What followed was a long silence while he tried to figure what to say. How to answer. Her question—maybe just her presence—had somehow slashed through the fragile defences he'd built over the last two years, exposing…nothing. An aching void.

But then he looked out at the water, at the kids who were now sitting in the shallows, messing around with the dogs, who seemed bemused by the few hopeful fish still nosing around them. These kids looked peaceful. Healthy. Happy. That was what he'd clung to over the last two years—his work, medicine, treating kids, fighting for the lives he couldn't give Harper. It was his reason for getting up in the morning. Maybe his only reason.

'My work,' he said. 'Thank God I'm a doctor.'

'And yet you still wanted to leave.'

'It's not enough.'

But then he caught himself. This was getting him nowhere, landing it all on this woman beside him. Any minute now she'd be suggesting antidepressants, he thought, and the last thing he wanted was another doctor suggesting…things. How many of his colleagues had tried to make things right, as if tragedy could ever be cured by medicine?

'So what about you?' he demanded, his voice rougher than it should be. 'You don't do family?'

'You're kidding me, right?' She motioned out to the kids. 'What is this but family, up to my neck and beyond?'

'But not by choice.' They were both watching the kids now, not looking at each other. Maybe focusing on the kids was the only way of coping with a discussion that was a bit too intimate and yet impossible to end. 'So before your brother's death…no partner?'

'No,' she told him, and a smile suddenly twitched at the corner of her mouth. 'Well, there was Hugh. We'd been dating for a whole six weeks when Chris and Harriet were killed. Hugh's a radiologist at Sydney Central, a gorgeous guy, every woman's dream date. He always says just the right thing, one of those guys who has the answer to everything. But when I told him I was taking on the care of three orphaned kids he was gobsmacked. His pride and self-consequence told him he ought to offer to help, but his base self couldn't get away fast enough. Money was his answer. He offered to pay out the lease on my apartment and then left for a conference in Sweden. A conference I swear he hadn't thought of attending before Chris and Harriet were killed.'

'Prat.'

'No.' She shrugged, her smile turning a little self-deprecating. 'It was a very generous offer, and how could I blame him for not wanting involvement? I felt a bit the same myself. My mum and dad split when I was six, and my brother and I split with them. I went with Mum to the mainland and Chris stayed here with Dad and his kelp. Then Mum was…'

She hesitated.

'My theory now is that she was damaged by the way she'd abandoned Chris, and I was a permanent reminder that she had two kids. She was…distant is probably the best way to describe it. I think even then I blamed her for dragging me away from Dad and Chris, and we were never close.' She hesitated. 'I guess that's one of the things that's driving me now. I need to keep these kids together and I need them to see I'll always be there for them.'

'Like your parents weren't there for you?'

'As you say,' she said shortly, and he heard the echo of long-ago pain.

And suddenly there it was again, that surge of grief, the vision of Charlotte driving away with Harper. Of Harper looking back at him.

Regrets, recriminations were coming at him, as they always did. Would it have killed him to accompany them?

'Silas? What's wrong?'

'Nothing,' he said, giving himself an inward shake. 'We were talking about you. Missing family.'

She gave him an odd look but moved on. 'I guess I didn't, after a while,' she told him. 'Losing Chris was hard, but I was only six. I made good friends at school. I was smart, I loved medicine and…well, I guess I turned into a bit of a party animal. I've had a great life. My apartment is…was…fabulous. I have a neat little sports car—bright crimson. It's still garaged in Sydney.' She gazed out at the kids. 'Maybe that's like kelp casseroles and stuffed toys—I can't bear to let it go yet. My friends used to say I need a poodle—something aristocratic—to sit beside me, but I've never needed anyone to sit beside me. And now…'

But then she paused as the youngest of the two dogs—Nipper—came tearing out of the shallows and up the beach, seemingly just to check on them. He jumped up on Jenny, got pushed down then proceeded to shake himself, sand and seawater flying everywhere. Finally he turned and hurled himself back down to the water.

'So now I have this lot and I'll love them whether or not they want me,' Jenny said, brushing water from her face but talking almost as if she hadn't been interrupted. 'But can you imagine me fitting everyone into my gorgeous little car? It's waiting for me to man up enough to sell it, and neither Pepper nor Nipper seem the least bit aristocratic. But it can't matter because here I am, Jenny Martin, part of a family, while you're heading back to the States to your career.' She gave a rueful grin. 'I'll swap lives if you like.'

It was said lightly, a joke, but both of them stayed looking at the kids in the water and there were undercurrents… The truth.

She was a woman with a family she'd never asked for.

He was a man who was desperate for…

Oh, cut it out. He wasn't desperate. He had a great life back home, a job that challenged him, great parents, lots of friends. All he had to do was get there.

While Jenny stayed here.

He thought of Hugh, the radiologist. He knew the type. Medicine was full of them. Ego-driven specialists, good at their job but they solved the world's problems with money.

Charlotte had been the same.

'So your chances of a boyfriend now?' he asked, trying to move on, but it was a crass question. He'd spoken without thought and he saw her face close. *Damn, of all the stupid things to ask.* 'No. Sorry. Jenny, that was dumb. Forget I asked. It's like the people who tell me I should date again—I want to slug them.'

'Yeah.' She managed a smile, but it was tight. Polite. Rigid with control. 'It is a dumb question, and I won't retaliate by asking about your future dating plans. But who knows? Maybe somewhere out there's a hunk who thinks a woman stuck on this island for ever, caring for three kids and two dogs with no money at all, would be the sexiest thing ever. Maybe there are thousands queued up on dating apps, all ready to get on the next plane. Meanwhile, I'm thinking these potatoes must be pretty much done, Dr Braden. Enough of the introspection. Let's eat.'

CHAPTER NINE

BAKED POTATOES WERE always a success. Apart from that one time Tom had burned himself, they were pretty much a guaranteed way to get them all to eat. Usually she served them with coleslaw and yoghurt. Tonight, with the prospect of a paying job and with a general store within walking distance, she'd lashed out and bought cheese, sour cream and bacon. Now she dug out the potatoes, still wrapped in their foil. Then she hauled a heap of coals from the edge of the fire, put some butter in the pan and fried the bacon while the potatoes cooled.

The smell of bacon brought the kids running, and they fell on the food as if they hadn't been fed for a week. And they talked. Mealtime usually meant stilted silence. Now they were hopping into their spuds, vying for more and more bacon—and talking so fast to Silas that she was having trouble keeping up.

'I fed the biggest one.' That was Ruby. 'Dad might have caught him for dinner if he'd been here, but Mum would have told him off and made him let it go…'

'Mine were slippery,' Tom broke in. 'But I catched three. I put them back though. They'll grow to be as big as Ruby's.'

'Will you come to the boatyard with me tomorrow?' That was Sam. 'After…after school, I mean.'

There was a moment's silence at that, the enormity of actually confronting school seemingly daunting. But, if it worked, a new home, new friends… It might lift these kids from the nightmare of grief they'd been living in.

And that made her collect herself. The sun was slipping towards the horizon, and tomorrow was the start of their new lives.

'Right, showers and bed,' she told them, standing up and brushing off sand. 'Now.'

'We don't have to go to bed until we're tired,' Ruby said mutinously, but, before she could answer, Silas stepped in.

'I have a surprise,' he told them. 'Tomorrow, because it's a huge day—Jenny's off to become the island doctor and you're off to meet your new classmates—I've stocked the fridge. I'm planning a buffet breakfast, all you can eat—eggs, sausages, fruit salad, two types of toast, four types of jam, you name it, it'll be on the veranda for anyone who's up early enough to enjoy it. And the best thing is… I've found strawberries.'

'Strawberries?' Tom said, sounding confused.

'Strawberries?' Jenny said faintly. Where had he sourced those? They certainly weren't stocked in the Albatross general store, and they'd be far too expensive to buy on Gannet. Had these kids ever eaten them?

'Last year Elsa bought us ice cream with frozen strawberries when Mum had to take us to Gannet for the dentist,' Ruby said. 'Are they like that?'

'Are they in jam?' Sam asked, suspicious.

'I have half a bucket of fresh ones,' Silas said and grinned, benevolent genie producing his miracle. 'And there'll be ice cream too. But you have to go to bed now, so you'll wake up in time.'

'Really?'

'Really.'

'Come on,' Tom yelled. 'Let's go!'

'Showers before bed,' Jenny yelled, and they waved acknowledgement as they took off towards the house.

Magic.

She turned to face Silas. He was still lying on the rug, smiling. Looking smugly up at her.

'How on earth…? Where did you source strawberries?'

'It seems Fred's wife, Wilma, has a greenhouse,' he said, smugness intensifying. 'It also seems that Wilma's three-year-old granddaughter has a lump on her forehead that the doctors say is harmless but Wilma worries about. Thus, seeing she'd heard I'm a paediatrician, she wondered if I wouldn't mind looking. So for the cost of confirming the diagnosis of one hemangioma, and reassuring her that yes, it'll disappear before Angelica turns four or five, I was given half a bucket of the world's best strawberries.'

She stared at him in stupefaction. 'The kids…you've blown their minds. What a way to send them to bed.'

'You're not supposed to be focusing on the kids,' he said, wounded. 'You're supposed to be thanking me. They'll be thinking strawberries all night instead of school…all because of my brilliance.'

'I am thanking you,' she said carefully, trying not to focus on his smile. 'But I'm also thinking… I'm pretty good at diagnosing hemangiomas as well.'

Every doctor was. Hemangiomas appeared in the first weeks after birth, raised bumps, turning bright crimson as they formed. They were capable of terrifying parents, but unless they formed too close to the eyes they seldom needed treatment and usually disappeared before the child reached school age. Angelica's parents would have been reassured by their treating doctor, but they'd obviously not been able to translate that reassurance to Wilma.

And now, at just the perfect moment, Silas had bartered his knowledge for strawberries for her kids. She wanted to laugh. She wanted to hug him.

She wanted…

No.

'I'll go make sure they're washed and tucked in,' she said hastily. She looked down at him, at his twinkling eyes, his smile… *Uh-oh.*

She needed to put kids to bed.

She did not need to think about his smile.

'Do you want a hand back to the house?' she managed, and he shook his head.

'You know, I don't. I'd prefer to lie here for a while and soak up the sunset. Jenny, there's a bottle of wine in the fridge. What about settling the kids and bringing it back to share?'

She shouldn't. She shouldn't, she shouldn't, she shouldn't.

'That's a lovely idea,' she said weakly and made her escape.

She headed back to the house slowly, then sat on the veranda for a while, giving the kids time to sort themselves out. They hated what they thought of as her nagging. Independence was their mantra.

It should be hers too, she told herself, thinking that returning to the beach was a bad idea. Silas was making her feel like she had no business feeling. It was surely sheer idiocy to take this one step further.

He was a sailor, stranded and wounded in more ways than one. He was stuck here for six weeks and then he'd be gone, off to carry on with a life she longed for.

But a life he didn't long for. His life seemed steeped in sadness and regret.

He'd get over it, she told herself. People did. Two years wasn't long enough to shake the grief for a wife and child. This whole episode might help, bring him out of his fog, send him home ready to start again.

How could she start again?

Oh, for heaven's sake, she *was* starting again. He'd rescued her from an endless nightmare of drying kelp for a living. They were therefore quits. They could now get on with their lives, hopefully living happily ever after.

He without his family. She with hers. A family, like it or not.

It's just the way it is, she told herself as she finally went to check on the kids.

The house was big. They'd offered Sam a room to himself, but the kids had decided they'd sleep together. They'd hauled a mattress from the single room into the bigger twin room, and now she stood in the doorway and looked down at three sleeping children.

They'd gone to sleep happy.

Because of Silas.

Who was waiting on the beach for her.

And that made her feel…

Stop it! What was wrong with her? He was just a friend, someone who'd helped her at just the right time.

She was tucking blankets around each of the children in turn, giving each of them a kiss as she did. Usually she felt emotional as she kissed them—they'd never allow her to kiss them if they were awake—but tonight she was too distracted to think about the difficulties of forming bonds with them. Her thoughts seemed to be filled with the image of Silas.

She had to go back—of course she did. With his leg

in a cast, with a wide beach and soft sand, he'd be stuck. He might even have trouble getting up from the picnic rug. As well as that, the debris from their picnic was still there and she needed to collect it.

There was also the matter of a bottle of wine in the fridge. That was a dangerous thought.

She could pretend she'd forgotten he'd asked her to bring it.

Why would she? Why did it seem so…dangerous?

She was being ridiculous. *Pull yourself together, woman,* she told herself, and the memory of Silas's smile was suddenly intensifying. A siren song.

Oh, what the heck. She cast a last long look at her three sleeping children, threw a silent blessing on them all—and then cast caution to the wind.

One bottle of wine. Two wine glasses.

And then she glanced down at what she was wearing. Shorts and T-shirt, salt and sand-encrusted.

She thought suddenly of what she'd have worn to the beach with friends in another life. Life before kids. She'd unpacked here, and as she did she'd looked at clothes she hadn't worn since she'd left Sydney. And never would?

She thought suddenly, incongruously, of Silas's handkerchief, an echo of his life before. He was still using handkerchiefs.

So, dammit, why not? She was still the same Jenny Martin—wasn't she? She was about to sit on the beach at sunset with another adult. If she'd been back in Sydney, back in her old life, she wouldn't be seen dead joining friends while wearing stained shorts and T-shirt.

So why did she need an excuse?

Okay. Deep breath, she told herself.

Go hit your wardrobe.

* * *

If she didn't come back he might be in trouble. The sand was soft, and he wasn't too flash on his crutches yet. Even standing was a hassle. Surely she'd remember he needed help.

But she'd come back. This wasn't a woman who avoided her responsibilities—far from it. He thought of the responsibilities she'd taken on, and it practically did his head in.

So she would come back, but would she bring wine? Would she return just to help him home, or would she come to stay?

But finally she emerged from the house, and yes, she was carrying a wine bottle and glasses. But he wasn't looking at the wine.

She was wearing a short, short skirt, crimson with white spots, bouncy and flared, with an oversized white shirt, tied to accentuate the tiny waist of the dress. It looked like a man's shirt but he knew it wasn't.

She'd combed her tangle of curls. They were damp but they looked great.

And on her feet… As she grew nearer he saw she was wearing flip-flops, but not just any flip-flops. Louboutins? One of his colleagues had worn a pair of these to a beach party he and Charlotte had hosted, and Charlotte had told him their price. Maybe they were worth it, he thought, looking at Jenny's feet. They were a riot of brilliant colour, a work of art all by themselves. They were fabulous.

Jenny looked fabulous. Younger. Sexy. Infinitely desirable!

That she'd decided to dress up a little took his breath away. He was suddenly feeling like a guy who'd asked a girl on her first date and been accepted.

Which was dumb. This was a transient relationship—it had to be. He was here for six weeks and the last thing Jenny needed was emotional involvement.

Still, as he watched her come in her gorgeous, bouncy riot of colour, her skin burnished from the sun, her curls bouncing as she walked, her eyes smiling as she saw him watching, he thought…

'Hey,' she said. 'Did you think I'd deserted you?'

It took him a minute to find his voice but somehow he managed it. 'I was figuring I'd call Pepper and Nipper, grab a collar apiece and have them tug me up to the house. Like sled dogs.'

'Well, good luck with that,' she said, plonking herself down beside him. The dogs, exhausted by their evening of fish-chasing and bacon-begging, looked like two black and white fur rugs, sprawled on the sand. 'I've never met two more useless dogs in my life. Pepper's got a heart condition too, and the last thing I need is a dead dog. They'll live for ever, though,' she said hastily as Nipper raised his head and gave her a look which Silas swore was reproachful. 'And we love them for what they are.'

'Well…thank you for coming anyway,' he told her. 'And…they're nice flip-flops.' He sounded lame but he was having trouble getting his voice to work.

'Aren't they great?' She wiggled her toes in satisfaction. 'Total extravagance. Bought when I hadn't a care in the world. I have them for sale online, but no one's bought them. By the way, we call them thongs over here,' she told him. 'You can see why.'

He stared at the flip flops and he had a sudden image of the same riot of colour worn as…a thong.

Cut it out! Think about something else!

He focused on pouring wine, trying very hard to shift his focus from thongs. He couldn't. 'Don't sell them,' he growled. 'They're great. Here's to your new life, flip-flops…um…thongs…included.'

'Yeah.' She was gazing at the flip-flops, but her smile had slipped. 'Hooray.'

'You're not feeling happy?'

She took a sip of her wine and stared at her toes. The sun was setting behind them and the sea was washed by a tangerine glow. The tide was washing in, a gentle hush-hush in the stillness of the evening. Behind them was a gorgeous house, sleeping children—a new life?

'Of course I'm happy. I have so much to be grateful for,' she said. 'I might even be able to afford to keep these. I can't thank you enough.'

'But you're still not where you want to be. I wish I could do more.'

'Well, there's two of us. I wish I could do more for you. And I'm getting parts of my life back.' She wiggled her toes once more. 'It's just what is. How's your leg? Hurting?'

'No,' he lied, and she grinned.

'I bet. You want me to take you home to bed?'

Almost involuntarily, his smile deepened. 'There's an invitation impossible to resist.'

Maybe he shouldn't have said that but, to his relief, she chuckled. 'In your dreams, mate,' she told him. 'We try that and someone will have a nightmare, the kids will wake up and join us, the dogs will investigate, everyone will discuss why we're sharing—and there's also the small matter of one bulky cast…'

'Hmm,' he said. 'I take it that's an invitation refused then?'

'I'm game if you're game,' she told him, and he blinked. But she was still smiling, and he thought, if they'd both been free... But he forced himself to rethink what she'd just said and bit back regret.

'Okay, maybe not.'

'There's a wise man. This wine is lovely.'

'Top shelf of Albatross general store. I asked for a white wine and she pointed to a no-name cask or this one. It was a tricky decision. I gather Albatross isn't a population of discerning sommeliers.'

'It's pretty much beer or whisky,' she told him. 'Plus Gloria on Wharf Road makes a fruity lexia which I believe is highly popular. There's also a rumour that supplies bound for one of the outer islands were washed overboard at the beginning of the storm you were trapped in. I hear someone's found a crate of French champagne, but good luck getting your hands on that. So it's beer now, Gloria's lexia when I feel like living dangerously, sherry to look forward to as I approach rocking chair status and whisky for emergencies.'

Her words had been said lightly—for fun—but he heard the underlying strain.

'Jenny...'

'Hey, no problem,' she told him. 'You've solved my biggest nightmare, collecting kelp for the rest of my life. The kids will be at school tomorrow—please heaven they like it—and I'll be checking out my new clinic. You want to come? I've never set up a doctor's clinic.'

'Neither have I. Hospital settings only.'

'Same. I'll admit the idea of practising medicine here without backup is scary. For me, I like a hospital full of medical specialists. *Ooh, this looks like a hemangioma,* I'll say. *Can you just pop along the hall and see our paediatrician? Nice Dr Braden will confirm it.*'

'And we'd both be able to charge, and live happily ever after,' he agreed, smiling.

'Yep.' She had another sip of wine and stretched her legs, wiggling her toes once more into the sun-warmed sand. And why that should make him feel…

'So,' she said. 'Plan? You'll stay here and supervise *Sea Raven* until you're ready to sail again?'

'Maybe not,' he said cautiously. 'I seem to have lost my appetite for lone sailing. But I'll stay until she's mended and then fly back to the States. Doug and Fred say they'll keep an eye on her. It might be a while, but we'll eventually find a crew to bring her home.'

And that was the end of his heroic gesture, he thought bitterly. 'I'll go fetch your yacht from Sydney and bring her home in time for your birthday,' he'd told his dad. Now it was, 'I just bashed your boat and almost killed myself. I've left her in harbour on a little-known island in the middle of the Pacific and come home without her. Happy Birthday.'

'I suspect,' Jenny said softly, 'that your dad's best birthday gift will be knowing you're safe. No?'

He sighed and raked his hair. But she was right. He'd rung his parents from hospital on Gannet—he'd had to, they'd been tracking his progress. He'd confessed all, but instead of distress, all he'd heard was relief.

'You're safe? That's all that matters.' His dad had been gruff with emotion. '*Sea Raven* can go to the bottom for all I care, as long as you're okay.'

'Yeah,' he told Jenny, and he couldn't quite keep the emotion from his own voice. 'When I started to apologise Mom came onto the line and scolded. "We weep over people, Silas, not things. *Sea Raven*'s beautiful, but in the end she's only wood and sail. A thing. You of all people should know that."'

'Your parents sound lovely.'

'They are,' he said. 'I've been lucky.' He closed his eyes. 'That was what I wanted to give Harper. Family.'

'I bet she knew she was loved.'

'But I didn't keep her safe. And here you are, giving up everything, walking away from a life you love, to keep these kids safe.'

'Let's not get high ideas,' she told him. 'If I get into trouble in the surf, it'll be them who pull me out. They're fiercely independent. They don't want…'

'They do want to be loved,' he said gently. 'Even I can see that.'

'I'll get there,' she said, almost fiercely. 'That's all I can do, love them, love them, love them. It's all I can give them.'

'I saw Sam's hug tonight. You're a family.'

'Well, we're the beginnings of a family.' She sounded brisk but he could hear the underlying emotion. 'I just… What happened to me… Our parents splitting, Chris and me being torn apart, Mum stopping caring… These kids will be loved if it kills me to do it. I'd even have eaten kelp curry if I had to.' And then she stopped and managed to smile again. 'But you've saved me from that. I have a gorgeous house, the chance to return to my career and right now the crabs and sandworms are demolishing every last trace of kelp casserole. If I wasn't so sensible I could kiss you, Silas Braden.'

'Do you have to be sensible?'

And that caused…silence.

This was dumb. Really, really dumb.

Kissing this man…why would she even want to?

Well, that was a no-brainer. She thought suddenly, ridiculously, of the line coined to describe the US servicemen stationed in Australia during the Second World War.

For Australia's young women the influx of young men had been a source of fun and distraction in those grim times, but the local lads had been less than delighted. They'd coined the phrase *They're overpaid, oversexed and over here.*

So here was Silas Braden and the phrase was suddenly right up there, almost in neon lights. Wealthy. Very, very sexy. And right here.

Unconsciously her lips twitched, and she couldn't stop a grin.

'What?' he demanded, and she told him, because why not? Thankfully, his dark eyes creased into responsive laughter. He had great eyes, she thought. Smiling eyes. And he laughed with her. These last months had been almost solidly dreary. To have these laughing, gentle eyes… This man.

The stupid line was still playing in her head.

Overpaid? He was wealthy. That shouldn't be an attraction, but he had organised her a great house.

Oversexed? Despite the cast on his leg—yeah, definitely, she thought. Or…should that description apply more to the way she was feeling?

And *over here*? He was right beside her. He was right…here.

'I believe they came with silk stockings,' he said, cutting through her totally inappropriate thoughts. 'Damn, I should have packed some.'

'Yeah, they'd be so useful. Instead you've bought me a house for a year, and happy kids.'

The laughter faded a little. His smile was still there but it was gentle, questioning. 'Jenny,' he said softly. 'I'm not buying a kiss. Gratitude doesn't come into what I'm feeling right now.'

Oh, help.

A kiss…

'We'd…we'd have to stop. Nothing else but…but a kiss is possible,' she said, almost helplessly.

'You think I don't know that?' His smile was suddenly teasing. 'As you've already pointed out, apart from anything else, I have a cast on my leg, which I imagine could make things impossible.'

'Not impossible,' she said and then caught herself. What was she saying? 'But…definitely unwise. So why a kiss if…if we can't take it further?'

'Because I really, really want to kiss you.' The lines around his eyes were creasing deeper, his smile a caress all on its own. 'And I admit I'm a stranger on a lonely beach, and what I'm saying may be taken as making a hit on a defenceless woman, but do take a look at my leg. You back away and I'll founder in soft sand. I'm at your mercy, Jenny Martin, so, as for a kiss… I believe it's your call.'

Her call.

Why not? There was that question again. There were a million reasons why not, but right now…those eyes… that smile.

Overpaid. Oversexed. Over here.

Oh, for heaven's sake, why not indeed?

She reached out and took his face between her hands. She kissed him.

What had he expected? A light kiss, a fun kiss between two consenting adults. A kiss of two adults who hadn't been near the other sex for…how long?

For him it had been since Charlotte died, or if he was honest since well before that. He and Charlotte had seemed to go into marriage with all the wrong ideas about what marriage was. They'd foundered almost from the start, but despite their marriage being…barren…he hadn't played around.

And that was what this must be, he thought as Jenny's lips touched his. Playing around. He had to leave in six weeks.

But as her mouth met his, as her hands firmed on his face, as her lips opened, as she kissed…like a woman hungry…he forgot the concept of playing around.

This was no playing. This was a woman laying her need on the line. This was a woman who knew what she wanted—and she wanted him.

He'd forgotten—or maybe he'd never known—that a woman could feel like this. She was melting into him, tasting him—devouring him. That was what this felt like—or maybe it was just that his body felt as if it was dissolving into hers. In one kiss.

Just the one kiss? This was so much more. His hands came around her waist, feeling the warmth of her. His hands were on the smooth, bare skin of her waist, tugging her into him, urgent with want, with desire, with need.

Where had this heat come from? One minute he was sitting on the beach, joking a little, smiling and taking pleasure in making her smile. Now though, it was as if a flame had flickered and flared…and was threatening to consume them.

This was crazy. Inappropriate. Mad. He was sitting on the beach, his damaged leg out before him. Jenny had leaned into him to kiss and now…he had her in his arms, he was cradling her, holding her against his chest, feeling her heartbeat. Or was that his own? His heart felt as if it was pumping out of his chest.

He wanted her so much. Damn this cast, this beach, a house full of kids, dependence, everything that was screaming that he was being dumb, nothing could come from this. He just wanted her.

Nothing was making sense. There was only this moment, this sensation, this man.

She'd kissed him…almost as a joke? Certainly it had started light-heartedly, but there was nothing light-hearted about the way she was feeling now. Her mouth was locked on his, and the heat between them made her feel as if her body was on fire. Her arms had found themselves entwined around his shoulders and she was curved into his chest. His lovely hands were on the bare skin at her waist, making her feel…making her feel… No, there was no word for it. This was indescribable. His hold was strong, sure, but there was underlying tenderness. He held her as if he was holding something of infinite worth.

And there was no pressure. She knew if she pulled back she'd be released in an instant.

There was no way she could—or would—pull back. The feel of him…the taste…the strength…

She pressed closer. His arms tightened and she felt…

As if she'd found her place.

Her home.

Well, there was a dumb thing to think. For Jenny, who'd been torn from the island at the age of six, who'd spent her childhood with an itinerant mother, home was a nebulous concept. For the last few months she'd been trying to provide a home for three children, but that home was where they had to feel safe and loved. It surely wasn't where she wanted to be.

But, in this man's arms, for some inexplicable reason, some reason she might have to figure out later but she couldn't now, right now she felt as if she was in the safest spot in the world.

Right now she never wanted to leave this man's arms. She wanted his strength. She wanted his warmth. She wanted *him*, and if circumstances had been different maybe she would've even begged him to take her to his bed.

But there was no way they could extend this moment. Circumstances were what they were, but when the kiss finally ended, as even the most amazing kisses eventually must, she looked into his eyes and all she felt was longing.

'Wow,' she managed, but she couldn't go on. She couldn't describe the way she was feeling, and it seemed neither could he.

'That was…amazing,' he told her, and his voice was husky.

'Yeah.' The word came out almost as a squeak, but it was all she could manage.

Somehow she succeeded in tugging her arms from around his neck and shifting back a little. Just a little. 'I… I have no idea what just happened,' she said, trying again. 'But this…this is scaring me.'

'Me too,' he agreed, and there was that smile again. That smile that made her insides seem to smoulder. 'You want to try and get more scared?'

But someone had to have sense. She had three kids up in the house, she reminded herself, even though it almost killed her to acknowledge it. But she'd taken them on, and after months of coping with their pain she knew she loved them. Their needs had to be her priority.

Love hurts. There was a song that belted those words out, and right now she knew it for an absolute truth. There was no way she was free to take this further.

She took a deep breath and forced herself to say it like it was. 'The kids… Silas, we need to pack up. I'll take the stuff back to the house and come back for you.'

'You could bring some pillows and we could settle in for the night?' And oh, that smile…

But she had herself in hand now…sort of.

'In your dreams,' she managed. 'The tide'll come in. You'll get sand in your cast. The kids will wake up and want me. So, moving on…'

'Jenny…'

'No, don't,' she said, cutting him off. 'Silas, that was great, awesome, fun, but life…life is simply what it is. We just have to take the bits left to us.'

'We might make those bits better,' he said softly, and she shook her head.

'Not tonight, Silas Braden. You've made enough of my life better. Tonight was great. Awesome…' Those eyes gleamed and he reached for her again but she shoved herself back.

'But there's no better to be had,' she managed. 'Certainly not tonight. And Silas, for me…maybe not for ever.'

CHAPTER TEN

WHEN JENNY WOKE, the first thing that came into her head was the memory of the kiss from the night before. Or maybe it had been with her all night, drifting in and out of her dreams. In another life…

But there wasn't another life. There was only this one, and if the thought of the kiss stayed with her as she showered and dressed, then she had to find a way to deal with it. She needed to put it in a compartment at the back of her mind. She might allow it to surface again in her dreams, but in real life it had no place.

She roused the kids and headed down the passage—and stopped, stunned. It seemed Silas had done exactly what he'd promised. And more.

Out on the veranda was a feast. He'd pulled a couple of outdoor tables together and covered them with… sheets? They didn't look like sheets, though. They looked like linen tablecloths from a fancy hotel. He'd gathered bunches of scarlet bottlebrush and put them in Joan's jam jars, bright splashes of colour all along the table. And the food…

It looked like a hotel buffet, she thought, stunned. The kids were emerging behind her, but they too stopped in their tracks, stunned by the sight ahead.

'Neat, eh?' Silas said, sounding smug, grinning at

their reaction. He was standing beside a barbecue at the side. 'I'm ready for egg orders—name your preference. Runny, oozy or solid—your wish is my command. The only thing I couldn't find was chef whites. I'd look much more professional in a hat.'

There was so much. The toaster was on the table, with a power lead stretching back into the house. A pile of bread sat ready to toast. Butter. Jam. No, make that jams, plural.

Bowls. Plates. Cutlery. Napkins, for heaven's sake!

Jugs of juice. A coffee pot.

Strawberries. A vast bowl of crimson goodness.

The kids just stood and gaped.

So did Jenny.

'Where...?'

'A call to Dianne and Ron at the general store,' he said, looking like he was trying for false modesty but smugness was coming through. 'Who knew that Albatross provided home delivery? And it seems Ron gets up at five to go surfing anyway. Today's a celebration—first day at school for you guys, first day as island doctor for Jenny, so I thought it should be first day of something for me. So first day as breakfast organiser.' He gazed along the table and his grin widened. 'We may well be eating leftovers for the rest of the week, but good, huh?'

Dammit, what was it with this man? He was wearing a faded T-shirt, shorts and—maybe because he was dealing with spitting fat?—he had a boot on his non-plastered foot and a sock pulled over the other. He looked a bit flushed—from cooking? Or maybe getting all this together had been a bit more effort than he'd planned. His hair was a bit unkempt. He obviously hadn't had time to shave.

But he looked better than breakfast, Jenny thought,

and then caught herself and tried desperately to fight back sensations that were totally inappropriate. Or she tried to fight them back.

They were refusing to go.

At least she didn't have to say anything. The kids were saying it all for her. They'd never seen such a feast and they were whooping and eating and talking like…like kids should, she thought. Silas was joining in, laughing, joking, and she thought, *This man's a paediatrician. He's healing them.*

But what he was doing for these kids had nothing to do with his medicine, she thought, and knew it for truth. It was just the way he was.

What had he said? All he'd wanted was family? It was what he was forming right here, she thought, and suddenly she was hit by a wave of what could only be described as panic.

'Jenny? What's wrong?' He must have seen the change on her face. He got it, this man. Empathy seemed to be his thing.

Somehow she had to find an answer. 'N…nothing,' she managed. 'This is…awesome. Thank you so much.'

'My pleasure,' he said, but there was a crease between his eyes that told her he was seeing more than she wanted him to see.

She shouldn't panic. Somehow he was showing her what life *could* be like—being a family. Living here. Loving these kids. Letting go of her dream of returning to Sydney for ever.

He'd helped her so much. She should be grateful and she was, but there was still that aching void of loss.

She ate, she even managed to enjoy it, but the remnants of panic were still there.

'We gotta go.' That was Sam, shaking her out of her

mental fog at last. He'd just finished his second huge bowl of strawberries. 'Fred says we gotta be at school at eight-thirty and it takes fifteen minutes to walk.' And then his voice faltered a little and Jenny thought, *There's panic on Sam's part too.*

'We're taking the car,' Silas told them. 'If Jenny thinks it's okay, first day at school I think you need an escort. But, before we go, I want you to pack yourselves a lunch. Paper bags are at the end of the table. There's bread, cheese, leftover bacon, fruit, paper cups you can put left-over strawberries in, anything that'll fit in your bags.'

And once again there was excitement. The kids relaxed again into the novelty of their first ever packed lunch, and Jenny thought this was Silas. He'd sensed panic and figured out to fix it.

Why couldn't he fix hers?

The locals, with the Gannet Island medical staff behind them, must have moved fast. Very fast. It was almost as if, having been told there might be a doctor available, they were trying to lock her in before she could change her mind. They'd had a mere five days' warning that she was moving into town but those five days had been used to astonishing effect. Marc had rung Jenny a few times so she sort of knew what to expect, but the end result astounded her.

The general store had originally been built with residence on the side, but Dianne and Ron who ran it had long since decided they didn't enjoy being woken at midnight because someone had run out of milk. They'd therefore built themselves a home on the far side of the little town, and the residence was no longer used. Or it hadn't been until now.

With the kids at school—and Jenny crossing every finger and toe that it went well—Silas and Jenny checked it out. And it was perfect.

What had been the living room was now set up as a waiting room, six comfy chairs, new floor-coverings, a television. Of the two bedrooms, the biggest was set up as a consulting room, the smaller as a storeroom with an additional examination table on the side—for a patient who might need to lie down while Jenny finished consulting with someone else. There was a serviceable bathroom. A decent laundry.

There was a box of toys in the waiting room, with a bacterial wipe dispenser beside it. A sign: 'Please wipe toys after use'. There was a mammoth box of tissues on the edge of Jenny's desk.

There was every piece of equipment she was likely to need.

'This is great,' Silas said as they checked it out. At least...' He looked doubtfully at her. 'I think it's great.'

'You've never run a solo practice either?'

'No,' he admitted.

Jenny was looking at the tissues with trepidation. 'There are usually nurses where I work,' she said faintly. 'Handing out tissues.'

'Hey, I know how to do that,' Silas said bracingly. 'A kid comes in with a runny nose, you hand one to the mum or dad and say deal.'

She smiled but the flutter of panic in her stomach didn't ease. 'And if it's the parent who needs the tissues?'

'Yeah,' he said, and his voice softened. 'I guess as an emergency doctor you don't get to deal with emotional aftermath. But you'll figure it out, Jen. You're one strong woman.' And suddenly his arm was around her and she was being hugged.

But maybe that made her feel even more scared.

Four months ago she'd been a singleton leading a fun, carefree life. She'd worked hard but she'd also played hard. Emotional issues were for others, not for her.

Now she had three kids totally dependent on her. She had…this tissue box. She had a community she was starting to realise would rely on her as their family doctor, who'd come to her with emotional issues as well as physical.

And right now she had this man, standing beside her. Holding her.

'I'll be here for the next few weeks,' he said, and he kissed her hair. It was a brush of his mouth, the merest hint of contact, meant to reassure, but for some reason it did the opposite. 'You'll manage, Jen. You'll be brilliant.'

'I don't think I want to be brilliant. I want…' But it didn't matter what she wanted. Her life was prescribed.

If she wanted to walk away from the kids, she couldn't. If she wanted to leave this island, she couldn't.

If she wanted to turn in to this man beside her and let herself be held, let herself fold into his body, let herself sink into the strength of him…

She couldn't. Or she mustn't. He was here for another few weeks and then he'd be gone.

She tugged away so hard, so fast that he staggered. He'd been leaning on one crutch while he'd held her and she realised what she'd done and had to move back in, fast, to hold him. Just for a moment. Just until he steadied.

'Silas, thank you,' she managed, and heaven knew how hard it was to get the words out. 'This is brilliant. You've been brilliant. But…can you manage to get back to the house? I can drive you if you like, but I need… I need time to sort myself out. I need to ring Marc, figure how to organise prescriptions, figure who's who for referral, that sort of thing.'

'I can help.'

'You've helped enough. Silas, you must be exhausted and I don't need you any more.' Her voice wobbled but she took a deep breath and forced herself to steady. He was unsteady because of crutches. She was unsteady for a whole bunch of other reasons, and she had to get over it.

'Go home, Silas,' she managed, gently but firmly. 'Your help's been awesome, but as your doctor I'm thinking you must be due for a nap—and from now on I need to learn to manage on my own.'

Joan's house was only three blocks away, a drive he could easily manage. Accelerator and brake were able to be handled by his right foot, though the cast on his left leg meant he was sitting awkwardly. He wasn't accustomed to driving on the right side either, but this wasn't exactly a major highway. He met one man on a tractor, who slowed and waved as if he was greeting another local. It should have been easy, but by the time he reached home and sank into a wicker chair on the veranda he felt as if he'd run a marathon.

The last few days had left him feeling weaker than he'd felt in his life, and, he had to admit, breakfast had been an effort. He lay back and let the sun play on his face and knew that Jenny was right. He did need to sleep.

But he felt good. He'd done good. He'd helped her. Here in this house, on this side of the island, with the kids at school, with her little clinic, she could surely be happy.

Except she wasn't. He'd seen the look of panic as she'd walked through her new clinic. This was yet another move to cement the loss of the life she'd once had.

And loss was something he recognised. The pain of losing Harper was still bone-deep. Charlotte's death had been dreadful, but he seemed to have lost Charlotte a long time ago. Their marriage had been a paper-thin construct, held together by both of them for pride, for convenience, for Harper. He'd been gutted by both their deaths, but the loss of Harper had left a void nothing could heal.

But this morning that loss had somehow eased. The enjoyment of the kids at breakfast. Their amazement, their laughter, even their trepidation as they'd walked into school... He was looking forward—a lot—to hearing how it all went. To figuring how to ease any problems.

To helping this little family.

Which included Jenny.

Jenny.

He was remembering the feel of her this morning, the hug. The sensation of her pulling away and him staggering—and Jenny catching him. Steadying him.

For some reason that was what this whole experience felt like. Being steadied. Charlotte and Harper's death had rocked his world, but here in this place, with this woman, somehow his foundations seemed to be settling.

Because he was needed?

But he wasn't needed, he thought, not any more. He'd done what he could. He could leave.

But not by boat. The idea of continuing solo navigation was out of the question.

'You get yourself home safely, that's all we ask,' his father had told him on their last phone call. 'The boat's the least of our concerns. When your cast's off, your leg's going to be wonky for months. Get on a plane and come home.'

He could do that as soon as he got the all clear on his lungs, he thought. *Sea Raven* was in the best of hands. Doug and Fred were skilled craftsmen who'd not only repair it, they'd also take care of it, even if it had to sit in the harbour here for a few months until a crew could be found to take it back.

There were flights from Gannet back to Sydney twice a week. From there he could fly home. An international flight would be a pain with a cast on his leg, but he could well afford two seats.

Maybe he could check in with Marc and fly home… maybe even tomorrow.

He didn't want to.

Because?

Because he could help Jenny.

Really? What else could he do? She needed to learn to run the clinic by herself. These kids were independent already, and she'd been caring for them herself since their parents' death. If he stayed, maybe they'd learn to be dependent on him, and that was dumb. Unless…

Unless what? Once again came that shaft of sensation, the moment when Jenny had caught him. The night before had been amazing—that kiss, the feel of her—but the lightning bolt had come today, when she'd caught him.

Why did it feel as if her stopping him from falling had changed things?

Because his fog of grief, the overwhelming grey he hadn't been able to shake had suddenly lifted. Now, resting with the morning rays on his face, he felt almost as if he was feeling the sun for the first time.

The sweep of lawns down to the sea, the sparkling water beyond, the cacophony of birds of every description in the trees around him… Yes, this place was amazing, but the place was nothing to do with how he was feeling.

Family.

He could almost taste it, the sensation of being needed, of being centred. Of loving and being loved.

But he couldn't go down that path, at least…not yet. Meanwhile, how else could he help?

This place, this house, was rented. Jenny would be operating as the sole doctor in a community of four hundred islanders, and being a lone practitioner scared her—he could see that. Surely this wasn't a long-term proposition.

But this island was the kids' home. They couldn't leave within the terms of their parents' will.

But that was all about money, he thought, and money wasn't a problem. He could fix this.

He was suddenly thinking about his home. His parents' house was magnificent, set on five acres of amazing beachfront garden. His house stood next door and it was similarly beautiful.

In the beginning Charlotte had hidden her dislike. She'd conceded it could be a great place for weekend parties, and had even enjoyed supervising the best architects, the best landscape gardeners. The end result was fantastic.

In those early years he'd imagined maybe three or four kids. They'd employ a nanny, he thought, because both he and Charlotte were committed to their careers, but they'd still be hands-on parents. His own parents would adore grandchildren living next door. He and Charlotte could commute. It would be a family home.

But then Harper had been born and the dream had faded. Or *his* dream. It seemed he and Charlotte had been operating on separate wavelengths.

'This place is okay for weekends, with guests,' she'd told him. 'But to keep ourselves buried here during the week, or at all during winter… No way. And if you think I'm up for any more children…one's enough. Moving on…'

So they'd lived in a glitzy apartment close to the hospital where they worked, but also close to the high life Charlotte intended to enjoy for the rest of her life.

And the rest of her life didn't include family.

Family.

And the thought came. He could give Jenny and her kids family.

He could give them his dream.

He lay in the sun, half asleep but conscious enough to let the dream grow. His career had taken off. He was—or he had been—head of paediatrics in one of California's most prestigious hospitals—but he'd quit to bring *Sea Raven* home. There were other jobs, though. There was a great hospital only ten minutes from his home. No, from his weekend retreat…

But if it wasn't a weekend retreat…

Jenny could work there too, he thought. Medical accreditation would be easy—Australian qualifications were recognised the world over. They'd find the kids a good school. There'd be the garden, the beach, a life that'd be fantastic for them. And for his parents. They missed Harper with a fierceness that matched his own, but he knew in Sam, in Tom, in Ruby, they'd find fun. It'd surely ease the aching pain they all carried.

Win-win for everyone, he thought, and finally he allowed himself to centre his thoughts on Jenny.

And there was the heart of his whole plan. Jenny, whose hands had steadied him. Jenny, whose kiss last night had blasted away fog, had pierced his pain—had set him free?

He wanted her.

It was too soon. Too fast. He saw that himself. He'd known her for a little over a week, half of which he'd spent in hospital on another island.

And yet there was a part of him that said he did know

her. The way she'd felt in his arms last night…it had felt as if she belonged.

As if he'd found his home.

The sun was growing warmer and his thoughts were getting fuzzier. His leg was aching and he'd taken painkillers when he'd got home. That must be what all this was, he thought, a dreamy vision of what could be if the stars aligned. And stars, in his experience, seldom aligned.

But maybe stars could be tweaked? If a man had patience. If a man thought staying here for six weeks and just…letting things take their course was sensible. In six weeks he'd surely know whether this was drug-induced desire or something deeper.

Finally he gave in to the warmth, the fatigue, the peace of his surroundings and let sleep overtake him. But in his heart there was a plan.

A family.

Jenny.

Home.

CHAPTER ELEVEN

FOR JENNY THE weeks that followed seemed like she'd stepped out of a nightmare into something verging on heaven.

Her world wasn't perfect. If she had her choice she wouldn't be sole carer for three orphaned children on a remote island far away from the life she'd known and loved. Nor would she be a solo doctor in such a place.

But right now she had Silas.

To her delight the kids had taken to school like ducks to water. Whatever fears and prejudices their parents had instilled into them seemed to have been allayed almost from the first day. The tiny school had two teachers. Mrs Graham was an artist; she had a studio overlooking the harbour where she painted abstract—and often peculiar—impressions of whatever was about her. She was a little bit crazy, a little bit wonderful, and she loved kids to bits. Mr Sanderson was an ex-marine scientist who'd decided Albatross was his idea of heaven.

Together they provided an awesome environment for the now seventeen children in their charge, and the kids came home on the first day already talking of friends.

'Lou has four kayaks under his house and he says his dad'll take us kayaking this weekend. Can I go, Jenny, *please…?*' Sam demanded on his first night. The change in him was extraordinary, and it was matched by similar excitement in Ruby and Tom.

Jenny's little clinic was likewise successful—almost too successful. From the day she'd declared it open she'd been booked solid.

'It's a lot of catch-up,' she told Silas as they sat on the veranda an evening two weeks into her new role. 'People have been sitting on what they think is trivial, complaints they don't think worth catching the ferry over to Gannet for. But some of it's not trivial. I had a guy come in today with what he says is a bit of a rub under his glasses. He's a pale-skinned fisherman, and that lesion on his face looks like an extensive carcinoma. If he'd left it any longer it could have moved into his eye. He's heading to Gannet tomorrow to see if the surgeon there thinks he can remove it, but he might need a plastic surgeon and a graft.'

'So you're doing good,' Silas said cautiously.

'There's surely a need.'

'Are you enjoying it?'

'I guess.'

The kids had gone to bed and Silas had carried a bottle of wine out to the veranda. The setting sun was casting its tangerine glow over the ocean—something she was getting used to. It might not be what she wanted, but it was so far from where she'd been stuck until two weeks ago that she felt blessed.

She'd have to move, she told herself. Joan might eventually want her home back. Even if she didn't, this house would surely be too expensive to buy. What sort of home could she afford when this twelve-month lease was up?

'Long-term?' he asked, and it was as if he was echoing her thoughts. And with that came a sense of inexplicable panic.

'One day at a time,' she managed. 'Who knows, another miracle might get washed up on the beach.'

'I'm not a miracle.'

'You have been to me.'

'Well, the feeling's mutual. Jenny…' He put his glass down and turned to her, but the weird panic was escalating. She rose, a bit too fast.

'I… I need to go to bed.'

'Because?'

'Because I'm tired.'

'Because you don't want to sit out here with me any more?'

'I…no.' She shook her head. 'Silas, I can't afford to get used to this.' She hesitated. 'You know, you could go home now. Your chest is clear.'

'I'll go when the cast is off—though I guess that depends on whether I'm welcome to stay until then.'

'You're paying for the lease. Of course you're welcome.'

'I don't think this is anything to do with money.' He rose and smiled. 'Jenny, this thing between us…'

'No.'

They hadn't kissed since that first night. They hadn't touched each other. Not because they didn't want to. *This thing...* It was like some magnetic pull, tugging them together. When they were close it was almost a physical connection. When they were apart… More and more he was in her thoughts.

In another time, another place, they might have a red-hot affair, she thought. But now… She had three kids, and this man was leaving in a few weeks. She had to adjust to a new reality, and taking this man to her bed would be a disaster.

She was doctor enough to realise that she'd been close

enough to despair for there to be a real risk of clinical depression. Somehow Silas had lifted her out of it with his huge practical help. Anything else though—emotional dependence, physical attachment to a man who had to leave—would be dangerous.

She was right to panic.

'Silas, there's no point going down that road,' she said bluntly. 'I can't afford to get any closer than I am now.'

'You don't want to?' He was watching her, those gorgeous eyes questioning yet empathic. How did he do it? How did he show that he cared just by looking at her?

'Silas, I do want you,' she said bluntly now because there seemed little choice but to be honest. 'You know I want you—that kiss seemed to blast me into another dimension, but frankly it's scared me stupid.'

'There's nothing to fear from me, Jen.' His smile turned teasing. 'Or…it might be like the tunnel of doom in the fairground. The first time you enter you're terrified. The next time you figure how the bells and whistles work and the terror fades.'

'So it'd be a mechanical exploration?'

'We could try it and see.'

'Yeah.' She managed to smile back at him. 'But if the tunnel of doom turned out not to be…a construct… If it turned out to be as amazing as…'

'As that kiss suggested,' he said helpfully. 'It may well be. I'm told I'm a very good kisser.'

'Me too,' she said, because there was no way she was letting him up the ante. She was trying desperately to keep it light. 'So let's just rest on our laurels. We're both surely kissers of Olympic standard. We both blew each other's minds, and anything else would be reaching for the stars.'

'There's nothing wrong with reaching for the stars.'

'Yes, there is, because if I reach them…' She caught herself, closed her eyes, struggled with sense. 'If I got so high, then in four weeks you'll leave and I'll need to get on with my life. And I can't afford to fall, for my sake, for the kids' sake, or just for simple necessity. So my feet need to stay firmly on the ground, and right now I'm going to bed. At my end of the house. So I'll leave you to your wine, Silas. Goodnight.'

Nothing had changed. Everything had changed.

He sat and stared out over the sea, watching the stars glitter over the ocean, and he let the embryonic ideas he'd had that first morning swirl and settle. The more he thought about it the more it seemed…like fate.

She wanted him. He knew it and he wanted her. To have Jenny in his bed… To hold her, to wake every morning to have her warmth, her laughter, her love…

It was an enticement all on its own, but there was more. Ideas had seeded and grown to a vision of the future—a house filled with kids, with noise, with dogs, with chaos. Some men might blench, but for Silas it was like a siren song. He missed Harper with an ache that could never be assuaged, and the hole in his life seemed to have been growing bigger as time went by. To have a family…

He had four more weeks. Time to think a bit more. Time to take the look of fear from Jenny's eyes. Time to convince her that the tunnel of doom wasn't even a remote description of what they could achieve together.

He rose and stretched. His leg had ceased to ache—it was now just an annoying impediment to his movement. The enforced idleness—no work, no sailing, none of the frenetic life he'd led trying to block out tragedy—was healing him mentally as well as physically.

It was time to move on. Time to find happiness?

He had it almost in his grasp, he thought, but he had to be patient. He had an excuse to stay here for now.

Enough time to form a family?

It was Saturday night two weeks later—or, to be more precise, very early Sunday morning. Jenny had been trying to sleep and it was getting harder and harder.

Which was dumb. Her life had been transformed. She was living in a great house, the kids were almost deliriously happy and her little clinic was going from strength to strength.

Silas's leg was healing nicely. This afternoon he'd even managed to join them in a game of soccer on the front lawn. He'd been goalkeeper while the kids had kicked ball after ball at him. With the help of his cast, he'd fielded most of them. Nipper had been going nuts with delight. Pepper, his age showing, had played for a while but then elected to sit on the veranda with Jenny. Jenny had hugged the old dog and felt...hungry. Aching. Desperate for something she knew she couldn't have.

She should be grateful for what she had—and she was—dogs to hug, kids to love—but, as the days wore on, as it got closer to the time Silas had to leave, the hunger got worse.

So now she lay in the dark and sleep wouldn't come, and when her phone rang she was almost grateful for the interruption.

'Doc?' It was Ron, owner of the general store, who also acted as the island's policeman. She'd treated his piles and he'd been pathetically grateful, but there was nothing of the patient in his voice now. 'Doc, we got trouble. You know all that stuff washed up on the beach in the storm? Seems a couple of kids—Luke Miles and

Toby Stafford—found a crate of high-end liqueur. Vodka, bloody highest alcohol content there is. Seems they hid it, and tonight they and their mates took it to the cave down from the boat ramp. Seems they mixed it with cola, enough to make it sweet and fizzy so they could drink it fast. And they did. Finally one of 'em realised what was happening, got scared and managed to stagger out to the road. Alfie Bligh found him almost passed out and got out of him where they were. Five kids, aged thirteen, fourteen. Doc, every one of 'em's all but unconscious. Alfie's phoned from the cave, and he sounds scared out of his wits. He says from a couple of 'em, he can't even get a response. Can you come? And I dunno what we're dealing with, but that other doc, Jen—if I send the missus over to your place to look after the kiddies, could he come too? Reckon we'll need all the help we can get. The missus can be at your place in two minutes.'

And all thoughts of Silas—all thoughts of anything else—were swept away. Five kids with alcohol poisoning. Vodka mixed with a little cola to make it palatable—maybe even taste good. If they'd been drinking it like soda… *No!*

'Tell Alfie to get them all on their sides if he can. The biggest danger is choking, so tell him to check their mouths over and over again. And tell him I'm on my way.'

Silas was a doctor and he responded as such. He was awake in an instant and two minutes later, as Ron's 'missus', Dianne, sped into the driveway he was fully dressed, limping out to join her.

'Can you ring Gannet and tell them what's happening?' Jenny asked Dianne as she reached her car. 'I'm imagining we'll need evacuation; put them on notice.

And if the kids wake up tell them…just that someone's very ill and Silas and I both needed to go.'

'Got it,' Dianne said calmly. She was dressed in a housecoat and fluffy slippers. Her head was covered with plastic curlers, but she was exuding practicality and sense. 'Go.'

And they went.

They stopped at the clinic and grabbed everything they thought they might need, then headed for the boatshed. Jenny's hands were gripped hard on the steering wheel, her knuckles white. Severe alcoholic poisoning. Five kids. Where was her ER department, the competence of her major teaching hospital, her team, when she needed them most?

But suddenly Silas's hand was on hers. 'Deep breath, Jen; this is what we were trained for. We can do this. You especially; you're used to ER. This is the same, only without the white coats and floodlights.'

'And without my team.'

'I'm your team.'

Maybe it was a flippant remark, but it steadied her.

In ER, when they got the call that a crisis had occurred and multiple patients were due to arrive, there was organised chaos while the department was cleared to receive them. But then there was often a moment of stillness, where the team stood silent, bracing, preparing for the doors to swing open, for their work to begin.

That was what this felt like now, she thought, as Silas's hand stayed on hers. She was a professional. She could do this.

What was more, she had a professional beside her.

'Do we know anything about the kids?' he asked.

'I don't know them.' Living on the far side of the island, she knew few people from this side. 'But I'm imagining they'll be kids who go to school over on Gannet. They'll have been home during the storm, found the alcohol and stashed it. This is a long weekend; it's a school holiday on Monday. They'll have headed to the cave to celebrate.'

'Some celebration.'

'As you say.'

They fell silent again. Vodka and cola… Just enough cola to make the vodka taste okay. Kids daring each other on. Drinking it like soda.

'Their blood alcohol level'll probably still be rising,' she said, thinking it through. 'I don't know how long ago they were drinking.'

'Stomach pump?'

'Not any more.' Her ER training was kicking in. She'd seen alcohol poisoning before—kids experimenting. 'It can cause more damage than it fixes. We just need to get as much fluid aboard as we can manage. Hydration's imperative, as is keeping up their blood sugars, but we need to focus on airways. Intubation if we must. Oxygen. Ventilators if we have to.' Though that'd be a nightmare if they were vomiting.

'Gannet…'

'We can evacuate—we'll have to. If some of them are unconscious already they'll need more care than we can give them.'

'So we keep them alive until the big guns arrive,' Silas said. 'At least it's not me they're taking off the island this time.'

They were met by Ron. He drove an ancient pickup, but in his role as part-time policeman he had a flashing light which he could attach to the top of his cab. As they rounded the corner to the cove beyond the boatshed they saw his lights flashing blue, and as soon as they stopped he came forward to meet them.

'We got one here,' he said briefly, pointing to a kid slumped by a tree. 'Craig got scared and came for help. He could talk when I found him, but he's pretty near passed out now. The rest are in the cave. Alfie's there now and he says things are bad. Doc...' He faced Silas, glancing down at the cast on his leg. 'Can you check Craig while I take Doc Martin to the cave? She'll get there faster. I've rung for backup—they'll be here in minutes and then I'll help you along the beach. Doc...' he turned to Jenny '...can we go?'

'Bags are in the back,' Silas said brusquely. They were both in full medical mode now. The worst cases would be in the cave, but Craig couldn't be left. 'Leave the bag on the left for me. Jen, I'll be with you as soon as I can.'

She wanted him with her.

What she wanted had nothing to do with it. There were lives at stake.

She went.

What followed was a nightmare.

The quantity of alcohol these kids had consumed was terrifying. The lack of flavour in vodka, the sweetness and fizz of the small amount of cola they'd added had meant the kids had drunk with ease. After one glass they'd have felt little effect, so they'd downed another. Then another. How many before the effects hit like a sledgehammer? The kids were far too far gone to tell.

What Jenny found were four kids in various stages of consciousness, with none in a state to talk. Alfie, a skinny, wiry fisherman, had managed to roll them onto their sides. Ron had brought a lantern in with him. The kids had lit a fire and Alfie was using his torch light, but it was about as far from Jenny's magnificently lit emergency department as it was possible to get.

She moved in, checking breathing, checking airways, moving fast.

'This one.' Alfie was obviously a man of few words, but as they'd entered he'd given a grunt of relief. He'd been stooped over the kid at the back of the cave, and as she checked the closer ones he called her over. 'Doc, he's choking. I reckon he's almost stopped breathing. Oh, hell…'

The kid was starting to fit. As Jenny moved swiftly to his side, the boy's body grew rigid, convulsing.

She hadn't finished checking the other three, but there was no time. With the boy on his side, with his airway as clear as she could make it, he was still frightening her. His skin was clammy, and when she found his pulse it was erratic and scarily slow.

And there were three others behind her, three who hadn't been assessed. She was intensely focused—she had to be to keep this kid alive—but panic was rising. How to block out the thought of other kids dying while she focused on one?

But suddenly Silas was beside her, his glance sweeping over the whole cave. He'd moved astonishingly swiftly for someone on crutches.

'Ellen Cross arrived just as you left,' he said brusquely. 'Seems Ron put out a call and she was a nurse twenty years back, competent and sensible. I left her with Craig, and Ron brought me in here.' As he talked his gaze was assessing the situation—or at least what was on the surface—and then he looked down at the boy Jen was treating.

'I need to intubate,' she said briefly, not stopping working. 'But I haven't had time for triage.'

'Right, we have four adults for four patients.' He raised his voice. 'Ron, Alfie, take one kid apiece. Keep their faces out of whatever they've brought up, keep airways clear and yell if there's any sign their breathing's compromised. Rotate with Jen as she assesses each; leave no one alone. I'll struggle to get up and down again, so I'll stay with this kid. His name?'

'Luke Miles,' Ron said shakily. 'Doc…we could lose 'em all.'

'We're not going to lose any of them,' Silas shot back, and it was a decree. 'Alfie, bring the lantern over here; the rest of us will share Ron's, or use our phones.' Then he put his hand on Luke's face. The kid was still convulsing but he talked as if he could hear him.

'Luke, you're safe now, you have all the help you need. Let's make your breathing easier. Jen, I'm intubating. I'll cope here, but can you set up drips for the rest? They'll still be absorbing alcohol. We need to get them hydrated as fast as possible—and we need to get their blood sugars up.' That had to be a priority. This amount of alcohol would be acting as an extreme diuretic and that alone could cause long-term brain damage. Luke's fitting would have been caused by the alcohol's side-effect of hypoglycaemia.

And as he spoke Jenny's panic eased. This was a disaster, but it was one they could cope with—together. There was still urgency, but she'd worked under these circumstances before. Multiple casualties and not enough staff. Multi car pile-ups in the small hours when staffing was lowest. Once, a fire in a multi-storey apartment complex. She was an ER doctor. She could cope.

Or…she could cope now Silas was here. What was it about his presence that had settled her so fast?

It was just because she was no longer the sole medic,

she told herself. It was just because Silas's presence turned them into a team.

Or…

Now wasn't the time to think about that, but somehow it stayed with her. The way she'd felt as he'd arrived at her side.

He was due to leave, she told herself. It was dumb—even dangerous—to think she needed him in order to be competent herself. She'd be the sole doctor here for as long as her kids needed to be on the island.

That thought stayed with her, but it could only occupy a tiny part of her mind. The rest of her was pure competence, a doctor doing her job.

A doctor not panicking, because she wasn't alone.

Because Silas was here.

CHAPTER TWELVE

AND THIRTY MINUTES later the cavalry arrived, in force. Ron had done his work well—he'd called everyone he thought could help.

Luckily the night was calm, it was low tide and once the kids could be moved out of the cave conditions were easier. Floodlights were set up on the beach and, with two people rostered onto the care of each boy, Silas and Jenny could move between them. With slowed heart rates and little gag reflex, every boy had to be monitored. Two of the boys were convulsing, but the rehydration seemed to be lessening the severity.

There was no fast cure for this, however. It'd take time to wash the alcohol from their systems, and there was a real risk of brain damage. Keeping the airways clear was the key—once breathing faltered or slowed to dangerous levels, the brain could be lethally deprived of oxygen.

They had two boys set up with oxygen masks but that invoked another level of care—the gagging didn't stop. Both doctors were working beyond their capacity and when they heard the helicopter overhead Jenny almost sagged with relief.

Here were the Gannet Island medics—two doctors and two paramedics, a chopper full of equipment.

A plan was already in place for evacuation to Sydney.

These kids would need intensive care, intubation, high level management. There was the possibility that they'd need that care for weeks, as any long-term effects started to become obvious.

The night wore on. Parents reached the beach in various states of distress. The plan was for the kids to be choppered back to Gannet and then be taken on to Sydney by plane. The plane was on its way but with no runway on Albatross, with each child needing critical care, with parents as well, the chopper had to make three runs.

It was almost dawn before Silas and Jenny could finally make their way home. They hardly talked. There seemed no need for words; what had happened was too dire. They'd done what they could. Now it was up to others to care—and to hope.

'Shower,' Jen said as she climbed wearily out of the car. It was all she could think of.

'Me too,' Silas agreed. To say they were filthy would be an understatement. 'But I won't sleep. Debrief time. Meet you on the veranda when we're clean?'

And she had to agree. She knew the drill—every doctor did. Major trauma could—did—cause trauma to the treating medics as well. Debriefing could be even more important than sleep.

They brought a concerned Dianne up to speed, thanked her and said goodbye, then headed for showers at their respective ends of the house. Fifteen minutes later Jenny joined Silas on the veranda. He was sitting on the steps, watching the first tinge of dawn colour the horizon. The dogs were with him, but they were flopped on the outside settee. Obviously it was still night time for them. A night with no nightmares.

Lucky dogs.

She sat down beside him, and he handed her a glass of orange juice. Fresh!

'You've had time to squeeze oranges?'

'Boys take less time to shower than girls,' he told her, in a voice that brooked no argument. 'You take a lot longer to get pretty.'

'Yeah?' She looked down at her faded pyjamas, ran her fingers through her tangle of damp curls and thought… pretty?

On the other hand, Silas was wearing shorts and a faded T-shirt. He also looked damp from the shower. His leg was stuck out in front of him, the cast white against his tanned skin. Pretty didn't begin to describe it.

Oh, for heaven's sake, there's enough emotion here to contend with, without adding lust to the mix. Get a grip.

'I… I admit it took ages to choose these PJs,' she managed. 'I'm only sorry you've abandoned your flamingos—they would have made a great match. As for my make-up—it takes real skill to look this natural.'

He chuckled and the world seemed to settle a little. They drank their juice, watching the tinge of dawn over the ocean, letting their kaleidoscope of emotion recede to something they could deal with.

'Thank you,' she said at last, and he took her empty glass and put it with his on the veranda behind them.

'For the juice? My pleasure.'

'No.' She closed her eyes for a moment and again, in swept the horrors of the night. Emotions hadn't settled far enough, and she was suddenly, terrifyingly letting herself imagine what might have been. 'For being here,' she said. 'If I'd been by myself I know we'd have lost lives. As it is…'

'As it is they have every chance of pulling through.'

'We don't know that.' Two of the boys had been deeply unconscious as they'd been loaded onto the chopper.

'We can hope,' he told her. 'We can even believe. Yes, they've done themselves damage, but they're in the best of hands. I'm betting we have five chastened teenagers back on the island in days, maybe all teetotal for life. It's a good result, Dr Martin. Let's not haunt ourselves with what-if. We did good.'

'I couldn't have done it without you.'

'Happy to be of service.'

'Yeah.' But she was reliving that moment of panic, the moment she'd realised that she couldn't cope. 'Silas, I don't think I can do this. Being sole doctor…'

'Events like this'll be rare as hens' teeth.'

'Yes, but they'll still happen. I just want…'

'To go home?' His voice had gentled now.

'Yes.' It was almost a wail. She needed to get a grip, but the night had been too long, too frightening, and her emotions were stripped raw. 'Oh, Silas, I don't want to be here. I don't want to be sole doctor. I want to be…me.'

When her brother had died she'd accepted this responsibility, this life, as inevitable, and it had been no use railing against fate.

But that acceptance had come when she'd been locked on the far side of the island. Silas's arrival, his generosity, his ability to make the kids happy, giving them all a great place to live, allowing her even to be a doctor again, had changed her life so much. But tonight it was as if a chasm had opened before her.

Chris and Harriet's deaths had left her responsible for three kids, but by moving here, right now she felt responsible for the whole island.

'I can't do it,' she whispered. 'Silas, I just…can't.'

'You don't need to.'

‘I have no choice.’ She gulped back a sob and swiped back stupid weak tears.

‘You do.’ And how it happened she didn’t know, but suddenly she was in his arms. Her face was tight against his chest and his arms were holding her…as if he’d never let her go.

And such were the emotions of the night that she let it happen. No, she wanted it to happen. Cradled against him, feeling his heartbeat, feeling the strength, the heat, the sheer maleness of him…

If this could be her home…

‘Jenny, come home with me,’ he said, and it was a statement that stopped the tears in their tracks.

She couldn’t answer. That might have meant lifting her face from his chest, and right now that seemed the most important thing in the world. She didn’t understand, but part of her seemed to stop, to become almost paralysed by his words.

‘Jen?’ His fingers were raking her hair, teasing out the damp curls. It was a sensation that was almost indescribable. ‘How I’m feeling about you…you and the kids…’ She heard a rueful chuckle but there was a catch in it, as if emotion was front and foremost. ‘Okay, the dogs too. One woman, three kids, two dogs. Jen, I’ve fallen in love.’

It was such a statement. Its vastness took her breath away. She didn’t move—indeed she couldn’t have moved if she’d wanted to. It was as if she was paralysed. She was held against his chest, feeling the beating of his heart, held by hands that were strong and sure.

In love...

‘These last weeks,’ he said, still stroking her hair and oh, what that did to her. ‘Jen, what you’re doing here has me stunned. You’ve abandoned your life and taken on these kids’ care. You’ve thrown everything you have into loving them, into providing them with a future, but you've left yourself out of the equation. So now you're facing a lifetime on this island, as lone parent, as lone doctor. Jen, I can't leave you like this, but there is an alternative. What I'm feeling for you… Every morning the first thing I think of is you. Every time I see you, there's a lurch inside that tells me that we belong together.'

'I don't… I can't…' There were no words for what she was feeling. She could only stay where she was and listen.

'Jen, what Charlotte and I had could never work,' he said gently. 'We never talked of the future, we didn't realise what each of us needed. But you and me… The things you need… We could have a marriage for all the right reasons. Even without the way I'm feeling, every path seems to lead to one conclusion. You and me, three kids, two dogs…we could be a family. In truth…' and there was definitely a quaver in his voice now '…maybe we already are.'

His words weren't making sense. What was he saying?

We could be a family.

I've fallen in love.

She needed to move, *now*. Cradled against him seemed the safest place in the world, but what he was saying was huge. Somehow she had to get her spinning mind to work.

With an almost herculean effort she managed to pull away. He let her go in an instant, and she sat back and looked at him. His eyes were gentle, kind, searching.

He meant it, she thought. This was serious.

We could be a family.

I've fallen in love.

It was so huge she couldn't take it in, but somehow she had to find a response. For the last few months, no matter what she'd felt, she'd been Sensible Jenny, Responsible Jenny, and she fought to find that Jenny now.

'How…? Silas, I don't understand.'

'Jenny, come home with me,' he said again. He was smiling at her now, seeing her confusion. A genie ready to grant her wish, already knowing the pleasure it could bring? 'Jenny, you know I'm wealthy. You know my family is wealthy.'

'Yes, but…'

'We can afford to make things happen,' he told her. 'And we will. Jen, I was brought up on my parents' property, five acres of garden running down to the sea, with its own private jetty, huge trees to climb, a comfortable, gracious home—pretty much the best place in the world to bring up kids. When Charlotte and I married I bought the property next door, because that was my dream—to have kids, dogs, boats, with my parents living next door, sharing our lives. But it wasn't Charlotte's dream. Charlotte hated the place and we ended up living in the city, close to the hospital where I worked, close to the social life Charlotte craved. But my house is still there.'

What was he suggesting? She didn't say anything. She could do nothing but wait while she struggled to figure how to breathe again.

'But Jen, the more I think of it, that dream could work for us.' His voice was growing urgent. 'The kids have transitioned well to here, so maybe they could transition well to there as well. As a permanent home. We have great schools, great universities, so many opportunities they'll never get here. We live near a fantastic harbour—if Sam ends up still dreaming of boats he could find an apprenticeship there. He could take any path he chooses. My parents would adore the kids, and I'd bet they'd be adored in turn. We've a great teaching hospital close by. Australian qualifications can be easily transferred. You could go back to work in a magnificent ER department, with a truly supportive, highly skilled team. In the same hospital as me. And Jen, you and me,' he said softly, 'I think that could work too.'

'You…and me?' It was a breathless whisper, but it was all she could manage.

'Us.' He took her hands in his, but her hands felt lifeless, limp with shock. 'Jen, the first time I saw you, leaning over me on the sand, I thought you were an angel.'

'You would have thought an overweight slob with whiskers was an angel right then,' she retorted, a surge of her normal self coming to her rescue. 'Man falls for rescuer… I'm no heroine, Silas Braden.'

'You are,' he said gently. 'That was the first moment, but ever since… You're brave and strong and funny. You're committed to these kids you hardly know. You're facing a future you never wanted but you'll stick with it, because these kids need you.'

'So you're saying you love me…because you think I'm brave.'

'No.' His hands firmed on hers, and his hold became more urgent. 'I love you because you're you. Because of the way you smile at me. Because of the way you feel when I hold you. Jen, the more I see you, the more I know I want to spend my life with you.'

There was so much in those words that her breath was taken away all over again, but somehow…somehow she had to keep her head.

Wow, it was hard to make her voice work, but she had to manage it. Sensible Jenny had to make her presence felt. 'So,' she managed, 'this place in America… You think…we could be the family it needs? The family you've always dreamed of?'

'Yes, I do.'

And why did that trouble her? Why did it make her meet his gaze and search for what was behind it?

'Silas…'

'Think about it,' he said, his words suddenly urgent. 'Jen, it's probably too soon, but I can wait. I can stay here until you think it's time. Maybe we could wait until the kids' summer break from school, then fly over so you can check it out. Once I have you home, you'll see.'

'Home,' she said slowly. 'Your home.'

'I hope it could be our home.'

'But here…the kids…the clinic…'

'You never wanted to be a lone doctor,' he said. 'And as for the kids' inheritance… Jenny, I can make up for that tenfold, I promise.'

'Silas…'

And his expression changed.

'Hell, I'm a fool. It's too soon. This isn't the time to be saying it. You're shocked and exhausted and you need to sleep. So do I. Jen, for now all I need you to understand is that I'm falling madly, deeply in love with you. With you and your adorable family. But sleep now. There'll be no pressure. Decisions are for the future.'

'I don't…'

'Don't say anything,' he told her, and his fingers cupped her chin, tilting her face so her troubled gaze met his. 'I love you, Jenny Martin, and that's all that matters. For now…sleep.'

Yes, sleep was what she needed. Sleep might make this crazy conversation sensible. She should therefore pull away, stand up, head into the house and fall into bed.

But the sensible Jenny Martin seemed to be shrinking. The non-sensible Jenny Martin was well in control—or out of control.

What this man was offering… It was too much. It was

entirely, absolutely too much and there was only one course of action available to her.

The not so sensible Jenny Martin lifted her face—and she kissed him.

And things fell into place.

She was sleep-deprived, shocked, confused. Her emotions were in turmoil, but when his mouth met hers, when she felt herself once more cradled against him, confusion, chaos fell away. This was surely no siren song, no mythical promise of a fairy tale. What he'd been saying made perfect sense. Here was her centre. Here was her future.

Her home?

How long the kiss lasted she could never afterwards tell—five seconds, ten minutes? Time was nothing. Everything was nothing except this man. This moment.

He loved her?

And when finally they parted just enough for her to see his gaze, his smile, his beautiful tender eyes, she thought, *There is nothing else.*

What he'd said… What he was offering… *Say yes*, her heart screamed. Let this man take on her problems, her anxieties. Let him heal her fractured life. Here was her happy ever after. *Just say yes.*

But a tiny bit of sensible Jenny was still there, and as she pulled away from him it started to swell. Maybe the Jenny of five months ago would have said yes, joyfully, instantly, but things had changed, were still changing.

She'd spent the last few months with kids whose lives depended on her, and they still depended on her. Their island home, their needs, even the memory of that freezer full of kelp—their images were with her, and now they were making her almost sag with emotions she had no hope of understanding.

'I can't… Silas, I can't…'

'No.' He smiled ruefully, snagged the veranda rail and pulled himself to his feet. Then he reached down and tugged her up after him. 'Of course you can't, not now.' His fingers brushed her cheek. 'I know it's too soon, but tonight I couldn't help saying…what's starting to feel so right. Sleep, my Jen, and think about things when you wake. Or in a week or a week after that. We have time, Jenny love, time for us, time for the future.'

Then he placed his finger on her lips, a touch that made her want to melt all over again.

'But for now, sleep well. Just know that you're no longer alone. If I have my way you'll never feel alone again.'

CHAPTER THIRTEEN

IT WAS ELEVEN O'CLOCK, a ridiculous time to still be in bed, but despite her exhaustion her sleep had been troubled.

At seven she'd heard the kids stir. She'd struggled out of bed, but Tom had met her in the hall. He'd obviously heard her open her door and zoomed down the passage in his pyjamas to intercept her.

'Silas says he's making us all breakfast,' he announced importantly. 'And he says you were brave last night and made kids better and he says go back to bed. And he says do you want pancakes 'cos we'll bring them to you, or do you want to sleep?'

She thought of Silas, who must be as exhausted as she was, supervising the kids, making pancakes—who would have guessed that he even knew how? She thought of the way he'd be looking, surely unshaven, maybe even still in his boxers, smiling at the kids, joking with them, discussing their day. It was Sunday. A day with no responsibilities. A day to be…together?

And part of her dissolved into panic. All she had to do was walk down the hall and join them and she'd be part of what he was offering. She'd sink into the sweet siren song he was holding out to her. Family.

Silas.

Oh, she wanted him. Every fibre of her being was screaming, *Yes*.

No.

What was she thinking? Why was this responsible side of her suddenly surfacing, screaming doubts?

Screaming yet more responsibility?

'I don't need breakfast,' she managed. 'I'm just going to the bathroom. Will you tell Silas I need to go back to sleep?'

'Sure,' Tom said happily, and Jenny thought—was that a trace of an American accent she was hearing?

That added to her confusion. She headed back to bed, slipped under the covers again and told herself she needed to sleep. Instead her mind raced in all different directions. Finally she rose, stood under the shower for far too long and forced herself to think. She needed to stay where she was for a while, away from anyone or anything that could sway her judgement. Especially away from a pair of smiling blue eyes—eyes that saw too much, eyes that were full of empathy, understanding…love?

Eyes that pulled her into his world. His fantasy. His happy ever after.

And when she finally stepped from the shower and wrapped herself in a towel, she'd come to the only decision she could make. She dressed and headed for the kitchen, made herself coffee and went out to the veranda. The kids were playing soccer. Silas was in his now normal spot as keeper, guarding with cast and crutches. The dogs were barking with excitement as the ball went everywhere, and for a moment Jenny felt a surge of pure panic. What was she about to do?

The sensible thing, she told herself. The only thing. The reasons she'd sorted in the shower still held.

Silas had seen her. He waved a crutch and the ball zoomed past and slammed into the net.

'Hooray!' Ruby yelled. 'Score!'

'Time out,' Silas called. 'Here's Jenny. Ready to referee, Jen?'

'Nope,' she called. 'I have an alternative plan. Kids, it's been weeks since we left Kelpcutter's Cove and we need to check on it. How about we head over there? We'll stop at the baker's and grab pies for lunch.'

'Yay!' She had their total agreement.

'Me too?' Silas was watching her, still smiling but his eyes were wary.

'If you would,' she told him. 'Silas, there's something I need to say to you, and Kelpcutter's Cove is the place to do it.'

He climbed from the car and was astonished.

He'd seen this place from two angles. The first was from the storm-ravaged beach and from the makeshift stretcher they'd used to drag him to the house. The second was from the rather more professional stretcher the paramedics had used to carry him to the helicopter. If he'd been asked to describe Kelpcutter's Cove he'd have used words such as remote, bleak, a storm-blasted outpost of civilisation.

It was none of those things—or maybe it was, but not today. The kids and dogs were out of the car almost before it stopped, racing down to the beach as he stood and took in the scene before him.

The house was a long, low, ramshackle building with sagging verandas. Piles of cray pots in various stages of repair were scattered around the yard, and a couple of old car bodies were rusting slowly into the sand. And yet it was…glorious?

The house was tucked into the cove, obviously built to give it protection from prevailing winds. Palms had been planted between house and beach and a wilderness of a garden led to the front door. The garden looked to hold every variety of flower and flowering bush he could imagine. A stand of frangipanis surrounded a vast water tank, and the water tank itself was covered with crimson bougainvillea.

'Wow,' he said softly and whistled and looked across to Jenny. She was watching him with a look he was unfamiliar with. Sadness? Regret?

'This is why I brought you here,' she said softly. 'Isn't it beautiful?'

'More than beautiful.' He looked past the house to the cove. He could see glimpses of the kids and dogs through the sandhills, whooping along the beach. There was an old stone jetty reaching out into the waves. That had been the mark on the map he'd been heading for. The night he'd arrived the water had been a churning maelstrom. Now it was sapphire, sparking in the midday sun.

The place looked like paradise.

'I never realised,' he said slowly.

'No.' She gave a rueful shrug. 'I think... I might just have talked of this as my prison but, as prisons go, it's pretty awesome. Silas, I can't take the kids away from this.'

'You have taken them away.'

She nodded. 'Not far, but yes, I have because, despite this place being beautiful, it doesn't work for us. You've given us a solution, and I'm so grateful I can't begin to thank you.'

She hesitated, but then forced herself to go on. 'Silas, I came here in a panic when Chris and Harriet died, and then I was stuck. The way the kids were, I couldn't imagine taking them back to Sydney, even if I had some means of housing them. So I came here, mourning my brother, trying to cope with three grief-stricken children. I was missing my job, my friends… Silas, I was as lost as the children. And then you came along and…fixed things.'

'I'm glad to be of service.' He felt wary, not sure where this was going. He was still gazing around, taking in the beauty of this place, awestruck. This was so not what he'd imagined.

'But Silas, I can't take them any further.'

There was silence at that. He waited, willing her to explain, but there was only stillness. She stood motionless on the driver's side of the car, staring down at the cove, carefully not looking at him.

It was up to him to ask the questions. He didn't want to, but he must.

'You can't think about making your home with me?'

'My home's with the kids and I've accepted that,' she said, and her voice was bleak. 'But Silas, the kids' home is here.'

'But you can't live here.'

'Not in Kelpcutter's Bay.' Still she wasn't looking at him. 'But on Albatross…in Joan's place or somewhere else, somewhere I can find and afford after a year's practising medicine.'

'You've said you can't practise medicine here alone.'

'I don't have a choice.'

'Jenny,' he said carefully, one word at a time. 'I'm offering you one.'

She sighed and closed her eyes, and he could see her almost visibly brace. The temptation to round the car and take her in his arms was almost irresistible, but the sight of her braced shoulders stopped him. She'd push him away, he thought. She was a strong woman and he loved her for it. Whatever she decided, his pressure would—should—make no difference.

And when she opened her eyes he saw that strength. And her voice held...implacability?

'Silas, the kids own this.' She gestured to the cove, but then turned and spread her arms wide, encompassing all the land behind them. 'My great-great-grandfather came here with the whalers and decided to stay. He marked off pretty much all this side of the island, then headed to Sydney, got himself legal title and found himself a bride. Four generations of my family have made a living from this land. They've owned it and they've loved it, and now, as long as the kids stay on the island, it's theirs to do with what they will. But, according to their parents' unfortunate will, until Tom's of age, if they leave the island then they lose it.'

'We can fight that, or we can compensate...'

'We can't compensate them for this. And I've had legal advice, though even that cost heaps. We might be able to bend the conditions if the kids want to leave for university, or for essentials they can't get while based on the island, but to take them now...they'd lose this.'

She turned to look at him then, her gaze suddenly sure. 'Do you remember I told you there's a tin mine in the middle of the island? That gave Grandpa enough money to build a decent house, but no one wants tin any more. What is desirable, though, and what companies can afford to pay any amount for is nickel. I think I told you there's nickel, lots of it, all over this side of the island. We walk away now, the miners move in and this will be gone for ever.'

'You're sure of that?'

'I'm sure,' she said bleakly. 'If we leave, it reverts to the marine research group Harriet found on the internet—

apparently she used it to track a turtle she named. On the surface it sounds great, but a little digging shows it's run by some sort of foundation that puts only ten per cent of their fundraising into turtle research. The rest goes into the founders' own pockets. This place would be a nickel mine within months of them getting their hands on it.'

'But…'

'There's no buts,' she told him. 'Just facts. If the kids leave then it'll be destroyed. You know, if it wasn't for the will we could make this work,' she said sadly. 'Its remoteness and beauty would mean we could lease or sell pockets of it, support ourselves that way, but the will prevents that. It can't be sold, and the maximum lease the trustees can get is fifteen years, until Tom comes of age. No one will build or settle with that time frame in mind.'

She hesitated again and sighed. 'Silas, Chris and Harriet gave custody to me for a reason. They knew—at least I hope they knew—that I have enough of this island in my blood to protect it. These few weeks…seeing the kids happy on the island… Silas, I can't take this away from them. This place is theirs and they have to keep it.'

'But where do you fit in that equation?' he asked, watching her face, and she shrugged.

'Here.'

'Here?'

'Oh, not in Kelpcutter's Bay. Thank heaven you saved me from that. I can't make a living from kelp, and to be honest I don't see how Chris and Harriet could have kept on with it either. They had a dream—Harriet left a diary and it showed what they ached for. If they'd had money they'd have repaired the damage made by the tin mine. They'd have rebuilt the jetty, built an eco-resort big enough to cover costs and converted the rest of the place into a sanctuary. That was their dream, to build it up for the kids. That may never be possible, no matter what I do now, but all I *can* do is hold it for them, keep them safe here until they decide for themselves. I can't have it destroyed on my watch.'

'So you'd sacrifice yourself,' he said slowly, 'for someone else's dream.'

'You tell me what choice I have?'

'Jen, I can provide the kids with a future. I have enough...'

'Do you have this?'

He didn't answer. They stood silent while the warm wind washed over them, while the kids' laughter echoed up from the beach.

He thought of his home, half a world away. They could be happy there too, he thought. He and Jenny could make them secure, give them every opportunity.

'Chris and Harriet were their parents,' Jen said softly into the stillness. 'And Chris was my brother.' She took a deep breath and forged on.

'Silas, dumb or not, I seem to have fallen in love with you—but there's been this overriding knowledge. These kids have been entrusted to my care. Their parents loved this place, kelp and all. If we take them away... I can't do it. I don't exactly think that Chris and Harriet would haunt me, but I'd know that this side of the island would become one massive mine. And the kids would know, and they'd know for ever. So...' She took a deep breath. 'What I feel...what I want...it can't matter. This is too big. Yes, I could make my future with you in America, but these kids are my family. I'm all they have and this... this has to be their heritage. So I'm sorry, Silas, but I must stay here.'

'Jen…'

'Please, stop,' she begged. 'Silas, there's nothing else to be said.'

He left a week later. Once he'd accepted the finality of Jenny's decision there seemed little point in staying. *Sea Raven*'s repairs were proceeding well. The kids were happy and settled. Jenny was working steadily at the clinic and there seemed no place for him.

He flew back to Sydney and then onto California. His parents were overjoyed to see him, and there was no reproach about the fact that he'd failed to bring their boat home. It felt great to see them, but he'd left them hoping to fill a void in his life and that void had only grown bigger.

He phoned Albatross as soon as he arrived. Jenny sounded cheerful, chatty, reassuring. 'Everything's fine, Silas. We're doing good.'

A couple of days later he phoned again, and she didn't sound so cheerful.

'Silas, please, let's keep in touch with email. I don't… There's nothing much to say. I'll put Sam on if you like and he can talk to you about the boat.'

'Jenny, I want…'

'We can't afford to want,' she said gently. 'I'm so grateful to you, I can't tell you, but I need to get on with my life as it is. Here's Sam.'

And did he detect the trace of tears in her voice as she handed over the phone?

There was nothing he could do about it.

His leg healed. With the cast removed he went back to work and threw himself into his medicine. He was dealing with sick kids, often very sick. He was needed. What he was doing was surely enough to fill his life, knowing that he was really helping.

As he'd helped Jenny. He'd done well there too, he told himself. Yes, she'd struggle with being a lone clinician, but she'd manage and it was a darn sight better than living on kelp.

But she stayed in his thoughts, always there. Harper's death was still a massive void but superimposed now was another loss. The memory of that night on the beach was with him in his dreams—the kids dispersing kelp casseroles in the water, the fish, the feeding frenzy, the dogs barking in the background.

The feel of Jenny in his arms. Her kiss…

Why couldn't he return, be with her for ever?

How could he? Here he had a job he loved. He had his parents to consider. He had his dream home.

His father's birthday was a brilliant affair. His mother had put all her considerable talents into organising an event that would be the talk of local society for months. She and his father had laboured in their garden—and in his garden next door—for months, making them picture perfect.

With the luncheon over, with the guests finally dispersed, Silas wandered out to the terrace alone, looking out over the garden to the sea beyond.

It should have been a day to make him proud. Why was he so flat? But a cloud of depression seemed not only to be hanging over him; his parents as well seemed almost to be operating automatically.

'You're missing Jenny?' He turned and it was his mother, coming out to join him. He'd told her about Jenny and the kids when he'd returned, of course he had, and she'd listened with enjoyment. But maybe she'd watched his face a shade too closely as he'd described Jen, because she'd been circling the issue ever since.

'I can't afford to miss her.'

'So could you go back?' his mother said gently into the stillness of early evening. 'Is that an option?'

He shrugged. 'To live on an island in the middle of the Pacific, an island that hardly supports one doctor? You know the work I'm doing here, the research. How could I leave that? And besides, what about you? Do you think I could live half a world away from…'

'The people you love?' his mother finished for him. 'Us?'

'Of course you,' he said, roughly now because emotions were surging that he was having trouble containing. 'Dad's not able to work. Harper's gone, your granddaughter. You're both hurting. How could I leave you?'

'Do you want to leave?'

He didn't answer. Instead he looked out over the garden, and then through to his garden next door. To his home. To the central gate, always left open. He could almost see Sam and Ruby and Tom playing in this garden. This was his dream, his solution to all their problems. His parents would be grandparents again. They'd be surrounded by kids and dogs and chaos.

And he'd have Jenny.

Jenny.

Why couldn't she agree?

'You know, I don't think it would have made much difference to your father's happiness if you had got *Sea Raven* home,' his mother said at last, and her tone was thoughtful. 'I didn't realise it until we saw the reports of the storm you were heading into. And then, when we knew you were safe… Silas, not one skerrick of our thoughts was for *Sea Raven*. It was all for you. She's just a boat, Silas. A thing.'

'You're kidding,' he said faintly. 'Would you be brave enough to say that in front of Dad?'

'Yes, I would,' she said stoutly. 'And what's more, I know he'd agree. And then there's place. This house, this garden… They're beautiful and we've loved living here, but in the end it's just a piece of land, a few plants, a house that's wood, nails, stuff. And stuff doesn't matter. Silas, your place next door has been sitting empty for years, making you miserable because it's a dream you can't get anyone to share.' She hesitated and then said very gently, 'So how about following a dream without *stuff* getting in the way?'

'You and Dad aren't *stuff*,' he managed. This was too close, too personal. His mother had always respected his boundaries, and she was well over the line now.

But she wasn't backing off. She put her hand on his and pressed, suddenly urgent.

'We're not,' she said. 'We're definitely not, and that's the problem. Your dad seemed happy today but he's not and you know why? Because deep down it's because you're not happy. Harper's death is a hole in all of our hearts. We can never fill that, but now, the way you talk of Jenny, the way your voice sounds when you say her name…'

'Mom, I can't afford to love her,' he said almost explosively, and she glared at him.

'What sort of statement is that from a Braden?' she demanded. 'Accepting defeat before you even try? Maybe we can help. What your father needs more than anything in the world is a challenge and I'm right behind him.'

'You're thinking you could help persuade Jenny to move here?'

'I'm thinking it's time to toss our entire pack of cards up in the air and see where they land,' she said. 'Let's brainstorm. Come on in and talk to your father.'

'I need to get back to the hospital.'

'You do not,' she retorted. 'You've been retreating to your medicine for far too long. Are there any patients who'll die if you don't head back tonight?'

'No, but…'

'There you are then. Come on, Silas, let's brainstorm. Now!'

'You make me sound like I'm three years old.'

'Well, you are a male,' she said with a trace of a teasing smile. 'As a species, maybe there are always times when you turn into three-year-olds. But your Jenny sounds all female to me, so she's part of my tribe, and it seems to me that she needs one of her tribe to put in her oar. So inside. Ten minutes, max,' she said darkly and left.

What was she suggesting?

He took longer than her stipulated ten minutes. He stood and looked out over his parents' little piece of paradise for longer. Then he turned and saw the expanse of land, of garden, the place he'd bought before he'd bought for…his family. He'd assumed Charlotte would be part of this. Part of his dream.

It hadn't been her dream. They'd been engaged when he'd bought it. He hadn't even asked her.

He hadn't been fair, he conceded. This hadn't been Charlotte's vision of home. They'd never had a shared dream, he realised. Maybe they'd never even tried to figure one out.

Maybe they hadn't cared enough? The thought made him feel infinitely sad. Charlotte… She'd been smart, bright, bubbly, a loving mother. A socialite who'd been determined to have her own life.

As he'd been determined to have his.

Maybe the same was happening now, he thought with sudden insight. His home, this place, this lifestyle—it was his life. His home.

So where should home be?

Where the heart was?

He thought of what his mother had said: '*...time to toss our entire pack of cards up in the air and see where they land.*'

The entire pack of cards... This place? This dream?

His world seemed to be shifting. His parents were inside, waiting for him, wanting him to be happy. Grey with heartache themselves.

If somehow between them they could find a solution... it'd be a miracle.

He pulled his phone out of his pocket. What time was it on Albatross? Midday, he thought. He could ring Jenny now, talk to her, try and find a plan...

That wouldn't be fair.

He thought of her months ago, hearing the news of her brother's death, abandoning her life to make three kids safe and happy. How could he put more pressure on her now...to make him happy?

He couldn't. It was up to him to find a solution. A solution...to make Jenny happy?

His parents were waiting. He had family already, he thought, family who were desperate to help.

Family... If only he could extend...

There had to be a solution. He had to find it.

He closed his eyes and then turned and went into the house—and at three in the morning he did.

She had the solution to all her problems—but it wasn't enough.

She had a great house. The kids were making friends,

spending their lives between school, home, the boatshed, the beach. The way they'd adjusted to their new lives was astounding.

Her clinic was working a treat. Most of what she saw was minor but there were enough challenges for her to accept that she was providing a real service. The community surely seemed to think so. Two months ago she'd felt so isolated she'd been bordering on depression. Now she seemed to have friends everywhere. Wherever she went she was greeted with pleasure.

She was Jenny Martin, their own doctor; Jenny Martin, who'd saved the lives of five of their own; Jenny Martin, make-do mum to three kids. She was making friends. She'd even had occasion to wear a couple of her cool Sydney outfits as *friends* invited her to join them for barbecues, picnics, life events. Her life should be satisfying.

And it was satisfying on one level. She thought about it as she dressed and wrapped Gloria Hyland's arm. Gloria made huge sculptures from rusty iron she scrounged wherever she could find it. The tear on her arm was full of dirt and had taken ages to clean, and Jenny had checked and found her last tetanus shot had been...well, never, as far as records showed.

'I'd normally wrap it up myself,' Gloria had told her. 'But, seeing you're here now, I thought I'd let you do it. Thanks, Doc.' And Jenny thought of infection and the possibility of tetanus and knew she'd been of real use.

So there she had it. She had a home. She had happy kids. She had a satisfying career, and she was making friends. It wasn't the life she'd have chosen, but it was what it was, and surely she could accept it as happy ever after.

Except for Silas, who was with her only in her dreams.

When would she get over him? How many months? How many years?

She could be with him right now, she thought bleakly. All she had to do was organise four tickets to the US, maybe a couple extra for the dogs, and ring him to tell him what she'd done. In her dreams she saw herself doing it, but every dawn saw her waking to reality, knowing she'd done the right thing in staying. The only possible thing.

She worked on, one step after another. There was no other way. The memory of Silas must surely fade. He was someone who'd stepped into her life, transformed it, given her a happy ever after—of sorts—and then, like the genie in the fairy tale, disappeared in a puff of smoke. He'd returned to his Very Important Work, of research, cutting-edge medicine that might surely make a difference to kids the world over.

While Jenny did what she'd been trained to do—sort of. She sat on a stool and carefully cleaned gravel out of seven-year-old Isabelle Islington's grazed knee and told herself someone had to do this. She could be happy. She *would* be happy.

And then the door of the clinic swung open with a bang, and it was Doug from the boatshed, beaming like an excited Father Christmas. And talking as if he could scarcely get the news out fast enough.

'Jen, sorry to interrupt, but you gotta come quick. The plane's just landed and guess who's on board? Doc Braden, that's who. There's a couple of others with him, they're his parents, Jeff said, and they've brought enough luggage for a month of Sundays. Seems they've organised to stay at Marie Lindrows's guesthouse and Marie's heading out to pick 'em up. But the first thing Doc Braden said when he got off the plane was, "Where's Jen?" So

Jeff rang me and said to get in the Jeep and bring you. And here I am.' He was beaming, and Cupid couldn't have matched his beatific smile.

Silas. Here. Her heart almost seemed to stop.

She was treating a patient.

'I'm working,' she managed. 'Doug…'

'Don't mind us,' Isabelle's mum said. 'This is just a grazed knee.'

'Isabelle's my patient,' Jenny told her. 'And Silas…' She swallowed. 'I guess he'll have come for his boat.'

'I guess,' Doug said. 'But Jen, he wants to see you right away, and we're betting his boat doesn't have anything to do with it. We're betting he's come for you.'

'Go,' Isabelle's mum said, beaming with excitement. 'You've cleaned the knee. I can bandage it.'

'I'll bandage it myself,' Jen said, fighting emotion that was threatening to overwhelm her. 'I have patients booked until one. Doug, can you tell him I'm pleased he's come but I'm busy. I'll catch up with him this afternoon.'

CHAPTER FOURTEEN

HER LAST PATIENT turned out to be complex. Niko Makris was yet another island artist, eighty years old, scruffy, bearded, unkempt. He was a loner who lived up in the hills with his dogs and his paints, and he saw the world only in rare runs into town for supplies. Twice a year an agent would arrive from Sydney and take away canvases that were said to sell for eye-watering amounts—apparently they were stunningly beautiful.

There was nothing beautiful about him now, though. Niko limped in, in obvious pain, and he tugged up the leg of his trousers to reveal a massive ulcer.

'Oh, Niko, how long's it been like this?'

'Weeks,' he said bluntly. 'Maybe more. I've put stuff on it, though, antiseptic. I don't like fuss, but I'm not an idiot.'

Her heart sank. This needed major work—local anaesthetic, debridement of the foul edges and careful cleaning.

She prepared equipment but she couldn't resist a glance at the clock. It was almost one.

It didn't matter. It mustn't matter. She wasn't a teenager, tearing off to meet a boy she fancied.

She mustn't even...fancy him.

And then there was a knock on the door. Not having a receptionist meant there was no barrier between Jen and her patients. At least whoever it was hadn't barged straight in, like Doug.

'Could you wait, please?' she called, and then there was the sound of a voice that had her heart missing a beat.

'I'll wait,' Silas said calmly. 'Unless I can help. There's two doctors here now, love. I'm here if you need me.'

Silas. Here.

'I don't mind two docs,' Niko said diffidently. 'If two docs could do it faster...'

She glanced again at his leg. This was a big job. She'd had half a mind to refer him on to the better facilities at Gannet, but she knew he'd hate that. He probably wouldn't go.

And Silas was...*here.*

'If you're sure you don't mind,' she asked the elderly artist, trying to sound as if this was just a normal day-to-day meeting of two doctors. 'Dr Braden could help me get this cleaned a lot faster. Yes?'

'Yes,' Niko said definitely.

'Silas,' Jenny called, and there was no way she could disguise the tremor in her voice. 'Niko would like you to help and...and so would I.'

So in the end it wasn't the reunion Silas had imagined during all these past weeks, as he'd planned, organised, hoped. There was no chance to say anything. Niko was lying on the treatment table, minus trousers. The local anaesthetic had taken effect and he and Jenny reverted to what they were, two medical professionals working as a team.

And in a way it helped. This reunion had been built up in his mind as something so huge, so important that it overrode everything.

He'd imagined...what? A blurry, rose-coloured image

of Jenny falling into his arms, of him carrying her away into the sunset, solving her problems, taking care of her for ever?

But this was Jen. She was the woman who'd saved him, who was caring for her kids, who was now caring for the whole island. She was a competent, talented colleague and right now he'd taken on the role of assistant. She was debriding what was truly a horrible wound, but she wasn't hesitating. Her hands were skilled and sure, and she kept up a stream of light banter with Niko as she worked.

'I won't be able to make your leg as pretty as your pictures,' she told him. 'But I'll do my best. Niko, your painting in the church is truly glorious.'

'It is,' he said with no false modesty. 'But I can't take credit. My fingers just paint what's in my heart, and my heart seems big enough to fit all the works I need to paint. And you...your fingers work the same. You got the skills—you just follow your heart. And Doc...' He hesitated, a shy man, obviously struggling to find what he wanted to say. 'Those kids you're looking after... I know what you've done. Your heart is maybe even bigger than mine.'

Silas was swabbing as Jenny worked, but for an instant his fingers stilled. The thought hit him, and it was almost overwhelming. What was he about to do, asking a woman such as this to marry him? How could he ever have thought he was worthy?

And then she smiled at Niko, and her smile was enough for him to know that he had no choice. His heart was hers, like it or not. If she wouldn't take him... The thought left him numb.

'How about you dress this while I clear up?' Jenny said, interrupting his thoughts. The ulcer was as clear as she could make it. 'Niko, you need to have this dressed every day. You can come down here, or I'll come up to you if you can't. I'd love to see your paintings.'

And there it was again, Jenny's generosity. The old man seemed fragile, even without his wounded leg. It must have taken a herculean effort for him to get to the clinic today. But Silas knew where he lived, way up on the ridge above the town. For Jen to go up there every day…

She'd do it, he thought. She was just… Jen.

'Thank you,' Niko said quietly. 'That would be most kind. And maybe in return… I could paint your children?'

'Wow,' Jen breathed, and suddenly, to Silas's astonishment, she leaned over and gave the old man a hug. 'That would be awesome.'

Niko turned almost pink with pleasure, and Silas wondered how many times this man ever hugged.

Jenny would do it.

His Jenny.

Please...

And then Niko was gone, but still they didn't talk. They didn't seem to be able to. Jenny had moved into clinical mode, cleaning, filing, setting the clinic up for the next day. Then she made two mugs of tea while he watched. Was she reinforcing her armour?

'Right,' she said in a tone that was almost businesslike. 'You're here. Why? Spill.'

And she headed out to the veranda, sat herself down on the steps and left him to follow.

It *was* armour, he thought. There'd be no sinking into arms and weeping in relief and happiness from this woman. That'd involve leaving her exposed—and she was exposed enough.

She was exposed because she loved him?

Please.

He sat beside her. The veranda looked out towards the sea. Lorikeets were squawking in the frangipanis overhead. The day was calm and still, and he could hear the faint wash of surf on the beach below the town.

It was so far from his life in California that it took his breath away.

But his life wasn't in California. He knew it.

'Jenny, I've come to ask you to marry me,' he said, because how could he lead up to a question like that? He couldn't. He just put it out there and hoped. 'Properly,' he added.

She didn't answer. How could she? She didn't know his thoughts—she had no way of knowing what was in his heart. She sat, silent, holding her mug as if it was very, very fragile and one slip would mean things would shatter into a million pieces.

'I want to live here,' he told her.

They were sitting side by side on the step. Their bodies were just touching. He felt her stiffen. He felt…fear?

'You want to live here?' It was a whisper, so faint he hardly heard it.

'Yes.'

'You can't.' She sounded almost panicked. 'Silas, there's nothing for you to do. You'd go stir-crazy. This is nonsense.'

'You want to hear my plan?' He hesitated and then added, 'No, that's wrong. You want to hear what I hope can be *our* plan?'

Once again there was silence. She was close to running, he thought. He could feel her panic.

'Yes,' she said at last, and tried and failed to take a sip of tea. She turned and set her mug far enough back so she couldn't inadvertently knock it, break it. Break something.

So get the practical side of things out of the way first, he told himself. The emotional stuff—what he really wanted—had to wait.

'My parents have made a tentative offer on a fifteen-year lease for your part of the island,' he told her. 'They've been in touch with the trustees in Sydney. They've agreed, but of course the offer is conditional on my parents seeing it, and on all of us talking to you and to the kids. Getting your approval. That's why we're here.'

'Your parents…?' She sounded bewildered and he didn't blame her. All he wanted was to sweep her into his arms, declare his love, hold her to him. It had been so long, but he had to go slowly. He had to make her see.

'Jen, my father had a stroke over four years ago,' he made himself say. Heaven only knew how hard it was to refrain from reaching out to her, but he must.

'Dad was a brilliant surgeon,' he managed. 'He recovered, but not enough to operate again. While he was still in rehab, Charlotte and Harper were killed. Then… what we did…what we all did was spiral into darkness we couldn't seem to escape. I buried myself in my work, blindly working on, in the hope that finally a direction would make sense. And maybe my parents did the same, filling emptiness with their garden, their social lives, their boat. They seemed to be in almost as dark a place as I was. But Jen, nothing worked. Finally I walked away from medicine, quitting my post to sail Dad's boat home. That was such a bad idea—but then I met you.'

There was silence at that. It stretched out, seemingly to the horizon and back again.

Time to say what was in his heart?

'And I fell in love.'

More silence.

'You don't need to say anything,' he said, urgently now. The look on her face still spoke of fear. It was as if there were a chasm between them and she was afraid of making a move. 'Just listen to my plan. But it's just a plan at the moment, Jen, love. We're not pressuring you.'

'But you want to marry me?'

'Yes.' He smiled then, but he still didn't reach out to touch her, even though his body was screaming that this was what he wanted more than life itself. She was putting him in mind of some wild creature, wary, watchful—ready to retreat?

'Jen, I love you.' He said it very softly, a declaration he was almost afraid to make. So much depended on these next few minutes. His whole life? He took a deep breath, steadied and made himself go on.

'From the first moment I saw you I fell in love,' he told her. 'They say patients often fall for their doctors. That's what I told myself at first, for who wouldn't fall for a nymph who saved them from the sea, who dragged them to safety?'

'Me and the kids.'

'Yeah, and I love you all,' he told her, smiling, because he was starting to see a glimmer of light in her eyes. A glimmer of hope? 'But I didn't just fall for the woman who saved me. I fell for a woman who'd sacrificed her world to keep three kids safe. Who'd walked away from the life she loved to a life of responsibility, of isolation, even of kelp casseroles.'

'I never ate 'em.'

'I bet you would if you'd had to.'

'I did,' she admitted, 'buy a cookbook online. *A Hun-*

dred Delicious Ways with Kelp. It lied,' she said darkly. 'But Silas…'

'Hear me out,' he told her, but there was a smile lurking behind her eyes now and he thought, *Yes!* Somehow he was breaking through.

'So now you're sole doctor here,' he said. 'You don't want to be, but you'll do it for as long as you need to because you love the kids. And you'll honour your brother and sister-in-law's wishes. I get that. Loyalty. Love. But then there was my dream. It was a fine dream, Jen—a wife, a family, in the place I've dreamed of living since I was a child. My dream included what I thought was my dream job, satisfying work in one of the best hospitals in the world. My dream had everything, or I thought it did. All I needed was a family to complete the picture.'

'We're never…we could never be that family.'

'And that's what I've figured. You can't have a family on one person's terms,' he told her. 'Follow one person's dreams. But I didn't see that, and because I was stupid I walked away. It took time, day after day of not seeing you, of not seeing the kids, of not even seeing your dumb dogs, to accept what you accepted almost the moment you heard your brother had died. That family encompasses everyone. That you need to follow your heart, no matter where that takes you.'

'Oh, Silas…'

'So I'm back,' he said softly. 'No pressure, Jen, love, but listen to my plan. I know you have a life here now. I know you don't need rescuing, but if you can find it in your heart to let me share…'

'H…how?' She sounded as if she was almost afraid to breathe, and once again he had that vision of a wild creature. He wouldn't scare her. He mustn't.

He loved her far too much.

'Jen, I've been offered a job on Gannet Island,' he told her. 'I've talked to Marc and confirmed there's an opening for a paediatrician. It's not a huge job—the island population isn't big enough to support a massive career. But the plan would be to run clinics four days a week.'

'We couldn't... I couldn't...'

'Live on Gannet? I know that. But the ferry does a run morning and night—it'd be much like a normal commute. In bad weather it wouldn't work, but the islanders understand that. The chopper's available to fetch me in an emergency, and meanwhile I'm available as your backup. I'll never be far away, and every night...if you let me...if you want me...every night I'll be with you. I'll be home.'

Home.

Who needed to breathe anyway? she thought wildly. Not her. Breathing was for those who hadn't just been handed the world. And now this man was looking at her as if she was the most precious thing he could ever imagine.

She looked into those gorgeous blue eyes and saw warmth, love, promise. But she also saw uncertainty. How could he know that he was everything to her, that it had almost killed her to see him go?

He hadn't tried to take her hands, to touch her, to pressure her. The decision was all hers.

She was struggling with the enormity of what he'd said, struggling with the details of what seemed far too massive a concept to take in. That he was here, that he wanted to spend the rest of his life with her. With her kids, her dogs, her chaos. With her medicine.

Her home could be his home. Here.

Home.

The word was in her heart and it sounded right. It expanded, filling the bleak crevices that had been there ever since her mother had taken her from the island, separating her from the father and brother she'd loved.

Home. Silas. For ever?

But when she spoke it was to ask about a side issue, something that took away emotional pressure—maybe a way she could catch her breath?

'Your…your parents?'

'Well, that might even be a bonus, if it works,' he told her, and the laughter was back in his eyes now. And suddenly—daringly—he took her hands. 'As I said, we were all in a bad place, and maybe one of the reasons I didn't think of staying here was because, for my parents, me moving away—I know how much that'd hurt. But Mom and Dad are aching for a challenge.'

'A challenge…?'

'They have money, and they have energy,' he told her. 'Dad's stroke has left him depressed but not incapacitated, and Mom is desperate for something she can sink her teeth into. My description of this island, this set-up, almost lit a fire under them. They have a boat that's already here. They have a son who hopes to live here.'

'Silas…'

'Hear me out,' he said, smiling at her bewilderment. 'I know it's a lot to take in. It's a dream at this time, but maybe it can even be more than a dream—for all of us.'

'I don't…'

'Shush,' he said, and put a finger on her lips. 'I need you just to listen. Right now, our thoughts are that we take on the lease of the kids' land. We have a plan, with the trustees' permission, which seems to be a given—and with the kids' enthusiasm. Mom and Dad will use their energy and their resources to restore the house and to rebuild the jetty. They've done a heap of research and they're so excited. They'd love to fix the mess the tin mine has left, to revegetate, restore, turn it into the gorgeous sanctuary it could be. If things work out, they're thinking maybe they could build ten or so eco-cabins. For select tourists? For scientists? The ultimate plan would be to leave the kids—our kids?—a legacy Chris and Harriet would be proud of.'

'Our kids?' she said faintly.

'Okay, we're getting ahead of ourselves, but Mom and Dad are already starting to feel proprietary. They have so many plans they're coming out of their ears, but they're here now just to see the place. To see the kids they hope might be their "sort of" grandkids. To see if they could possibly start a life here. And, of course, to meet you. But no pressure, Jen. Nothing's set in stone. Everything depends on…'

'On whether I'll marry you.' How hard was it to get those words out?

'On whether you feel you could love me.' He said it surely, strongly. 'Jen, marriage is just a contract. It's an end, Jen, a declaration of what's come before. You don't have to take my family. You don't have to commit to anything. For now, all I'm saying is that I love you more than I thought I could ever love anyone. We have all these plans, my parents, me, the medics on Gannet, the trustees, your kids, but you need your own plans, my Jen. I'm here now, with plans that may or may not be part of yours. But all that matters now, all that has to matter, is that I'm a guy looking at a woman he loves with all his heart and hoping she can love him back. Could you?'

And there was only one answer to that. 'Of course I could,' she murmured. 'I already do. Oh, Silas… But…'

'No buts,' he told her and his gaze was a caress all by itself. He put his finger back on her lips, gentle, loving. 'No buts, not now. Let's take this moment just for us. Plans can wait for tomorrow, for next week, for next year. For this moment…it's just us, my Jen. I love you with all my heart. You love me?'

'Yes, I do.'

'Then that's a very good start,' he told her, and he smiled.

And then he kissed her, and there was no room for words. There was no room for plans.

There was no room for anything for a very long time.

CHAPTER FIFTEEN

THE OPENING OF the Albatross Wildlife Eco Resort was one of the most talked about events in the history of the Birding Isles. Its building, its conservation ethics and its astounding beauty had attracted international attention, and a tiny, select group of media had been invited for the occasion.

The guest list had to be tiny because this was a place of invitation only, a place where scientists could study an eco-system returning to its natural state, where wildlife and vegetation were being allowed, encouraged, invited to return.

The ten eco-cabins, nestled into the hills, were now full of paying guests, and the old house, restored now and used as a nerve centre for rehabilitation efforts, was, for this occasion, full to bursting as well.

Normally only the two senior Braden doctors lived here. This was the couple whose passion had built this place, but for the opening their entire extended family was present. Silas and Jenny, Sam and Ruby and Tom—and one small baby called Grace, eight months old, adored by the entire island.

Jenny and Silas normally lived on the town side of the island, still in Joan's old house, still gloriously happy. But of course they were in and out of this place, seeing it grow, helping all they could, watching the kids fall even more in love with it than they'd been when their parents were alive. In time it would revert to their care, if they wanted it, and that was the way it should be.

Marc, head of the Birding Isles medical group and now the unofficial representative of the entire island chain, was about to make a speech. They could have had a mainland politician, but this was a local effort, a Birding Isles treasure, and asking Marc seemed right. They were now standing under the palms, waiting for him to speak to the assembled crowd.

The kids were flying up from the beach—they'd raced down to check out *Sea Raven*, now anchored in the little cove below the house—and also to check their old haunts. But even they knew the seriousness of this occasion and Sam, now aged fourteen, almost a young man, had dragged them up to listen.

They were growing up to be fine people, Jenny thought mistily, and then she looked down at the baby in her arms and she thought, *This is a fine family. My family.*

'Chris and Harriet would be so happy to see this,' she murmured, gazing at the rebuilt house, at the gorgeous beach with its restored jetty, at the landscape cleared of non-native vegetation, at the natural beauty of the place, which was almost breathtaking. 'They'd be so proud.'

'Not as proud as us.' Silas was right beside her, his arm around her waist. 'I think we must be the proudest people on this island.'

'Yeah? Look at your Mom and Dad.' She smiled, misty-eyed. The older couple were standing beside Marc. They'd put their heart and soul into this place, only leaving it when they needed to be part of their grandchildren's lives. Grandchildren plural, Jenny thought. They adored tiny Grace, but they'd taken Sam, Ruby and Tom seamlessly into their lives. They were all islanders now.

Not just islanders. *Family.*

And this place only accentuated it, in more ways than one, for the local artists had produced minor miracles.

Inland, beside the waterfall that had once marked tragedy, there were now two sculptures, carved from Australia's native beech. The sculptures were smooth and tactile, life-sized, designed and carved by a consortium of the island's best artists and woodworkers. They stood together, looking out over the island with obvious pride. They were abstract forms, but they were Harriet and Chris.

On the headland overlooking Kelpcutter's Cove there were two more sculptures. These, too, were an abstract representation, Charlotte and Harper, on skis, looking out over the ocean towards the US, but standing together with love. They depicted peace, maybe even joy.

Finally, back near the house where dog kennels had once stood, there was one more sculpture, this time of Pepper, whose old heart had finally given out, but he had a place here for ever. A half-grown collie pup was now bounding along with Nipper and the kids, because love… well, love continued.

'What have I done to deserve this?' Jenny murmured. This seemed her perfect life, with medicine, with family, and now this place, built to give the kids the options their parents had wanted. They were all blending together into such a rich tapestry she could scarcely take it in.

There was also—unbelievably—the icing on the cake—her little red sports car in the garage beside their home. She used it on house calls—family doctor with style! Since Pepper's death Nipper had decided to sit beside her wherever she went, aristocratic dog doing his duty. She loved it and the locals loved it. Doctor and Dog. It was over-the-top dumb for a place like this, but Silas had decreed it needed to be here.

Silas. She woke every morning in her husband's arms, and every morning she had to almost pinch herself to believe it was real.

What had she done to deserve this?

'What have any of us done to deserve this?' Silas responded, and then his arm tightened. 'What have I done to deserve you?'

'Just been you,' she said serenely, watching as Marc approached the microphone and held up his hand for silence. 'How could I have ever wanted anything different?'

'Then that's just as well,' Silas murmured, and he kissed her hair as Marc started to speak. 'Because everything else is a bonus. A magnificent bonus, but still a bonus. This is amazing, Jenny, love. It's a home, a life for all of us, but when all's said and done...*you* are where I need to be. Home is *you*.'

* * * * *

IN BALI WITH THE SINGLE DAD

ANNIE O'NEIL

MILLS & BOON

To Chantal:

Your friendship is a permanent ray of sunshine to me.
xx

CHAPTER ONE

UP UNTIL NOW, life had never given Rebecca Stone cause to believe in lust at first sight, let alone love at first sight. Sensible was as sensible did, in her book. But today she was a believer. In the lust part anyway.

Flickers of heat were dancing about her erogenous zones as if she were a teenage girl about to be kissed by the lead singer of a boy band. Extraordinary, considering mere seconds ago her hormones were behaving very much like the pragmatic, heartbroken, thirty-seven-year-old English doctor she was. One who was forcing herself out of her comfort zone by trying to find her Zen on a surfboard in Bali.

She looked down at her nipples. Yup. They were definitely feeling it. The sea water was simply too perfect a temperature to blame for their…erm…peaked interest. The gentle movements of the water underneath her surfboard weren't bad either. Better than the spin cycle on her washing machine, anyway. Not that she'd actually *done* that. Well… Apart from that once. Research, obviously. For science.

She looked back at the beach, hunting for the man who had triggered the initial flare of electric current.

Mmm. There he was. *Ai caramba.*

Admittedly, he wasn't exactly close, and she wasn't

wearing her glasses, so there was a lot more fantasy than reality at play, but…

If gorgeous Zen gods came in six-foot-something, ebony-haired, sexily-inked, golden-skinned packages she was ready for the universe to bring them.

And the universe did. From where she sat he looked like a walking, talking action hero. Lean, fit, lethal if he wanted to be—but only because his ability to protect himself came via a martial art born of an ancient philosophy of peace that only resorted to hand-to-hand combat as a last and regretful resort.

Her secret weakness.

Not your usual go-to fantasy man for a girl born and raised in the depths of the English countryside…but everyone had their buttons, right? And hers were being pushed.

Rather than let reality deflate the fizz of lust bubbles effervescing round her insides, she lay back on her surfboard and closed her eyes, letting the ocean gently tip its warm sensations around her as if she were a lava lamp.

Ah, now… If this was what her serenity coach meant by feeling 'at one with the ocean'…*splish-splash*…she was pretty sure she was getting the hang of it. Finally.

How interesting that this newfound peaceful feeling had arrived the day before she had to decide whether to keep her ticket as it was—open-ended—or change it and head back to reality in England.

She had to pick up where she'd left off at some point. Newly single. In need of a job. At a hospital, probably. It would be different enough from what she was meant to be doing to take away some of the sting.

It wasn't as if the world and the life she'd left behind had entirely evaporated simply because she was thousands of miles away.

No. It would still be there. But it wouldn't be the same.

Her thumb shifted to her ring finger and felt the absence of the ring anew.

A skittering of unwelcome goosebumps surfaced as she tried to picture herself getting off the plane in England.

Could she even rely on her gut instinct any more? The one that had led her to paediatric surgery but then taken a hard right into general practice.

The core-deep instinct she'd relied on when she'd worked with her young patients had definitely been broken when she picked her fiancé. She'd been so *sensible* about their relationship. So *practical.*

Maybe that had been the problem.

She tried to imagine their last moments together with a new fictional twist. One in which she swept the ring off her finger and coolly placed it on the counter. Throwing it was a step too far into melodrama for her sensibilities. *Have your ring,* she'd say in this version, continuing in a calm, powerful, yet astonishingly sultry movie-star-style voice. *May it serve as a bittersweet reminder of everything you've left behind.*

She grinned and gave the air a little victory punch, letting her fingers splash back into the sea with a satisfying *splosh.* Yes, that version of herself was rather delightful. One worth pursuing. Definitely better than the version who'd been blotchy-faced and tear-streaked as she'd soaped her finger so she could yank the ring off her finger, repeating over and over, 'You found someone else? Wasn't I enough?' She'd happily leave that girl behind.

If only this new version of herself could empty her brain of practical thoughts and be more whimsical and carefree, like her new surf buddy Kylie. Kylie wouldn't be thinking about the tide being about to shift, and the fact that falling asleep on top of a surfboard not only increased her chances of sunburn but meant she might literally be swept out into the vast expanse that was the Indian Ocean, never to be found again.

And just like that here calamity brain kicked into gear. What if she got so Zenned out the waves crashed over her and she drowned? What would become of her beloved Nanny Bea? The patients she was meant to help? The soulmate she was—*please, God*—destined to meet? The children she was meant to have even though the clock was ticking insanely fast on that front and realistically, as a doctor, she knew her chances were dwindling—

Stop!

None of that was happening. Not here. Not now.

She forced herself to take slow, deep breaths with her eyes closed. Maybe if she counted down from ten in time with the swish-swish of the sea. Ten…nine…eight… lucky seven…

Perhaps Mr Tall, Dark and Dangerously Sexy would come out and save her. She cracked her eyes open again and, as if he'd been a mirage, there was no sign of him. Hope plummeted heavily into her belly. No chance of a rescue, then.

At least the cove was every bit as beautiful.

There were a bounty of idyllic tropical coves here in Bali, but this one was particularly divine. Steep rock cliffs covered in lush jungle greenery cocooned an immaculate white beach. It was perfect for swimmers of all levels, and had some ace waves if you swam out further, and it had the added bonus of being only a short walk from the all-female surfing school and resort where she was staying.

'Bex!'

Rebecca pushed herself up and waved at Kylie. She

still wasn't used to being called by the nickname. Any nickname, really. She'd never had one. Had always been plain old Rebecca Stone.

That's Dr *Rebecca Stone, young lady,* she heard her Nan counter. *No one can take that away from you.*

'Earth to The Bexinator?' Kylie spoke in a robotic voice. 'The ocean is calling me. Is it calling you?'

'Seriously?' Rebecca frowned out at the surf, then at Kylie. They'd surfed all morning, eaten like wolves, sweated through so-called Recovery Yoga, and then, at Kylie's request, come out to the cove for another hour of intense surfing. With the tide receding, swimming out to the rideable waves would be a longer, more dangerous paddle—hello, riptides! As much as twenty-something Kylie seemed like the Energizer Bunny, everyone had their limits. Especially newer surfers. Like Rebecca.

'Are you sure you're not too tired?' Rebecca swung her hands in invitation. 'Come here. Bob alongside me and soak in the sights. Maybe we can spot some new eye candy.'

She tipped her head towards the cove, where… *Ooh!* Her eyes caught and snagged on her sexy mystery man. Only this time he had company. Two little ebony-haired girls were balancing on his feet and clutching his hands as he floated them through gales of laughter onto the beach. She sighed. He looked like a living statue made of precious metals. If she wasn't completely rusty in the flirtation department, she'd—

A blonde woman with alabaster skin peeking out from a sarong entered the cove and ran towards him with a couple of beach towels.

Rebecca's breath caught in her throat like shards of glass. Whether or not she could flirt didn't matter. He wasn't available. If only she'd known that about her fiancé.

Oblivious, Kylie clucked. 'No eye candy for me. Remember? I'm all loved-up.'

'Hmmm...' Rebecca feigned ignorance. 'Remind me?'

Kylie play-punched her arm.

Rebecca laughed good-naturedly and they air-boxed for a minute.

There wasn't a soul on Bali who wasn't aware that Kylie was loved-up. Except maybe the guy on the beach. From her vantage point there wasn't a thing in the world he needed, let alone tourist love gossip. Or, in her case, a lack thereof.

Her eyes drifted from him to the little girls. To their glossy black hair, swinging along their backs. The way they were practically glued to his side, looking up at him, laughing, dangling off his muscled forearms like pretty giggling ornaments. She ached to know what that felt like. That deep, biological love that only came from being a family—

You've got your gran. Some people don't even have that.

She tore her eyes away before unwelcome tears began to trickle down her cheeks. You'd think by now she'd be immune to seeing men with children without her ovaries waving and doing silly dances, screaming, *Me, too! Me, too! I want to go to that party!* But, no. It appeared her ovaries were still very much wanting to join the party, despite their decreasing ability to make babies of her own.

Thanks, life.

She caught the dark thought and forced it into a new form—just as the resort's serenity coach had recommended. *'Take unwelcome thoughts and turn them into mind clay. Reshape them into something different. Something positive.'*

Wrapping the blob of dark thoughts in a swatch of

happy thoughts was simple enough on a practical level. She was two weeks into her holiday on Bali. One she could easily extend as there was literally nothing waiting for her at home—apart from her nan, who had offered to come out to Bali if she wanted to stay longer. She had always been a sensible saver, never over-extending her finances—not even on her wedding dress, returned now, courtesy of the wedding insurance she'd purchased. The wedding fund she'd begun the day she'd turned eighteen had now been renamed The No More Comfort Zone Fund, and still had a fair amount of savings in it.

It was an enviable place to be. She had the whole of the rest of her life ahead of her. Minus the thirty-seven years she'd already had. But if she lived to a hundred, thirty-seven wasn't even half her life.

Hmmm… The dark thoughts were still peeking out.

She scraped around for one more thing to cover up the darkness.

Her hair! Her hair was like a different creature here. Maybe it was something in the water. Maybe it was the fact that she'd forgotten her straighteners and blow dryer and was wearing it wild and free, like a costume drama heroine. Whatever it was, her hair had transformed itself from the bane of her existence into a huge wavy halo of fire-coloured locks.

So! She had her health, a savings account, and she was bossing it on the hair front. Just because David, his solitaire diamond ring and the entire, very specific future they'd planned together weren't on the cards any more, it didn't mean her future couldn't be rose-coloured.

Sure. The break-up might have changed her from a proactive, list-making, uber-achiever into something cracked and fragile. But, courtesy of an intervention from her grandmother in the form of a plane ticket to the most exotic place she could think of, the drowning her sorrows phase was over.

'It's a life gift,' her grandmother had said. *'And life,'* she had reminded her granddaughter with a tap on the nose, *'is for living.'*

So here she was, slowly rebuilding herself, relighting her internal fires, and in the process trying to learn how to become more flexible and resilient. She'd learnt the hard way that keeping her eyes on one solitary prize had blinkered her to the things she should have noticed. Like the fact her ex didn't love her any more and had been having a year-long affair with someone he *did* love.

Anyway…

Her eyes slipped back to the shore. There were other prizes out there. Better, more appropriate prizes. Not that a husband was a prize. Or a gift. Or something that finally made you whole. A husband—any partner, really—should be a soulmate. A kindred spirit. A best friend. And David hadn't been any of those things in the end. A good actor was what he'd been.

None of which meant she couldn't enjoy a little bit of eye candy from a distance, right?

Straight away she found him again. The sexy dad.

A hot, biological jolt of connection sparked through her when he turned to face the sea and—against the odds—appeared to be looking directly at her. He was still too far away for her to properly read his expression, but…and she didn't know why…the funniest feeling came over her. One of empathy. A sense that Mr Perfect hadn't always been that way.

Perhaps he, too, had been someone entirely different before he'd arrived here on this beach with his two beautiful daughters and his gorgeous blonde wife. A monk? A soldier fighting for his life? A clueless fiancé who had thought his life was perfect only to find out everything he'd been working towards had been an illusion?

She pulled a face. She was definitely going to have to work on her positive visualisation.

Rebecca summoned up a smile and retrained her gaze on Kylie, who was checking her board leash was secure. 'Kylie…? I'm knackered. You've surfed as much as me today. Are you sure you're up for another run?'

Kylie gave a huge affirmative nod. 'I told the Surf God I wasn't going to meet him until I've done it properly.'

'Because you want to prove to *yourself* you can do it, right?'

Rebecca was all for a holiday romance, but not the kind that meant you'd do something stupid. The Surf God—aka Antonio, an Italian beach bum—was the most recent of Kylie's *innamoratos*. Something about him seemed a bit too slippery eel for Rebecca. Or maybe she was just jaded.

Kylie rolled her eyes and scoffed. 'Totes. Who else would I do this for?' She gave Rebecca a cautionary look. Kylie knew her history courtesy of one too many margaritas the other night. 'Surf gods come and go, Bex. But I'm the one who lives in my skin, so this is for me and those juicy little waves out there. The ones with my name written all over them.'

Rebecca grinned and met Kylie's fist-bump. Whatever happened, the one thing Rebecca was certain of was that Kylie was a gift from the universe.

When she'd first arrived at the resort, all sad and heartbroken, Kylie had been sitting out on the shared deck and had invited her over for sundowners. Over brightly coloured cocktails she'd waxed lyrical about meeting her 'for ever man' on her very first night out in Kuta, the island's biggest resort town. A bartender who made a mean Sex on the Beach. Stefan? Sven? Didn't matter. He'd taken up with someone else, and so had Kylie.

Who knew who next week might bring? Conor the chiropractor? Declan the dentist? Both? Whomsoever she chose, Kylie always made one thing very, very clear. Kylie was in charge of Kylie's heart. No one else. It was a lesson Rebecca had vowed to put into practice if and when she ever fell in love again. If that was what she'd even shared with David. Had it been love? Her nipples had never pinged to attention when David was within kissing distance.

Kylie shadowed her eyes against the afternoon sun. 'You're not going to your dark place, are you?'

Rebecca wasn't sure where she was. But it definitely wasn't dark.

When she didn't answer, Kylie flicked her thumb out towards the setting sun. 'Sure you don't want a final ride?'

Rebecca raised her arms then let them flop back to her sides, 'Honestly. I'm good. My arms have had their fill of fighting the waves today.'

'Noodled, are you?'

Rebecca grinned. She had doubled her surf slang since she'd arrived, and this was one of her favourite words: noodled. 'Tired arms, but I'm a happy little camper. Go on. The sooner you catch that wave, the sooner we can have sundowners back at the resort.'

Non-alcoholic sundowners. She'd had enough of chasing the blues away with vodka.

She gave Kylie a jaunty farewell salute and watched as her holiday friend paddled off.

Kylie was not only ten years younger than her, she was positively alight with oxytocin—the so-called 'love hormone'. A definite advantage. Not Rebecca. No oxytocin in her. Not so much as a droplet. Oxytocin was dead to her.

And just like that she was hunting for Hot Dad and his little girls again.

Ping!

There they were. Building a sandcastle.

She closed her eyes as a twist of something too close to envy tightened in her belly. Jagged shards of broken dreams crashed through her like pieces of icy dislodged metal. Harsh and bruising. Destabilising.

She let out a small growl and shook the sensation away. She had the sun on her shoulders, a tropical sea lapping round her legs and a hotel room on stilts waiting for her. And cocktail hour with a top-rate gal-pal who had never once blown off their sundowner sessions for a guy. From here on out she'd take her cues from Kylie. She would be spontaneous, carefree, and pay attention to the gifts the universe was offering.

Sure, Sexy Dad was unavailable. But perhaps she was meant simply to enjoy the aesthetic pleasure of him. It wasn't like he was the type of man she went for in 'real' life.

The thought snagged in her mind and made her double back.

Her serenity coach had repeatedly told Rebecca she was too closed off to things she wasn't familiar with. Change-resistant.

A smile twitched at her lips. Well, then… Sexy Dad's mission was complete. She officially knew what it was like to have her body gripped by lust at first sight.

Her smile stretched into a self-effacing grimace as she remembered the childish tantrum she'd had in front of her nan. *'Never Again! No more men! Not even if the man of my dreams walks through that door! I am done!'*

Well… At the time she'd meant it.

Who was she to fight it if the universe was offering her a man wearing board shorts as if they'd been specially tailored for him? One who had a six-pack and enigmatic script inked round his to-die-for biceps? Not to mention the ebony clutch of man bun resting at the top of his head. She'd always been a 'short haircuts for guys' kind of woman, but this guy? He was the exception to the unwritten rule.

See? *Ha!* Step by step…wave by wave…gorgeous unavailable sex god by sex god…the nightmare that had been her life back in England was being churned out of her system. One scrumptious man bun at a time.

She nodded in the direction she thought the UK was and lifted her hands in a prayer of thanks to her grandmother.

If it hadn't been for Nanny Bea she would've been climbing up Machu Picchu about now. Getting blisters and altitude sickness, most likely. Sleeping in a tent instead of a teak four-poster bed with mosquito netting wafting gently in the breeze. Or, more likely, not sleeping, and wondering why on earth she'd tortured herself by going on her honeymoon on her own. So the switch to Bali had been a good thing. Far better than wallowing in misery under her duvet after her fiancé had got someone else pregnant and moved to London so they could live out their lives in wedded bliss.

She closed her eyes, instantly hearing her grandmother's strong country brogue countering the dark thoughts pressing for head space.

'Life's what you make of it, Rebecca. If you want a prize for sitting out the next fifty-odd years in that tatty old armchair so be it, but I won't be the one handing out ribbons.'

The admonishment had been enough to make her take a shower. Which had been a win at that juncture. The next day she'd combed her hair. The next she'd actually gone to the shops. Sure, it had only been to buy ingredients to make brownies, which she'd eaten straight from the pan, but even so… She was learning to count her blessings where she found them these days. Not counting her chickens before they hatched.

She looked back to the shore.

Beach Towel Woman had disappeared, and it was just Hot Dad and his little girls now. His back was to her—exquisite musculature, undulating beneath skin that was a warm copper hue and then inch by inch disappearing beneath a long-sleeved shirt. *Sigh.*

After they'd taken turns painting one another's faces with sunblock, he stretched out and propped himself up on his elbows, whereupon the girls delighted in making his long, distinctly muscular, and very attractive legs and torso disappear under handful after handful of white sand.

Not that she was letting her gaze linger, or anything, but she couldn't help but notice the way he held his shoulders. The proud lift of his spine. There was a tautness to it that spoke of… She shook her head, unable to put her finger on it. Discipline? Penance? Whatever it was, that peculiar sense of familiarity took flight again and rippled through her central nervous system.

Another wave caught the edge of her board, reminding her that bobbing about in the thick of things probably wasn't the best of ideas when other surfers might be whizzing in off some of the bigger waves.

She pressed her palms onto the board, and was just about to start paddling to shore when she saw Kylie coming in on a wave, her face beaming with joy at having finally managed to stand up.

Another surfer, a young man wearing flower print board shorts, joined the wave from the other side. Uh-oh. Rookie error. This wasn't good. She could tell Kylie thought she was on the wave alone, and the other guy, from the way he was manipulating his board to ride the wave all the way to shore, thought he had the advantage. They didn't call that kind of move snaking for no reason.

She tried to call out to Kylie, but the crashing of the surf drowned out her warning. She was too late to stop the inevitable. The front of the guy's board clipped the back of Kylie's. Both boards flipped up, obscuring her view of the surfers.

Rebecca flattened herself to her board and began to paddle with everything she had.

CHAPTER TWO

NOAH WHIPPED ROUND, his sand 'blanket' sliding down his legs, to the obvious disappointment of his nieces. But the sharp chorus of groans and cries of alarm that had just swept across the cove had him on high alert.

'Uncle Noah!' Isla cried. 'Where are you going?'

Ruby grabbed his hand. 'You're not going to leave us, are you?'

Noah froze, the small little-girl hands in his making more of an impression than he could have ever predicted.

The man he'd been two months ago would've been halfway down the beach by now. Ready to launch himself into the sea and plough through the waves to help. He'd operated on enough surfers to know how bad some of their injuries could be.

But he couldn't be that guy any more. Mr Drop Everything and Run. Or, more accurately, Mr Drop Every-*one* and Run.

He had responsibilities now. Beyond anything he'd ever shouldered. Dependents. Little girls with his sister's big black eyes looking up at him, their anxiety cutting through the fun they'd just been sharing. Feeling the fear that, yet again, someone they loved would never come back.

'No. I'm staying here with you two, but…'

Their eyes widened, then creased with fear. Any sentence that had a 'but' wasn't making a turn for the better.

'But we might have to head to the clinic, okay? Together.'

'What about the picnic?'

'We can still eat it,' Noah assured them. 'Just…maybe in the Jeep.'

His suggestion was met with forlorn little 'ohs'.

He scrambled to think of something they'd like even while steering them back onto his feet, so he could edge his way closer to the shore in case he was needed. 'What if we have it by the pool back at the villa? Or try again tomorrow?'

'I suppose…' sighed Isla.

'Okay,' Ruby managed, through a chin-quiver.

He pulled her in close and dropped an awkward kiss on her head. It was what his sister would've done, right?

Not for the first time he cursed himself for delaying, and then skipping, her multiple invitations to come to the island for family time with them. It wasn't as if he was a stranger to the place. He'd used to come every year when his mum was—

Anyway… Too late, he finally saw that all of the time he'd spent in the operating theatre back in Sydney, instead of here getting to know his sister's children, would have been worth its weight in gold.

Big fat tears began to streak down six-year-old Ruby's cheeks.

Crumbs. He pulled them both in close but said nothing. He owed these two some fun time. He'd relied on his brother-in-law's relatives and his cousin too much over the past couple of months. *He* was meant to be their guardian now. Their de facto father. And he'd promised them an afternoon at the beach.

Failed at the first hurdle. Nice one.

More shouts erupted from the shore.

'We'll come back tomorrow,' he assured them, as he tried to figure out who was in trouble and where. 'And tonight we can have…um…. ice cream? Ice cream sundaes.' He knew he sounded distracted. Was plucking things from the *Parenting from Hell* rulebook, but…

'They're both down!'

'I see blood.'

'Aren't there sharks round here?'

'Someone should call an ambulance!'

'Are there any doctors here?'

What the hell was he supposed to do?

Did he stay there, safe on the beach with the girls, or follow his oath as a doctor to prioritise the patient?

He didn't have a patient yet. And he'd also pledged to maintain the utmost respect for human life. Didn't that include Ruby and Isla? He didn't know any more. The lines between his professional and personal lives had more than blurred over the past ten years. They'd pretty much disappeared. His professional life had *been* his personal life right up until he'd got that phone call.

He felt as if he was being ripped in half. How the hell did parents do anything beyond prioritising their kids?

He forced his brain to stop whirling. He was a sought-after surgeon, for heaven's sake. He knew how to prioritise.

Right. Number one: he wasn't the only able-bodied swimmer in the small cove. There were multiple people out on the water already. And now that his cousin Mel had gone back to the clinic there was no one here he knew—let alone trusted to look after the girls. Which meant the only person they had to protect them was him.

Much to his horror, his first instinct hadn't been to

stay glued to their sides. Already he was failing them. Failing his sister's memory.

Today was meant to have been just for them. His first full day off since he'd arrived in Bali—excluding the funeral, of course. A huge, elaborate multi-day affair, complete with a ceremonial burial, a procession and a funeral pyre, then a ceremony by the sea where the waves had escorted his sister and his brother-in-law's souls to a higher plane.

Half the island's population had come out to pay their respects. Except, of course, the driver of the four-by-four that had sent their car over the edge of the narrow mountain road and tumbling down a ravine. He was in prison now. Serving a life sentence during which the erstwhile tourist could reflect on just how wise his decision to get stoned and barrel down a road full of switchbacks 'just to see what the rental car could handle' had been.

Noah's first instinct had been to close the clinic to tourists. Screw the lot of them.

Then pragmatics had kicked in. Now that he wasn't sending money from Sydney it needed an income. If the tourists' travel insurance money didn't help fund the other half of its work—the one that offered expensive surgeries to deprived local families…

He swept his hand through his hair until it jammed at the base of his bun. It went against everything he stood for to stand here and watch other people swim out to help the surfers.

'Uncle Noah?'

He looked down at Isla's sweet face. 'Yes, darlin'?'

'You can go if you want. We'll be okay. As long as you promise to come back.'

He ribcage all but caved in on itself.

'No, darlin'. I'm going to stick here with you. If they

need medical help it'll be here on the beach or back at the clinic.'

Ruby's face crumpled. 'What about our bedtime stories?'

'Hey…' He dropped down onto one knee, using his thumbs to wipe the tears away. 'We'll still have story time.'

'Promise?' She held out a little finger.

'Promise.' They linked fingers and it just about destroyed him to see the relief in her eyes.

He rose and tugged his T-shirt on, silently cursing himself. This was his fault. The tears. The anxiety. Since the funeral he'd buried himself in work at the clinic, as if that would bring his sister and her husband back. Thank God his cousin had foreseen his inability to juggle both the clinic and the girls from the get-go, but now it was time to step into shoes he didn't even begin to know how to fill.

Mel had to go home to her family in Oz. His late brother-in-law's family, whilst Indonesian, lived on another island, and had left a week ago amidst a flurry of promises to come back regularly. There had been talk of sending the girls to live in Jakarta with them. Talk Noah had refused to give any sort of definitive response to. Mostly because he had no idea what was best for the girls, and that had to be his number one priority right now.

Sure. He could hire a nanny. In fact, he'd *have* to hire a nanny. Someone, anyway. He couldn't work *and* be there for them the way he wanted to. Not that work was filling the dark void inside him the way it had used to. No matter how many broken bones he set, or wounds he stitched, or coral rashes he cleaned at the clinic, nothing would bring his sister and her husband back. The same way his punishing work schedule back in Sydney hadn't cured his mother or turned his father into the kind of man who led by example. Work had come first—family second.

The past few years Noah had felt himself falling into the same trap. *Do as I say. Not as I do.*

At least he hadn't had affairs.

He screwed the memories up tight and crammed them out of sight. What his dad did in his private time wasn't Noah's concern any more. He barely considered the man a member of his family.

The girls were his family now. This very morning he'd made a silent promise to his sister, as he and the girls had laid flowers at her shrine. A vow to ensure Ruby and Isla would know beyond a shadow of a doubt that he was there for them as much as he was for the clinic.

No.

He checked himself.

The clinic would have to—

Hell. He didn't know.

The list of things he'd do differently if he could live his life over again began to press against his temporal lobes. He'd be married with kids of his own if he hadn't been so hellbent on—on what, exactly?

Not hurting anyone the way his father had?

He looked down at the near identical pairs of ebony eyes looking up at him. Real life was here and now and shaped like two perfect little girls. Little girls who needed to know that they were loved and, just as importantly, safe.

'The guy's gonna need medical help, for sure!'

'I'm a doctor.'

He couldn't stop himself. He'd sworn an oath.

He'd also signed a fifteen-page document assuring his sister that, in the unlikely event of her death, he'd become guardian to her children.

'It's all right, girls. I'm going to be right here within sight, yeah?'

'Fan-bloody-tastic, mate.' A fellow Australian jogged over to him. 'A Quimby wave hog hit the tube and blasted straight into the kook. Real sketchy. Look. There.' He pointed out to sea. 'I reckon the girl is tombstoning.'

Noah stared at him. Despite doing countless surgeries on surfers, their lingo was not his native tongue. 'Translate.'

'Idiot bloke hit a wave, thought he could outrun the newbie girl, and crashed into her instead. She's still attached to her board but must've been knocked out. Because it's surfacing and she isn't.'

Noah took a step towards the sea and felt the surfer's arm restrain him. 'No, mate. There's a couple of people already paddling out there. If you're the one who's going to stitch 'em up or blast the water out of their lungs you need to stay safe here with your little ones, yeah?'

Noah swore under his breath. Fancy getting told how to look after his nieces by a surfer dude.

The bloke continued, oblivious to the short, sharp knife-blow he'd delivered to Noah's confidence. 'I predict a smashed nose or a fin slash for him. And a concussion for her.'

Now, that was language he could understand. Orthopaedic surgeons in Australia were well acquainted with noses that had met their surfboards face-forward. He'd realigned more than one deviated septum whilst avoiding fresh sutures applied after the back fin of a surfboard had done its best to scar the surfer for life.

Why the hell people thought they could outwit the ocean was beyond him.

Running. That was more his speed. Cycling. Swimming. In a pool.

And long walks at sunset on the beach...

He could practically hear his sister dissolving into giggles as she pretended to type up imaginary profiles for him on the dating apps he'd refused to let her sign him up to after Alice had given him his walking papers.

The reminder of those moments he'd never have again made him instinctively tighten his grip on his nieces' shoulders. With one tucked under each arm, Noah squinted out to the bay, his dark eyes arrowing in on a guy flipping over his surfboard and awkwardly climbing on, face-planting on the board as a wave crashed over him. When he lifted his head, he saw his face was streaming with blood.

'Ha!' crowed the surfer dude. 'Can I call it or what?'

Noah gave him a grudging smile. It felt strange, as lately it hadn't been in his practice to smile. Anyway… Whatever… Work. Broken nose. He could probably set it here on the beach if that was all that had happened to him. If it was anything else they'd have to head back to the clinic.

His real concern was for the woman.

He could see the other board bobbing up and down nearby, but no sign of its owner. *Not good.* Riders usually wore an ankle leash that kept them and the board together. He saw an auburn-haired woman—the one he'd caught looking at him earlier—approaching the scene on a colourful board. She was wearing a long-sleeved swimsuit.

He'd told himself that it was her suit that had caught his attention. But it hadn't been. Something about her had seemed familiar.

He leaned in, as if it would help him hear. It didn't. He watched as she checked in with the guy, asked him a couple of questions, then gestured to one of the other surfers to come over.

What *was* it about her that seemed so familiar?

He lost sight of her for a moment, as she slipped off her board and dived under, just as a wave crested and crashed over her board.

Broken Nose Bloke was now being towed to shore by another surfer.

He hadn't realised he'd been holding his breath until the redhead resurfaced with a blonde who, with the help of the other surfers, was soon loaded onto her board and also towed in.

Noah's brain kicked into gear. Weaving elements of his old life into his new one was the only way he could see this working. 'C'mon, girls. You up for a run? Who can make it to the Jeep to grab Uncle Noah's medical bag first?'

Amidst a chorus of 'Me! Me!' and 'I can do it!' they ran.

Noah jogged into the surf and began to do the one thing he knew he was good at. Practising medicine.

Noah had done a quick reset of the lad's nose almost before he'd even hit the shore. Now that his nieces had returned with his medical bag, he popped a temporary bandage over the nasty gash on the young man's cheek. As predicted, it was from his board fin—the laser-sharp steering device. He'd definitely need stitches.

Noah felt a punch of pride that his nieces, who had virtually grown up in the medical clinic his sister ran—he checked himself, *had run*—were more fascinated than grossed out, and were now standing by waiting to help with the next patient.

Noah looked out to the water just as the surfers were

pulling the board with the blonde woman on it to shore. Walking alongside the board was the redhead. She was giving the blonde a sternal rub.

Interesting… Not your bog-standard first aid knowledge.

'Come on, Kylie. This isn't the way this is going to end. Not today. Not on my watch.'

Her cheeks were streaked with tears, or maybe droplets from the ocean. Difficult to tell. Her expression was dark. She knew the young woman's name, so chances were high they were friends. Although there was a bit of an age gap. Mother? No. Not that much. Didn't matter. Age-guessing wasn't his priority.

'What's wrong with her?' one of the crowd asked.

'She's unconscious,' the redhead answered. 'I'm not sure if she's inhaled water or been knocked on the head by the board.' She did one more sternal rub, then pressed her fingers to Kylie's throat and paled. 'No pulse.'

No pulse indicated that she'd inhaled water and had begun to drown. She needed CPR straight away. Water blocking the airway meant no oxygen, and if that were the case it was possible she'd been without oxygen for several minutes now. Too long meant permanent brain damage or worse.

'Can someone take the leash off?' Noah asked as he waded in and grabbed one end of Kylie's board, easily hoisting her towards the safety of the beach. Two other surf dudes had the other end, while the auburn-haired woman began to shoo people back.

When they'd set the board down, Noah did a lightning-fast visual check. The sternal rub had produced some foam at her mouth. A good sign, in this case. Her body was expelling water. Forty seconds underwater after an involuntary inhalation was enough to drown an adult. Twenty seconds could take a child's life.

Reflexively, Noah glanced round and checked that the girls were well clear of the surf. It was receding. He didn't know the cove intimately, but he knew enough about tides to know there was a tug to the waves, and those precious little humans simply did not have the strength to fight it.

'She needs CPR! Clear the space,' the woman demanded.

Noah took a step forward.

'I said clear the space,' she repeated firmly.

Their eyes met and locked. It couldn't have been for more than a second that their gazes meshed, maybe less, but something about the passage of time changed in that instant.

Some people said fear made time appear to stand still, while others claimed it could be anything new—making the brain strain to register and understand what was happening. In medical terms, it was the cerebral cortex making a faulty overestimation of the duration of a stimuli connected to the fight-or-flight response. He didn't feel like fighting. And he wasn't, despite her request, going to move.

There was another option. One his sister would've pounced on because it would explain why his heart was crashing against his chest. Why he could feel his pulse in his throat. An oxytocin surge. Love at first sight.

He blinked the thought away.

Something at first sight, maybe.

Recognition?

He *saw* himself in her forest-green eyes. Not literally, of course, but…

Hand on heart, he could see a version of himself deep within the flecks of her gold and green irises. Felt an affinity shift between them…energy syncing with the sparks flashing in her pupils.

He had no idea how he knew—*déjà-vu*?—but he knew that, like him, she had grounded her life in facts, only to have her reality upended by one of life's blunt U-turns. A traumatic event had destroyed the path she'd prepared for herself. A path as straight and well-laid-out as his had been. She was, in short, a kindred spirit.

Where the hell did he know her from?

The moment ended as quickly as it had begun.

'I'm a doctor,' they both said at the same time.

Again, their eyes met and locked, this time with a shared understanding. They could both help Kylie.

'Rebecca.' She pointed at herself.

'Noah.'

There was another microsecond of connection. More complex this time. Something that ingrained itself in him on a cellular level. An exchange of energy that clarified something they both knew to be true: Kylie's life was in their hands.

Together they dropped to their knees beside Kylie. Rebecca spoke as she pressed two fingers together and made a quick swoop of Kylie's mouth, clearing it of the foam.

'She wanted to do one last run. She was over-tired, but against my advice went out anyway. Broken Nose Bloke dropped in on her wave. His board clipped hers. She went under and didn't resurface for a good ninety seconds. She's a strong swimmer but she was caught off guard.'

There was no anger or frustration in her voice. Just facts. The perfect 'doctor' tone.

In another textbook re-enactment of her medical training, Rebecca kept saying her patient's name. 'Kylie? Kylie, can you hear me?' No response. 'We're here with you, Kylie.'

His eyes snapped to hers. How had they become a 'we'?

'I can't do this alone,' she said.

The words exploded in him like a grenade.

She had more strength of character than he did.

A couple of years back, when his sister and her husband had been doing their wills, she'd suggested he take some time to think about whether he really was happy to be named their guardian. He'd been newly single, and his sister had her doubts. He'd struggle to do it on his own, she'd warned him. She and her husband had trouble balancing everything, and they were a team.

'Don't be ridiculous,' he'd retorted, grabbing the paperwork and signing it. *'It's not as if it'll ever happen,'* he'd said.

Another grenade went off.

It was something he knew to do in his operating theatre—to expect the unexpected. But somehow he hadn't trained himself to brace for it in real life.

'You okay?'

Rebecca was looking at him as if she was reading his thoughts. He nodded, annoyed with himself that he'd faltered, even for a nanosecond. Each fraction of time was precious to this woman. So they got to work.

With Noah's help, Rebecca rolled the young woman onto her back, still on the surfboard—a better surface for compressions than the sand.

'I'll do rescue breaths—you do compressions.' She pointed at her arms as a signal that hers were tired after swimming into shore.

No ego. She earned another notch of his respect. Some people might have insisted on performing the 'glory' job. She clearly knew the real glory came from getting it right.

Without waiting for an answer, she tilted Kylie's chin and head backwards, to keep the airway as wide open as possible. A swathe of auburn hair swept down as she leant forward.

Noah's fingers twitched with an absurd desire to push it across her shoulder to her back. He cursed himself for the lack of focus, tugged his phone out of his pocket and got one of his nieces to hold it so he could get the staff at the clinic to prep a room for them.

The most up-to-date CPR advice was to forgo the rescue breaths, but in the case of drowning a handful of breaths could make the critical difference. Rebecca gave Kylie five rescue breaths.

Noah had already woven his fingers together, one palm over the other, and as soon as she'd finished he began compressions.

As he neared the end of the minute-long cycle, Rebecca began counting out loud. 'One-eighteen, one-nineteen, one-twenty.' She leant forward as he held his hands up and gave two more rescue breaths.

He did another sixty compressions. This time, before Rebecca could count him out, Kylie lurched forward, and the water that had been trapped in her lungs began to be expelled. They swiftly shifted her into the recovery position as the crowd around them burst into spontaneous applause, complete with a round of back-slapping and hugs and *Thank Gods*.

There were a couple of foil blankets in his kit but, not wanting to put them directly against Kylie's skin, Noah pulled his shirt off and tucked it around her shoulders.

When he looked up again, Rebecca's gaze wasn't on his face.

CHAPTER THREE

REBECCA BIT DOWN on the inside of her cheek so hard she drew blood. It was the only way she could stop herself from reaching across and touching Noah to make sure he wasn't a mirage.

A man this perfect couldn't be mortal. Could he? Who even *had* a physique like that? Certainly not her ex. It wasn't gym-built. No. That kind of beauty was… It was… He was…

Not. Available.

'Did I ace the wave?' Kylie's weak voice broke through the silence and, mercifully, ended Rebecca's staring contest with Noah's pin-up-ready torso.

'You were perfect,' Rebecca whispered.

And then, of course, her eyes met Noah's.

He arched an inquisitive eyebrow. She practically felt his gaze drop down to her lips…just as she was licking them. His eyes pinged back to hers and her body lit up as if she were a one-woman advertisement for holiday romances.

Rather than launch herself at him, she made herself focus on Kylie, even though her body was practically vibrating with a life-force she'd never known she possessed.

Was this what living outside her comfort zone was

meant to make her feel like? Charged like a thousand-watt bulb?

After checking that Kylie's skin wasn't cold, or tinted with the tell-tale blue of hypothermia, she had checked for any unusual abdominal swellings and made sure she felt well enough to travel. Then they'd bundled the lad with the broken nose and Kylie into the Jeep Noah's little girls had guided them to.

All this while she had been averting her gaze from Noah's chest. And his back. And his sexy arm tattoos. But most of all his face. Apart from the fact he was like vitamins for the eyes, she couldn't shake the feeling of having met him before.

Like a soulmate.

Rebecca kept one hand on Kylie's pulse and, as she was now seated in the back of the Jeep, her eyes on what she could see of Noah's profile. The man was clearly off-limits, but no matter how much she chastised herself she couldn't stop herself from staring.

This was a serious moth-to-the-flame situation. Obvious enough to draw Kylie's attention. Because, even though she was exhausted, and still experiencing a jagged-sounding cough, she had enough energy to start whisper-singing. 'Rebecca and Noah, sitting in a tree…'

Rebecca gently pressed a finger to her friend's lips and, through a smirk of her own, intoned, 'Hush. Save your energy. You've been through a serious trauma.'

Which, to be fair, she had. If they'd been at the last hospital where she'd worked, before she'd decamped to Cornwall, she'd be demanding a full neurological work-up and scans galore. Of her lungs, her stomach, her brain. A lot could go wrong when you were without oxygen—but, seeing as Kylie was well enough to tease her, she was pretty sure twenty-four hours of observation would conclude that she'd had a very near miss.

She gave her friend's hand a squeeze and smoothed her blonde hair back from her forehead. Poor love. How terrifying.

And then she went right back to staring at Noah.

As the vehicle wove beneath the canopy of thick jungle foliage, Rebecca tried to figure out what the universe was doing by gifting her someone she couldn't have. It seemed mean.

Anyway… She doubted she could handle getting naked in front of someone who looked *that* divine, let alone orgasm in front of him. She wasn't exactly a supermodel. Plus-sizes and comfort clothes were her normal apparel. And scrubs. In fact, mostly scrubs. This whole 'swimsuit as daywear' thing was only because she knew she'd never see anyone she met here again.

And why was she even thinking about things like that? It wasn't as if they were on their way to his secret mountain lair, where he would have his wicked way to her. This presumably married father of two was driving them to a medical clinic to check her friend hadn't sustained brain damage.

And yet…

Every time her eyes connected with Noah's it felt as if he'd zapped her with something. A live current. When their hands had accidentally brushed against each other's when they'd loaded Kylie into his very fancy Jeep spontaneous combustion had seemed a genuine possibility.

Being the gifted flirt she wasn't, she'd done the sexiest thing possible and asked him if he was happy for Kylie to throw up in the back of this vehicle. Because, if she wasn't mistaken, it still had that new car smell. Her ex would've called an ambulance to do the job. He was very precious about his vehicles. Too bad he hadn't felt that way about her heart.

Noah had given her a look that spoke volumes.

A person's life trumps that new car smell.

And that had set a whole new raft of butterflies into flight in her tummy.

Unlike her ex, who had become a doctor because that was what generations of the men in his family before him had done, Noah seemed to have arrived on earth pre-programmed to want to fix what was broken.

As if he was reading her mind, his eyes met hers in the rear-view mirror and he gave her a tight nod of affirmation.

Her heart skipped a beat. And then a few more. She fanned herself with the back of her hand. Who needed AEDs when you had a Noah? He'd done more to her nervous system in the span of ten minutes than David had ever done over the course of five entire years. Had she ever even known what love was?

The thought threatened to crack her in half. She quickly corseted it and returned to her safe place: pragmatics.

Regardless of all these carnal thoughts and feelings, Noah was no-go territory. Unlike her ex's new wife, Rebecca didn't stray into territory that wasn't hers. She knew how deep those wounds cut.

Besides, Noah was literally perfect, so even the idea that he would consider cheating on his trim blonde wife with Rebecca—a taller than average 'big-boned' girl from the West Country, with a dedication to spreadsheeting—was ludicrous. Especially not with two gorgeous inky-haired chatterbox daughters who, at present, were sitting up front on the bench seat asking Broken Nose Bloke—aka Mack Redding, a surfer and plumber from Brisbane—if, when he had stitches, which in their estimation was a sure thing, they could watch.

He gave a quick glance at Noah, as if to say *Is that okay?* Noah rolled his eyes and nodded. Mack said it was the least he could do. 'How about you do them for me, little ladies? Which one of you are up for it?' he asked.

They dissolved into gales of laughter.

Rebecca had done about a million stitches in her time. She was about to volunteer when Mack flicked his thumb back in her direction.

'Can Red do them?' Mack asked Noah. 'No offence, Doc, but she's got smaller hands.'

He dropped her a wink and made a noise Rebecca was fairly certain was meant to be flirtatious. But, as much as she was trying to follow the universe's hints, he was definitely not her type.

Noah spread his palms wide against the steering wheel, then tightened them round the leather. Rebecca saw what Mack couldn't. Those were surgeon's hands. Or maybe… Was he jealous?

No. He was married. It was more likely that he was annoyed this guy couldn't tell one quality set of doctor's hands from another.

It suddenly struck her that she hadn't asked Noah what his connection to the clinic was. She knew the one he'd mentioned. Simply called The Island Clinic, it was on the edge of a village halfway between the cove where they'd just been and the much more heavily frequented surfer beach adjacent to Rebecca's resort. She rode one of the resort bicycles to the village every day, to a place that made amazing coffee and even more delicious fruit smoothies.

And then, as her eyes connected with Noah's in the

rear-view mirror and his frown dug a furrow between his eyebrows, she knew exactly where she'd seen him before.

'You're Mr Guava, Lime and Pineapple Crush!'

She clapped her hand over her mouth, horrified that the words had leapt out like that.

She'd told Kylie all about him. The man who appeared like clockwork at the juice bar at eleven every morning, wearing black scrubs and a frown. He was never rude. And it wasn't an angry frown. It was more…haunted. As if he'd seen things in the operating theatre no mortal should ever have to witness.

She bit down on her lip as his eyes bored into hers until the horn from a passing car sounded. He returned his gaze to the road—but not for long. They flicked back and forth between the road and her as his mind visibly whirred, trying to connect the dots.

'What?' Kylie squawked. 'Your sexy surly doc gave me the kiss of life?'

'Er… No. I did that,' she whispered making a hand gesture so Kylie would keep the volume down.

'Phew! I mean, not that he's gross—he's totally hot. But I'm obvs taken.'

'He's also driving this vehicle,' Rebecca growled. 'Shh.'

Kylie smirked, and in a loud clear voice said, 'Get in there, girl!'

Noah's eyes snapped to Rebecca's in the rear-view mirror. He wasn't smiling.

A flush of embarrassment swept up her neck, illuminating her cheeks like a harvest moon. Just last night she had—very uncharacteristically—brought herself to orgasm thinking about him. Her face went a darker shade of crimson. She never did that sort of thing. One minute she'd been thinking about smoothies, and the next she'd been turning Mr Guava, Lime and Pineapple Crush into a smooth talker who knew how to slip a girl's sundress off her shoulders with a heavenly effect on her erogenous zones.

This was humiliation of the highest order. Thank God she hadn't mentioned *that* to Kylie.

Kylie tried to press herself up, but began coughing so hard that Rebecca got her to lie back on her side. Flirting, or whatever this was—angry staring?—while ignoring your friend, who might be suffering from dry drowning, wasn't really the sort of incident she'd like hung out to dry in front of the medical board.

Well, Your Honour. You see... There was this super-hot guy I kept seeing when I was sitting outside this bijou medical clinic that, in a tropical way, reminded me of the sort of thing I once wanted to run, before my fiancé stomped all over my heart and destroyed our shared hopes and dreams by getting another woman pregnant with twins and moving to London to be with them.

Sorry, what? What was I doing outside the medical clinic? I suppose you could call it loitering with intent. Was I hurt? No. I mean, apart from the heartbreak side of things. But, look... The truth is, I was deciding whether or not to beg the people at the clinic for a job, so I could start my life over again here in Bali rather than move back to the UK and face my demons head-on, but—like I said—there was this super-hot doctor who gave me tingles even thinking about—

You what, now? Yes, that's right. I sat outside the clinic for several days. At the juice bar, actually. Why did I stop? My friend Kylie made me go surfing with her, because she said the juice bar wasn't helping me find my Zen.

It had seemed such a good idea at the time. Dreaming about a future so entirely different from the GP surgery she and her ex had planned on opening. But she'd kept seeing this glowering, gorgeous man hunk, and the thought of working with someone so…so scrumptiously scowly—Heathcliff *sur la mer*—seemed bordering on insanity.

He gave her butterflies. Everywhere. In *public*.

Kylie had decided for her in the end, announcing that men who frowned when ordering a drink that sounded like the punchline to a joke were not suitable rebound material. And 'jumping back on the horse' was something Kylie had been actively encouraging her to do since the day they'd met. With a happy go-lucky type. Like Mack.

Rebecca glanced at the surfer, who was now delighting the little girls by making faces.

A sigh hoisted up her shoulders, then wilted them.

Now that she knew Noah was married, she thought that at least she'd spared herself the humiliation of asking him for a job. Because working with this walking, talking, surgical example of everything she'd ever wanted—apart from the frowning—would have been torture.

How could she not have recognised him on the beach?

Maybe because he was half-naked and about a thousand times more gorgeous than he looked in his black scrubs, you idiot.

Plus, he'd been smiling when she'd spotted him with the girls. So she wasn't a complete idiot. The smile had changed his entire aura. And it had been a beautiful thing to behold.

'Mr Guava, Lime and Pineapple Crush, eh?' Mack mimicked when he caught Rebecca staring again. He obviously thought Rebecca was backing the wrong horse. 'Sounds like someone fancies someone else.' He made some *boom-chica-boom* noises, instantly regretting the impact the movement had on his face.

'Ooh!' The little girls twisted round in their seats in tandem, to stare at Rebecca.

'No! No one fancies anyone. I just—' She took in a shaky breath and continued in a voice that was so British she was surprised the words didn't etch themselves into the windows. 'I happen to have noticed that Noah buys juice. That is all.'

She glanced towards the rear-view mirror again and cringed. Noah was suppressing a smile. Did he *like* it that she'd noticed him at the juice bar?

Stop it! You cannot be a lust monster. Not with a married father of two.

He gave his chin a rub and said, 'Perhaps the girls will run over and get you a turmeric, ginger and coconut water while my cousin does the stitches. You might've seen her down at the beach? She's waiting for us at the clinic.'

Each word tumbled through her as if she was a pinball machine. He knew *her* drink, too.

'What about me?' whined Mack. 'I'm thirsty, too.'

Wait a minute… Cousin? Was the blonde she'd seen at the beach his *cousin*?

Her stomach swirled and lifted in a pirouette of joy.

'Get in there, girlfriend.' Kylie poked her with a finger.

'No way,' Rebecca whispered. 'I have to stay with you.'

Not that she could ever look Noah in the eye again. Not since she'd remembered…you know… Okay, fine. It had been a double orgasm. Fictional Noah was a terrific lover. But real-life Noah had two little girls who had to have a mother out there somewhere.

Kylie narrowed her eyes and tried to pull her backpack from Rebecca's lap. 'I'm going to text the Surf God. He can sit with me.' She flicked her fingers at Rebecca. 'You get on with crushing some tropical fruits.'

Just as Rebecca was going to begin a lecture on all the reasons why prancing off to a juice bar with a married stranger was ridiculous, Noah shifted down a gear and swung the Jeep into an alley away from the bustling high street.

At the back of the clinic, two enormous carved wooden doors were opened by a pair of uniformed men waiting in a small sentry house.

'Blimey, mate.' Mack climbed out of the Jeep and whistled. 'This place is a bit of a surprise.'

Mack wasn't kidding.

For starters, the clinic building was about a thousand times larger than it appeared from the front. Perhaps it was because the sun had hit that magical hour where everything was bathed in a diaphanous cloud of gold. Or maybe it was because this was like no clinic she'd ever seen before. It might also be because the man who had turned her body into a hotbed of molten hormones was looking directly at her with an intensity that demanded an honest reaction.

Whatever it was, Rebecca felt as if she'd entered an entirely different universe.

The modest stone wall and human-sized red door she'd stared at from the juice bar clearly hid a Tardis. Here, round the back, verdant palms arched over an enormous drive that led into a flourishing and expansive tropical garden, complete with soothing water features and a beautifully tiled infinity pool.

Nooks and crannies were carved into the bougainvillea-covered stone walls. Thick teak shelves supported shrines bedecked with offerings of fresh flowers and fruit. Individual villas were dotted about the gardens, each made from traditional materials in keeping with the large central building.

Noah was out of the driver's seat and opening the back door just as she leant forward to push the door open. Like a tropically dressed knight in shining armour, Noah somehow foresaw her lack of balance and scooped one arm under her legs and the other round her back so that she tumbled into his chest.

Rather than set her on the ground at once, or make an unfunny joke about her weight like her ex would have done, Noah continued to hold her, and for a curiously private-feeling moment it was as if the only people in the world who existed were the two of them.

His eyes—squid-ink-black from a distance—were actually more like lapis lazuli, gem-like in their blue-black ability to reflect light. He had freckles on his nose. A light smattering. She'd never known freckles seem masculine before. All of him was, actually. He was made of muscle and strength, without seeming as hard and inaccessible as that frown he sometimes wore.

A ripple of heat ran through her as his fingers shifted against her thigh. This was far superior to the fantasy she'd conjured up last night. His warm skin glowed with the scents she had come to associate with the island. Coconut. Sea-salted air. Lemongrass and pepper.

She met his gaze again, and in that instant a miracle occurred. She felt feminine for the first time in she didn't know how long. Possibly ever.

She wasn't a tiny woman—something her ex had never let her forget whenever she'd hinted that she might wear heels to an event. She didn't know why she'd bothered. It wasn't *her* fault he couldn't make six foot even in boots. She'd always worn ballet pumps in the end.

Relationships were meant to be about compromise,

right? But maybe that had been part of the problem. Perhaps they'd pushed the definition of compromise into territory more akin to acquiescence. Pushed it to the point where neither of them had ended up happy.

Noah didn't strike her as a man who would make her wear ballet flats to avoid bruising his ego. Then again, Noah would be able to rest his chin on her head even if she wore heels.

'Oh, for the love of Pete!' Kylie was crouching in the doorframe, waiting to climb out. 'Will you two stop staring at one another and move, so I can get out of this caboose and back to the resort?'

Noah released Rebecca to the ground with an awkward clearing of the throat, and when he went to lift Kylie out was met with a feminist lecture on how she didn't need a man to help her even if she had been half dead—

'Whoa!'

Rebecca and Noah lunged for Kylie as she pitched forward.

'Maybe I could do with a little bit of help.'

'You and me both, mate,' Mack said, rounding the corner of the Jeep.

They turned around to see that his temporary bandage was soaked through, and that what blood was left in his face had drained away.

'Good heavens, Noah! Did you get into a fist fight down at the beach?'

The beautiful blonde from the beach appeared on the wide porch at the back of the main building with a wheelchair.

'Girls. It's time for your supper and then baths, all right? I'll be over to the villa to help in a few moments.' She turned her gaze back to Noah, then shrugged. 'I guess I don't have to ask if you had a fun time at the beach, then, do I?'

A flurry of motion ensued.

Rebecca received a sharp 'get in there' elbow in her ribs from Kylie, just before the blonde scuttled the wheelchair down to them and introduced herself as Mel McKindry, Noah's cousin.

Kylie gave Rebecca a look.

Rebecca turned fuchsia.

Noah grabbed the tablet that had been on the wheelchair seat and started furiously typing.

Mel beamed at Rebecca. 'New friend of Noah's?' She flicked her gaze at her cousin, still tapping his tablet. 'Well done, mate. It's about time you brought someone back.'

If Rebecca wasn't mistaken, Noah growled.

Before either of them could explain, Mel called out to a colleague to bring another wheelchair and then shot a series of rapid-fire questions at the lot of them—medically based—while somehow managing to pull Rebecca's history from her as well.

Her nationality—British—the amount of time she'd been in Bali—a fortnight—whether she planned to stay—that was up in the air right now—and what sort of medicine she practised—trained as a paediatric surgeon then retrained as a GP.

'So that's what you're doing now? Working in general practice back in England?'

'Um…' Her eyes flicked to Noah's. 'Not exactly.'

'She's single, doesn't have a job, and is currently at one of life's more significant crossroads,' Kylie supplied, with a beam and a knowing wink at Noah. Rebecca jabbed her in the ribs only to receive a wounded, '*What?* It's the truth. Oh!' She brightened. 'And she has an open-ended ticket that she needs to change tomorrow. Just saying...'

As if Noah's cousin had received all the information she required, she beamed at Mack. 'I've got just the doctor to sort out your stitches, mate.' An artfully tattooed black-haired doctor who looked as if he spent most of his spare time in a boxing ring appeared and wheeled Mack off.

'Well, then...' Mel gave Kylie's hand a pat. 'I think I'll leave you under my *single* cousin Noah's care, with Rebecca accompanying you to ensure you feel comfortable with a male doctor, yeah?' To Rebecca she added, 'If you're happy staying in your swimsuit, please do. Otherwise I'm sure Noah could set you up with some scrubs.'

She gave Kylie a complicit wink, as if her almost drowning had all been part of an elaborate plan to get the two doctors to meet one another.

Rebecca managed to surface from her mortification for long enough to absorb the fact that Dr Noah Cameron was single.

Kylie hummed a happy little tune as Noah wheeled her up a ramp and into the main building.

For what appeared to be a simple tourist clinic from the outside, The Island Clinic had a lot of bells and whistles. And, twenty minutes in, Rebecca was pleased to see Noah was making use of most of them. He'd earned Rebecca's approval by ordering a number of scans, as well as running several simple neurological tests to ensure the absence of oxygen hadn't had any derogatory effect on Kylie.

Later, as the cicadas took up their night song and wafts of citronella drifted in with the breeze billowing the mosquito netting on the windows, Rebecca was struck by how ultra-romantic this setting could be. Which she took as her cue to get a move on. If she was looking at hospitals as romantic it was definitely time to leave.

'I'll be in tomorrow morning, once you've had a second round of neuro tests,' she told Kylie.

Kylie groaned. 'Don't go! Who am I going to talk to?'

Rebecca glanced around the room. There was a shelf with some well-worn books on it. Romances, from the looks of things. 'Here. Read one of these.'

She handed her a book, which Kylie refused to take.

'I bet you were a really bossy doctor back home,' Kylie whined. 'Why can't I go back to the resort and show the Surf God there's nothing wrong with me?'

'Maybe because it's an all-female resort and you need to rest?'

'You're not a nice doctor.' Kylie pouted.

'And you're a terrible patient,' Rebecca countered with a grin.

'If you won't listen to the lovely doctor, you'll have to listen to the grumpy one.'

Noah's deep Australian-accented voice came from the doorway, once again sending his words ricocheting through Rebecca's nervous system.

Lovely?

She felt like the ugly duckling on the brink of turning into a swan. What would happen if he spoke actual *sexy* words to her? She might lose control all together. She blushed remembering the moment when, alone in her bed, she had. And that had just been *thinking* about him.

'I don't think it'll surprise you to hear that we want to keep you in overnight for observation.' Noah gave the doorframe a knock, as if to say the matter was set in stone.

Rebecca smirked.

Kylie growled. 'I won't stay unless Rebecca stays, too.'

Rebecca glared at Kylie. If she hadn't nearly drowned today, she would definitely have hit her with a pillow. She couldn't stay here! Not with Dr Dangerously Delicious within arm's reach. *And his two perfect children.*

There was definitely a story there. One that mysteriously involved his cousin wanting to set him up with a complete stranger.

Noah's eyes flicked between the two of them, his eyebrows quirking as he tried to puzzle out which way this conversation was going to go.

Mel appeared in the doorway and did a lightning-fast reading of the scene.

'Hi, gang. Those scrubs suit you, Rebecca. They really bring out the green in your eyes. Don't they Noah?' She didn't wait for an answer. 'Hey… They're just about to bring supper round to all the patients. Kylie, I was hoping I might trade you one Rebecca for one of these…' She stepped to the side and in walked the Surf God.

Kylie squealed, then coughed, then clapped her hands and scooted over in her bed so that there was room for her holiday beau. A space he promptly filled.

'Well, then…' Mel grinned. 'I guess that leaves us three free to discuss who's going to take over from me when I head back to Sydney.'

CHAPTER FOUR

'SO...' REBECCA WAS staring doggedly at the menu the clinic's restaurant staff had just provided. 'What do you recommend?'

Leaving before my cousin commandeers your entire life!

Noah swallowed the words before they could gain traction. It was an unkind thought and it wasn't even aimed at Rebecca—a woman he would definitely be trying to charm into staying if this were a different time and a different place. A time when all the responsibility he'd had in life was his job and sending money here to the clinic to assuage his guilty conscience.

But it wasn't. It was here and now, and his guilty conscience had been pulled up sharply, forcing him to fulfil promises he'd never imagined would become his reality. Mostly because he'd never thought of a world without his sister in it. But that was the reality. One he and the girls had been left to survive.

Despite his newly established routine of perching on one of the kitchen stools in his sister's house—one ear on the girls' room, one on his pager, with a stack of patient reports as his reading material—his cousin had steered Noah and Rebecca out here to the courtyard restaurant to 'discuss employment possibilities', only for her to remember she'd promised the girls she'd help them with their baths.

He wasn't an idiot. She was obviously trying to set him up with Rebecca despite the spectacularly bad timing. Or because of it? He didn't know any more.

A few months ago his life had been as predictable as sunshine in Bali. Hell, a few *years* ago his life had been as predictable. Work, eat, sleep, repeat. The odd girlfriend had been factored into his schedule—right up until she figured out he wasn't going to propose or start a family, in an abbreviated version of what had happened to him and Alice—his med school girlfriend—after eight years of going out together. They'd been all work and some play, and he'd thought that was enough.

When his mum had died Alice had finally called his bluff after his promises that 'it'll happen one day'.

It had. But not with him. She was now happily married, had three cute little kids, and was living out in Perth with a husband who prized family time above all else.

Since then he hadn't bothered with false promises. As a result, his relationships were short and mostly sweet. When you dated in your thirties it was best to be honest with women, because he knew for them the biological clock ticked louder and faster. Now he was forty-one, and effectively a single dad…

In theory, he wanted a soulmate and children. But for reasons he couldn't explain he just hadn't felt that 'click' his sister had spoken about when she'd met her husband. That magic moment when she'd known she was ready to start a family.

'Anything I'd regret not trying?' Rebecca tapped her menu, reminding him that she had asked for a recommendation.

He rubbed his face. He was making a proper hash of

things. Rebecca was one of those 'league of her own' women. Someone who deserved the cream of the dating crop. Not an emotionally unavailable orthopaedic surgeon trying to figure out whether to stay here or pack up his nieces and head back to Sydney.

And just like that his long 'To Do' list reared its ugly head. He'd have to sell his condo if they moved. Too much glass. Too many sharp corners. Not enough bedrooms. Was it even near a school? He had no idea.

'Am I to take your silence as a no?' Rebecca asked, bemused.

'No, sorry. Everything's good.'

Get your act together, man!

'I was just—' His eyes snagged on her full mouth again, almost expecting the peek of her tongue as it swept along her bottom lip.

'Distracted?' She filled in for him.

His eyes flicked back up to hers. Beautiful. Calm in a crisis. A loyal friend. She was someone he could see himself having a kid with.

What? Where the hell had that come from?

He picked up his menu, cutting off his view of her. 'Let's take a look.'

The words blurred in front of his eyes. He owed this woman more than sub-par chitchat. He also owed his cousin the indulgence of thinking she'd done the right thing by pairing him up with someone so he wouldn't feel abandoned when she headed back to Oz.

As interfering as she could be, Mel had been an epic heroine these past couple of months.

Keeping his father and his third wife busy enough to ensure they rarely crossed paths with him at the funeral had been just one of Mel's superpowers. The fact his father had shown up at all was galling. Yeah, okay, he had been Indah's biological dad, and his, but had he ever really been a father to them?

How Mel had bundled him back to Oz without one fight erupting between father and son had been little short of a miracle.

It had been hard to imagine a man as flawed as his father witnessing a purification ceremony. The memory of it churned in his gut. As if his sister had needed any improvement. Or her husband. They'd been the good ones. The kind ones. The generous ones. Probably like Rebecca. After all, how many women would sit here with a man who seemed to have had all of the words he knew sucked out of him?

'Would you suggest a starter?' Rebecca prompted now, with saintlike patience. 'Or go straight to the main course?'

He looked at her then. Really looked at her. She was a beautiful woman. She had a glow about her that wasn't just aesthetic. It spoke of a personal warmth. A strength of character. If he'd been back in Sydney, maybe that 'click' would've latched into place…

But he wasn't, and it wouldn't.

And all she wants is a recommendation for what to eat so she can get the heck out of here, you idiot.

'I always start with the satay,' he said lamely.

Everyone started with the satay.

C'mon, man! Your mother was Indonesian. You grew up with this food. He'd also grown up with an Australian father who'd insisted upon a 'proper Sunday lunch' every week after church. The same man who had preached loyalty as the most essential of traits, only to be revealed as a serial philanderer. Even when his mum had been dying of cancer. Class in a glass, his father. Class in a glass.

Somehow what he lacked in fidelity he made up for in charm. A real modern-day Casanova.

At least his second wife had told him where to stuff it. It'd be interesting to see how long the third one hung in there. She'd not looked all that happy when they'd come over last month. Then again, it had been a funeral.

Rebecca generously pretended they were having a lively conversation and soldiered on. 'I adore a good satay. Is it just me, or does the Balinese one have an extra kick? Spicy…'

She ducked her head so that her eyes met his, and just like that they shared one of those jolts of electric current that seemed to pass between them every time their gazes intersected. As quickly as their eyes meshed they were torn apart, hers dropping back to her menu, his lifting up to the thatched palm roof of the outdoor dining area.

Was she feeling it, too? This…*connection*?

He'd had forty-one years to feel the 'click' with a woman and it was happening now. When his life was chaos. It didn't make sense. Bones, joints, ligaments and tendons… Those were the things he'd dedicated his professional career to. Those made sense. They didn't come with double meanings or hidden subtext. They were ripped, torn, broken, bruised. Things he could repair. Orthopaedics was straightforward. Honest.

Was his response to Rebecca an honest one, or a panicked reaction to his new circumstances?

All work and no play...

He crushed his sister's oft-repeated words in his hand.

Rebecca looked at him, startled. She set her menu down, shifting her chair away from the table. 'I'm going to be honest with you. I am getting the distinct impression you have somewhere else you need to be.'

The gold flecks in her eyes flared in the candlelight.

Her top teeth took purchase on her bottom lip. A current of electricity ran through his veins.

'No. Please stay. I'm being a jackass. You've done nothing wrong.'

Her skin turned a deep shade of pink, exposing a side of her he hadn't seen before. It was less protected than the version he'd first met. Raw, almost. He related to it. This glimpse of vulnerability.

What if you show her you're as vulnerable as she is?

And what if he tore off his shirt, beat his chest and admitted that he was clinging to every cell of inner alpha male he could? Because if he didn't, it'd be clear for all to see that he didn't have a clue what he was doing, and that for the first time in his life he wished he had a loved one by his side who knew him inside and out. Someone who could assure him he could do this. Someone like Rebecca.

After a moment's silence she squinted at him. 'I might be humiliating myself here, but do you get the feeling that your cousin is trying to set us up?'

And just like that the tension in the air dissipated.

Noah burst out laughing. 'She's not exactly subtle, is she?'

Rebecca shook her head, then scrunched her features up before releasing them into an expression he hadn't seen on her before. Feistiness. It suited her.

'Shame,' she said, almost wistfully.

'What is?'

'That you're not my type.'

He was shocked to feel his heart drop down to his gut. He wasn't in any place to be with anyone, but it stung that she wouldn't even give him a chance.

Before he could respond she continued, 'You're all gorgeous and broody and…' She waved her hands in front of him, as if that finished off the definition. 'Suffice it to say you're not someone I'd normally be set up with.'

He sat back and rubbed his jaw. 'I'm not sure if I'm meant to take that as a compliment or not.'

She shrugged. 'It's just a statement of fact.'

He smiled. He liked facts. He also liked honesty. So he did what he should've done the moment his cousin had left them alone. He said, 'I have a pretty complicated situation right now.'

She nodded, as if it wasn't a surprise to her.

He continued, 'My sister Indah was killed a couple of months ago. Both her and her husband.'

Rebecca gasped and pressed her hands to her chest. 'The two little girls…?'

He nodded. 'They're hers. *Were* hers,' he corrected reluctantly. 'I'm their guardian now…so you've caught me in the middle of deciding whether to stay here and run the clinic, which was basically my sister's thing, or whether to find a nanny in Sydney and go back to the life I know there.'

'Which is…?'

'I'm chief orthopaedic surgeon at Sydney Orthopaedics.' Getting that job had been his goal. He'd attained it just a few short months before Indah had been killed.

'Gosh.' She blew out a big breath, as if living his experiences herself. 'That's a big life-change. And I thought mine was big.'

He gave her a curious look.

She pointed at her ring finger. 'That had something on it a few months ago.'

'You broke it off?'

She winced. 'Well, technically, yes—but the fact he was in love with someone else who was bearing his child made it feel like less of a win.'

'Ouch.'

'You can say that again.' She took a sip of her water, then decisively put the glass down. 'Anyway. Rather than grieving for the family I don't have right now, I'm trying to look at it as a close shave with the wrong gene pool. It's nothing like what you're going through.'

It was, actually. They'd both been hurt. Deeply so. And they were both doing their best to find a future with some joy in it.

'I actually think we have more in common than you think.' He put on his scowling face. 'Apart from my broodiness, obviously.'

She laughed, then gave him a sidelong look. 'What on earth do we have in common?'

'Neither of us is living the life we thought we would be.'

She lifted her glass to his and they clinked.

'Look,' she said, after a moment's companionable silence, 'I don't know if this was a date set-up or a job set-up, but please don't think you have to ask me to work here. I'm pretty sure there are plenty of Indonesian doctors who would be thrilled to work in a beautiful place like this.'

'Most of our staff are local,' he admitted. 'Although, saying that, the clinic runs almost like two clinics. We serve the tourist population, but we also like to offer free medical care and more complex treatments to the poorer local population, courtesy of specialist surgeons who fly in to donate their time and expertise. So we actually need a mix of staff. Local and international. Do you know any languages?'

She answered without pausing to think about it. 'French and Spanish.'

Impressive. And useful. He should hire her. Here and now. But he fancied her.

So? He'd fancied women before.

Not women he could easily picture being a mother. He had the girls to think of. They wouldn't be able to bear another loss if this didn't work out. And there were Rebecca's broken dreams to consider.

'Come to Bali. Find some balance. Make peace with yourself.'

His sister's words rang in his ears. The old him hadn't had time for all that hippy nonsense. But he had to be a parent. Now. And figure out what the hell to do with this clinic. Also now.

So, no. He wouldn't be hiring Rebecca.

He opened his mouth to say as much, but instead something different came out. 'We're an international charity so we can avoid some of the visa hurdles. It does mean that the work you'd do would be largely voluntary. We could offer housing, food and a small stipend in exchange for consultancy—' He saw her eyes grow wider and wider as he continued. He pulled a quick U-turn. 'But the fact you're staying in a resort strongly suggests you're here on holiday. Not job-hunting. So it's all irrelevant, right?'

She scrunched up her nose. 'True…'

She drew out the vowels until they faded away, in a manner that filled him with a stupid helium hit of hope.

'Is there a "but" in there?'

'Let's just say I haven't been going to the juice bar across the street from the clinic solely because of the beverages.'

He frowned. 'Are you sick? Do you need medical care?'

'No.' She waved away his concern. 'I—' She took in

a deep breath, then put on a brave smile. 'This trip is me regrouping. I have a pretty big savings account, courtesy of the GP surgery I'm no longer opening. I thought I'd surf a bit and then go home, but I think I'm still…you know…' She pinched her fingers together into a yoga relaxation position. 'Finding myself? Or finding a new self?' She held her hands up in a *Who knows?* gesture.

'Any progress on that front?'

She lifted her shoulders up to her ears. 'Not sure. At this point I don't even know if I want to find the old me.'

'I hear you,' Noah said emphatically. 'I don't know if the old me can do what the new me needs to do.'

'Sounds like we both have some decisions to make.'

He nodded.

The waitress approached and they both ordered. Neither of them chose the satay. For some reason it made them both giggle.

Since when did he *giggle*?

When the waitress had left he asked, 'What made you come here? To Bali?'

She took a sip of her drink—ginger and lemongrass iced tea—gave a self-deprecating laugh, then answered his question. 'I came to Bali because I found an all-women's surf and yoga resort, promising to help me find my Zen.'

'And have you?' He was surprised to realise he really wanted to know. Was it even possible? To find this unachievable 'Zen'?

'Well, I'm not wallowing under my childhood duvet at my grandmother's house any more, but I wouldn't say I'm the most serene person on earth. I still love a good spreadsheet!' The smile wilted. 'Spreadsheets were an issue in my last relationship.'

'What's wrong with spreadsheets?'

'I know!' She laughed again. 'My ex said they hemmed him in. He obviously did not understand that spreadsheets create order and order means progress.'

'That's a big yes in my book.'

Her smile was a flash of sunshine.

He doubled back to something she'd glossed over. 'Were you raised by your grandmother?'

She nodded. 'Nanny Bea. She stepped in when my parents died.'

'Oh, I'm sorry.' Losing parents was terrain he didn't enjoy revisiting.

Well, done, Noah. You're batting a thousand here.

Rebecca waved off his apology. 'Don't be. I mean, it would've been great to have had my parents, but I haven't ever really known differently. Besides, who can fight the ocean and win?'

'Sorry. I'm not following.'

'My dad and my granddad were fishermen,' she explained. 'My mum went out with them one day because she said she never saw them enough and…' Her voice grew hollow as she continued. 'There was a big storm. No one came back.'

'And yet you surf?'

She gave a sad smile. 'What is it they say? Know thine enemy?' She cleared her throat and brightened her smile. 'I don't surf the crazy big waves. Just enough to know my limits. Anyway, I can't really remember them it was so long ago. Just snippets. I've always tried to focus on what I *do* have rather than what I don't.'

The comment lodged in his heart, and again he raised his glass to hers.

'Not that I've been a shining example of that ethos lately,' she said. 'To be honest, these past few months I've made an art of focusing on everything my ex has that I don't. A spouse. A child. A house with a garden and a job he—' Abruptly she stopped herself. 'I'm sorry. I think I've got verbal diarrhoea. Or someone gave me truth serum.' She held up her glass and gave it an accusing look. 'What do they put in this tea? Sorry, I'm really oversharing. Ding-ding!' She rang an imaginary bell. 'Taxi for one!'

'No.' He put his hand on hers. 'Stay. I like it.'

It was better than listening to his own thoughts. To the self-admonishments running on a loop in his head. *Woulda, shoulda, coulda...* So many things he would've done differently if only he'd seen what was coming.

She gave a low whistle. 'Wow. You're like— You're a rare mythical creature.'

Their eyes met, and once again he felt an electric current pass between them.

Suddenly she schooched forward, perched on the edge of her seat and, eyes glistening said, 'I've got an idea.'

He leant forward, his arms on the table. 'I'm all ears.'

'You know all this "finding myself" stuff? Letting the universe "gift" me with what I need?'

'Yes…' he answered, not entirely sure where this was going.

'Well, it seems you've got to do some of that, too. And as we both like lists and spreadsheets and plans so much…' She paused, her eyes alight with excitement about whatever it was she was going to propose. 'What if we let the universe call it with a coin toss? You know—whether or not I work here.'

He couldn't hide his shock. 'You'd do that? Stay based on the flip of a coin?'

'Sure. I agreed to give up a job I loved at Nottingham Children's Hospital to move to Cornwall for a man who turned out to be a weasel, so why not let a coin decide whether or not I stay in Bali and do some voluntary work for a good cause?' She gave his hand a pat. 'And don't worry. You're not the good cause. I'm sure you can do just fine without me.'

He gave her a rueful smile. 'I'm not so sure about that. It'd make my cousin happy.'

She shot him a look. One that he was pretty sure meant he'd stuck his foot in it.

'Go for it,' he said definitively. 'I'd love a list-making, spreadsheet-loving plan-maker on staff.'

Rebecca grinned and picked up her backpack. She dug around for a second, then produced a British coin with Queen Elizabeth on one side and what appeared to be a female warrior on the other. He smiled. If Rebecca were on a coin this would be how he'd portray her. Fiery and proud when she needed to be. Vulnerable and open when she'd decided to trust someone.

How had it come so easily to her? Trusting him in the way she had?

She handed the coin to Noah, her eyes bright. 'I'll call it—you flip it. Heads I'm staying. Tails I head back to Blighty the day after tomorrow.'

A sense of urgency gripped him. He couldn't let this woman go. Not now. Not yet.

He flipped the coin. They watched it twirl up into the air. Heads, then tails. Heads, then tails.

He caught the coin in one hand and flipped it onto the back of the other. He lifted his fingers away and held the coin out so they could both see.

Rebecca blinked her surprise.

Noah wondered if he should start leaving everything up to the flip of a coin. He met Rebecca's gaze head-on and said, 'Well, would you take a look at that…?'

CHAPTER FIVE

REBECCA HELD OUT the clipboard for her patient's mum to sign, then knelt down so she was at eye level with Miriam, an adorable little French girl who had quite an impressive sunburn. It wouldn't blister or scar, but judging from the tears that had been shed during the examination it definitely stung.

In her admittedly rusty French, Rebecca said, 'And you're going to be heading right back to your hotel to drink plenty of water in the shade, right? Maybe have a rest?'

The gap-toothed little girl nodded, tears clinging to her dark lashes, then sniffed. 'Will I still get to swim with the dolphins before I go?'

It was all Rebecca could do not to pull the poor little thing into her arms for a consolation hug. But there was the sunburn…and also her mum had said the reason the sunburn had come about was because the little girl had refused to put on the protective top and hat she'd brought with her to keep the sun off her child's delicate skin.

She remembered the advice Noah had given his nieces yesterday afternoon, when they'd run into the clinic and begged to go snorkelling to make up for the session they were meant to have had the other day, when Kylie had her accident. She repeated it now. 'Good things come to those who wait.'

A tiny little shiver slipped down her spine as she remembered how he'd glanced across at her, their eyes clashing as they always did, sparking the thought that he might not just be talking about snorkelling. Then he'd steered the children out to the courtyard as if he said suggestive things to her all the time.

Which, if her first week at the clinic was anything to go by, he didn't.

After their shared moment of insanity—leaving whether or not she stayed in Bali up to a coin toss—practicalities had taken over. Rebecca had seen Kylie off at the airport, packed up her things at the resort and relocated to the clinic. Since then, Noah had only spoken to her when absolutely necessary. Which made all her patient appointments a blessed relief from the tension she felt whenever she was near him.

Whatever had possessed her? Not only to tell him he was gorgeous and that she fancied the pants off him, but also that he wasn't her type?

She'd clearly been gripped by a moment's insanity. The break-up of her relationship, her dream to open a GP surgery that had never got off the ground and her subsequent wallowing had finally taken their toll.

Mercifully, he'd made sure all the 'settling in' jobs had been doled out to her, which was handy for getting to know everyone. But Rebecca was fairly certain that hadn't been his aim. The aim had been to avoid her.

Now she had two men on two different islands who wanted nothing to do with her. Terrific. At least she hadn't planned her entire future with Noah. She cringed as she remembered showing her ex the retirement plans she'd thought they should start following, so that they'd be able to help their future children onto the housing ladder whilst ensuring that their golden years together would be trouble-free.

Anyway, thank God she genuinely loved the work. It would tide her over until they found someone to replace her.

The job was quite bespoke. So far she'd been using a mix of her GP and paediatric skills. No surgeries yet, but there were some being scheduled. But right now sunburn was the name of the game.

A few teardrops plopped onto Miriam's chubby little-girl cheeks. Her mum moved in.

'Mon cherie. Ne pleure pas, ma petite.'

Don't cry, little one.

The woman carefully drew her daughter to her, swept the tears away with her thumbs and pressed a kiss onto her forehead.

'I wanted to see the dolphins,' the little girl wailed.

An increasingly familiar pinch in her heart caused Rebecca's smile to flicker. Then came the rush of longing. And…yes…there it was…the deep ache in her core.

The Noah Effect.

The man had ridiculously powerful pheromones. They were practically pleading with Rebecca's reproductive system to stage a coup and make good on the world's need for little baby Noahs.

The mum, clearly misinterpreting Rebecca's maternal pangs, offered an apologetic smile. 'She's been talking about the dolphins ever since we landed, but we had so much pre-booked. You know how it is… You make plans. You feel you should see them through. Anyhow, we thought we'd save the dolphins for last, as a sort of farewell treat.'

'When do you leave?'

'Demain.'

Tomorrow.

Rebecca nodded and made commiserating noises. Her eyes flicked between the two. The sunburn was bad, but not so bad that it had blistered. There was the chance of a fever setting in—or, if the skin broke, an infection, but…

What was it her grandmother was always saying? *'Life's for living,'* That was the first part. And then, when she knew Rebecca needed reminding that not everything went according to plan, she would add, *'Even if it does hurt sometimes'*.

She sat back on her heels and suggested to Miriam, knowing her mum was tuned in to every word, 'Perhaps if you stay in today, make sure you use the gel, give the anti-inflammatories some time to take effect and always wear a long-sleeved T-shirt with one of those hats that has a neck guard, you could go?' She gave Miriam's arm a light touch. 'You could do that, couldn't you? Wear a hat and a T-shirt if it means swimming with the dolphins?'

Happy tears ran down her cheeks into her wide gap-toothed grin. *'Oui. Absolutement! Oh, Maman, les dauphins!'*

After a few more precautions about what to watch out for, Rebecca waved them off from her examination room door. Her breath caught in her throat when Noah appeared from around the corner. He clearly hadn't been expecting to see her, because for the first time that week when their eyes met his instinct was to smile. And then, as if he'd given himself a lightning-fast telling-off, the smile was pressed into a thin, concentrated frown.

For goodness' sake! She got that he didn't want to be her boyfriend, but it didn't mean he had to scowl every time he saw her. What was the point in her staying if it made him uncomfortable? The man had enough on his plate without feeling he also had to keep her at arm's length.

She decided to put some more of Nanny Bea's advice into play. She pulled a coin out of her pocket. The same one that had landed her here in the clinic.

'Catch.' She threw it before he could dissuade her.

He caught it in one hand and slapped it down on the back of the other. Something lit in his eyes that she hadn't seen since the last time she'd left her fate to the toss of a coin. Engagement. An active interest in what she wanted.

Ooh… This was a bit more like it.

'What are you calling?' he asked, his low voice humming along her spine so it was almost as if he'd stroked it with his hand.

'Heads I stay. Tails I get out of your hair.'

His eyes snapped to hers. 'Why would you leave? Aren't you happy?'

'I like the *work* well enough,' she countered, with a bravura she wasn't entirely sure she felt.

She put a hand on her hip to make herself look more cavalier. His gaze dropped to her hip, then took its time working its way back up to her eyes. Her smile twitched.

'What are you saying?' he demanded. 'The accommodation isn't good enough?'

She pursed her lips. He knew damn straight she wasn't talking about the villa. The clinic, it turned out, had been a luxury resort up until the financial crisis a while back. Noah's father, a property developer, had bought it as an investment and then, after his mum had died, Noah and his sister had been gifted the site, refashioning it into a clinic.

Not that she'd learnt this from Noah. Dr Karja, the doctor she'd met on that first day, had told her. She still had a lot of unanswered questions about the place, but the state of it was not one of them.

No. It was Noah who was the problem.

'I want to help you,' she said.

A divot formed between his brows. 'You *are* helping. You work every day.'

Great. He was going to make her say it. *Okay. Fine.* 'Yes. I know. But I'm getting the feeling my presence here isn't helping *you*.'

'What? Don't be ridiculous,' he blustered, and then, after a long hard stare at the coin in his hand, he clenched it tight and put it in his pocket. He closed the space between them. 'I've got a lot going on right now.'

'I'm not contesting that,' she countered. 'Losing your sister and brother-in-law as well as gaining two children and a busy health clinic isn't exactly a small blip on the life-change chart.'

His expression barely changed, but she saw something. Something she hadn't noticed before. His pain went deeper than that. Straight to his marrow.

Why are you holding everything that hurts you so close to your heart?

Every pore in her body ached to help him. She'd felt it, too. That need to punish herself when her world had fallen to pieces. The pain had been visceral. Traumatic. As if the memories themselves had morphed into malignant cells, eating away at her ability to see life through anything but a grey, miserable lens. But couldn't he see it wouldn't help?

She readjusted her pose, crossing her arms over her chest, and said, 'Look, I'm all for seeing what the universe throws in my lap, but not if it comes at the expense of your happiness. Be honest. Is my being here adding to your list of problems?'

He continued to stare into her eyes, as if seeking the answer there. 'No.'

'Then why are you avoiding me?'

'I'm not! I—' He stopped himself and put up his hands. 'I am. I have been. I—' He gave a self-effacing laugh, lifting his eyes up to the ceiling. 'My sister would have a field-day with this.'

Rebecca leant against the wall, indicating that she was prepared to listen.

'Did Mel tell you what she and my sister nicknamed me after med school?'

This should be interesting. She was pretty sure it wasn't Mr Guava, Lime and Pineapple Crush.

'The Ostrich,' he said.

'What? Why?'

'They claimed that whenever anything happened that hadn't been added to my diary months in advance, I stuck my head in the sand.'

'You're a doctor. A *surgeon.* You have to act spontaneously all the time!'

He held his hands out. 'That's what *I* said!'

They stared at one another for a moment, then laughed. How was it that they leapt to one another's defence so easily?

Because somehow you already know *each other.*

His laugh died away and then, self-effacingly he added, 'I did the same thing with relationships.'

She nodded, bracing herself for news of a girlfriend waiting back in Sydney.

'I had a relationship. A long one.'

'And…?'

'And she wanted to get married, and I never asked.'

A lightbulb popped on. 'And you're regretting it now?'

He shook his head. 'No. Maybe… I mean, having

some help with the girls would be good, but—' He shook his head again and said more solidly, 'No. The point I'm trying to make is that I didn't ever really have what you'd call a steady girlfriend after that.'

She thought for a moment, then asked Noah a question she'd had to ask herself. 'Do you push everything in your life to the side for medicine? Use it as an excuse for not dealing with the other aspects of your life?'

'Wow.' Noah stuffed his hands in his pockets and took a step back. 'I feel seen.'

'You have to know it to call it,' she said gently.

He leant against the wall, mirroring her pose. 'I don't trust myself right now. You know…' He pointed with one of his fingers between the two of them.

She frowned. Was he trying to say he liked her, too?

Before the thought could find purchase, he continued, 'I don't know how to juggle it all. I feel like I'm failing the girls already. I don't know what to do and I've only just begun.'

The confession bashed into her like a wrecking ball. He might as well have reached into his chest, handed her his heart and said, *Here. Do what you can with it. I don't know how it works any more.*

She almost laughed.

'Who does?' she parried. 'It isn't like any parent knows how to do it beforehand. There aren't manuals for what you're going through. No instructional videos you can watch to figure it out—' She stopped herself. 'Well, there are…' She rattled off a few romcoms she'd binge-watched during the darker days of her post-break-up despair. 'They're fictional, of course, but do you know what they all have in common?'

'Tell me,' he said, and his body language was practically screaming, *I'll take any advice right now, so long as it helps.*

'For a while, everything goes unbelievably wrong.' Especially with the romance.

'Wow.' He pulled a face. 'Thanks for the pep talk.'

'No, listen. That's not the endgame. Yes, there's chaos—but you know what else almost always happens?'

'Go on, then, Miss The Universe Already Knows My Fate.'

She smiled, pleased he wasn't turning on his heels and stomping away. 'The hero realises he can't do it all alone.'

'You mean he can't go all ostrich and hope when he pulls his head out of the sand everything will be okay again?'

This was good. He was still able to poke fun at himself.

''Fraid not. Not in your case, anyway.' She pressed her hands to her heart. 'I know I've kind of pushed my way into your life—'

He held up a hand. 'No, you didn't. The universe guided you to me.'

She searched his voice and his face for hints of sarcasm, and was surprised to be met with a warm, grateful smile. 'Well,' she began, not wanting to overstep the mark, 'as it has guided me here, I'm sure it's for more reasons than my medical skills. So if it doesn't stress you out…if there is any way I can help share your load, I will do it. I'm a great babysitter. I can do arts and crafts. Finger-painting is one of my specialties.'

Why are you doing a testimonial on your skills with children? You're a paediatrician.

But she couldn't stop herself. This was definitely her reproductive system staging that coup.

To her shock, it seemed to be working.

The more she spoke, the more it seemed her words were physically entering him. Chipping away at whatever was holding him together. He parted his lips, as if to say something that had been dredged up from the depths of his soul—and then the Tannoy sounded.

An urgent call to the emergency entrance.

The shutters fell over his eyes. Work Noah was back.

He turned to go, glancing at his watch as he did so. Abruptly he froze, his face twisted in pain.

'What?'

'I'm supposed to meet the girls at five at the villa.'

'I'll do it,' she offered reflexively.

His eyes snapped to hers and held them. 'No. I'll see if I can find someone—'

'Noah,' she cut in. 'This isn't me trying to be the next girlfriend you'll have to ghost.'

Okay, that was a tiny white lie. She really wouldn't be sad if she was his girlfriend and he snogged her, but she genuinely did want to help.

'You've helped me by giving me work. Reminding me of my purpose.' As the words came out, she realised how true they were. Her voice caught in her throat. 'Let me return the favour. It's nothing more than that.'

He opened his mouth, presumably to protest, but nothing came out.

She opened her palms to show she was feeling as vulnerable as he was. 'Even ostriches need to ask for help.'

The Tannoy sounded again.

They stared at one another. It was decision time.

He bowed his head in acknowledgement. 'Thank you.'

He gave her directions to his place, which lay at the far end of the property, and said he'd text the girls' babysitter to let her know Rebecca would be coming.

'Thank you,' he said again, turning to head back to the clinic.

'Not a problem. Hey!' She called after him. 'What did it say? The coin?'

He blinked deliberately, as if debating whether or not to tell her. 'Stay.'

When he'd gone, Rebecca had the strangest feeling that he hadn't been telling her what was on the coin at all, but what was in his heart.

'And then what?' Ruby asked, her eyes glistening with delight.

And Isla cried, 'Tell us!'

'And then he asked if I'd had a facelift!'

Ruby and Isla frowned in confusion, until Rebecca put her hands on her cheeks and drew them back, so she looked as if she was caught in a wind tunnel. The girls fell about laughing, as if she'd just told them the funniest thing in the world.

'What's everyone laughing about?'

Rebecca's spine instantly turned buttery as Noah's rich Australian drawl poured warmth through her. When their eyes met, she felt as though a bottle of champagne had opened up inside her.

'Everything all right?'

She nodded, to stop herself from giggling coquettishly.

How had she gone from thirty-seven to seventeen in a millisecond?

No mystery there.

Noah wanted her to stay. And she liked it.

Since they'd last seen one another she'd elbowed a raft of insecurities to one side to make room for something far more pleasurable. A crush.

A practical one, of course. There were very strict 'look

but don't touch' rules. 'Enjoy but don't get attached.' It actually made sense to allow herself the butterflies that took flight every time she saw him. Seeing him should be a joy—not torture. And as she'd be leaving Bali in a few months a secret crush wouldn't hurt anyone.

She stood back as the girls flew across the small patio area towards him.

His smile became unchecked. This version of him was more open. Less taut and prepared for attack, and more guardian warrior prepared to protect. Her crush doubled in size. Who wouldn't be smitten by a man prepared to take on the world for his sister's children?

Isla threw her arms around his waist. 'Paman!' she cooed

And her sister followed suit with her own impassioned, 'You came back!'

Their depth of emotion made tears prick at the back of Rebecca's throat. It was the same love she felt for her grandmother.

With the loss of their parents, and their worlds sent topsy-turvy, these girls didn't only love him—they needed him. He was their rock. And he was doing everything in his power to be strong for them, no matter how new it was to him. No wonder he didn't have time for a girlfriend. She didn't think she'd have the brain power to absorb becoming an instant parent as well as someone's partner.

But that was the thing, wasn't it? Brains didn't fall in love. Hearts did.

Noah picked one girl up with each arm and twirled them round, to their absolute delight.

Her heart melted.

This, she thought. *This is what I wanted when I dreamt of having a family.*

She squinted up at the sky, wondering if the universe was reminding her that families didn't always come via the traditional path. Love, marriage, baby carriage.

Families could come shaped like this. Or, in fact, like her own tiny family of two.

Perhaps her childhood dream of having what society deemed traditional had overridden her gut instinct that her ex might not be The One.

They'd had shared interests. Similar jobs. They'd found one another attractive enough.

She'd been so *sensible* about it all.

Maybe that had been the problem.

She pressed her hands to her heart as the girls begged Noah to twirl them round again—which, of course, he did, making it crystal-clear that he needed them every bit as much as they needed him. How could he not? They were proof his sister and brother-in-law had existed. Prescient reminders that the simple things—like a loved one returning home from work—were what really made a relationship strong. That sort of thing couldn't be put on a spreadsheet.

Flashes of just how wrong she and her ex had got it crackled painfully through her. Their lives had been so busy with work they'd had only snatched moments together, careers taking precedence over everything else to the point where their actual romance hadn't been much more than a highlights reel. None of the depth and glue of real-life events that held couples together.

And then she'd issued an ultimatum. *Marry me and let's build our lives together or let's break up.*

She winced. Hadn't Noah's girlfriend done the same thing to him? *Ouch.*

Only her boyfriend *had* proposed. They'd drawn up practical plans, retrained as GPs, all the while scraping together whatever money they could to buy a practice in Cornwall and be near her grandmother. It had all been going perfectly to plan—right up until it had all fallen apart.

Although honestly… A niggle had lodged in her chest the moment David had slid that ring on her finger. One that had scratched and pushed against her conscience, virtually begging her to acknowledge the fact that they weren't following their hearts. That this wasn't how love worked. Structuring their lives—effectively cornering one another—into a lifestyle that wouldn't allow them to grow.

That niggle, of course, had turned out to be foresight, but heigh-ho. She gave her shoulders a shake and popped her eyes open. It wasn't always fun to be right.

'Paman!' Isla tugged on Noah's hand. 'We're hungry!'

'Are you?' He crouched into a wild animal pose. 'As hungry as a bear?'

He roared. They screamed and squealed. Isla literally jumped into his arms, begging him never to do that again, whilst Ruby jumped up and down shouting, 'Again! Again! I'm a hungry bear!'

He roared and chased them round the patio until they all collapsed in a heap on the small arc of grass that outlined a beautiful koi pond, the three of them giggling and catching their breath.

Watching Noah with the girls, stepping outside his comfort zone—or perhaps stepping into it?—felt like witnessing living proof that you couldn't *organise* someone into loving you. No matter how good the spreadsheet. It had to happen naturally.

A sharp stab of loneliness pierced her heart as she watched them disentangle themselves from one another. It was something she'd never experienced. Or she didn't remember anyway. A rough and tumble with her parents. It was something she'd ached for. The big, boisterous, love-infused silliness that only family members could share.

She caught herself with a terse reminder that these girls weren't with their parents either. They were resilient. Just as she had been. And with this version of Noah they'd flourish.

As if sensing her gaze on them, Noah looked up, instinctively wrapping his arms round each of the girls' shoulders.

'Thanks for looking after them. I wouldn't have accepted your offer, but—'

She stopped him there, before the tears pricking at the back of her eyes came. 'You can't help it if an urgent call comes in when you're meant to leave.' She was going to leave it there, but then, remembering their earlier conversation, forced herself to maintain eye contact and said, 'You can always ask me. Any time. I want to help.'

Something passed between them. Something understood.

The feeling was so intense she smiled and took a step forward, half expecting Noah to open up his arms and pull her in to join them, before remembering that, even though he'd peeled off one layer of himself, he hadn't exactly split himself in half and revealed all. He hadn't said he wanted to be friends. He definitely hadn't said he wanted to be lovers.

Wait! What?

And just like that she was mentally disrobing him.

Stay.

The word circled round her chest like warm honey. A sensation far too sexy for anyone's good.

She was about to make her apologies and leave, see

what sort of takeout meal she could find on the high street, when Noah cleared his throat and said, 'We were going to have an Aussie dinner night.'

Ruby cheered and Isla started marching around, saying, 'Shrimp on the barbie! Shrimp on the barbie!'

Noah rubbed his jaw and said, 'It won't be much more than that, but you're welcome to stay.'

Rebecca hesitated.

Stay.

To work? To play? Both?

She didn't have what Kylie did. The ability to live in the moment, enjoy her body and the men who wanted to pleasure it, only to move on to the next one when that didn't pan out.

She wanted love. Not lust. No matter how many intense looks they shared, the truth was Noah wasn't in any place to offer her anything more than a plate full of grilled shrimp and a few months' voluntary work.

'Life's for living, my little cupcake!' Her grandmother's voice rang in her ear. *'Find the zest!'*

But what if 'the zest' was tall, dark, grieving his sister, and trying to figure out how to balance work and raising two little girls?

Before she could pull some sort of excuse out of the ether, Ruby and Isla each grabbed one of her hands and guided her round the villa to a back patio she hadn't seen yet. She gasped. It was so beautiful. The whole area was strung with fairy lights, creating a magical feeling. And the thick stone slabs of the patio extended to a huge, modern, open-air kitchen.

Beneath soaring arched beams there was a gorgeous teak table, a massive kitchen island made out of a huge tree round, and everything a cooking obsessive could ever want hanging from the wooden dowels strategically placed along the immaculate countertops. A wooden staircase ran the length of the back wall up to a thatch-and-beam-covered room where, beneath a broad ceiling fan, she could glimpse invitingly deep sofas and low bookshelves stuffed to bursting. It was her kind of room.

'Don't get too excited,' Noah cautioned when he saw her gaze return to the kitchen. 'My sister's husband was the chef. Not me. They had this wonderland added on to the villa when they moved in to run the clinic. I cook bachelor food, caveman style, and other than that I can pour a mean bowl of cereal.'

As her lips twitched into a smile at the warning, a woman dressed in the clinic's restaurant uniform came through a discreet bamboo gate at the edge of the patio and set a tray of clingfilm-covered plates on a table next to the barbecue.

They all gathered round.

Shrimp. Chicken. Vegetables. All threaded onto tidy skewers. There were little bowls filled with dips. Satay. Chilli oil. And a few other things she recognised but couldn't name.

'Australian, you say?' She grinned across at Noah, who rubbed his jaw again, this time in embarrassment.

'Well, Australia's pretty multicultural. Myself included.' He gave her a sheepish smile. 'I'm not much of a cook, but if my Aussie father taught me one thing, it was how to grill meat.'

The fact he'd mentioned his father felt significant. There'd been no mention of him before. Perhaps Noah was unpeeling more layers of himself than she'd thought. Testing the waters to see how much he could trust her with his carefully protected private life.

'Well, in that case I'd be grateful to accept your invitation,' she said with a small curtsey.

'Good.' He spread his hand across his chest in a show of gratitude. *'Good.'*

CHAPTER SIX

'ARE YOU SURE?' Noah shook his head. 'You don't have to.'

'Absolutely.' Rebecca held out her palm and flicked her fingers in a *Hand it over* gesture. 'You made dinner—the least I can do is dry the dishes you are so gallantly washing.'

Noah gave her a bemused side-eye. 'It's not really gallant when there isn't anyone else to do it, is there?'

'My—' she began, and then rephrased the sentence. 'I know people who would rely on the restaurant staff to do them.'

Noah said nothing, but wondered if 'people' meant her ex. Even the veiled mention of him made his skin itch with distaste. Cheating was bad enough. But this guy sounded as if he'd set up a whole other family before informing Rebecca. No wonder she didn't want to go back to the UK.

He had to admit he had a bit of the same feeling about going back to Oz. Sydney was technically home, but his happiest memories were actually here in Bali. They'd only come once a year as children, during the long school holidays, but his dad had never come and along with his mum and his sister, Bali had always managed to feel more like home than Sydney ever had.

The houses they'd lived in growing up had always

been more of an advertisement for his father's success than a home. Bigger, showier, with less and less freedom to play, for fear of messing something up or breaking something. The fact that he'd moved into a condominium that pretty much said the same thing—*I'm so good at my job I live in a house that looks like it should be in a magazine spread*—was suddenly discomfiting.

Had he spent his career trying to prove to his dad he was good enough, despite his decision not to follow him into the family business?

'Come on.' Rebecca grinned at him, hand still extended. 'Many hands make light work.'

He gave her a fresh tea towel and turned the taps on full-blast to fill up the sink. 'I really should be getting the girls to help,' he said. 'My sister and I were always on drying duty with my mum, but—'

He closed his eyes, not knowing if he was trying to stop the memories or summon them. Him and his sister, standing on step stools as their mum handed them dishes and cutlery, while their dad kicked back in the sound-proof home cinema, watching whatever sport was on that night. For a man who purported to adore women, he had never respected them very much. Especially not their mother.

Noah started when Rebecca reached over to turn the hot tap off.

'I hope you're going to wear those.' Rebecca nodded to the pink washing up gloves hanging on a wooden rod to the left of the large butler's sink.

He snorted and then, considering the steam rising from the froth of bubbles, reconsidered. Putting on a comedic suave voice he intoned, 'I'm comfortable enough with my masculinity to wear pastels.'

Her smile widened as she watched him put on the pink

washing up gloves. 'Would that extend to changing out of your dour black scrubs into adorable pink paediatric scrubs?'

His answer was swift. 'No.'

'Okay…' She looked away, stung.

'Sorry. I didn't mean to snap, I—'

He had a choice here. Clam up like he usually did. Pound his emotions into submission. Push her away. Or take the path he normally didn't, as he had this afternoon when he'd found himself admitting he was in over his head.

'The black scrubs…they're not "mourning scrubs"…'

'I shouldn't have asked. It's not my business,' Rebecca began fastidiously drying a plate and placing it on the bamboo stand beside the sink. She held out her hand. 'Next dish, please. I've got an early start tomorrow, so I should push off soon.'

He swore to himself. *Nice one, Noah. Hurt the woman who's doing her best to help.*

It was a pointed reminder that his universe wasn't the only one. She'd been hurt, too. Had the rug pulled straight out from under her. Sure, in a totally different way from him, but they were both grieving for futures they'd never have.

Which made him stop in his tracks. What sort of future had he been planning for, exactly? One where he told himself he was a good man because he sent money from a job he loved to a sister he loved but never visited, just in case she asked him what the hell he was doing with his life?

That was definitely the track he'd been on.

Why did the idea of having a family of his own scare him so much?

Because caring meant loss. Or betrayal.

Loss of his mother. Betrayal from his father.

He hadn't grown up in the ideal family. Hadn't been set good examples. How the hell was he supposed to know how to get any of it right?

His sister hadn't let that scare her.

He turned off the cold tap and faced Rebecca. 'I'm sorry. I— My fallback position is defensiveness. To shut things down. It's not a good trait.'

'It's fine. You're stressed, and I'm pushing buttons I don't know about. Plate, please.' Her voice was bright. Too chirpy to be genuine.

Fix it, Noah.

How? Whenever he'd upset a girlfriend before he'd usually just called an end to it. Told her things were getting too complicated.

Ostrich!

Rebecca wasn't his girlfriend! She was his… Colleague didn't seem right, even though it was accurate. She was… He heard his sister's voice: *She's your sign from the universe.*

He began scrubbing the plates, turning over options as to how to get the conversation started again.

Sorry, I'm such an asshole.

Nope.

Pink scrubs don't really match my complexion.

Double no.

Do you know this is the longest amount of time I've spent in Bali since my mum passed away?

Closer…

I'm not sure I want to go home, but I don't know if staying is an option.

He had the girls to think of. At this very moment his cousin was back in Sydney, drawing up a list of candidates for the position of full-time nanny. He'd be able to lean on Mel for a bit of support there. Though he had his doubts. Chances were his father would be more likely to want to see the girls in Sydney than here. And here he had the clinic. And the girls had their friends. And his brother-in-law's family were only a short flight away.

After a few moments Rebecca said, 'I become useful when I'm stressed. Too useful. I make charts and lists and offer solutions to problems that people may not want fixing. Or, if they do, they probably need to fix them themselves. I also talk too much.'

She shot him a shy, apologetic smile, then grabbed a handful of spoons and began to dry them fastidiously.

This had gone from bad to worse.

He turned to her. 'I wear black scrubs because they make me feel like a ninja.'

She snorted and rolled her eyes. 'Yeah, right.'

'Seriously.'

She threw him a *Try again, pal* look.

Screw it. He was going to walk right out to the end of the plank on this one.

'I know it sounds completely ridiculous, but as a kid, when I first started thinking of becoming a doctor, I used to think if I became a superhero doctor I'd be the Samurai Surgeon.'

Her lips began to twitch. 'You did what?'

He couldn't believe he was actually admitting this. It was a childhood dream that could have died with his sister if he'd let it, but something about Rebecca made him want her to know him. The *real* him.

He relaxed into the storytelling. 'It's completely true. I used to want to do martial arts as a kid, like my Indonesian uncles.'

He sliced the air between them in a couple of moves

that might've looked cool if he hadn't been wearing pink washing up gloves.

'I am deeply jealous of your ninja skills,' Rebecca grinned. 'Come on, then. Show us some more moves.'

The playful mood drained out of him. He pulled the washing up gloves off and hung them on the rack. 'My dad pushed me into playing footie, rugby, Aussie rules… You know—tough guy sports.' He lowered his voice to mimic his father's. '"What the use of being built like you are if you're not going to put it to good use?"'

Rebecca frowned. 'He's seen *Crouching Tiger, Hidden Dragon*, hasn't he? Or *Karate Kid*? Please tell me he's seen *Karate Kid*.'

'Right?' Noah held his hands out, gratified that someone else understood his childhood dream.

He was going to leave it at that, but decided, *What the hell? In for a penny and all that.*

'I think it'd be fair to say my father was never one to bend like the willow.' He hoped the phrase translated. It was a sort of catch-all for many Eastern philosophical doctrines that recommended going with the flow rather than fighting the inevitable.

Rebeca frowned. 'But isn't your mum—?'

'Indonesian. Yes.' He cleared his throat and added. 'She was. She died seven years back.'

Rebecca's hands flew to cover her mouth as he explained about the illness that had taken her. Bone cancer, of all things. And he'd been completely powerless to stop it.

'I'm so sorry, Noah. I…' She took a step back, as if needing to give this new information some room to settle, then met his eyes straight on. 'For what it's worth I think you look kick-ass in those scrubs. They make you look…erm…' She waved her hand up and down at him, as if it would help the word come to her, before settling on, 'Good.'

The flush sweeping across her cheeks made him fairly certain she'd been thinking of a different word.

He made another chopping move with his hand, to cover up the fact that he liked it that she thought he looked kick-ass in his scrubs. Or maybe he was showing off.

Struth. He hadn't shown off for a girl in he didn't know in how long. School, maybe?

Rebecca gave the space between them a bit of a kick, and somehow they ended up doing a slow motion martial arts fight, culminating in a massive case of the giggles.

Was this what honesty did? Evoke joy?

Rather than feeling exposed, stupid, and desperately wishing he'd kept his mouth shut, he was laughing and enjoying being in his own skin.

They stopped, both panting a bit, and as their laughter died away it morphed into something else. Something… sexier. Heated.

The feelings tore at his heart. Old Noah would've asked if she fancied a bit of 'adult time', but this Noah couldn't. He had responsibilities beyond his work life now. And, just as importantly, he respected Rebecca too much to start something he knew he couldn't finish.

She must've seen the shift in his eyes, because the smile fell from her face. 'Well, I'd better get going.'

He tried to speak, but everything he wanted to say jammed in his throat.

What was it about her that made him want to reach into his chest, pull out his ragged heart and say, *Here. This is what's left of it. Atrophied in parts. Shredded in others. But the core is still beating. Improving, even. And part of the reason it's healing is because of you.*

Who even said stuff like that? TV characters, maybe. But this was real life.

'Fair enough.' He took the tea towel she handed back to him, too aware of the moment when they each had hold of one end.

Rebecca stared at him for a moment, and then, as if she needed to physically break away from the magnetic energy that kept tugging them together, abruptly pulled her huge swathe of hair back and, releasing an elastic band from her wrist, piled it up into a messy knot on top of her head. Loose tendrils of flame-coloured hair shifted round the curves of her face like firelight.

'What?' Rebecca asked, misreading the intensity of his gaze. She started dabbing at her face. 'Do I have food on my face? Bubbles from the washing up?'

He shook his head. She was perfect. 'You're hygienic.'

Nice, Noah. Just what every girl wants to hear. That she's hygienic.

Rebecca dipped her head and to his surprise gave him a shy smile. 'Thanks for letting me join you. It was nice having a family-style meal.'

The words landed in his chest like an arrow with a bittersweet sting.

It was a life he'd never imagined for himself, and quite clearly a life Rebecca had long dreamt of. Kids. A family. Chances were it might have been more painful than pleasurable for Rebecca to spend time with him and the girls. A visual visceral taunt. *Here's what you aren't getting!*

Now that it was over, he had to admit it *had* been really nice to play happy families. Natural, even. Probably the first night together when he and the girls had been this relaxed. Everyone had pitched in with the cooking, the girls donning aprons and white chef's toques they'd unearthed from somewhere. Rebecca had used some of the hairbands from the collection on her wrist to secure thick oven gloves onto the girls' small hands after they'd insisted on turning the barbecuing meat, and then used the same oven gloves as puppets, reducing the girls to streams of laughter as they tried to teach her how to count to ten in Balinese.

Conversation had flowed easily. In fact, making chit-chat with the girls had been much easier with Rebecca there. She didn't do the thing his cousin did—talk to him as if he were a child, too, speaking slowly and clearly about safety and boundaries and bedtimes and structure. He was a bachelor, not an idiot.

Rebecca was different. She spoke to everyone naturally about anything and everything. Enabled the girls to do things helicopter parents like his cousin might not allow. Like turning the meat on a hot barbecue. She turned the safety aspects into fun. It was easy to see why she'd been drawn to paediatrics. She was a natural with children.

And she deserved someone who wanted to give them to her.

At the end of the corridor a huge gale of laughter erupted from the bathroom, where the girls were taking a very splashy-sounding bath. His eyes met Rebecca's.

She flicked her thumb towards the gate that led out into the clinic gardens. 'I'll just sneak off before they're finished.'

'No, please.' The last thing he wanted her to feel like was a spare part. 'Stay. They'll want to say goodnight.'

In truth, sudden departures didn't go down well with the girls since their parents had been killed.

He got it. They wanted assurances. At six and eight, they weren't unaware of what was going on, and on the face of it were showing remarkable fortitude. But they had nightmares. Tensed when things didn't go strictly to plan. They were too young and too fragile to be reminded on a regular basis that life didn't come with assurances.

So what made you allow Rebecca to be with them this afternoon when you could've sent her to the emergency room in your place?

He knew the answer.

But he couldn't be an ostrich any more. It wasn't Rebecca's job to take care of the children. It was his.

A pitter-patter of feet sounded in the corridor and the girls appeared in their cotton pyjamas, faces scrubbed clean. 'Is she still here?'

Their eyes gleamed when they saw her. They ran over and hugged her round the waist.

Rebecca knelt down to their level. 'I couldn't leave without saying goodbye to you two flower-faces, could I?' She shot a quick look at Noah. 'I'm afraid I've got to go now, but I'll see you again soon, yeah?'

The girls made matching sad noises.

Ruby looked up at Noah, her expression one of complete innocence. 'Is Rebecca your girlfriend?'

A flush swept up Rebecca's neck to her cheeks.

Noah rubbed the back of his neck. 'No, honey. We work together.'

'But…' Isla began. 'Mummy and Daddy worked together, and they were married.'

'True, but—'

'I should definitely be hitting the road.' Rebecca grabbed her backpack from one of the kitchen chairs and was halfway across the patio before Noah could protest. 'Goodnight, girls. See you tomorrow, okay?'

She didn't bother saying goodbye to him.

After a chorus of goodnights had followed her down

the low-lit path, the girls tugged Noah to the sofa for their night-time story ritual.

All of them were clearly feeling Rebecca's absence, because their newly established routine—supper, bath, then sofa time with a story—was considerably more subdued.

'What will it be tonight, then, girls? A fairy tale? Or one of the books your auntie brought over from Australia?'

The girls listlessly pawed through the pile of books he showed them.

Then Ruby pushed them down onto his lap and said, 'Uncle Noah?'

'Yes, poppet?'

'Would you make Rebecca your girlfriend?'

He faltered, trying to come up with some sort of answer. He chose a question instead. 'We're doing all right, aren't we? Us three?'

'Yeah, but…' Isla traced her finger along one of the tattoos on his arm. A dragon. 'It'd be nice if there was someone here who was like a mummy, the same way you're sort of like an *ayah*.'

The Indonesian word for father barely made it out of her mouth before tears began to trickle down her cheeks.

Oh, hell. If Isla was crying that meant— Yup. Ruby was crying, too.

He pulled the girls in close, dropping kisses atop each of their heads. He hadn't even bothered trying to soothe them with words when he'd first flown over, and the tradition, if you could call it that, had stuck. Hugs and kisses had become his language for the times when words would never do. It was what his own mother had done. His father had placated and charmed with words, and they had all been lies in the end.

The girls burrowed into his chest as if they were kittens, each seeking a snuggly purchase as they wept into his shirt. He looked out into the darkness, wishing like hell that Rebecca had stayed.

CHAPTER SEVEN

REBECCA'S SMILE CAME unbidden as Noah appeared at the charge nurse's desk. And then, embarrassingly, a blush. Why did she always turn the colour of a beet when she was near him? She wasn't a twelve-year-old girl any more.

She gave herself a little shoulder-shake, as if that would remind her of the facts here. She was a grown woman trying to put her past behind her with a very interesting job. A job she should be focussing on instead of staring at Noah's hands and wondering what it would feel like if he ran just one of those beautiful surgeon's fingers along her collarbone and—

'Good morning, Dr Stone.'

Ah. So she was Dr Stone again. No more Rebecca. Okay. Cool. She could roll with that. She gave him what she hoped was an officious-looking nod.

He gave her an inquisitive look. 'You're up bright and early.'

Her smile remained fixed as her flush deepened. 'Certainly am!'

That was what happened when sleeping involved having erotic dreams about your new boss. You woke up early and had lots and lots of energy to expend.

Which was fairly different from how she'd used to be. Clinging to every ounce of sleep she could schedule.

Noah reached across the counter, his arm accidentally brushing hers as she reached for a notepad. Her eyes snapped to his as a rippling of goosebumps skittered up her arm.

His gaze quickly dropped away, and she wondered if he'd been imagining her naked, too.

Oh, Lordy.

She began to scribble on the pad as if writing a prescription. *You have a raging case of I-fancy-the-pants-off-you.*

'That's it,' she murmured as her hand started involuntarily drawing little love hearts.

'Rebecca?' Noah's expression turned into a concerned frown and he moved closer to the desk, as if to try and read what she was writing. 'Is everything all right? Do you need help with a patient?'

'Nope. Grand. Everything's lovely.' She crumpled up the paper and stuffed it into her pocket. 'Tickety-boo, in fact. Thank you for enquiring, Dr Cameron. Just off for a spot of tea in the staffroom. If you'll excuse me?' The Britishisms fell out of her mouth and she barely stopped herself from offering him a curtsey.

Looking at him only made her heart-rate spike, so she did what any mature woman hoping to make a positive impression would—picked up a nearby pamphlet on a monkey sanctuary and tapped it, as if it explained her very odd behaviour, then high-tailed it to the staffroom.

'Thanks for another great day.' The charge nurse, a friendly local woman called Jhoti, took Rebecca's tablet from her and waved it as if it was a trophy. 'You don't know how much it means to us to have you here.'

Rebecca stopped in her tracks. 'I thought you had loads of doctors right now?'

The nurse smiled, then leant in and spoke in a whisper. 'There are a few surgeons around…' Her smile faded away. 'Sort of, anyway.'

'What does that mean?' Rebecca asked. 'Sort of?'

'Well…' The nurse drew out the word, her eyes flicking down the corridor. 'With everything in flux…you know… Dr Cameron hasn't exactly made it clear whether or not the clinic's going to stay open. So we've got some surgeons on holiday here in Bali who've volunteered to do the odd surgery, but no one like you who has committed to working for a few months. He can't shut it down while you're working here.'

Rebecca blinked in surprise. First of all, she was pretty sure she didn't wield that kind of power. Second of all… 'You don't think he'd actually close it, do you?'

The nurse shrugged, then leaned in a bit closer. 'We have no idea. He never really seemed that into it when his sister was running the place. We thought it was for both of them, you know… Given that the place was opened in their mother's memory.'

Rebecca nodded as if she had known, but this was all news to her. It helped a lot of pieces fit into place. Noah's mum had passed away around the time when he'd said he had his last long-term relationship. The two had to be connected. But his not wanting to come here… That wouldn't make sense unless—oh, God—unless he blamed himself for not being able to cure his mother's cancer.

Jhoti looked over her shoulder again. 'It was definitely Indah's passion project. And her husband's. We actually used to call Dr Cameron Dr Cheques and Balances up until the last couple of months, when we discovered how great a doctor he actually is.'

Rebecca knew the comment wasn't mean. It simply spoke to the fact that they didn't know him.

'Maybe if you could let him know how much we love working here...'

'Me?' Rebecca pulled back.

'Yes.' Jhoti gave Rebecca a look, suggesting she was missing something obvious. 'He listens to you. When he talks to us he's always a bit removed, but with you... he really listens.'

Another nurse came up to the counter then, ending the conversation, but Rebecca was reeling.

Noah listened to her?

It was a fairly big headline, considering she barely had the skills to chat with him without her face turning tomato-red.

But the reality of how big a decision Noah had to make made her concerns about whether or not he had a crush on her pale in comparison. All of this—the clinic, her volunteer work here and, more to the point, the jobs of the two dozen or so locals who offered invaluable medical aid to the local community—could be shut down in an instant.

Noah could've closed it the day his sister had died, but hadn't. He had a life back in Australia. A high-powered job that had brought him international renown. And the girls' future to think of. Of course he'd go back. It wasn't a question of if. It was a question of when.

The thought twisted her in two.

In such a short time she'd grown to love this place. The cottage hospital feel of the clinic married the two things she loved most about medicine—personalised service and the power to see a medical situation through, no matter the cost.

What if...? What if *she* offered to run it?

The thought gripped her stomach in a way that felt a lot more like excitement than panic. But just as quickly it reversed course.

Was she hoping to fill the gaping void in her life with something that would distract her? Trying to be useful in the way she had been in taking over all the planning for the GP surgery back home? Well, that had ended in epic failure…so perhaps she needed to adopt another tack. Self-preservation.

Rebecca distractedly gave the nurse a wave goodnight, then scuttled out to the garden to call Nanny Bea. Her homing beacon. She might be letting this whole 'taking what the universe presented to her' thing run away with itself.

She tucked herself into a shady nook out in the garden, pulled her phone out of her pocket and dialled the one and only number in 'Favourites'.

After a few moments, she pulled the phone away from her ear and frowned.

Weird.

Her nan always answered the phone at the first ring when she made her daily check-in.

It had rung seven times now.

Rebecca checked her watch. It was ten a.m. back home. She'd always been at home pretty much round the clock when Rebecca had been there.

A shiver of panic swept through her. Maybe something was wrong. What if something had happened to her and no one from the village had checked? Her nan wasn't exactly elderly—she was a vital seventy-seven, and most folk thought she was in her sixties. She regularly won her age category in the local half-marathon, but—

No. This wasn't right. Nanny Bea always answered the phone straight away.

Guilt swept into the cracks of her conscience that anxiety had opened.

What if something had happened to Nanny Bea?

The answering machine clicked in and Rebecca did her best to leave a chirpy message, but she knew it sounded false. She was just about to search for the number for her nan's best friend when she heard footsteps.

'Hey.' Noah stopped in his tracks. His eyes went to the phone and Rebecca's peculiar expression. 'Everything all right?'

She shook her head. 'I—I don't know.'

CHAPTER EIGHT

NOAH'S NERVE-ENDINGS SHOT to high alert in a way they normally wouldn't for a colleague. 'What's wrong? Is there anything I can do?'

Rebecca shook her head and held up her phone. 'I don't think so. It's my nan. She's not answering the phone.'

'Is that unusual?'

'Yes. But—' Rebecca gave him a pained wince. 'I could be blowing things out of proportion.'

'How do you mean?'

'She could be at the shops. She could be out watering her flowers. She could be—I don't know… Having a life now that her messed-up granddaughter isn't there any more?' She threw up her hands and then let them flop back into her lap, giving an emotive cross between a sigh and fear-laden squeak. 'She's just always there for me, and now she's—she's not.'

Her voice hitched in a way that tugged at Noah's heart. He sat down beside her and took one of her hands in his. 'Do you need to speak to her urgently? Is something wrong?'

Rebecca opened her mouth then quickly pressed her lips together.

'What? You can tell me.'

'I don't think I can.'

'Why?'

'Because it's about you. Well, you and the clinic.' She pulled her hand from his and began to fret at the skin on her thumb.

'What about the clinic? Everything seemed fine when I left.' He threw a look back at the main building and then in the direction of his villa, where he was meant to be meeting the girls.

'No, sorry. I didn't mean—' She tipped her head into her hands. 'Oh, man. I'm really sticking my foot in my mouth. Do you need to go? You look like you have to get home. I'll just— Let's pretend this never happened.'

'Rebecca. What is going on?'

She looked at him then—really looked at him. Her body language shifted, grew stronger, as if she'd made a decision.

'The staff are wondering whether or not you are going to close the clinic down. They're worried for their futures and for some mad reason they think you listen to me. That you trust me.' She waved her hands. 'I don't know… It's probably all nonsense.'

'No. They're right.' It was empowering, putting words to the mysterious energy that had gripped him since Rebecca had come into his life. 'I do trust you.'

He respected her, too, which was why he was trying to ignore the obvious sexual chemistry they shared. Rebecca deserved better than this version of him.

She pressed her hands to her heart. 'That means a lot to me. Believe me. But…why not them? You've got an amazingly dedicated staff here. Ready and willing to do anything they can to make sure this place stays open.'

He threw another look back at the clinic. 'It isn't that I don't trust them. It's more…' He looked into her beautiful green eyes. 'I don't trust *me*.'

Today it felt doubly true. His cousin was starting to send through the CVs of very well-regarded nannies. Men and women much more qualified than him to raise two little girls. He'd also had a call from his boss back in Sydney, asking when he was thinking about coming back. Noah had said he needed more time, but he could tell there was a limit to his boss's patience. Noah brought in high-profile patients, and without him there they'd need to employ some other big-shot surgeon. One who wasn't juggling all the feelings he'd put on hold for the last couple of decades.

'Why don't you trust yourself?' she asked.

Because I've met you.

It was a mad thought, but it was true. She believed in him in the way his sister had. She saw through all his bravura and…what had she called it?…his broodiness. She saw a kind man. One with a big heart.

He wanted to be that man for the girls and for Rebecca.

Heading back to Sydney meant that man would disappear.

He leant back against the stone wall and threw her a sad smile. 'Have you ever wished you could go back in time and make some changes to the decisions you made?'

She laughed. 'Just about every day of the week! Mostly on the personal front. Being a doctor was always my goal.' Her brow furrowed as she tipped her head to the side to consider him, as if she could see straight into his mind. 'What would you change? You're a successful surgeon. You've got a thriving clinic here—'

'Let me stop you there. The clinic exists because of my sister. I didn't want to have anything to do with it.'

'Why not?'

He held up a hand. 'It isn't caring for the patients that's

the problem.' He swept his hand across the gardens. 'It's the packaging.'

Rebecca looked confused. 'Seriously? You have a problem with paradise?'

'I do,' he admitted. 'Because this particular paradise comes with a bunch of conditions.'

She tucked her knees under her chin and gave him an *I'm all ears* look.

It was a story he hadn't told much—if ever. 'My dad isn't what you would call a faithful man.'

Rebecca nodded. She wasn't judging. Just listening. And for that he was grateful. He surprised himself by letting the whole story pour out.

'He's a property developer. Buys beautiful artisan places like this and does them up to high spec for Western tourists.'

'Is that how he met your mother?' Rebecca asked.

He nodded. 'A long time ago, when he didn't have much more than two coins to rub together. He had come here on a surfing holiday with a couple of friends, stayed in a guest house with a ramshackle seafront bar that the owner didn't want to run any more. My mum worked there doing odd jobs. Bartending some days. Cleaning on others.'

He glanced at Rebecca. Not everyone knew he came from such humble roots. Rebecca gave him another encouraging nod, clearly keen for him to continue. So he did. He told her how his dad had convinced the owner to let him run the bar in exchange for a free room. His father had somehow turned the place around and made it one of the most popular tourist nightspots on the island. It had been the beginning of what was to become a massive property empire. One he ran to this day.

'So that's when your parents fell in love?'

He nodded. 'My mum had a really amazing eye for interior decor and helped him design all his places until we were born.' He gave a tight huff of indignation. 'Not that he gave her much credit for either thing. But praise and adulation wasn't something she ever craved, you know? She was just happy knowing we were being looked after and getting amazing educations. Things she hadn't really ever had.'

'Did she have family here?'

He shook his head. 'She was actually an orphan. If she hadn't caught my dad's eye, she might've stayed a cleaner here her whole life.'

'So, that's a good thing, right? That they met? She got to discover some hidden talents. She had you.'

The comment was a pointed one. A reminder that he wouldn't be here if his parents hadn't got together.

'You say your dad has an eye for the ladies?'

He nodded. 'We weren't really aware of it as kids. He was always off on one business trip or another. Mum always stayed with us. If he needed her for design work he'd send her the briefs or, if it was the school holidays, fly us all out to join him—after he'd had all the lipstick dry cleaned out of his collars, if you get my meaning.'

Rebecca nodded.

He cut to the chase. 'Just as I was fresh out of med school and making my mark in the world of orthopaedics my mum got bone cancer. Stage four.'

She winced.

'All she wanted to do was come back here. Dad had just bought this place for a song after one of the financial crashes, so we thought—why not? If what she really needed was palliative care, my sister and I could sort that out with help from the local hospital, and she could design a last, final tribute to her homeland.'

'So…is that what happened?'

'Nope.' He knew he sounded bitter. 'Dad kept making excuses. Saying he couldn't get a construction team. That it wouldn't be restful for Mum.' He twirled his finger. 'A ream of excuses, all of which were Class-A bull.'

Rebecca looked alarmed. 'Why would he lie about that?'

'Because he was keeping his latest mistress here.' He nodded towards one of the bungalows that his sister, rather hilariously, had used for putting the rubbish in. 'She'd come to Bali to "get over" a divorce and my dad helped her with that.' He huffed out a disbelieving laugh. 'He kept making excuses as to why Mum couldn't come just yet. One more week this… Next month that… He actually said to me, "As the doctor in the family, it's your job to keep her alive."'

He still didn't begin to know how to forgive his father for that. He was an orthopaedic surgeon, not an oncologist. Not to mention they hadn't even found out about the cancer until it was too late. Not even oncologists were wizards.

'Anyway…' He tugged this hand through his hair. 'Mum died in Australia.'

'Oh, Noah.' Rebecca had tears in her eyes, and her expression was wreathed in compassion when it should've been etched with contempt. 'I'm so sorry.'

He was too. The cancer had been cruel and swift, and even though he couldn't have cured it he was her son. A doctor who should've made her journey more comfortable. And it wasn't as if there hadn't been other places to stay in Bali. He'd just… He'd wanted his dad—just once—to act like a man whose wife, the mother of his children, was the centre of his universe. And he hadn't. Not even knowing she was dying.

Noah knew he'd carry the shame of not standing up to his father to his grave.

In a monotone he explained how, after his mum's death, his dad had given him and his sister the half-developed resort hotel. His sister, an ICU nurse, had come up with the idea of turning it into a clinic that served the local community and helped people like their mum, whose parents had both died of malaria—a disease that was easily curable with access to proper medical care. Care they'd been unable to afford. Noah had suggested it also treated tourists, so that there'd be a steady revenue stream. Then he'd left his sister to it.

'I just—' He stopped.

'What?'

Rebecca gave his hand a squeeze. Sympathy he didn't deserve.

'I did what I always do. Stuck my head in the sand and told myself that I was doing the right thing by staying in Sydney, working my ass off to buy fancy equipment so volunteer surgeons could come in and perform lifesaving surgeries for people who deserved them.'

'The clinic's got amazing resources because of all your hard work,' Rebecca insisted.

'I should have been here,' Noah said, in a voice he barely recognised.

He should have been here helping his sister. Being a good big brother. Helping her and her husband with the clinic, their children—all of it. And then, very possibly, they might not have been on that road, on that day, at the moment that idiot had raced down the switchbacks and driven their car off the road and into a ravine.

Rebecca took a deep breath. 'Want to know what I've been telling myself these past few weeks?'

He gave her a soft, teasing smile. 'That the universe will sort it all out for you?'

She gave him a *ha-ha-very-funny* look, then softened. 'A little bit that, but mostly I've been thinking how the only way I can change things in the past is by living proactively in the present.'

'That sounds very philosophical for a woman who comes prepared with three hairbands on her wrist at all times.'

They both looked at her wrist where, sure enough, there were spare hairbands. She took the light-hearted jibe and ran with it. 'Living in the present doesn't have to mean not being prepared for it. It's more…' She shifted her legs round so that she was facing him. 'The fact that you didn't shut this place down the day your sister died means something.'

Noah tipped his head in affirmation. 'Go on.'

'I think you believe that the work done here is important.'

'Of course.'

'And, if I'm right, you also believe it honours your mother's legacy. She sounds like she was a caring, loving woman, who put her family first.'

'That was her, all right. She was the essence of maternal love.'

Rebecca's smile softened. 'You're fortunate to have had that.'

He was. It was something Rebecca hadn't had, and he saw what she was trying to point out. He should be grateful for what he *had* had, not for what he hadn't. Which did mean maybe the clinic could be run in a different way. Right now it didn't need more fancy machines. It needed someone who cared at the helm.

Rebecca gave him another thoughtful look, then asked, 'If you decided to stay here, how much would you be leaving behind in Sydney?'

He could've laid out all the facts. Told her how he was

regularly wooed by elite hospitals across Australia and beyond. How he was requested by name by the country's biggest sports stars and often invited to restaurant openings and other high society events. But there was a flipside to that lifestyle. The absence of any time for socialising. His lack of interest in anything beyond a casual relationship. The occasional dark nights of the soul when he'd wonder what the hell he was doing with his life and, worse, whether or not he would end up alone if he continued in this vein.

He looked Rebecca in the eye and, trusting in their friendship said, 'Beyond a couple of unopened bottles of beer in a fridge in a soulless bachelor pad, not much.'

It was a stark admission. He did love his job. But he could do it here just as easily. And without the pressure of television interviews with sports stars and tech gurus, and all the other high-profile patients the hospital regularly dangled in front of him more for their kudos than his professional satisfaction, he'd have that feeling he enjoyed with every patient he treated here in Bali, because he was giving precisely the type of care his mother would have loved to have given in her name.

'Are you sure you didn't also study psychology?' he asked.

Rebecca rolled her eyes. 'Let's just say I've been asking myself a lot of deep and meaningful questions lately. I've just turned that looking glass on to you to see if it helps.'

'It has.' He smiled and then, as if it was the most natural thing in the world, swept the backs of his fingers along her cheek, as if she were a girlfriend or a lover.

She flushed under his touch.

The energy between them surged and grew thick with promise. 'You've been a good friend to me,' he said.

She looked down, her dark lashes brushing against her cheeks. When she lifted her eyes up to meet his again, they were glistening.

Something that felt like hope gave a fist-pump in his chest. Was this what it was like to meet your kindred spirit? To meet The One?

Just as quickly the fist bashed into his conscience.

What could he offer her?

Friendship. He wanted something more, but the two little girls waiting for him a few hundred metres away were his reminder that he was not in a place to make promises. What if she wanted children of her own? He had no idea where he stood on that. Not with the plates he was spinning.

'Is that what we are?' she asked. 'Friends?'

The air between them hummed with anticipation. 'I'm not sure what we are,' he answered honestly.

His eyes stayed locked to hers for a moment and then, as if summoned, dropped to her lips.

He'd been wanting to pull her into his arms and make good on his instinct to kiss her ever since he'd met her. A primitive indicator that friendship wasn't all he was after.

'I'd like to be friends,' he said, tugging his eyes back up to meet hers. 'You say things I need to hear. And I would hate for that to stop for any reason.'

His eyes dropped to her lips again, practically spelling out what he wasn't saying. If they made this relationship physical he was giving no guarantees that he'd be able to see it through into a relationship.

Rebecca cleared her throat and, obviously feeling awkward, made a one-eighty change in conversation. 'I know I'm supposed to be flipping coins and leaving stuff up to the universe to make decisions for me, but if you're genuinely struggling with which way to go—Sydney or staying here—sometimes I find writing lists really helps clear things up for me. You know—putting stuff in black and white.'

He laughed and tipped an invisible cap. 'On your advice, I will sit down tonight to make one.' He knew what the first item should be: *Don't fall in love.*

He rose and pointed to the phone by her side. 'I'm afraid my woes have steered us off track. Weren't we trying to figure out what's going on with your grandmother?'

Rebecca went ashen at the reminder. 'Nanny Bea! Sorry. I've got to ring her again.' She threw him a pleading look. 'Do you mind staying while I ring? Just in case—you know….'

Just in case something was wrong.

The vulnerability of her request wrapped round his heart. 'Not at all.'

She thumbed an app open. 'Oh! She's sent a text message.' She pressed a button, her brows arrowing together and then, just as quickly, flying up to her forehead. 'Oh, my goodness!' She turned the phone towards him, her face wreathed in smiles. 'Nanny Bea's been on a date!'

He pressed his hands to his chest, as if he'd been struck by an arrow, then dropped them when Rebecca began to frown at the message. 'What?'

'It's just a bit weird, that's all.' She tried to put on a smile but didn't entirely succeed. 'But I guess this is more evidence that the world works in mysterious ways.' She frowned again and added, almost to herself, 'I guess even if the universe gives us things it's still up to us to decide what to do about them.'

Yes, thought Noah, his fingers finding the coin he'd kept in his pocket ever since Rebecca had tossed it to him. *It certainly is.*

CHAPTER NINE

'BYE, NAN. HAVE fun and be safe. Love you.'

After a wave and an air-kiss, Rebecca ended the video call, slipped her phone into the pocket of her backpack and gave Noah at not entirely apologetic smile.

'Sorry about that. Just doing my daily check-in.' She rubbed her hands together in a show of excitement. 'Okay! Let's go and see this monkey temple.'

It was a Saturday afternoon. When the girls had joined Rebecca at the pool for a morning swim—something they'd taken to doing most mornings before school—they'd discovered that Rebecca hadn't yet been to the Sacred Monkey Sanctuary.

The girls had run back to the villa and dragged Noah out to the pool, along with a pile of notebooks so he could make a list of all of the places they thought Rebecca should see, and then they'd insisted he take them all out.

So here they were, backpacks filled with sunblock and water, all set to head off to the sanctuary. It was the closest to a family outing Rebecca had ever had as an adult, and it was impossible not to remember the moment when the girls had asked Noah if she was his girlfriend. And then, of course, the moment he'd made it very clear that she was in The Friend Zone.

'Everything all right at home?' Tiny lines of concern fanned out from Noah's eyes.

'I don't think I've ever heard Nan so happy,' Rebecca admitted, smiling her thanks to Noah who, gentleman that he was, had just opened the Jeep's passenger door for her. The girls were already in the back, ready for their outing. When Noah had climbed into the driver's seat she continued. 'She and Nathan are off to visit an art gallery.'

Nathan Parker was her Nan's new beau. A widower and retired civil engineer, Nathan had moved to the seaside to be near his daughter and grandchildren. The pair had met at the library, when they'd each reached for the same copy of *Jane Eyre* and it had been, according to her Nan, love at first sight.

'It's a bit further down the coast from her village and it's rumoured to have the best tearoom in Cornwall. Apparently, the carrot cake is to die for.'

'Are they going for the art or the cake?' Noah asked as he pulled his own door shut and clicked his safety belt into place, after triple-checking that the girls had done the same.

Her heart gave a little squeeze. He was obviously trying not to smother the girls with protective measures, but clearly had a safety-first checklist going on in his head. Bless him… She adored the girls, but she could also see insta-parenting from Noah's perspective. Panic-inducing. Proper 'in at the deep end' stuff.

It did make her wonder… Would he ever want children of his own or, now that he had the girls, was he drawing a line under that possibility? The fact he'd properly Friend Zoned her probably meant she should make her hormones do the same. She wanted children. At least the option to try. But if it didn't work she was open to other options.

Sensing Noah's gaze on her, Rebecca made herself

laugh and continue in a light-hearted tone. 'My grandmother is a very competitive cake-maker. If she hears someone else is offering cakes to die for she'll drive from one end of Britain to the other to investigate.'

'What is carrot cake?' Isla asked. 'Does it taste like supper or dessert?'

Noah glanced into the rear-view mirror. 'Didn't your mum ever make it for you?'

Both girls shook their heads.

'What about Lamingtons?' he asked. 'Our mum used to make them for us all the time. Did she make those?'

Again, two dark haired heads shook back and forth.

'What *did* she make for you?'

'Mummy didn't cook,' Isla said matter-of-factly. 'She said she was like you, Uncle Noah.'

'Oh?' He shot Rebecca a mystified look. 'And what is that, exactly?'

Ruby piped up. 'Mummy said you could burn water.'

Rebecca stifled a laugh. Obviously his culinary skills were better than that. The barbecue had been delicious.

Noah pretended to look hurt. 'I'm sure I could manage something slightly better than burnt water. It's just—I've never really allowed time for cooking.' He tightened his hands round the steering wheel and pressed his arms out to their full length, as if creating space between himself and the memories.

Almost to himself, he explained, 'My mum—your grandmother—was an amazing cook. She despaired at the two of us, always trying and failing to get us to cook with her.'

When he fell silent Rebecca volunteered, 'I was pretty much tied to my nan's apron strings.'

Noah shot her a quick forlorn smile. 'Mum always conceded to whatever things my father wanted, and us learning how to cook wasn't one of them. We were always doing sport, or going to some sort of after-school club. She did try.'

He laughed quietly, but Rebecca could tell it wasn't because his memories were happy.

'There was one time she tried to get me in the kitchen with her when I was home from med school. She insisted learning to make her nasi goreng was the way I'd win a wife. Suffice it to say her cunning plan didn't work.' He held up his left hand and wiggled his empty ring finger at her.

Rebecca studied him as he fixed his gaze on the road. She was pretty sure Noah's lack of cooking skills was not the reason why he was single.

A cloud of sadness hung over him as he navigated the vehicle out of the village and drove deeper into the island, where the road was shrouded by thick jungle canopy.

Isla said, 'Mummy always took us to the bakery if we wanted anything. She said that was what bakeries were for.'

'Daddy made us Laklak cakes once,' Ruby reminded her.

'They were burnt,' Isla said sombrely, and then, to Rebecca's astonishment, they both began to giggle at the memory.

Noah and Rebecca exchanged a look. It was the first time Rebecca had known the girls to openly talk about their parents and not get tearful. Noah looked panicked. Rebecca instantly understood. He wanted it to continue, but didn't know how.

She twisted in her seat as much as the seatbelt would allow and asked, 'What's a Laklak cake?'

The girls grinned and spoke over one another, explaining about cakes made of rice flour that they were small—like the size of their hands, not Noah's—and how, depending upon where you got them, they came with grated coconut or sweetened condensed milk. They were often bright green and, most of all, they were delicious even if they were burnt.

'They do sound delicious,' Rebecca said. 'Noah, what do you think? Could we hunt down some Laklak cakes on the way to the monkey temple?'

He threw her a grateful look. 'Sounds perfect. Let's do it.'

They proceeded to have one of the most perfect afternoons Rebecca had ever had.

Fuelled by the delicious coconutty cakes they'd found at a roadside bakery, they went to the Sacred Monkey Sanctuary. When they saw how huge it was Isla grabbed Noah by the hand and Ruby did the same to Rebecca. The girls insisted that Noah and Rebecca hold hands as well as they walked round the vast sanctuary.

'We don't want anyone to get lost,' Ruby said gravely.

So, Noah held out his hand to Rebecca and she took it.

'Is this all right?' he asked as he wove his fingers through hers.

'Fine,' she squeaked.

It wasn't just all right—it was perfection. She felt contented, in a way she'd never imagined possible. As if she'd come home. It made her wonder if home could actually be a person—not a place.

She'd been so intent on setting up the GP surgery in Cornwall she hadn't stopped to consider if it was a place that would make them both happy. With her hand in Noah's she felt safe in a way she hadn't in years. Not that being raised by her nan or that any of her other relationships had been frightening. Far from it. It was more that she'd always felt as if her young life had been a quest to create the one thing that was missing: a big, happy, family.

And here on this day, in this place—even though she knew it wasn't really true—she felt like she was part of one. They laughed at silly things. Noticed who'd left a pocket of their backpack unzipped. And Noah was the one who, as they were approaching a group of monkeys, suggested she twist her thick hair into a bun, so that the monkeys didn't make a grab for it.

'It's very beautiful,' he said, his eyes not quite meeting hers as he spoke. 'Monkeys are renowned for wanting beautiful things.'

A warm glow lit in her. A tiny flicker of hope that maybe one day this friendship could bloom into something else.

She unearthed a few hairpins from her bag, and the girls made a big show of tucking them all into place, then standing back and waiting for Noah's approval—which, to their combined satisfaction, he gave.

All tiny little building blocks that created the strong, safe, foundation of a family.

Though the girls had soon forgotten their insistence that they all hold hands, Noah reached out for hers and gave it a squeeze as the girls closed their eyes shut tight to make wishes and flip coins into the Holy Spring Temple Pool. 'You okay?'

She smiled at him. 'More than okay.'

The rest of the world blurred as they continued to look into one another's eyes. Someone jostled against Noah, pushing him closer to Rebecca. He wrapped a protective arm around her as he regained his balance.

'You okay?' he asked again as her hands landed on his chest.

She looked up at him, her heart-rate spiking as their

gazes synced. She parted her lips to say something, but couldn't. How could she explain to him that from the moment she'd laid eyes on him she'd known he would always be more than a friend to her? That when he touched her she felt more alive than she had seconds earlier? That he could trust her to love the girls as much as he did even if trusting felt like stepping off a cliff into the great unknown?

She had no idea why, but the way he was looking at her made her feel as if he was thinking exactly same thing: *I want you...but I don't know how to begin.*

'Rebecca!' Isla grabbed her free hand and gave it a tug. 'Want to make a wish?'

'I do,' she whispered, her eyes still locked on Noah's.

Her wish ran through her head on a loop. *Fall in love with me. Fall in love with me. Fall in love with me.*

His hands shifted so that they rested loosely on her hips, as casually as if he'd done it a thousand times before and would a thousand times again. If he were to tip his head down to hers…

'What're you wishing for?' he asked.

This, she thought. *This and so much more.*

'Can't tell you,' she said, still close enough to kiss him. 'Otherwise it might not come true.'

'Well, then…' Noah locked her lips with a twist of his fingers. 'Better not say a word.'

Noah grimaced as he punched the 'accept' symbol on his phone. 'Hey, Dad. What's up?'

It was a curt greeting for a bereaved father. Not that his father had won any prizes for parenting over the years, or shown all that much heartache that his only daughter had had her life cut short—but still… Noah was the only blood relative he had left. He should do better.

'How's it going?' he asked, and then, after getting a neutral 'Fine…' that didn't really send the conversation anywhere, he asked about his father's wife.

'Ah, yes…about her…'

His father said something about his wife 'developing other interests'—which, Noah had learnt, was code for the marriage being over.

He felt the wind leave his chest. Wow. He really was all his father had left now.

Two bachelors and two little girls were all that remained of the Cameron clan.

He glanced over at the kitchen, where Rebecca was teaching the girls how to make a simple pasta dish. He felt himself soften as he took in the scene, barely hearing his father as he said something about being in the area—Singapore first, then somewhere else.

'So I thought I'd pop over to Bali after.'

'After what?'

'Jakarta, son. I just said.'

Skeins of guilt lanced through him. He'd just done to his father what his father had done to Noah as a boy. Pretended to listen while thinking of something else. With his father it had always been business, bank accounts, and whatever girlfriend he'd had on the go.

For Noah it was—

Hell. He let out a low whistle. He was being distracted by the simple but powerful joy of being part of something bigger than himself. A makeshift family. If that was what you could call it.

To be honest, it scared the hell out of him to put a label on it.

Ever since they'd started working their way through the girls' 'must-see' list for Rebecca, he'd felt more and more as if he, the girls and Rebecca were a unit. A foursome who worked better as a whole. No one tried to make anyone be anything they weren't. Noah wasn't their father. Rebecca wasn't their mother. And yet with the care they offered one another, and the compassion, it felt exactly like what he imagined being part of a 'real' family would.

But there was a part of him that worried he was leaning into Rebecca's ease with the children just to lighten his own load. Again, something his father had always done. Leaving 'women's work' to someone else. But this was different. Noah was the one who hated being left out. He loved being part of the foursome. The one they all picked on and teased. The one who brought a blush to Rebecca's cheeks with little more than a glance. The one who, despite it being a horrendous idea, was falling in love.

'Son?' His father's voice broke the silence.

'Yeah, sorry. You were saying?'

'I was saying I've booked a flight to Bali so I can have a talk with you.'

'Oh.' He couldn't think of anything he'd like less. His father's arrival would be like throwing a stone at the fragile new existence they'd formed. 'Right.'

'Don't worry, mate.' He could practically see his father rolling his eyes. 'I think you'll like what I'm going to propose. It should help you in your…you know…your circumstances.'

He was about to say, *No, Dad, what situation?* Just to get him to acknowledge that his granddaughters didn't have parents any more. But getting into a shouting match with his father had never solved anything.

'Fair enough. When will we see you?'

'We?' His father crowed. 'So you've found yourself a little lady to look after the girls, then? About time, son.

A nanny with benefits. I'm impressed… I wondered how you were going to sort out that little situation.'

'Situation?' He barely kept the contempt out of his voice. 'I'd hardly call it that.'

'Call it what you like, son. It wasn't what you were born to.'

Noah's eyes flicked to Rebecca and the girls. They were stirring something on the stove, giggling away about who knew what. It looked fun. He wanted to be there. Be part of the fun. But his dad's words felt like a stark reminder that, of all the people his sister could have asked to be the girls' guardian, he was the least likely candidate. He wasn't a dad. A husband. He barely knew how to refer to the girls when they were out. They weren't his daughters. They were simply a legally binding unit. One Rebecca was not a part of.

'There's no one,' he said, wanting to dead-end his father's inaccurate and antiquated views on women. 'I meant me and the girls.'

But it hurt to omit Rebecca from the equation.

He told himself the white lie was to protect her from his dad's presumptions. But the truth was he knew he was protecting his own heart. He couldn't just assume that Rebecca, who was nursing a broken heart of her own, would take him on, and the girls, not to mention a clinic that was a far cry from the children's hospital where she'd worked back in the UK. Maybe he'd move to Sydney. Maybe stay here. There were a million 'maybes' in his future, and that wasn't fair on her.

For all he knew, Rebecca was still planning on using that plane ticket of hers. He could ask her, of course. Ask her what she really wanted. But the truth was he didn't want to know. Not just yet. The part of him that was still reeling from his sister's death wanted this…whatever it was…to have a bit more time.

'Whatever you say, son. If you want to be PC about it, go for it,' his father continued. 'But you and I both know you will not be getting back on the work horse in Sydney without a woman by your side. Paid or otherwise. You're like me. Not built for it—the whole parenting lark. Heaven knows what your sister was thinking when she picked *you* as the girls' guardian.'

Bloody hell! He turned his back on the cosy scene in the kitchen and strode out deeper into the gardens.

'I don't really think you're in the best place to judge what I'm capable of, Dad.'

His father whistled. 'Ooh! So he *can* fight back.'

'Seriously? You want me to fight with you about whether or not I can look after the girls?'

'You've been faffing about there for three months, son. Reputations have been gained and lost in less time. You've got to get yourself back to Sydney. Remind people who you are. What would your mother think if you let yourself down like this? Let the Cameron name disappear without so much as a whimper?'

Noah grunted as if he'd been physically punched. His father really knew how to swing hard with the low blows.

At least Noah was here. *Trying.* Yanking the girls out of their comfort zone would be a last resort option for him. The girls were in their school, their home, in the only country they'd ever really known.

And it wasn't exactly as if his father was in any place to cast aspersions. He'd flown in to Bali, holding his Panama hat to his chest as his daughter's ashes were absorbed into the sea, then jumped on the earliest plane out, leaving Noah to deal with the aftermath of a horrific situation. One that should've cut any normal father to the bone.

'What does your boss make of this, son? This leave of absence you've taken?'

'She's not got a problem with it.'

'She?' His father hooted. 'What? Does she have you on one of those "compassionate leave" stints? Let me tell you, son…that'll come back to bite you in the ass.'

Noah tuned his father out. He'd had this lecture enough times during his childhood to be able to recite it by rote. *Win at sport. Excel at school. Never rely on anyone. Be king of whatever mountain you climb.*

It was the Aussie male form of encouragement.

Or was it time he called a spade a spade?

It was bullying disguised as parenting.

Even *thinking* it felt too close to the bone.

He took a mental swing at the thought and bashed it out of his mind.

'Right, Dad. Gotta go. Text me your flight details and I'll send a car.'

'There's a good lad.'

Noah hung up the call.

He walked back into the kitchen once he'd shaken off his rage.

Rebecca looked over. 'Everything all right?'

'Yup. My father's coming for a visit in a couple of weeks.'

'Oh!' Rebecca's face lit up. 'That's great news.'

He tried to get his expression to match hers, but knew he was failing. She was clearly waiting for an invitation to meet him, but there was no chance he was going to subject her to that man.

She gave the girls some quiet instructions and then, clearly sensing he wasn't over the moon, crossed to him, her smile tipping at the edges. 'It *is* good news, right?'

He caught the stream of insults he could have unleashed and said, 'Yeah. It'll be good for him to see the girls.'

Rebecca's smile faltered. She understood what he was saying. She wasn't invited.

He was about to explain about his dad, and how he wanted to set him straight on a few things before he met her, but Rebecca beat him to it.

'Right, then. Well… How about you come and look at what the girls have magicked up? You just need to sprinkle some of these herbs on top and you can sit down and enjoy.'

'You're not staying?'

She gave him a wide-eyed look. 'I don't think that's a good idea. Do you?'

Noah knew what she was really asking. What was he playing at? Letting her into their day-to-day lives, but not inviting her to meet his father? From her point of view it was a big slight. Family meant everything to her.

He reached out and took her hand in his. 'Please. Stay for dinner. We'd like it.'

'We?' she asked, eyebrows raised.

'Me,' he answered honestly. 'I'd like it. You already know the girls would have moved you in weeks ago if they could.'

He hoped she knew what he was really saying. That he cared for her, but he needed time.

She looked down, then up. 'I don't know, Noah. It's—'

'It's *dinner*,' he finished for her. 'Please stay. And tomorrow we'll talk. I'll explain about my dad.'

She let the comment simmer between them for a moment and then, when the girls called her to check on the dish, she gave him a conditional smile. 'I'll stay for the girls. For dinner.'

The decision was a premium display of her strength

of character. He could tell he'd hurt her, and yet she'd put those feelings to the side for the girls. And, with any luck, for him. She deserved more from him. He owed her a decision, one way or another.

He gave her hand a light caress, then lifted it to his lips, giving the back of it a soft kiss. 'Thank you.'

She stiffened, and then, to his surprise, relaxed and laughed. 'You make disliking you very difficult.'

'You want to *dislike* me?'

To be fair, he didn't blame her. Flirty one minute. Distant the next. Welcoming her into the family home and then shutting the door in her face. He wouldn't like himself very much if he were in her shoes.

'I don't want to get hurt again,' she said honestly. 'But maybe that's not how life works. Maybe it's pain that makes us stronger. Come on.' She hooked her arm and gestured for him to follow her. 'It's best when it's hot.'

After she'd turned to the girls he put his hand in his pocket, his fingers catching on the British coin that had already decided so much. In his heart he knew he was well past the point of leaving his fate up to a flip of a coin. It was time to make a decision.

CHAPTER TEN

REBECCA SHOOK HER finger at her telephone screen. 'You make sure he gets you home at a respectable hour, young lady.'

Her nan, whom she'd video called a few minutes earlier, giggled as if Rebecca had just told her not to ride home on a unicorn. 'Don't you worry about that, love. We're in our seventies—not seventeen!'

'So long as you're sensible,' Rebecca continued with mock authority. 'Otherwise I'll have to fly home and chaperone.'

'Rebecca Stone! Have I taught you nothing? I don't want you even *thinking* about leaving that lovely tropical island of yours,' her nan chided, with her own well-practised finger-wag. 'I've not seen you look this happy in actual years.'

Rebecca was about to protest, but as she caught a glimpse of Noah, moving from one patient's cubicle to another, and felt the increasingly familiar rush of tingles course through her, she knew deep down that her nan was right. She was happy.

Sure, things were weird with Noah. She didn't just fancy him. She cared for him. She was pretty sure he felt the same way, too. But if this was the universe gifting them to one another the universe's timing was awful.

She'd only come out of a wretched long-term relationship a few months ago. How on earth was she ready to fall in love again?

And as for Noah…

Falling in love whilst grieving for his sister and trying to be a parent… How would that work?

She nipped the thought in the bud. Shifting from friends to lovers was her fantasy and hers alone.

At best, this was an intense holiday friendship that she was endowing with way too much meaning. As for expecting an invitation to meet his dad…? What had she been thinking?

Hormones.

For sure.

Her tummy felt like a butterfly sanctuary whenever she was near Noah.

Nothing, however, compared to what her nan was experiencing. At long last her grandmother had met her perfect match. Nathan. Her septuagenarian stallion, she called him. And after thirty-three years of widowhood, heaven knew she deserved to meet someone.

It had been just two weeks since Nan had met Nathan. And in that short period of time, they'd gone from being 'two old codgers' who enjoyed one another's company to 'a silver fox and a vixen' who were, by their own admission, madly in love.

If she weren't so charmed by it, Rebecca thought, she might be a tiny bit envious. Things with Noah weren't nearly as straightforward.

Yes, he'd said they would talk, but that had been days ago, and each time they'd sat down something or someone had aborted it. Although their friendship had definitely built in strength, and that meant the world to her. If she really wanted to do right by him she should draw a line in the sand for him. Tell him it was friends or nothing.

If only her body wasn't head over heels in lust with him.

'Dr Stone?' The charge nurse handed Rebecca a tablet with her next patient's information up on the screen, then pointed to a cubicle.

'Oh, love!' Nanny Bea chided. 'Are you keeping patients waiting just to gossip with your lovestruck nan?'

'Not at all,' Rebecca protested. 'It's important to make sure my lovestruck nan is behaving sensibly.'

Her grandmother tsked away the notion. 'I'm perfectly fine, and if there's any time to lose my marbles for a handsome man who treats me like a queen, it's now.' She grinned mischievously. 'Take it from me, love. Losing your marbles over someone who treats you like a queen is worth it at any time in life.' She made a shooing gesture. 'Go on. Don't keep your patients waiting on my account.'

Rebecca blew her nan a kiss then ended the call, still smiling as she pulled back the curtain to see her next patient.

The second she laid eyes on the little boy in the cubicle, she knew what the problem was.

Gastroenteritis.

His lips were dry. His eyes had a sunken look. And one glance at his body language showed he was both irritable and lethargic.

'Finally!' his mother cried over Rebecca's introduction. 'We've been waiting for twenty minutes.'

Rebecca smiled apologetically, then stepped into the cubicle, pulling the curtain behind her. The clinic was obviously busy, but parents were always stressed in situations like this. Even at the best of times—at home with a familiar doctor. On holiday, she was quickly learning, that tension was doubled. They were frightened about language barriers, different treatment methods, substandard care practices—none of which they'd have to worry about here in this clinic. Or anywhere on Bali for that matter.

She and Noah had taken a child down to the main hospital the other day, for some specialised scans, and the facilities there were marvellous. What had surprised her, when he'd circled around the back of the hospital, had been the *very* fancy private wing he'd pointed out. The one where foreigners discreetly dipped in for a bit of a holiday nip and tuck holiday.

She'd heard about places like it, of course, but had never come face to face with one. From what she'd seen there were a fair few people who'd be returning home extolling the 'rejuvenating effects' of their holiday.

She sat down on her wheeled stool, and after a quick round of questions with the mum, to ascertain where they were from—Holland—where they were staying in Bali—a resort down the road—what they'd been eating and any activities they'd been up to, she turned her attention to the boy, gave him a soft smile and introduced herself.

Before he could say his name, she felt her stool begin to move across the floor. The low murmur of voices around the clinic rose in volume.

Aftershock. Must be. There had been an earthquake earlier that morning which, mercifully, hadn't taken any lives. It had left their part of the island unscathed, but she knew the main hospital an hour or so south of them couldn't take any extra patients as they were dealing with a bit of structural damage to their casualty unit.

She held out her hand to shake the little boy's. 'That was interesting, wasn't it?' She smiled.

Hmm… Her comment hadn't really registered. She

held his hand in hers. It was cool, but not cold, which was good. His skin was pale, but not mottled. Also good. She'd run a few more tests before deciding whether or not to put him on an IV drip. Sometimes a steady intake of rehydration solution did the trick.

She kept hold of his hand, wanting to check for capillary refill. 'I'm just going to give your finger a bit of a squeeze to see how fast your body responds, all right?'

He nodded, a vacant look in his eyes. Poor little chap was exhausted. She pressed until the blood left the tip of his fingers then released. A normal finger would've bounced back straight away. Johann's didn't.

Unfortunately, gastroenteritis—or, as tourists often referred to it, Bali Belly—wasn't uncommon in foreign visitors, and it looked as if this poor lad was no exception.

'Johann's been sick for four days now,' the mother said with a crisp note of displeasure. 'All those surf lessons we pre-booked—wasted.' She fixed her gaze on Rebecca. 'I tell him to wash his hands a thousand times a day, and to stay away from food he can't identify. But does he listen? No.'

Rebecca bit her tongue. This sort of comment arose with surprising frequency amongst parents who were frustrated that their children's illness had somehow ruined their holiday. Rebecca had always thought the whole point of coming to a place like this was to experience new things. Try new things.

Like falling in love with an emotionally unavailable ninja surgeon and his two little girls?

Unbidden, an image of Noah piggybacking both girls round the garden yesterday as they all played tag sprang to mind. They always had such fun together. They'd always organically find themselves gathering at the end of the day for a bit of a giggle…and then something else would always happen. A spark of connection. A moment of physical contact. Something that tugged her and Noah together then pushed them apart—as if they both knew that whatever it was they shared was short term.

She cornered the thought and stuffed it behind a mental door, then took a slow breath and made a few notes on the tablet she'd been given for the patient's records.

The mother tapped at the screen to get Rebecca's attention. 'I gave him vodka yesterday and this morning, on the recommendation of one of the other guests.'

'Sorry?' She had Rebecca's attention now. Not only was Johann seven years old—vodka was *not* a cure for gastroenteritis.

The woman explained, as if to a child, that she'd had it on *excellent* authority from another guest at their hotel that a shot of vodka every morning was the answer, and if that didn't work a beer. She was a nurse, the woman told her. Swore by it.

Rebecca tipped her head to one side and as neutrally as she could said, 'Rehydrating is very important, and whilst many adults like to think alcohol will kill any bacterial bugs they may have picked up the infection could be viral, so not "killable" as such. Also, alcohol dehydrates.' She managed to dial back a very sharp reprimand about the dangers of giving a child alcohol and closed with a simple sentence. 'As a paediatric doctor, I wouldn't recommend it—ever.'

'This vodka had electrolytes,' the woman countered vehemently, stepping towards Rebecca. She glanced at Rebecca's left hand which, of course, was ring-free. 'I know my child. Someone who doesn't have children wouldn't ever understand the risks you're prepared to take to look after them.'

Ouch. Well, that certainly stung. Less so, seeing as

she'd spent over a decade of her life training to be a paediatric surgeon, but…the woman had chosen a target and hit it.

Rebecca said nothing, which only seemed to enrage the woman more. Rebecca put her hands up between them and took a step back, just dodging the finger now poking in her face.

'I'm not a bad mother.'

This was another pronouncement Rebecca encountered a lot. Along with defensiveness. Bullying. Insistence that they were good parents. It was stress, she reminded herself.

She's belittling you to make herself feel big because she's frightened.

'The vodka I gave him,' the mother continued, 'was *electrolyte* enhanced. Same stuff as all those fancy drinks down at the pharmacy, and we didn't even need to leave the hotel.'

Rebecca looked the woman straight in the eye. 'Two million children a year die from gastroenteritis. It was a wise decision to bring your son here.'

The mum all but choked on her rage. She knew Rebecca wasn't giving her a compliment.

Rebecca regretted having spoken so sharply, but seriously… Vodka? Here in Bali, an island geared towards tourism, it was simple to get a doctor to come to a hotel. It was a service they offered themselves at the clinic. Not to mention the fact that any member of hotel staff would happily go to the pharmacy for you. Why choose electrolyte-enhanced vodka designed for party hounds to 'cure' your seven-year-old child?

She returned to her examination of the boy, reminding herself that she didn't know the whole picture. Perhaps this lady was a single mum, on holiday for the first time and feeling out of her element. Perhaps she'd saved for years for this break and now that she was here, all her efforts felt ruined. At least she'd come to the clinic…

As she took Johann's temperature and pulse, a commotion sounded down at the intake area. Noah was paged on the Tannoy. She heard footsteps running past.

His?

Focus!

'Have you been able to keep anything down, Johann? Any fluids?'

'It all comes right back up,' the mother answered for him. 'Or out, if you know what I mean.'

Rebecca gave her a polite nod. 'Any blood in the stools?'

The mother recoiled. 'I didn't look at it!'

Rebecca pulled her stethoscope from around her neck and gave Johann a smile. 'I'm going to have a listen to your tummy, all right?'

The boy let out a sigh and flopped back onto the immaculate white pillow. He was knackered, poor thing.

Just as she popped the earpieces in, Noah stuck his head into the curtained area.

Her heart-rate quickened. No matter how frequently she saw him, each appearance elicited a new, fresh burst of attraction. As if someone had opened a cold bottle of fizzy drink inside her chest.

'Sorry to interrupt,' Noah said. 'But I'm going to need an extra pair of hands in the OR as soon as you're able. Up for it?'

Her pulse leapt, then hit that old familiar rhythm it used to have when she'd worked as a surgeon. A rhythm that slowed down time so that she could see, frame by frame, every move she had to make before she did it, ensuring the child brought into her care survived.

'Absolutely.'

She was about to ask what had happened when the irritable mother cut in, 'What about Johann?'

Despite a niggle that something seriously wrong must have happened—a worse aftershock somewhere else on the island, an incoming tsunami—she kept her voice calm.

'We're going to set Johann up on an IV drip. Get him rehydrated.' Rebecca informed her in her 'non-negotiable' voice. 'We'll also take stool and urine samples and give him an antiemetic. It'll help settle his stomach enough to curb the vomiting.' Before the mum could interject again, Rebecca waved a colleague over. 'One of our nurses will sit here with you—this is Nurse Kartika.' To Johann she added, 'Her name means shining star and she has the personality to match.'

She quickly explained the situation to Kartika, then shared a complicit look with the nurse. International medical personnel silent speak for *Tread carefully. This one's a live wire.*

'She'll make sure a doctor checks over the results before he is released.'

There was shouting, and then the sound of a woman keening from towards the entrance to the clinic.

'And how long will all that take?' Johann's mother cried.

'An hour. Maybe two. It depends upon how your son's health is after treatment.' She fixed the mum with her steeliest gaze. 'That *is* why you brought him here? To make sure your son's condition doesn't worsen?'

The woman stared at her for a moment and then, completely unexpectedly, burst into tears. 'I'm sorry. I know I'm being horrid. It's just—' She lowered her voice and nodded at Johann. 'His new stepfather... This is supposed to be our honeymoon.' She flashed a very shiny diamond ring, then covered it as if she was ashamed to be wearing it. 'His new dad isn't the hugest fan of children, but he made an exception for Johann because he's usually such a good boy. Doesn't need to be shouted at. Do you Jo-Jo?'

She walked over to her son and gently stroked his blond fringe away from his forehead before planting a soft kiss on his cheek. She looked back up at Rebecca.

'I just— I'd made plans, you know? Jo-Jo was supposed to be being looked after by his father while we were on this trip, but of course he flaked. I'd made sure every single detail of this trip was going to be perfect, so Karl—that's my new husband—wouldn't have any reason to think he'd made a mistake in marrying me, and—'

'Am I the reason he made the mistake, Mummy?' Johann asked.

'No, darling. No, no, no.' The tears flowed even more freely now as she pulled her son into her arms and held him close.

Rebecca's heart squeezed tight. The poor woman. And poor Johann. It didn't sound like a dream arrangement for any of them.

It wasn't as if Rebecca was in a place to give marital advice, but something told her she should take this as a sign that the collapse of her own relationship had actually been a blessing.

Something deep inside her shifted.

It was time to step away from the self-pity she'd been feeling about her broken engagement and start proactively walking towards her future.

One that involved Noah?

Another round of shouting and crying erupted at the far end of the clinic.

'I'm really sorry. I'm going to have to dash. But you're in good hands with Nurse Kartika.'

She took off at a jog towards the operating theatres.

Noah intercepted her just as she was about to enter the scrub room. 'Family of six riding a scooter involved in a car crash.'

She winced. She'd seen drivers precariously balance entire extended families on small motorcycles meant for one, maybe two people max. This wasn't going to be pretty. 'Was it the aftershock?'

He shook his head, confused. 'What aftershock?'

She was about to explain, then realised whatever had been going on for him had trumped her feeling a bit of a wobble. 'I presume you need me to scrub in?'

'Yes. A four-by-four didn't stop at a junction—smashed right into them.' He pushed the door to the scrub room open, and she saw a specialist nurse already preparing two sets of surgical gowns. 'They're doing CT scans now. Murray and Irawan are in the trauma units with two of them.'

She nodded. It was a fortunate time to have the extra volunteer surgeons on staff.

'Grandmother, dad, mother and three children aged four, two and an infant—all piled on, along with the family's shopping. No helmets.'

She sucked in a sharp breath as she ran a line of surgical solution along her nails. Noah's eyes snapped to hers. He would know she wasn't feeling the sting of the medicated soap. It was the knowledge of what was to come. Children rarely wore bike helmets here. Adults did—but not always. Her heart was crumpling in on itself over that family, but she couldn't afford to let herself become emotional. Not with lives at stake.

'Grandmother is getting CPR. Dad has at least two compound fractures in his leg—took the brunt of the collision. Mum has a broken arm and suspected internal bleeding. I'll be seeing the two of them. The baby and the four and two-year-olds are getting scans, but you'll need to—'

'Wait. They're *all* here?' She knew they didn't have the resources to operate on everyone.

Noah's expression was grim. 'Also the driver of the car. After the earthquake the trauma centre at the main hospital has had to send everyone to other clinics and smaller hospitals. We're all that's left. And we were the closest. For whatever reason, today seems to be accident day. Lots of idiot drivers out on the road.'

His eyes darkened to a fathomless black. It was impossible to read if he was feeling rage or grief.

She wouldn't blame him for either, but knew there was no way he should go into surgery with either mindset. Sure, he'd lost his family to an idiot driver—but, as she'd just been reminded, it was best not to judge before you knew the whole story. Heck. If Noah had met her three months ago he would've thought she was a pathetic sloth who never left her bed.

'You can't enjoy the ups if you don't have the downs!'

Her grandmother's voice sing-songed through her head.

Nanny Bea's wisdom was usually pretty spot-on and today was no different.

'The driver?' she asked, wincing in advance of the answer.

'He had a stroke. Lost control. I've got Rahman and Nikolaides working on him.'

Ah. There you go. Not all drivers were idiots.

And if there was ever a good time for someone to

have a stroke, now was it. Those two specialists had volunteered a few months back. Rahman was a vascular specialist and Nikolaides a neurosurgeon. They'd met at Cambridge years ago, and always promised each other they'd learn how to surf by the time they turned fifty. Last year they'd each celebrated their forty-ninth birthdays.

'Okay. Got it.' She turned off the tap with her elbow, hands raised as she prepared to glove up. 'I presume you have a masterplan?'

'All hands on deck. I'll see Dad and Mum in the next room. You'll see to the children in here.'

'All three?' Her eyes went wide.

'Unless you can magic some other surgeons out of the ether. We'll all pop in as and when we can.'

His tone was brusque, but the look in his eyes said something else altogether. It said he trusted her. He believed in her.

He stepped in close and leant in, his cheek brushing against hers as he whispered in her ear. 'I'll be right next door.'

It was all the pep talk she needed.

Rebecca had survived busy days at work before. Eighteen-hour shifts at the hospital with only a few hours of snatched sleep. Twenty-four-hour days. Even less sleep. Junk food to fuel it all. A thousand broken dates with friends and would-be suitors. Little wonder she'd ended up with a doctor whose own schedule was just as busy.

The all-consuming demands of the job was one of the reasons she'd decided to step away from surgical work and into family practice, but from the moment she stepped into the clinic's operating theatre she felt a life-force surge through her that she hadn't experienced in years.

All three children had sustained severe road rash and other traumatic injuries.

The infant was the least harmed, though still badly hurt, despite having been cushioned in her mother's arms as the car crashed into them. Fractures to her tiny left arm. Possible whiplash. Cerebral bruising, but nothing to indicate an internal bleed. *Yet.* She'd need more scans, and an urgent consult from Nikolaides. Most pressingly, the tiny little girl had broken three ribs, one of which had caused a lung puncture.

As she called out preparatory instructions for the other two children, Rebecca swiftly inserted a needle into the infant's pleural space to release the trapped air, then instructed a junior doctor visiting from Singapore to stay with her until the lung had been reinflated. When it was safe, she'd repair the injury to the lung tissue via the bronchial airways.

Much more seriously, the two-year-old and four-year-old boys had both sustained traumatic brain injuries. The eldest had a frightening skull fracture and the two-year-old had a depressed skull bone fracture. He'd also sustained a potentially lethal puncture wound. In his heart.

As she stepped towards the two-year-old's table an alarm sounded at the baby's table. Alarms had been sounding from the four-year-old's table from the moment he'd arrived.

She couldn't be in three places at once—but nor could she give up on any of these tiny lives. Panic began to rise from her gut to her chest. These children would need surgeries she hadn't performed in years. Could she remember the detailed procedures? Noah obviously believed in her, trusted her. And from a man like him, she had to believe it was trust well-placed.

She closed her eyes and allowed herself to count to

one. These children didn't have time for her to make it all the way to ten. And then she got to work.

An hour later Noah pushed through the operating theatre door, holding a mask over his face.

Instead of saying what her heart was screaming—*It's so good to see you*—she said 'Aren't you meant to be operating?'

'Done the initial exams. They're both with the anaesthetist now. I'm just checking in.'

He might as well have told her he loved her for the comfort it gave her.

Was that what she wanted? For Noah to fall in love with her?

'Dr Stone?' her nurse prompted, handing her the scalpel.

'Yes. Sorry.' She began opening up the abdominal wall of the two-year-old, whose swollen tummy indicated... yup...massive internal bleeding.

'You okay?' Noah asked as multiple alarms began to sound.

'I will be when I can stem the flow...' She grabbed a few pads to soak up the excess blood, then snapped a small clamp into place. 'There!' She waited a moment, to ensure the clamp wouldn't put too much pressure on the other blood vessels around it. It stayed fixed. The big problem was going to be the piece of bamboo still in the little boy's heart. Ironically, or perhaps cruelly, it was probably the one thing keeping him alive.

She raised her eyebrows to him. 'I'm going to need Nikolaides in here. Is that possible?'

He nodded. 'Absolutely. Stroke victim wasn't as bad as he could've been. I'll send him in now. Will you need me?'

Alarms sounded at one of her other tables.

'We're losing him!'

She whipped around and saw the four-year-old's tiny body was seizing.

'Yes,' she said, almost to herself.

She'd need him. But not now. After.

This was one of those moments where her skill as a surgeon was all that stood between life and death for a child. And no matter how confident she was in her skills she already knew in her bones that not all of these children were going to make it out of here alive.

CHAPTER ELEVEN

'CLAMP.'

Noah's eyes were glued to the screen that was showing each of Rebecca's precise movements. She was clearly a surgeon at the top of her game, and he was impressed. His operations were finished, and he'd come in to assist her, but she didn't need his help. It was almost impossible to believe she hadn't done this type of surgery in over five years.

'You sure you haven't done this recently?' he asked.

'Like riding a bicycle,' she said grimly.

He didn't begrudge her the tone. She'd just called time of death on the four-year-old, whose internal injuries had proved too devastating to fix. Without being able to obtain the permission of his parents—both barely out of surgery themselves and still under anaesthetic—she had made the executive decision to use the boy's heart to replace the devastated remains of his little brother's.

It was the kind of decision he'd heard a handful of his army buddies talking about. Operating on one fallen comrade only to use their organs for someone else as a matter of urgency. War, natural disasters, car accidents—nothing about them was fair. And today was no different. But it felt different. And the reason was standing in front of him, lifting a small, perfect heart out of a chest that would never take a breath of life again.

'Scalpel.'

Rebecca had command of the operating theatre in a way he'd never borne witness to before. And he was pretty used to giving command performances himself. Not that that was the aim.

He could tell she wasn't doing this for the glory. And definitely not the pay cheque. There wasn't one.

No. Her entire aura was infused with respect for the life she'd just lost and the one she was hoping to save.

Her movements were gentle, deliberate. As if the boy was aware of them—which, of course, he couldn't possibly be. But Noah got it. She was honouring the four-year-old boy who would never laugh again, never cry, never be cuddled in his parents' arms again. She was honouring the reality that his loss of life meant he would be able to give the gift of it to his brother.

As he watched Rebecca he imagined his nieces reaching up to him, their small hands seeking comfort in his larger ones. His fingers balled into protective fists and then opened, feeling the gaping emptiness left behind.

The sensation all but cracked him in half. Enough to open up his brain and, more importantly, his heart to the message he clearly needed to receive: Life was too damn short to put living on hold. If he felt something for someone he was going to show it from now on. And by 'someone' he meant Rebecca.

After she'd placed the heart in a surgical bowl filled with ice, their eyes met. That increasingly familiar flare of heat he felt whenever they looked at one another all but scorched his own living, beating heart.

He kept his stance solid. His gaze unblinking. He wasn't going to shy away from the attraction they shared any more. Life was too precious. Too large a gift to fritter away on anything that didn't make him a better man.

'Right.' Rebecca was standing across from Noah at the two-year-old's table now. 'Let's give this heart a new home.'

Her eyes met his, and after a short nod of confirmation that they were both ready they began to prepare the area around the two-year-old's perforated heart, so that cardio-pulmonary bypass could be initiated.

Once the cannulas and clamps were in place they removed the old heart, devastated by the clump of bamboo skewers he'd landed on when he'd been thrown from the Moto. The skewers had effectively become miniature spears, shredding the tiny heart beyond repair.

His brother's healthy heart was brought into place. The atmosphere in the room grew taut. If this failed, that would be two lives lost today.

Sensing the shift in mood, Rebecca brightened her voice and said, 'Let's see if my grandmother's attempts to teach me how to sew are up to the task.'

There was a murmur of laughter—the best sign of support from her team. They'd been watching her these last few hours and knew for a fact that her suturing was up to it.

Noah knew it was ridiculous, but he felt proud by proxy. The way a boyfriend might of his girlfriend. A husband of his wife.

He instantly took the thought and tried file it where he usually did—in the Do Not Revisit cupboard. But watching her replace a savaged heart with the new one made it impossible.

'I'll start with the left atrium…' She deftly stitched the four heart chambers into place, following suit with the ascending aorta. She removed the aortic cross clamp, and they all held their breath until…

Beep. Beep. Beep.

The soft crinkles around her eyes indicated that she was smiling. A chorus of cheers and sighs of relief filled the air. Losing one life had been devastating. Losing both would have been an unimaginable blow.

'Bravo, Dr Stone,' he said.

She blinked and drew in a sharp breath, as if she was about to admit something—something from the heart—but then said, 'Thank you for your help.'

Together they sutured the pulmonary artery, and the inferior and superior vena cavas to their corresponding valves. The heart was weaned from cardio pulmonary bypass. Using the echocardiogram, they ensured all the valves were functioning well, and that both of the ventricles were performing.

When she stepped back from the table after putting the final stitch in the boy's chest she said, 'Now comes the hard part.'

Freshly showered, Noah couldn't say he felt like a new man, but he knew they'd met the challenges of the day head-on and had done the best they could with a fraction of the staff a hospital would have had. And the worst part was over: telling the boys' parents.

He'd stood alongside Rebecca as she, at her own insistence, had informed the children's parents that two of their three children were in the ICU but that they'd been unable to save their eldest son. When they'd left the room she'd disappeared into the women's changing room before he could offer her a hug or a word of condolence.

He got it. Sometimes you needed to process things alone. But there were other times, like now, when you needed to know there was someone in your life who understood what you were going through.

Which was why he was waiting out here in the corridor.

When Rebecca eventually came out of the women's changing room her eyes snapped to his. She was clearly surprised to see him. She scanned him as if checking for damage, her eyes doing a double-take as they reached his shoulders.

'Your hair—' she said.

He gave his scalp a rough rub, and then, pre-programmed by his father's disapproving glares, made light of it. 'I know. Needs a cut.'

Rebecca frowned at him, confused by the comment. 'Why?'

'Not exactly surgery-friendly.'

'Plenty of surgeons have long hair.' She pointed at her own.

He shrugged, then pulled a swathe of it into his fist and feigned hacking it off with two of his fingers, more angry with himself for succumbing to his father's archaic stance than anything.

'Don't cut it,' she said. Her voice was lower than normal. As if the words had rasped up her throat against her will.

And just like that an image of a towel-clad Rebecca crashed into his head. She was playing with his hair. Combing her fingers through it, her face close to his as he gently tipped her chin up to see if a kiss would taste as good as he imagined it.

He shifted from one hip to the other. 'It's just about the same length as yours, I think.'

Seriously? That was all he had?

This new life plan of his to seize the day wasn't exactly turning him into a sparkling conversationalist.

She stared at him, then tugged her damp ponytail over her shoulder, studying it as if she'd never seen it before. 'I grew mine when I stopped doing surgery.'

Her voice carried a note of something he couldn't put his finger on. It wasn't regret, exactly…

Her eyes flicked back to his. 'I always wish I'd been braver.'

'Yeah. Me, too.'

He was pretty sure neither of them were talking about hair any more.

The air crackled between them—invisible bursts of electricity sweeping through parts of his body that would make wearing scrubs very awkward in about thirty seconds.

He wanted her. Now. And if he was reading the energy right she wanted him, too.

Making love to Rebecca Stone wasn't the sensible thing to do. But he'd done enough pragmatic thinking to last him a lifetime.

His toes practically curled with horror at his own ineptness as he heard himself say, 'The girls are asleep now. Would you like to come to mine for a cup of tea?'

What the hell? Since when had he turned into an idiot nineteen-year-old?

Rebecca looked at him askance, as if weighing up her options. 'Do you want tea?' she asked simply. 'Or me?'

And just like that all the blood in his brain crashed below his waistline.

The space between them evaporated, and before one more rational thought could enter his head they were kissing as if their lives depended upon it. Hungry, intense, exploratory kisses that doubled the shared energy surging between them.

Holding Rebecca in his arms felt like coming home. A feeling he'd never had with another woman. How could they know so little about one another's history and yet know in their guts that what they were doing was right? That moving their relationship to a physical level was a risk worth taking?

They knew enough, he told himself. *They knew what was important.*

He grabbed her hand and pulled her into a nearby examination room. 'Okay if I lock the door?'

She gave him a look that said, *It'd be foolish not to*, then reached across him to lock it herself. As she drew back her sweet scent filled his senses with burnt sugar and frangipani.

'Now, then…' She smiled. 'Where were we?'

He completely lost himself in her touch. Her caresses. The way she kissed. Soft and then urgent. Insatiable then teasing. It was like playing Russian roulette with his sanity. He'd never lost control with or for a woman before, but something about Rebecca made him believe he could trust her with everything. His body. His intellect. His heart.

But was the trust strong enough to risk his fragile new beginning with the girls?

As if she'd heard his thoughts she pulled away and pressed one of her hands against his chest, her fingers shifting softly against the fabric of his clean scrubs until she'd found what she'd been seeking. The racing beat of his heart.

'Do you want to go to them?' she asked, tipping her head in the direction of his villa.

He shook his head, then stopped to explain. 'I asked

the sitter to stay with them overnight when I didn't know how long we'd be in the OR.'

She nodded, absorbing what the subtext of that was. *I'm free to be with you if that's what you want.*

They looked into one another's eyes, seeking answers, until he couldn't stand the distance between them any more. He dipped his head down and kissed her again.

'You taste as good as I imagined,' he whispered against her lips.

'You've imagined kissing me?' She nipped at his lower lip with her teeth, clearly emboldened by the admission.

'Don't sound so surprised.' He returned the gesture, pleased when it drew a mew of pleasure from her. He pulled back and gently shifted a few stray strands of hair off her cheek. 'Look at you… You've got to know you're sexy.'

Her bottom lip grated against her top teeth as her gaze dropped away from his.

Hell. Maybe she didn't. Well, that wouldn't do, would it? He tasked himself with showing her precisely how sexy she was.

He cupped her shoulders in his hands and waited until she met his eyes. 'I've wanted you from the moment I laid eyes on you, Dr Rebecca Stone.'

Her cheeks pinkened. 'I thought I was the only one carrying a flame.'

'No, you didn't,' Noah gently chastised.

She hadn't been the only one sending heated looks and she knew it. He'd also blatantly lied about that last coin toss. The one that had convinced her to stay. And he was pretty sure she knew it.

'There's been a fair amount of flirtation between the two of us over the past couple of weeks. And, though I know I've been wrestling with a lot of other issues, the attraction hasn't been one-way.'

Her expression was still shrouded in disbelief. 'There's simply no way someone like you could fancy me as much as I fancy them.'

'What do you mean. "someone like me"? A cantankerous ostrich who's floundering in a world he never thought he'd find himself in?'

'See!' she said, as if the fact he'd admitted he was floundering meant she'd been right to put herself down.

'See, what?'

'You're not yourself. You don't know what you're doing. You don't even want your father to meet me.'

He winced. Definitely not one of his finer moments. 'Meet him. He's a Class-A jackass, so maybe it'll be useful for you in figuring out why I am the way I am.'

'Hmm, no. I feel like I just begged for it.'

'The only thing I want you begging for is more of this.'

He tugged her back to him and gave her a kiss that defied the constraints of time.

When they came up for air he said, 'How was that for proof I'm interested?'

'Pretty good.' She scrunched up her nose and grinned up at him. 'I might need a bit more convincing, though.'

He laughed. 'Convincing of what? That I find you completely irresistible?' He gave a low growl, hoping she would translate that into a display of his desire.

'Ooh. Nice start.'

'But…?'

'But you're just…' She patted his chest, then squeezed his biceps and shoulders with a dreamy sigh. 'You're so perfect.'

'And so are you.'

She snorted and gave a little eye-roll.

'Hey. Enough of that.'

He didn't know if it was her ex who'd made her think so poorly of herself, or life in general, but whoever it was had a lot to answer for. He ran his thumb along her lips, pleased when she didn't miss the opportunity to give it a saucy little bite. She was frightened of rejection. He got that. He was terrified of commitment. But wanting her to feel good about herself overrode whatever it was happening between the two of them in the here and now.

'Listen to me.' He swept his hand across her hairline, tracing his fingers along her cheek. 'You're a talented, intelligent, funny, beautiful woman. You do a mean oven glove sock puppet and you seriously rocked in the operating theatre today.' He held up a hand. 'Life isn't perfect. Nor am I. But so far as I can see, your only flaw is your insecurity.'

She pointed at her bare ring finger. 'He didn't exactly leave me feeling good about myself.'

'Well…' Noah looked her straight in the eye. 'He doesn't count any more, does he?'

She gave her head a slow shake.

Noah dropped a few light kisses on her lips, her nose, her brow. 'My darling woman. I don't know if it's a safety blanket you've put on after everything you've been through, but you don't need it. You're amazing. And today you excelled yourself. I was in awe. If anyone has made you think you are anything less than one of the wonders of the world, I'll be more than happy to set them straight.'

He did a couple of silly martial arts moves, gratified to see a smile tease at the corners of her lips.

'Besides,' he added. 'If you think I'm so perfect, why would I lower my perfection standards to slum it?'

'Convenience?'

She was grinning. He ran his hands along her sides and drew her to him for another delicious kiss. 'That wasn't convenience,' he growled. 'That was perfection.'

Her smile shifted into something more sober. 'I guess I told myself that was what I had to believe. That you didn't fancy me. It made the possibility that nothing would happen easier to bear.'

He shook his head confused. 'You're exquisite. Why wouldn't I want you?'

'Uh, apart from the fact I'm not exactly a swimsuit model?' She pressed a finger to his lips to stop his interruption. 'I could hardly pounce on a man grieving for his sister and wrestling with his new identity as guardian to the world's cutest little girls, could I?'

'Oh, I don't know…' he began jokingly, and then, wanting to honour the honesty she'd offered him, he told her the truth. 'If you've sensed anything from me, it was only about *me*. I was scared. I *am* scared. This—' he moved his hand between the two of them '—whatever this is… It feels bigger than anything I've ever known, and I guess I thought ignoring it might be better than screwing it up.'

'That makes two of us.'

He could see she wasn't saying it just to make him feel better. She was saying it because she meant it.

'What scares you the most?' he asked.

'That I'll lose myself in you.'

'Is that what happened in your last relationship?'

She nodded. 'I changed my life in a big way to make that relationship happen, and the idea of having to start all over again if this goes wrong—'

'We don't even know what "this" is yet.'

It wasn't exactly a romantic sentiment, but it needed to be said. She took a moment to let the thought settle and then flashed him a smile. 'There's no harm in finding out, right?'

He laughed and ran his thumbs along her jawline, pulling her in for a soft kiss. Then another. And another until he couldn't bear it any more. He wanted more of her. He wanted skin on skin. Breath tangling with sighs. The hot, fluid union of his body melding with hers. And by the way she was responding to his touch, she wanted the same thing.

Low moans of approbation reverberated against her throat as he tasted and explored her. He dropped kisses on her jawline, her neck, her throat. His hands enjoyed the purchase they had on those sweet curves between her waist and hips. Anyone who'd made her feel anything other than proud of this body deserved a very stern talking-to.

Her groans became his as she pressed her hips to his, their kisses deepening as she ran her hands over his shoulders and slid them up and around his neck.

'It is so nice to kiss a man who makes me have to go on tiptoe,' she whispered.

'Is that what I've got going for me?' He pulled her in close. 'My height?'

She tipped her head to the side, as if considering the question, and smiled, her lips brushing against his mouth as she said, 'You might have one or two other assets I wouldn't mind having access to.'

The words dropped a firebomb directly into his erogenous zones. His erection pulsed with desire. The naughty smile on her lips showed she'd felt it and liked knowing she was the reason he was hard.

Where the hell had this version of Rebecca risen from? Talk about phoenix from the ashes.

'Want to get out of here?' he asked.

'No,' she said. 'I just want you.'

CHAPTER TWELVE

Rebecca traced her fingers round the neckline of Noah's scrubs feeling like an emboldened goddess. Aphrodite? Maybe. Whichever one was filled to the brim with pent-up lust.

As she tugged him in for the most scorching kiss she'd ever stolen from a man she curled her fingers tight around the vee of the cotton fabric—then ripped it.

To their mutual astonishment the fabric tore right in half—just as she'd hoped. A minor miracle if ever there was one. Not as miraculous as being locked in an examination room snogging the man of her dreams, but… *mmm*…her brain turned to mush as he tugged her in for another kiss.

When he pulled back, she hovered her hands over his golden skin. 'Can I?' she asked.

'I'd be very upset if you didn't.' He swallowed, his Adam's apple all but spelling out the question he wasn't asking: Who the hell had stolen Rebecca and replaced her with this sex kitten?

It was a good question. One she didn't have the answer to. And frankly she didn't much care. She liked this version of herself. She was sassy.

She scraped her nails across the span of Noah's shoulders, shifting the rest of the thick cotton out of the way. 'We won't be needing that,' she said as it slid to the ground.

Noah murmured something she didn't quite catch, but she caught the gist of it. *Please don't stop.*

So she carried on.

She shamelessly admired his bare chest and then, pushing him back across the room so that he was forced to hoist himself up onto the counter, she grinned. 'There...' She ran the tip of one of her nails around the dark areola of his nipple, instantly making it go hard. 'Just the perfect height to do this.' She swept her tongue round the same nipple, skidding her fingers over the other one until it, too, went hard.

'Who even *are* you?' he breathed through a moan as she pressed her hand onto his erection.

'I'm your gift from the universe.' She smiled, then ran her fingertips along his six-pack, thrilling in the response of his musculature as she touched him.

Rebecca felt, for the very first time, as if her body, mind and spirit were at one with themselves. But she realised with startling clarity that she wasn't different. She was finally herself. And she liked who she was. This version of her would never undress in the dark and run to hide under the covers so her lover wouldn't see her body, as she had with her ex. This one would wear high heels when she wanted. This one would never turn crimson in shame because of her Rubenesque curves. This one enjoyed being in Noah's arms. She felt sensual and desired. Powerful. It was a delicious elixir like the fabled milk and honey...and she was ready to drink from its cup.

She pinched the fabric waist tie of Noah's scrubs between two of her fingers and tugged as she met his eyes. 'I don't think we'll be needing these either.'

Noah's eyes blinked wide. A flicker of fear ran

through her that she'd taken this whole emboldened-like-a-goddess thing a step too far, but... *Hmm*. What was that pressing against her thigh? She smiled as he pulled her in closer. If the strength of his erection was anything to go by, he liked it.

'Let's even the playing field, shall we?'

He teased his fingers beneath the hem of her scrubs top. She hadn't bothered putting on a bra, and just the idea of his fingers reaching her breasts sent a surge of heat through her.

Noah took his time, shifting the cotton away with the backs of his hands as his fingertips whispered along her skin with tantalising slowness. He teased goosebumps out of the delicate indentations at her waist...the soft skin along her sides. She arched towards him as his fingers neared her breasts. As if sensing she wanted nothing more than to feel his skin against hers, he whipped her top up and over her head, slipped off the countertop, pulled her to him.

The effect on her body was instantaneous. As if her bones had turned to rubber and heated fistfuls of glitter had been released into her nervous system. He slid his hands to her bum, and before she could figure out what he was doing he'd lifted her up and round and placed her on the counter, where he'd just been.

A richly satisfied look flickered through his eyes as he repeated her phrase. 'Ah...just the perfect height to do this.'

He cupped one of her breasts with his hand and, while lightly stroking the other with the backs of his fingers, began to lazily twirl his tongue round her nipple. Again, she arched towards him, enjoying the pleasure he was openly taking in increasing her desire. She'd not experienced this before. An equality of passion. Desire to please. Two equals with one mutual interest at heart. To bring the other person joy.

Beneath Noah's caresses, his tongue, his mouth, her breasts felt plump and full. Not that they'd ever been tiny, but she felt no shame in the luxurious opulence of them now. His physique was such that she felt feminine in his arms. Delicate from the way he touched her. And positively primal when he slid her scrubs bottoms off her legs and ran his hands up along between her thighs until he reached the triangle between her legs, slipping first one, then two fingers into her to dizzying effect.

Not having a shirt to grab hold of any more, she ran her fingers through his soft black hair, curling them into small fistfuls of the silky ebony depths. When his touch threatened to overwhelm her, she tugged him away from her, her voice shaking as she said, 'I want you. Now.'

He didn't need any more encouragement. What followed was fast and delicious. Two voracious appetites sating themselves…pleasuring each other's body.

Mercifully, they'd tumbled into a room that had an ample supply of protection. She would've taken her time sheathing him, but the pulsing between her legs demanded urgent action.

He turned her so that her back was to him. The warmth from his chest radiated through her. Her breath hitched as his erection teased apart her legs. Her core turned molten as, once again, his fingers slipped through her soft curls to her clitoris. Her heart lurched around her ribcage… her body was physically aching with unfulfilled desire until she all but begged him to enter her.

Though she hadn't ever had sex this way before—her ex had been quite a traditionalist when it came to those things: bed, covers, one of two positions and this wasn't one of them—she already knew she liked it.

Noah spread his hands along the sides of her waist and, after a few gentle, teasing entrances, slid his full length into her. His hands swept up her sides and cupped her breasts as she pushed back into him, wriggling her bum until the very tip of his erection hit the magic spot that lit her up like the Eiffel Tower. They groaned in tandem, and then an organic rhythm took hold of them as they began to move.

They were beyond language now. Beyond instructions. Instinct took over in a way she'd never imagined possible. This was the type of magic she'd expect between two seasoned lovers. Not lust-filled, half-exhausted, adrenaline-fuelled surgeons so far out of their depth neither of them could see beyond today, let along the next month or year.

And yet…none of it mattered. Not the fear, the fatigue, the future. Because for the first time in her life she was living in the moment. Not for a spreadsheet, not for a deadline. She was living for the here and now with Noah. For his touch. His deep thrust and his rich groans of desire. Noah *knew* her. Her body. Her rhythms. The perfect place to hold her hips as he increased the shared rhythm building between their bodies.

All at once she felt a sea change in their movements. As if they had literally become one. Noah's intense, organic thrusts came more intuitively, matching the undulations of her hips. Intellectually, she knew they were both moving faster, more urgently, but something in her brain was processing the pulsing of their bodies as a sybaritic decadence. As if each thrust was unveiling another pleasure zone deep within her. Until wave after wave of heat swept through her and Noah clasped her to him, his hips trying and failing to contain the fundamental thrusts his body was succumbing to as they reached their climaxes in tandem.

As the waves of pleasure eased, leaving her body humming with pleasure, Rebecca felt an extraordinary combination of drained and elated. As if she were literally floating on air. Noah turned her round, his body warm with exertion, and pulled her to him. He dropped a light kiss on her lips, then rested his chin on her head as they wrapped their arms around one another and allowed their breathing to settle.

After a few moments of silence, Rebecca pulled back and smiled up at him. 'Did you want to get back to the girls?'

He tugged his discarded scrubs from the floor and pulled his mobile phone out of the pocket and checked for messages.

'Looks like they went to sleep after a double dose of story time.'

He scanned her, as if reliving the sex they'd just shared. If she'd thought she might be able to head off to sleep, she'd been wrong.

'Fancy a midnight snack?'

'Absolutely.' She gave him a cheeky grin. 'How about we have it at my villa, just in case we make any noise?'

He play-growled his approval and pulled her in for another groan-inducing kiss. Which, of course, made them laugh. It felt so good to do this. To laugh. To feel as if she belonged in someone's arms.

They both pulled on their scrubs and gave the room a quick tidy, dissolving into giggles when they examined the ripped remains of Noah's top.

'I think I'm going to have to make a donation to the clinic for destroying clinic property.' Rebecca laughed.

Noah held up the remains of his top and then gave her a look that suggested he hoped this wouldn't be the first and only time she ripped his clothes off. 'What do you say we open a tab?'

* * *

The second time they made love, it was as gentle as the breeze undulating the mosquito netting around Rebecca's four-poster bed. They had all the shuttered windows wide open to the night sky. Their movements fell naturally in sync with the sound of the distant waves, lulling them into a beautiful organic place where their bodies might as well have been filled with phosphorescence.

Getting to touch and kiss Noah's body in this way felt luxurious. Even more so to have him explore her body in the same way. While there was no chance she would've traded in that frantic, voracious lovemaking back at the clinic, this felt less like getting access to an entire chocolate cake for one minute and more like being offered an all-day brunch with an open champagne bar.

It felt new to indulge in touching and being touched—to put life and all its craziness on hold while they explored one another's bodies as if they had all the time in the world. No. It didn't just feel good. It felt right.

When they'd reached an all-consuming climax, luxuriating in the waves of pleasure they'd unleashed in the other's body, they fell asleep in one another's arms, spent from a day that had seen them at both extremes.

Rebecca felt the sun on her face before she opened her eyes. She yawned and stretched like a cat, her eyes popping wide open when she realised Noah had gone.

Her blood ran cold.

It was the one thought she hadn't allowed herself. The one fear.

That Noah would regret what had happened between them.

She was about to go into a tailspin of panic—and then her eyes lit on the clock.

Gah!

Lovers' remorse was one thing, but being late for work when the man she'd bared her soul to was her boss was an entirely different affair.

She flew into the shower and tugged on a pair of scrubs.

She was stuffing her hair into a topknot as she came down the stairs from her bedroom, wishing she had time to run across the street for one of the fruit drinks she'd become addicted to—and, of course, a coffee—when she saw a steaming cup of takeaway coffee sitting next to a smoothie on the kitchen counter, along with a note.

She picked it up, hands shaking with nerves. Before she'd read anything more than her name, she closed her eyes against the neat script.

Please, please, please don't let it be a goodbye.

Having wild, spontaneous sex, then making slow, mesmeric love was so far outside her experience she barely recognised the body she was walking around in, let alone the woman who'd ravished Noah last night. She had investigated his body as if he was a sexy crime scene. Explored each millimetre of his body. The tattoos, the curves, the taut musculature…

But it wasn't just his body she'd fallen head over heels for—because that was what she'd done. It wasn't a crush. It wasn't lust. It wasn't a holiday romance. She'd taken a step off a cliff she'd never thought she'd step off again and done the unimaginable. She'd fallen in love with Noah Cameron, knowing his was a heart she'd never be able to call her own.

She forced herself to open her eyes, steeling her heart for the inevitable.

Wanted to take the girls to school. See you at the clinic. I think we need to talk before they get home.

All the insecurities she'd thought she'd dealt with crashed in on her like a tsunami.

Her professional goals.

Her desire for a family.

Her desire to be loved *for* her quirks, not despite them.

None of it was enough.

Noah hadn't spelled it out because he hadn't needed to.

A 'talk' before the girls came home meant only one thing. Noah wanted to shut down what had happened between them before the girls got attached.

The coffee was a nice touch. Considerate. It showed he was trying to be respectful of her feelings. But Rebecca knew now that a coffee and a smoothie had never been the endgame. Love had.

She clutched her arms round her stomach, doubling over on herself. What was it about her that made men walk away? The pain was unimaginable. She felt it on a cellular level. Straight through to her essence.

Because it wasn't just Noah rejecting her—it was history repeating itself. Once again Rebecca had chosen a man who didn't want to be 'pinned down'. Not by her, anyway.

After she and her ex had done everything by the book, literally—they'd even had a planner detailing how their futures would pan out—she'd taken her broken heart and tried to heal it by throwing it in the polar opposite direction. She'd harnessed her trust, her compassion, her willingness to let the universe do its work on her behalf, and had still been proved to have the instincts of a moth to a flame.

She couldn't face another rejection. Not from Noah. Not after opening her heart up to him the way she had.

The pain twisted in on itself. She couldn't even blame him. The girls had to come first for him. She was free to pick up her life and relocate it wherever she wanted—but he didn't have the same luxury.

There was only one solution for it. She'd have to end things so he didn't have to bear the extra burden of guilt.

She grabbed her backpack and set off for the clinic, grateful to her grapefruit shower gel for taking Noah's scent away from her skin. It would have been one reminder too many of what she was letting go.

She forced herself to become the sensible, fact-based woman she'd been when she'd flown into Bali. The one who honoured science and statistics and empirical evidence. The one who devoted her life to medicine. She had that to thank him for. Giving her a job that had reminded her where her energies were best spent: on other people's children.

Perhaps that was what last night had really been. A thank-you shag for reminding her of her true passion: paediatric surgery.

The emotion of yesterday's intense surgeries had clearly made them lose perspective on life. They'd lost and saved lives and, although they were trained to maintain a clinical distance—especially in the operating theatre—occasionally the human drama of a case crept into their bones and made itself heard. Yesterday had been one of those occasions.

It must've been particularly hard going for Noah, who knew exactly what it felt like to think everything was perfectly fine one minute and then, with just one poorly driven vehicle, have everything change. She could've kicked herself for not taking that into account last night. Of *course* he'd been feeling vulnerable. And she'd *launched* herself at him.

Shame deepened her misery.

How could she have been so blind? So insensitive?

Of course last night had been nothing more than a fluke. A one-off to dilute the painful memories that must surely have been at play when he'd pulled her into his arms.

She'd never been his endgame.

He had children to look after. Enormous decisions to make. Like whether or not he'd move back to Australia, for example. Or keep the clinic a going concern. They were just the tip of an enormous iceberg's worth of decisions. There was no chance a woman trying to find her 'true self' after being epically dumped registered anywhere but in the fathomless icy depths of his To Do list.

But he treated you like a queen. He made you feel beautiful.

It was true. He had. She'd never felt more desired. And that should be what she took away from this. Not sorrow.

He'd done nothing to make her feel horrible about herself. This was a holiday romance. Nothing more. Nothing less. Nothing to feel ashamed about. Not yet anyway.

All of which made now the perfect time to draw a line under it all and move on.

In an emotional about-face her serenity coach would've applauded, Rebecca chucked out the filter of self-pity she'd been using and vowed to do the right thing by Noah.

She would take the decision-making out of his hands and make it crystal-clear that the night had been a one-off. She would shoulder the blame for their hedonistic lovemaking sessions. The moans, the groans, the ripped shirt. She'd taken advantage of him at a time when they'd both been vulnerable.

He'd openly told her he was floundering. That he was struggling to make decisions. Well, this was one decision he wouldn't have to make.

Would her heart crack in two as she stepped back into the friend zone? *Definitely.* But their friendship had empowered her. Reminded her that she was a woman with her own mind, her own profession, her own voice.

It was time she used all of them.

She took a sip of the coffee and sighed. *So good.*

Despite her determination to see her decision through, prickles of sadness teased at the back of her throat. Bringing her coffee and inviting her to lunch to tell her he just wasn't that into her was gentlemanly. Miles better than her ex's lack of consideration. Leaving his laptop on the kitchen table, open to his girlfriend's pregnancy scans, had been a fairly traumatic way of finding out her intended had other intentions.

If Noah was to be her solitary rebound experience she should thank heaven above that it had been as celestial as it had. How could she regret learning just how sublime lovemaking could be? It had never been like that with her ex, or anyone before him. It had set a whole new bar. One she would insist upon in any future lovers.

When she arrived at the clinic she checked in with the charge nurse, who gave her an update on the infant and the two-year-old boy. They were both still in the clinic's cobbled-together version of an intensive care unit, and would be transferred to the main hospital with its better staffed unit later this afternoon, as soon as the building got its all-clear. Noah was down there now.

'Great!' Rebecca chirped. 'Grand.'

More time to come up with the perfect way to release him from any commitment he might feel he owed her.

* * *

Two cases of Bali Belly, one monkey bite that hadn't broken the skin and three rather savage coral cuts later, Rebecca looked up at the sound of a knock on the door to the office she'd been using to make notes.

Noah.

All her vows to be a brand-new version of herself evaporated.

How could they not?

He was all golden-skinned and ebony-haired. Blue-black eyes glittering like the night sky. His tattoos, each of which she'd run her tongue along, were peeking out from beneath the sleeves of his black scrubs.

Her eyes darted to the door.

He saw the move.

'Don't worry,' he said, pushing it even wider open. 'You're safe.'

Her face must've looked stricken, because his virtually mirrored hers when their eyes met.

They both spoke at once, their hurried apologies tumbling over each other.

'Sorry. I—I meant I probably shouldn't have instigated—' he began.

'I should be the one assuring you that you're safe with—' she said.

They both pulled themselves up short. Their eyes caught and locked, each of them actively searching the other's gaze for answers.

Noah looked different today. Softer. More approachable. Surely it couldn't be because he was falling for her the same way she had fallen for him?

Why did you dump the man of your dreams?

Because you knew it was the right thing to do.

'We should probably draw a line under what happened last night,' she said.

His expression remained neutral, but something flared in his eyes that made it clear he had not seen that coming. Not from her, anyway.

'Fair enough.' He nodded, and then, as if closing the door on that very brief, incredibly perfect chapter in their lives, said in a voice almost bereft of emotion, 'The girls have to be my priority.'

Tears stung at the back of her throat. He'd tried to disguise it, but she heard the regret in his voice. So she said the only thing she could. 'Of course they do.'

'They woke up last night and couldn't find me.'

The information pierced through what she now realised was a gossamer-thin layer of confidence. The tears she'd been holding back skidded down her cheeks. 'I'm so sorry. Are they all right?'

'They are now.'

She heard what he was saying. Now that he'd reassured them he would always be there for them. Exclusively. As he should be. They'd all experienced too much loss to endure any moments of unnecessary pain. Of course she wanted Noah. But not at the expense of the girls' happiness and security.

'I'm so sorry. I didn't know.'

'And yet you pipped me to the post.' He tipped his finger towards her, then to himself, before curling his hand into a fist. 'Calling an end to this.'

'I—I just thought, as you've got so much on your plate, you don't need extra complications.'

'Is that how you see what's been developing between us? As a complication?'

'Not for me…' She floundered, suddenly panicked that she'd read the situation incorrectly. 'I think you're amazing. I have from the moment I very first saw you. But…yesterday was intense. Before we…' She threw her hands up in the air. 'When you weren't there this morning, I guess I thought I was one extra thing on your list of things to do that you didn't need to worry about. There's a lot I need to sort out in my life too. You shouldn't have to deal with that as well.'

Noah seemed to let the comment sink in. Then, to her sorrow, she watched as he morphed back into the man she'd first met a few weeks ago. The one who kept his emotions in check. Whose smiles were rare. The one whose thoughts were impossible to read.

'Fair enough,' he said, as if she'd casually mentioned she was becoming a vegetarian after having a bad steak. 'Probably just as well. My dad's arriving today, and the girls and I are out to dinner with him tonight, so…'

He didn't need to finish the sentence.

As you weren't invited anyway, it's best not to muddy the waters more than we already have.

'Okay.'

She wove her fingers together, too aware that what she really wanted to do was to wrap her arms around him. Hug him. Kiss him. Ask him to sit down and talk, see if there wasn't some way they could work this out. But she knew in her heart he had to do what he thought best. Just because he'd given her a three-month contract, several delicious weeks of frisson and one night of bliss, it didn't mean he owed her a happily-ever-after. This wasn't real life for either of them. It was time to face reality and move on.

She put on what she hoped was a friendly smile and asked, 'Would it be best if I left now? Or would you like me to see out the last few weeks of my contract?'

CHAPTER THIRTEEN

NOAH FELT AWFUL. He'd never experienced the sensation of being utterly torn in two, but something was telling him this was exactly what it felt like.

'The staff would be delighted if you stayed. I know the girls would like it, too. As you know, they're not good with abrupt departures.'

A fresh crop of tears glistened in her eyes. She didn't say anything, but he could see the question in her eyes. The one he wasn't answering. What did he want?

Of course he wanted her to stay. But it would only make her inevitable departure more difficult.

Last night he'd felt connected to Rebecca in a way he'd never experienced before. They were on a professional par. She was amazing with the girls. And, more importantly, she was balm to his soul. She made him want to be a better man.

For the first time in his life he'd had those three precious words floating on the tip of his tongue all night long. He was grateful now he hadn't said them. How could he have told her he loved her and then explained a handful of hours later that he wasn't strong enough to both love Rebecca *and* do what was best for the girls?

Falling on the 'men aren't multi-taskers' stereotype simply wasn't good enough.

He dug into his pocket and handed her a fresh handkerchief.

She took it, but refused to meet his eyes.

He wanted to tell her he'd woken up *happy*. That wasn't something that had come pre-packed in his toolbox. Straight-up happiness. And, goddammit, he'd woken up at *peace*. For the first time ever he had been genuinely looking forward to seeing his father, so he could introduce him to the woman he hoped would be in his life…well, for ever.

He'd never introduced his father to anyone. There'd never been any point. And today there wasn't either. Because the time had finally come for him to start making those difficult decisions about the girls, the clinic, and all their futures. Decisions he'd have to make independent of Rebecca. Decisions he knew his father would've made the day Indah died.

'What do *you* want, Noah?' Rebecca pressed.

He wanted her. But he couldn't have her. Not now. Not like this. Not when he couldn't give her everything she deserved.

He took the British coin out of his pocket, gave the proud warrior a look, then placed it on the desk between them. 'It's your life, Rebecca. So this should be your call.'

And then he walked away.

She called out after him, but he kept walking. He had a clinic to run. News to break to the girls. A father's disappointment to shoulder. Might as well lose himself in a few hours' work, first.

A few long-legged strides later he was in front of the charge nurse. He nodded at the patient board. 'Right. Where do I start?'

* * *

A few hours later, with not enough patients to wipe what had happened from his brain, Noah was buttoning up a fresh shirt when Isla and Ruby knocked on his door.

'Hey, girls, come on in.'

He'd already broken the news that Rebecca wouldn't be joining them later and, as expected, it hadn't gone down a storm. He hadn't told them the real reason, of course. He'd said she had to work late and she was sorry she wouldn't be making it.

They'd been gutted. He knew they loved him, but they lit up whenever Rebecca was about. She had that effect on kids. She was a natural hugger. Loved board games. Knew when to tease, when to back off. She was good with them. She made him a better parent to them, and it was killing him that it couldn't continue.

Because as much as she improved him she also threw him off balance. And that simply wasn't an option. Especially with everything they'd gone through.

Was this how he'd always handled things? Waiting for the right place? The right time? Only to realise there never was one?

He silently cursed himself as the girls wrapped their arms round his waist. He'd known how he felt about Rebecca from the first day he'd met her. And for some idiot reason he'd thought keeping those feelings to himself had been the smart thing to do.

No wonder she wanted out. Who wanted a man who couldn't make a decision and stick to it? One who fell head over heels in love only to pull the plug.

His cousin was right. He was a structured, routine-orientated guy, who excelled in the workplace. And that was it. It was time to head back to Australia and give the girls a solid foundation for their futures. Fancy schools.

Elite country clubs. A stay-at-home mum… Well… They'd have whatever nanny his cousin had chosen, anyway. Someone far better qualified to give these girls the TLC they deserved.

'Uncle Noah?' Ruby was giving him one of her most soulful, pleading looks.

'Yes, darlin'?'

'Do you think if we made Rebecca a carrot cake she would come to supper with us tonight?'

Noah swept his hand across Ruby's hair and gave Isla's shoulder a squeeze. 'I don't think we have time, love. Your granddad is due to meet us at the restaurant in half an hour.'

'Maybe we should leave her a note to tell her where we are?' Isla's little brow crinkled with concern. 'Just in case she finishes in time?'

Noah squatted down so he was at the girls' eye level, using the pads of his thumbs to smooth the furrows away. 'I'm sure she would've joined us if she could. She's got a lot of patients to see today.'

'Maybe they'll all feel better soon and she'll be hungry.' Isla threw a look at Ruby, who nodded. They'd obviously been discussing this. 'We should probably tell her.'

He was going to say no, but their little faces were so filled with hope he thought *Why not?*

After they'd spoken this afternoon she hadn't stropped off to pack her bags and leave. She'd made it clear to the charge nurse, who'd passed on the news to him, that she was going to see through the three-month commitment she'd made. The last thing she'd do was begrudge the girls a hug and a kiss goodbye.

'She's with her patients right now, but why don't you make her a card or a drawing? She'd like that.'

The girls oohed and told him that was a good idea. 'Do you want to make her one, too?'

He smiled and shook his head. The only thing he wanted to do right now was to ask Rebecca to stay. But he'd be asking her to live her life in limbo. To maybe live in Bali. Maybe live in Sydney. Definitely give up her life in England, the way his own mother had given up her life here to follow a man. It hadn't worked out well for his mother. And he simply couldn't abide the thought of anything similar happening to Rebecca. Which was why the sensible decision to end things now had to be the path they chose.

'Uncle Noah, you look sad,' Ruby said. 'Do you wish Rebecca was coming, too?'

'Yeah,' he admitted. 'I do. But she can't, so it's just going to be the three of us.'

The girls threw their arms around his neck and squeezed. This would work. The three of them. There was enough love here to make whatever path they chose the right one. Wasn't there?

'Well, go on, then,' he said to the girls, shooing them out of his room with a semi-stern warning that they had ten minutes.

The girls ran off to find their crayons to draw Rebecca a card. Time Noah spent glaring at his own reflection. He briefly considered cutting off his hair. A classic 'man in crisis' move. But he knew if he did his father would make some jibe or another. *Finally seen the light and become a real man, have you son?* So he left it. Besides, he'd used Rebecca's shampoo that morning and, as stupid and romantic as it was, he liked having that essence of her with him. However fleeting.

After the girls had run across to her villa and delivered the card, Noah bundled them into the Jeep to meet his father. Just a few more hours to grit his teeth through before he could go home and figure out how the hell he was going to confront the rest of his life.

CHAPTER FOURTEEN

'HERE'S YOUR VALET parking slip, Dr Cameron.'

'Thank you.'

'Ooh,' said Isla as she slipped her hand into his after handing her light sweater to the cloakroom girl. 'Fancy.'

'Sure is,' Noah said.

It always was if his father had chosen it. For as long as he could remember, his father had only dined in fancy Michelin-starred restaurants. 'Research', he called it. But Noah knew what it really was. Posing.

Though his father rarely mentioned it, he came from a humble background. Downright poor, if they were going to be truthful. He'd been a jobbing farm labourer's son. His father had picked up contract work on vast estates owned by barely there owners. People so rich they could helicopter in from the city to check up on their staff in between jaunts to holiday hotspots.

Being one of the have-nots had fuelled Noah's father to become the driven, highly successful businessman he was today. At last count he'd owned twenty A-list resorts, tactically dotted around the globe.

Noah scanned the restaurant, instinctively looking for the chef's table—the only place his father would sit. Ah. There he was, looking every bit the patriarch, lording it over the rest of the diners. Shock of white hair.

Piercing blue eyes. The same steely build. From a distance, anyway.

He forced himself to remember that his dad was on his own again, and very possibly would be feeling just the slightest bit vulnerable. Then again…this was his dad they were talking about. Probably not.

Noah steered the girls across the room towards their grandfather, willing the meal to be à la carte rather than one of those endless chef's menus. Whatever his father had to say, he could say over the appetisers.

'Hello, Noah.' His bright blue eyes made a quick scan of his son, and in a rare turn of events he kept his observations to himself.

'Father,' Noah replied in a stiff, formal voice he only used for—well, his father.

Though they didn't maintain eye contact for long, for a fraction of a second Noah thought he saw a frailty he'd never noted in his father before. Old age? His father was a fairly robust sixty-five, so he doubted that.

Loneliness?

The word popped into his head and stuck. Newly single. Deceased daughter. Estranged son. Maybe his instinct to be concerned had been the right one.

'Girls.' His father gave each of the girls a nod rather than pulling them into his arms.

They looked up at him, confused. Noah gave both girls a quick tight hug before pointing them towards chairs, realising as he did so that it was a gesture he might not have done before meeting Rebecca. He zipped up the memory and set it aside. Tonight wasn't the night to rehash his failings.

As they got themselves settled, Noah asked the waiter for some soft drinks for the girls and a large bottle of water for himself.

'I've ordered a rather delightful Chablis,' his father cut in.

The last thing he and his father needed to maintain a civilised conversation was alcohol. 'Thanks, Dad. I'm driving. Water's fine.'

His father drew in a sharp breath, presumably to remind Noah that fine food was best enjoyed with fine wine, when his eyes lit on someone at the entrance to the restaurant. Noah's back was to the door, but the girls followed their grandfather's eyeline, their dark eyes widening as they hit the entrance.

'Rebecca!' the girls squealed in tandem, jumping down from their chairs and racing across the restaurant floor to hug her.

Noah turned, his lungs taking a hit as he saw her.

She was beautiful any day of the week, but tonight she looked out of this world.

She'd left her hair loose, allowing it to flow over her shoulders in flame-coloured pre-Raphaelite waves. She was wearing an aqua-blue dress that draped over one shoulder, leaving the other bare. The silky fabric skidded over her curves and fluttered in her wake as she walked towards them, her feet tucked into delicate heels the colour of the sea.

She met Noah's gaze head-on, with a smile and a proud confidence that suited her. 'Sorry I'm late. I hope the invitation still stands.'

'What are you doing here?' he asked quietly.

'Friends don't let friends dine with estranged fathers alone.'

Before he could respond, she handed him the card the girls had drawn for her.

It showed two little girls holding hands with two adults. One with dark hair and dark blue eyes and one with bright red hair and green eyes. There were hearts drawn all around the family.

Underneath the drawing, written in childlike handwriting were the words *Family = Love.*

Noah's father, characteristically using his arsenal of charm, rose from his chair and signalled to a waiter to bring a chair for Rebecca. 'We can't deny a beautiful woman like this a place at our table—can we, Noah?' He pointedly looked to his son for an explanation.

'This is Rebecca,' Noah began, instantly floundering when it came to deciding how to describe her.

'She's Uncle Noah's girlfriend,' Ruby said.

Noah's heart froze in place.

Rebecca's eyes flicked between Ruby's and Isla's. She smiled, and then, in a move he wasn't expecting, crossed her fingers and gave a hopeful little shrug.

Noah's eyes snapped to hers, and in that instant he saw what he should've seen back when they were at the clinic. She loved him, too.

His heart crashed against his ribcage, over and over, drumming out clamorous thumps of gratitude, relief and wonder.

But if she loved him why had she cut things short?

His mind flashed back to the note he'd written.

We need to talk.

He'd meant he'd wanted to talk to her about his father. Because if there was one thing in the world Noah could predict it was that his father only visited when he had plans, and Noah had wanted the two of them to be braced for it, armed with a plan of their own. A united front.

We need to talk.

In a sudden flash of understanding, he realised Rebecca had thought he'd given her the beginnings of a *Dear John* letter.

So of course she'd called it quits. She'd been treated horrifically by her ex and having been so brave, so bold, as to open up her heart to *him*, the last thing she was going to do was let him crush it under his foot like dirt. Or, from another angle, she'd done what she'd thought best. Made a complicated situation simpler. She knew he was struggling. She'd been trying to help.

'Before you sit…' Her expression remained unchanged, but her eyes snapped to his, flaring when they met and meshed. How the hell could he have walked away from her…? It was a mistake he was never going to make again. 'I just want to ask you a couple of things about a patient, if you don't mind.'

'Not at all.' Her smile remained an enchanting combination of soft and strong. As if she'd found her happy place and nothing would take it away.

She gave the girls a quick kiss on the tops of their heads and somehow bewitched his father into asking the waiter for colouring pencils, to help him explain to the girls what all the fancy dishes were.

They walked out into the garden at the back of the restaurant. There were palm trees wrapped with swirls of fairy lights. A koi pond with a bridge over it beckoned a few metres away from the building.

He held his hand out to guide her there.

'I hope I haven't overstepped,' she said before he could say anything. 'I was thinking if you and your father needed some alone time the girls and I could leave early. But if I've read the situation incorrectly again…' She winced. 'Oh, God. I have, haven't I? I'm sorry. I—'

He held up his hand, then dragged it through his hair

before looking her in the eye. 'I'm the one who owes you an apology.'

She took one of his hands in hers, weaving her fingers through his as she shook her head. She lifted her gaze to meet his. 'I—I think I might have jumped the gun this morning.'

'I think we *both* might have jumped the gun this morning.'

'The note,' she said. 'The one you wrote—'

'It was meant to be the *beginning* of something,' Noah explained. 'Not the end.'

Her cheeks pinkened as she gave him a sheepish smile. 'That occurred to me later. Much later.' She flicked her eyes towards the restaurant. 'As you can see, I still have insecurities.'

'Hey…' He reached out to give her arm a squeeze. 'All this is new to both of us. We're bound to misunderstand one another from time to time. But let me be clear: I am very happy that our friendship has developed into something more…' He selected the word carefully, pressing his hands to his heart as he said it. 'Meaningful.'

She held up the card the girls had drawn for her. 'Before today I didn't think crayon drawings were powerful, but…but this one showed me something I needed to be reminded of.'

'What's that?'

'That real love—true love—is strong. It's about being a friend, more than a lover. It endures misunderstandings. It stands up against hurt and pain and it doesn't crumble at the first mishap.' She looked down at her hands, then back up at him. 'I love you, Noah. I wanted to tell you that this morning. But even thinking that you might not love me back—'

He didn't leave her hanging this time. 'I do, my darling. My beautiful, beautiful gift from the universe.' They laughed and, as the sound sighed away, Noah continued. 'I love you, Rebecca Stone. Something I was too thick-headed to realise until you were strong enough to walk away from me.'

'Strong?' She grimaced. 'I think that was cowardice at work.'

He shook his head. 'No. It was strong to let me know you wanted to be loved the way you deserve to be loved. Wholly. With commitment and openness.'

Rebecca pressed a hand to his heart, letting the gesture do the talking for her. Their lives would be woven together now. Stronger because they were two.

'You said you wanted to talk to me about your dad?'

He grimaced as he tipped his head towards the dining room. 'I'm fairly certain he's going to offer to buy the clinic back from me. Turn it back into a hotel so the girls and I can move to Sydney "unencumbered."'

Rebecca paled, her face frozen in alarm. 'Is that what you want?'

'It's what I thought I wanted when I first flew out here, but…' He pulled her in closer to him. 'Then I met you.'

Her lips tipped into a smile. 'What does your meeting me have to do with the clinic?'

'The clinic was set up to be a legacy to my mother and her commitment to us. But if I'm being honest it never would have become anything if my sister hadn't put the plan into action.'

'You paid for everything!' Rebecca protested.

He shrugged the fact away. 'There are loads of people I could have gone to to be donors.'

'Like your father?'

'Like my father.'

'But you didn't want his money?'

Noah shook his head. 'No.' He clenched his jaw tight before admitting, 'It was his approval I was after.'

Rebecca closed her eyes, and when she opened them they glistened with un-spilt emotion.

Noah leant forward and gave her a soft kiss. 'I don't need it any more,' he said, adding, 'Someone very wise suggested I open my eyes to what the universe is offering, and it turns out it's giving me closure on that part of my life.'

'Noah… That's wonderful.'

'And that's why I wanted to talk to you. With closure comes new beginnings. And I'm wondering if you'd like to make a new beginning here, with me and the girls?'

Rebecca's eyes began to rapid blink. 'In Bali?'

He nodded. 'Yup.'

'What about your life back in Sydney?'

'It's not much of a life, to be honest. I've a couple of ideas I can run past the director about setting up an adjunct orthopaedic clinic here…but I'd feel a lot better working it out together with you, if you're willing.'

Her smile turned mischievous. 'Are you saying you want to work it out with your *girlfriend*?'

'If you're happy to be my girlfriend.' The line was cheesy, but at this exact moment he didn't care. He felt like a lovestruck teen. Rebecca was the woman he wanted. To work with, to play with, to love.

'How's this for an answer?' she asked, and went up on tiptoe to give him a long, slow, delicious kiss.

As coolly as he could manage, he whispered against her lips, 'That'll do. For now.' He swept his hands along her hips, then gave her bum a cheeky squeeze. 'We'd probably better get in there and rescue the girls.'

'Let's do that,' she agreed.

And after another sweeter than honey kiss, hand in hand, they went into the restaurant to face their future as a couple.

CHAPTER FIFTEEN

A FEW DAYS LATER, Noah finished tucking the girls in, then went back downstairs, where his father was laughing at some anecdote Rebecca was telling him about her grandmother.

'So the old bird's grown some new wings?' His father guffawed, instantly lowering his voice when he saw Noah—a reminder that there were two little girls trying to go to sleep upstairs.

Noah shook his head, astonished at the dozens of tiny little miracles that had materialised since he'd opened his heart to Rebecca. Wrapping his father round her little finger for one.

His father hadn't unveiled a grand plan, in the end. They'd simply done what his family had never done. Enjoyed a meal together. Laughed. Caught up on general news. Shared bites of their genuinely delicious food. It had felt both normal and extraordinary. And it continued to catch him out as each day passed.

Rebecca looked up, her smile brightening as she caught Noah's eye. 'Everything all right?'

Noah nodded and joined Rebecca on the sofa across from his father. 'Apart from the girls asking if they can have truffled risotto for their lunch tomorrow, everything's grand.'

He gave his father a begrudging smile. 'Thanks for yet another meal out, Dad. It was delicious.'

His father went through a strange throat-clearing exercise, and Noah was just about to get up and give him a thump on the back when he realised his dad was fighting back a swell of emotion.

He felt Rebecca's hand slip into his and give it a squeeze before she rose and got his father some water. There really was strength in numbers. Especially if that number was two.

'Here you are, Mr Cameron.'

'Reggie.'

The instruction was a plea. Devoid of his father's usual put-on charm and panache. He really wanted Rebecca to treat him like family.

Noah crossed to him. 'Are you all right, Dad?' They both knew he wasn't asking about his throat.

'Yes, son.' His father leant forward, elbows on knees, and after a few moments said, 'I've received a few wake-up calls these past few months.'

'Oh?'

'It's not my health. That's fine.'

The relief in Noah's chest caught him by surprise. He'd certainly never wished his father ill, but the fact he wasn't unwell was an enormous relief. 'Good. Good…'

'It's more I think it's time I smelt the roses a bit. Do you hear what I'm saying?'

'I think you'd better spell it out.'

His dad glanced across at Rebecca. 'You're happy for Rebecca to hear my plan?'

Noah nodded. 'She's a smart woman. I look to her for advice.' Though he kept his eyes on his father, he felt the warmth of Rebecca's smile.

'Right. Well, then… I've sold the business.'

'What?'

'That's right. The whole lot. It's why Caroline upped and left me. Thought she'd be jetting round all of the hotels and acting the Empress.'

That wasn't breaking news. She'd certainly passed on quite a few 'style choices' to Noah she had thought his father should make in the exclusive hotel he owned in Sydney. All of them in direct contrast to the elegant, discreet interior decor his mother had chosen. Caroline had been overruled.

His father gave his head a rub. 'That's a lot of spare dosh I've got floating around, and I'd like to see it put to good use.'

Noah went on the defensive. 'I'm not moving back to Sydney.'

'And I'm not asking you to.'

Both he and Rebecca back, surprised. 'What *are* you asking?' they said as one. Then turned to each other and laughed. 'Snap!'

'Oh, for heaven's sake…' Noah's father waved his hands. 'You two lovebirds…' His expression softened.

'What, Dad?'

'You remind me of me and your mother back in the day.'

Now, this was another surprise.

His dad leant back in his chair, and after a moment tugging at an invisible thread he said, 'I know I was a horrible husband. Unfaithful. Unkind. I took out all my insecurities on your mother when she was my number one champion. She gave me you two kids.' He winced at his turn of phrase. 'I should've been a much better father. I'll never be able to make up for the father I was, but I plan to start becoming the one I should have been.'

'Right…' Noah was wary. 'And what does that involve?'

'I'd like to invest in the clinic here. Donate, really. And also start a school. One the girls can go to for a Class-A education.'

'There are already schools here, Dad.'

'Yeah, but not ones that offer scholarships to the type of kiddies you're treating here.'

Rebecca jumped in. 'You want to subsidise medical treatment and education for the poor?'

'That's right.' Noah's dad pointed at Rebecca while nodding at Noah. 'She's got the idea. Bright one, this little chicken. You'd better tell me she's a keeper.'

Though he was still reeling from his father's about-face—from global entrepreneur to local philanthropist—Noah had enough wherewithal to know what his priority was. 'I'm going to do everything in my power to keep her by my side.'

Rebecca grinned and gave him a playful elbow in the ribs. 'I think we've got a few particulars to iron out first.'

'Like?'

'Like you receiving my nan's stamp of approval, for one.'

He grinned, looking forward to the moment when the woman who'd raised the love of his life arrived. 'I'll be buffing all my shoes in the morning.' He pretended to write it down. 'Anything else she'll want to see ship-shape?'

'Definitely. But I don't want to scare you off.' She made a scary face.

He could tell from her cheeky smile that she was joking…but also not joking. She wanted to be taken seriously. To be treated as a partner, not as the person who put in all the graft to lay the foundations for a relationship only to discover she'd built something her other half had never wanted to stand on.

'Don't you worry. It'll take an army of nay-sayers to frighten me off. And even then…' He made a couple of martial arts moves, to her obvious amusement.

Rebecca grinned, holding up her phone. 'You'd better get yourself battle-ready, because she's arriving here in a week.'

'Hold still, Nan. I just need to straighten these flowers in your hair.' Rebecca pinned the tropical flowers in place, their scent mingling organically with her grandmother's familiar perfume as she did. It was still so hard to believe her nan had flown all the way out here with Nathan and announce they were also getting married. When she finished, they both stepped back, hand in hand, to look at one another.

'You look beautiful,' her nan pronounced.

'Well, so do you. And, as the bride to be, you're the one who matters the most.'

Noah knocked on the door, letting out a low whistle of approval. 'Nathan is one lucky man!'

Nanny Bea cackled, waving away Noah's approval. 'You're just saying that to get on my good side, young man.' She fixed him with her best steely gaze. 'You know, the minister said he's happy to do a double wedding.'

Rebecca and Noah looked at one another's matching expressions of horror and then, after Nanny Bea had excused herself to the spare room to finish her make-up, realised they were actually letting the idea sink in and marinate.

'You are dressed very beautifully,' Noah said with an appreciative wink. 'Best-looking bridesmaid I've ever seen.'

'And your suit's very nice. Linen suits you.' Rebecca wasn't even looking at the suit. She was staring directly into Noah's eyes, trying to see if he was feeling what she was. Fear and excitement. Hope and possibility. 'Not that I've imagined it much…' she teased. 'For some reason I pictured you in scrubs when— I mean if we were ever to marry.'

'I'm happy to change,' Noah volunteered, half turning towards the stairs. 'I'm sure I can find a bow tie somewhere. Dad's probably brought one.'

They both grinned at the image.

'Would your father approve?'

'Of the bow tie?' Noah asked. 'Probably not. Of you?' he added more seriously. 'From the moment he saw you. Just like me.'

'And there's the girls to tell. Do you think they'll be happy?'

Noah tipped his head back and forth, nodding, and said, 'Actually, they brought me this this morning…just in case.' He dipped into his pocket and pulled out a seashell that had been worn through by the sea so that it was shaped like a ring.

Rebecca's hands flew to cover her mouth. 'It's beautiful.'

'Born from the sea. Just as I first saw you. My very own Amphitrite.'

A goddess of the sea. It wasn't how she'd ever once imagined herself. Then again, six months ago she never would have believed she would have left her future to a coin-toss and ended up in love with her soul mate in Bali.

'What if the universe delivers bad things?'

'The universe brings good and bad all the time,' Noah reminded her as he closed the space between them and took her hands in his. 'We never would have met if my sister hadn't died. Or if your ex hadn't left you. We met each other when neither of us was at our best, and yet somehow we knew we could be better. Together.'

It was true. She closed her eyes and tried to imagine what her world would be like if things had gone according to her spreadsheet. To her astonishment, nothing appeared. When she opened her eyes, her heart skipped a beat. He was still there, holding her hands, offering himself as a pillar to lean on when she wavered.

She put on a mock-officious voice. 'Nanny Bea will need new witnesses for her marriage.'

Noah gave her a hard, serious look. 'Let's witness this wedding for her. Let her bask in the sunlight today with Nathan. Then, later,' he nuzzled into the nook between her ear and her collarbone and gave her a kiss, 'We'll marry with the pair of them as our witnesses.' He pulled back and looked at her. 'I want to ask you to marry me properly.'

Rebecca held up the shell ring then signalled to Noah to slip it onto her finger. 'Shall we call this a promise ring?'

'A promise of a lifetime together? Absolutely.' He slid the ring on her finger and as it shifted into place Rebecca felt something shift inside her heart. She felt lighter and more secure all at the same time. She felt whole.

A flight of butterflies lifted and fluttered round her tummy as she lost herself in Noah's eyes. They glittered with a happiness she hadn't seen in them before. Perhaps it was something deeper. Something approaching the contentment, the peace they both sought. Perhaps this was what her serenity coach had been guiding her towards all along: harmony. Because that was what she felt when she was with Noah Cameron.

Through the window she could see the minister taking his place and the musicians begin to warm up their instruments for the bridal march her nan had insisted on them playing.

'Shall we go watch two little lovebirds tie the knot?' she asked.

'I couldn't think of anything I'd rather do,' Noah dropped a kiss on her lips that promised so much more. A lifetime of love, happiness and mutual respect.

'C'mon.' She tugged his hands. 'Let's get the rest of our lives started.'

EPILOGUE

REBECCA LOOKED AROUND the newly refurbished children's ward at The Island Clinic. The walls had been painted in beautiful murals that made it look as if it was in the heart of the Sacred Monkey Sanctuary. Large, wonderfully equipped aquariums were built right into the walls, skylights glowed with the filtered light coming through the palm trees, and in the centre of the waiting area was a wishing well.

Most of the furniture was for children—small tables and chairs for arts and crafts, bean bags and all sorts—but there were discreet nooks where parents could tuck themselves away from it all if they needed some time to regroup before putting on a smile for their child.

While it could not be more perfect—beautifully designed and kitted out precisely for the needs of children unfortunate enough to need to stay in hospital—it was strange seeing it from her current perspective: wearing a hospital gown and being pushed round in a wheelchair. Then again, it was also completely unfamiliar to be holding her own child in her arms.

She looked down at the tiny little baby in her arms, then traced her finger along her infant's cheek. 'What do you think, love? Has your granddad done your namesake proud?'

'I'll say he has.' Noah pulled a chair over so that he was sitting beside them. He gently put his arm round Rebecca's shoulder and held out one of his fingers so that Indah, their two-day-old little girl, could clasp it in her tiny hand.

Ruby, who had been pushing Rebecca's wheelchair, came round to stand in front of the pair of them and asked if she and Isla could take the baby over to one of the aquariums.

'Of course, love. Here you go.'

Ruby smiled up at her grandfather, who had become a bit of a permanent fixture around the clinic. Even though he'd bought a very ritzy house a few miles away, 'to give them space', more often than not he was here at the clinic, now an impressive hospital, 'popping in'. He said it was to make sure things were being done to his specs, but Rebecca knew better. He was loving being part of a happy, growing family. He'd even built a bungalow in his garden for Nanny Bea and Nathan to stay in during their visits.

'Will wonders never cease?' Noah nodded towards his father, who was being taught how to skip by Isla as Ruby carefully carried the baby over to one of the huge aquariums.

Rebecca smiled at her husband. 'You know what? I don't think they do cease. It seems like the more we open our eyes to the good things in life, the more they just keep on appearing.'

Noah swept a couple of locks of hair away from her forehead. 'You had me worried the other day.'

She tipped her forehead to his. 'I know…' Her labour had been long and difficult, and in the end she'd had to have a Caesarean section in the brand-new maternity ward. 'I had me worried too. But…' She popped a kiss on Noah's nose. 'It was kind of amazing that we had the first baby on the new ward, wasn't it?'

'It wasn't just amazing, my love,' Noah said decisively. 'It was destiny.' He brushed her cheek with his lips and whispered, 'I hope you know how much I love you.'

'I do,' she whispered back. 'I do, I do, I do, I do, I *do*.'

* * * * *

COMING SOON!

We really hope you enjoyed reading this book. If you're looking for more romance, be sure to head to the shops when new books are available on

Thursday 23rd June

To see which titles are coming soon, please visit

millsandboon.co.uk/nextmonth

MILLS & BOON

Coming next month

THE NIGHT THEY NEVER FORGOT
Scarlet Wilson

She met his gaze. There was so much there. Twelve lost years between them. She lifted a muffin from the plate and walked around her desk, gesturing to the seat at the other side as she moved to flick some switches on her coffee machine.

He could sense she was trying to decide how to play this. He'd turned up unexpectedly. They'd had literally no contact since that last awkward morning after graduation. He'd replayed that day over and over in his head so many times. It had seemed clear that Caitlin had thought they'd made a mistake; she'd made a quick comment—'at least we got that out of our system'—and that they could get back to being rivals again. He hadn't said a word. Hadn't told her how much that cheapened what had happened between them and how, after one taste of Caitlin, she would never be out of his system. He'd let the hurt feelings go; he'd wanted to respect her wishes. The embarrassing retreat and hasty exit he'd had to make had been imprinted in his soul. He'd lost the person he'd been closest to for six years. It shouldn't have been worth it. Not for one night.

But, strangely, that night had meant everything. And he was still glad they had gone there. Even if the next morning had been a disaster.

He couldn't help it. His eyes went to her left hand. No ring. The sense of relief was unexpectedly overwhelming.

Ridiculous. And he knew that. He also knew he couldn't take a lack of ring to mean anything at all. Caitlin might well be married and just not want to wear a ring—she was a surgeon after all. She could also be in a long-term relationship. But he couldn't help but hope not…no matter how shallow that might make him.

He swept his arm around the room. 'Corner office? They must like you.'

'Of course they do. I'm their shining star.'

It was the way she said those words. The confidence in herself that had brought him here.

He glanced out at the dark view of the beautiful city of Barcelona, with all the familiar structures easy to pick out.

'You've done really well for yourself.' He said the words with a hint of pride. When any other physician mentioned Caitlin he always said that they'd trained together, and that she was a fine surgeon.

'I like to think so.' Her gaze narrowed slightly. She was getting suspicious of the small talk.

'We should catch up?'

Her eyebrows raised.

'I mean, twelve years is a long time. You could be married, divorced, a mother of ten.'

Her eyes widened.

Continue reading
THE NIGHT THEY NEVER FORGOT
Scarlet Wilson

Available next month
www.millsandboon.co.uk

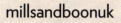